I0783276

EBenezer

A GLOBALIST'S CHRISTMAS CAROL

MARK HANNA

MarkusPartners Publishing

Published by MarkusPartners Publishing™
MarkusPartners Publishing is a trademark of Markus Partners LLC, An Arizona Corporation

First edition

Cover design by Nick Castle - Author photograph by Devyn Wiley

ISBN 979-8-9873331-4-3 (hardcover)
ISBN 979-8-9873331-1-2 (paperback)
ISBN 979-8-9873331-2-9 (ebook)

http://www.markhanna.tv

Printing 1, 2023
Printed in the United States of America
Soli Deo Gloria

DEDICATION

To my mother, who always inspired me, always believed in me
and was always there for me.
Marguerite Agnes Hanna (1931-2021)

STAVE 1

ELEVATION

CHAPTER 1

Is Marley really dead? Bobby wasn't the only one wondering as he gazed forward, waiting, along with several thousand other company employees, most of them strangers to him, for the ceremony to begin.

"It sure would've been nice to have attended in person," he whispered to the smartly dressed company woman next to him.

"Seriously? You have to have the right Rating for that, which, clearly, none of us have," she shot back, somewhat mechanically. Bobby didn't know her personally, but had noticed her a few times on the third floor—the Marketing floor—of their massive high-rise company complex. She looked a bit different now, not moving and ever so slightly distorted.

"So true. What's your Rating?" Bobby continued in a hushed tone.

"NE1," the young woman replied as she continued to stare directly forward. "You?"

"Same. I was NE2 until just last year, but thankfully I was promoted to Director of Operations & Accounting, which bumps me up."

"Wow, that's a fantastic position, especially your being so young! Whose office are you DOA for?" she asked, still looking straight ahead.

"I'm DOA for the executives. No doubt, it's really a great position, except for the money. I don't get paid squat—at least for this city."

"So you work directly with EB?"

"Yes, started with him three years ago," Bobby said, proud and ashamed at the same time. "Working directly for EB is a dream come true." Bobby fibbed a little, but not about the pay.

"That's incredible. You really scored. You must be some kind of a genius!" She turned her head slightly for the first time, and with a new level of interest, coyly smiled at him.

"I'm pretty good with numbers, and that seems to be EB's main use for me. I keep track of all the company's finances and check everything that crosses his desk. Saves him time. To EB, time is money."

"So you're like a CFO?"

"Except for my paycheck! Actually, I do the brunt of the number crunching and budget reconciliations that the CFO uses for the company's financial disclosures, forecasts, and long-term operational planning."

"You really are a genius! I'm surprised you don't have an Essential Rating. I would think you could be an ER1 or 2 if EB relies on you so much," the nameless woman said as she reached over to seemingly touch Bobby's leg in a gesture of approval. Out of habit and his deep love for his wife, Olivia, Bobby jerked his leg to try to avoid the contact. Caught off guard by what he saw as her forwardness, he couldn't move it fast enough. But instead of feeling her perfectly smooth and manicured hand on his thigh, there was nothing. Her long, slender fingers went right through his leg as though he were not really there. *I'll never get used to Ghosting,* Bobby chuckled to himself as he adjusted his helmet and a few settings on his desk chair's arm. *Such is the nature of the Pod.*

Bobby knew that she was right, and that she wasn't actually sitting next to him. Most likely, she was also at her desk many floors down, helmeted as he was to virtually connect to the ceremony through the Pod. But it was interesting that she had said what Bobby had been thinking every day for the last year: he really should be at an Essential Rating.

EB had already informed him that, though he was eligible, he would keep his Non-essential NE1 status and not receive an upgrade to ER until he had really proven himself to EB—whatever that meant. Bobby had been striving day and night to please EB since he joined the company and had won the full trust and confidence of all the other executives. But not EB, apparently. Loyalty was one of EB's most basic requirements in the company, most importantly among his executives, the top-floor group Bobby served. Any hint of betrayal or dissatisfaction by EB would send him packing. There had been several others before him in the DOA position that didn't last for this very reason. Though it was one of the most coveted jobs in the company, it was one of the most soul destroying too. Bobby knew EB would discard him like a pen without ink, just like all the others, if EB didn't have complete, unwavering confidence in him. But in spite of his over-the-top efforts and spotless reputation, gaining EB's full trust somehow eluded him. Daily, Bobby had to fight bitterness toward EB because of this.

It's possible this woman isn't even an employee, but a program planted to test me. Be careful, Bobby, and watch every word you say, he thought as the woman looked forward toward the ceremony podium again. Since everything in the Pod was recorded, down to eye movements, brain waves, and pulse rate, he knew that anything he said while plugged in to the Pod would be eternal, forever stored in one of EB's massive data cities located across the country.

The data farms were only a part of EB's information empire and consisted of acres and acres of artificial intelligence servers to hold, parse, and analyze every one of his customers', clients', and employees' data, and any data he could purchase from others. He didn't spend much money to buy up data, however, since nearly every American and a vast majority of the world's population were in one way or another connected into one of EB's companies or products. So massive was Bobby's boss's base that he had even achieved another accolade this year that he could shamelessly market and promote: he was now the largest owner of data warehouses, server farms, and private fusion centers on the planet.

Back in the moment at hand, Bobby realized he had neglected his small-town manners and hadn't introduced himself. "By the way, my name is Bobby, Bobby Cratchit," he said as he gave a nod to greet her, then quickly looked straight ahead, again to avoid eye contact.

"I'm Anna Strong," she replied. "Nice to meet you—virtually, anyway."

"And yes," Bobby said after a quick smile, "you're right—EB does rely on me. More than you'd imagine. But there's a cost, Anna, like on Monday. Even though it was Christmas Eve, I had to burn the midnight oil for him instead of spending it with my wife and children. He doesn't care much for Christmas, you know. But hey, if sacrificing a Christmas Eve gets me up to ER1 or 2, it's worth it, right?"

"I suppose," Anna responded with some hesitation. "I get it, that since the end of the Second Pandemic, we all need to have our place in society so it will function smoothly, especially in emergencies. But have you ever wondered if this whole rating system is a bit too much?"

Bobby hesitated, knowing that the conversation was approaching dangerous grounds. He wasn't afraid to delve in on the subject with her, but knew that since all their words were recorded and archived—and even the thought patterns behind the words—the conversation could come back to haunt him, especially with EB. But what good was free speech if it couldn't be employed to criticize the very system that was supposed to protect it?

"I've thought the same thing," he finally said after making the decision to exercise his ever dwindling First Amendment right. "It seems that everyone has become obsessed with whether they are Essential or Non-essential in our new so-called 'Technocracy'—myself included! But how else can we feel when we Non-essentials are the new serfs, no more than second-class citizens relegated to the back of society's bus? The Essentials never frame it this way, of course, but we all know that's what's happened. And it's becoming more and more difficult every day to break free and obtain the higher status."

"And keep it!" Anna interjected. "It's all over the news that a record number of people lost their Essential status this year."

"Exactly. Talk about social control. Any deviation from their rules, social regulations, and behavioral stipulations—or if the right recommendations or accommodations aren't obtained—to the bottom of the social pile you go!".

"And the new National ID and Total Life Social Credit System has pretty much solidified this control," Anna agreed. "I was too young to remember the First Pandemic, but isn't that where all this Ratings stuff started?"

"I don't think I'm much older than you, but that's my understanding too," Bobby replied. "After COVID had mutated itself to be the equivalent of the flu during the First Pandemic, small businesses, churches, community groups, and private enterprises became furious at how unequally they had been treated and the costs they had to incur because of the lockdowns and mandated closures. But big business, government, public education, and the healthcare establishment had argued that the mandates and shutdowns were a necessary evil to keep people safe. It took years and the Second COVID Pandemic to fully realize that categorizing businesses, organizations, and offices into 'essential' and 'non-essential' had been a terrible idea and error."

"Yeah, my father's restaurant chain in Michigan was ruined after the Second Pandemic lockdowns," she said, shaking her head. "The politicians' completely random categorizing of my family's business as Non-essential was not only elitist and anti-democratic, but communistic—a page right out of Lenin's playbook. I remember it well as we were drained of our income and wondered if we were even going to survive. But not so for the politicians, pundits, and power brokers that had been able to place themselves at the top of the 'essential' pyramid. They made sure their income was secure by issuing king-like dictates outside of laws or legislation as to what work was most important in a 'society'—and what work wasn't. How is it that laws everywhere were so easily and indiscriminately discarded or ignored by these ruling elite?"

"Simple," Bobby said, now looking at Anna who still stared straight ahead. "They bypassed our constitutional system of consent of the governed in the name of following the science for the greater good of social protection and progress."

"But that's what I don't understand," Anna responded after turning toward Bobby and looking directly into his eyes. "If setting up the Essential and Non-essential dichotomy was so damaging to smaller businesses and organizations, why do the same thing now on an individual level?"

Bobby knew the answer to this question as well, for it had been an active topic of discussion between EB and him since its implementation—or, more accurately, an active topic for EB to lecture him on. "The elite were cutting off their nose to spite their face," he said as he virtually touched his own nose to emphasize the point. "Putting businesses into these categories ended up cratering productivity. Economies all around the world crumbled, and with them tax revenues. The very social control the ruling class had sought through the mandates and lockdowns was evaporating as their income tax, sales tax, VAT tax, and all other tax sources were drying up. So, to save themselves and preserve their power, after the Second Pandemic, they pivoted to a different system, one that never again would bring them to the brink of being overthrown by the anger of the people, or put their revenues in jeopardy.

"The new system that emerged," he continued, "eradicated the designation of companies and organizations as Essential or Non-essential, and instead created a social credit and rating system that applied to individuals. They based this new system on the communist's model in China by establishing a very detailed set of rules that every individual citizen was required to follow in order to have a good social rating. You know the rest from there: school curriculums were adjusted so all children would learn how to think and act in order to achieve an Essential Rating themselves, and policy shifted and companies were required to change their advertising away from strict market dynamics to emphasize this new way. Even labor laws and other general regulations were all reset so there would never again be such severe corporate discrimination and economic disruption."

"And so here we are, slaving away trying to obtain E1 status," Anna observed, still looking directly into Bobby's eyes as though she were trying to break through the digital barrier and peer into his soul. "Like I said, maybe we've gone too far. I know the constant messaging from the powers that be is that we've achieved the greatest level of democracy in human history now that we're all interconnected. But I've got to say, it feels more like autocracy than democracy!"

"I totally agree," Bobby said, again turning away from her

uncomfortable stare. "We're supposed to have a government with a built-in system of real checks and balances to prevent despotism or tyranny. But where are the checks against the rules and regulations of the Technocracy's new top-down rating system? A quote by Patrick Henry comes to mind: 'The Constitution is not an instrument for the government to restrain the people; it is an instrument for the people to restrain the government—lest it come to dominate our lives and interests.'"

"Amen! That should have been on billboards all across the country during the two pandemics," she added. "I wouldn't be surprised if the pandemics were planned all along as the catalyst to accelerate and even bring about the Technocracy. And now all this technological interconnectivity that you and I are laboring day and night to create is rapidly shrinking the world, only furthering their power and control. It's like we've become slaves on their global electronic plantation, bound in their social and financial credit chains in order to produce the digital crops they're using to enrich themselves and expand the Technocracy."

At that point, Bobby froze. Although their conversation had already veered into gray areas the government had categorized as misinformation or social hate speech, to question whether the pandemics were a planned event was nothing short of sedition according to the new Technocrats. But Bobby's fire had been lit, and for the first time in a long time, someone else in the company had some of the same suspicions he had. He wasn't about to back out of the conversation now—risky as it was—but would certainly choose his phrasing carefully.

"That's an interesting perspective, Anna. Why would you think that?" Bobby asked, proud of himself that he deflected it back to her so it would be her words recorded, and not his, on the topic.

"I'm no expert, but by using such harsh and drastic measures during the pandemics to control the people, the ruling elite tipped their hand. They proved to me by what they did to my family that unless you were part of their world, you were nothing more than cattle to them to be herded wherever they commanded. Their disregard and blatant violations of the law showed me that they would use any means at their disposal to grab power and control—even a series of pandemics."

"But that doesn't mean they actually orchestrated the pandemics," Bobby replied back, playing the devil's advocate.

"True, but it wasn't just in this country. All over the world governments seemed to get in line and march lockstep to the orders of the global organizations and international powers on how to respond to the pandemics. This was especially true in the Second Pandemic when the first ever global lockdown was implemented and everyone in the world was required to use that lockdown tracking software. No discussion, no votes, no debates or deliberations. Just an immediate, coordinated total planetary lockdown by order of the global scientific elites in control."

"I have to admit, I thought that might be the end of our Constitution and republic," Bobby confided.

"Me too! It's pretty straightforward, Bobby. Look at the power and control they have now after the pandemics. And their power is only growing as technology advances—the very technology you and I spend all our brainpower and energy trying to deploy. They never would have been able to achieve this if it hadn't been for the pandemics. And I'm supposed to believe that it all just happened by accident?"

"Are you familiar with the three theories of the pandemics?" Bobby asked her.

"Three theories?" she asked with a shrug.

"Yeah. After all these years, still no one has definitively proven that the pandemics were deliberately orchestrated. But a lot of evidence has emerged that they came about in one of three ways. The first theory is that the First Pandemic was a deliberate and coordinated bioweapon attack released by communist China on the world to advance a united and cohesive international socialist order that China, under the Chinese Communist Party, would dominate and lead."

"Sure, I'm familiar with that one and know a lot of people who think that's how it all started," Anna agreed.

"The second theory disputes that it was a deliberate attack by communist China and posits that the virus's escape from the Wuhan Institute of Virology was accidental. But once it had escaped and spread, the Western democratic leftists, socialists, and globalists—of mainly the US and Europe—capitalized on the leak as an unprecedented opportunity to reset the global order to be more socialistic, collectivist, and centralized. *Never let a crisis go to waste* had been their motto."

"And then with the Second Pandemic, they solidified the Great Reset. That one seems to make sense too," Anna added.

"They all seem to make sense in one way or another," Bobby said carefully, making sure his words were hypothetical and couched in intellectual inquiry. "Then there's the third hypothesis. In this view, the communists, led by China and Russia, and the democratic socialists of the West, all coordinated with multinational corporations—especially the Big Tech, Big Pharma and Big Data companies—to either launch the pandemics (which is how the term "plan-demic" came about) or take advantage of the Wuhan lab leak to bring about a global system and order. In this scenario, the world's elites in government, central banks, the media, and corporations—together with other major 'stakeholders'—would all work together because of their similar worldviews to finish what was started in World War II."

"World War II?" Anna asked.

"Yes, the primary purpose of World War II was not just to stop Nazi Germany and the Axis powers, but to smash the entire nation-state system, replacing it with a top-down, United Nations–ruled globalist system of regions and countries."

"Wow, that sounds like the plantation I'm talking about," Anna said, fully engaged in Bobby's theorizing.

"You see, Anna," Bobby continued, sensing her hunger to understand what he had spent an extraordinary amount of time researching and contemplating, "although different in means and participants, the end goal of all three of these concepts was the same: use the fear and ignorance of the masses to demolish the old, largely Christian, decentralized order of individual freedom and rights under God and replace them with collectivistic, socialistic, and modernist laws under a single, unified global state. To do this, the Constitution as one of the last major governmental bulwarks against globalism and socialism had to be weakened inch by inch, step by step, until overthrown. And so, to your point, what better way to do this than via a worldwide pandemic or two that terrorizes people so they'll allow, even beg for, democratically established laws and the Constitution on which they were founded to be discarded?"

Anna was silent and just continued to stare at Bobby for a several moments. "You know, there are others in the company that think like this. Many others," she finally said after sensing Bobby was becoming tense because of her gaze. "Would you like to—" But before she could finish her sentence, a booming voice filled their Pod helmets and their inter-Pod conversation feature was automatically disabled.

"Good people from literally all around the world, thank you for being here with us, whether in person or electronically, at this solemn but truly celebratory occasion!"

The announcement startled Bobby, and annoyed him as he wanted to hear what else Anna was about to say. But their inter-Pod communications had been disabled, as with all of the ceremony's virtual attendees, so everyone's full attention would be on the event at hand.

Probably for the better, he thought to himself. *I've said too much. What am I thinking? I don't even know this woman! What if this was all a setup to see if I'm really loyal to EB, the company, and the new Technocratic way?*

Keeping his eyes straight ahead, even though Anna continued to glance at him as if trying to get his attention, Bobby pretended to focus on the global event before him. All eyes—those of the several hundred that were actually at the event, as well as the millions who were attending virtually like Bobby—were now riveted toward the podium where California's governor-president stood.

"We're here to honor, celebrate, and eternalize one of the great minds and lives of our generation, Jacob Marley," he eulogized. "And who better to lead us than his best friend, his eBeja cofounder, and his amazing partner in crime who, together with Jacob, literally changed our lives and, probably more than any single person on the planet, united the post-pandemic world. Global citizens everywhere, please welcome EB."

CHAPTER 2

The applause was thunderous, though most of it electronically created. EB didn't mind as he glided to the center of the stage getting drenched by the ovation and praise that rained down upon him. Dressed expensively in his usual modernist attire, the chief executive's wardrobe was the leading edge of fashion. Dazzling yet intimidating at the same time, his custom-tailored, two-thousand-dollar collared black Gucci button-up shirt was shrouded by a shimmering night-black unbuttoned black Cucinelli coat and completed with matching black jeans. Narrowing as they descended toward his feet, his costly pant legs ended just slightly above his kicks to reveal just a flash of his naked ankles when he walked.

Though only in his late forties, EB's short hair had already started graying and thinning, giving him a salt-and-pepper look around the sides. It made him appear distinguished in a way, contrasting against his pale white skin. But it was the unwelcomed balding that EB despised, becoming the primary reason he usually wore a cap of some kind. On special occasions, like this one, he would cover his head with a sleek, modern-styled top hat that made him look like a wizard of sorts, or maybe an undertaker. No one in the Bay Area, or in America for that matter, really wore top hats anymore. But EB was never one to follow trends. Instead he set them, and was doing that very thing bringing the top hat back into vogue among the technological and financial elite, who revered him like a Roman god.

His facial features, however, were far from Romanesque and

instead were rather thin and pointy. He deliberately covered his slender jawline with a short cut beard and mustache, also salt and pepper, and his eyes—indoors or out—with a pair of custom-made round-framed Dolce & Gabbana sunglasses. What made the pair special was their emerald lenses. Not just the extraordinary green color, but that they were made with an extremely thin layer of real emeralds, through which EB could see perfectly, but which blocked the outside world from seeing his eyes.

Completing his ensemble were his shoes. He still wore, almost everywhere, the same brand of sneakers he had worn for most of his life. They had become one of his hallmarks with Converse taking note and creating a line of All Star high-tops sporting his name, which became best sellers around the world. For this occasion, he had a special pair of Chucks made that were stripeless and, as usual, completely red except for the white shoelaces. Unlike his closet full of others, this special pair's words "All Star" on the back heel lit up, as did the famous red Converse star, both appearing to pulse a bit brighter, then dimmer, with each step.

"We are all now global citizens in a post-pandemic world," EB orated from center stage, after the crowd finally quieted, "and are more united than ever and more determined to make our diverse planet more equitable, more integrated, and more socially just. And while we all suffered from the scourge of the worst series of pandemics since the Black Plague, we have overcome! But let's be clear, our victory was not by accident. No, it came by the life and by the innovations of great and extraordinary individuals who dedicated their time, talents, and treasure to defeating this pernicious enemy. Jacob Marley is one of these heroes whose technological contributions made us more confident than ever that no matter what difficulties, obstacles, or seeming impossibilities nature throws at us, we will as a human race, together, always overcome!"

With that, the attending audience, as well as the millions connected in through the Pod network, erupted in applause. Except for Bobby. He wanted to cheer EB on, but knew EB too well. EB's views on what Marley had done to help "overcome" the pandemics were quite different from his. And on top of that, Bobby knew that when EB commended Marley, he was really exalting himself. It's true that the two had made all their innovations, inventions, and contributions together as a partnership. But everyone knew that EB was the real brain behind all of it. And Bobby knew that when this ceremony was all over and they were back in the office, EB would test him to make sure he acknowledged that it was really EB who was the hero and who had been at the forefront of developing the technologies to overcome the pandemics.

This had been one of the ways their company's influence and profits had skyrocketed. Though their pandemic plan had been a mutual effort of both EB and Jacob, it was EB that led the development of the applications that could flawlessly monitor each citizen's infection status, location, and whether they were violating lockdown regulations. And it was EB who secured the exclusive government contracts so these applications were deployed nationwide during the Second Pandemic. Although Bobby had also assisted in their development, he hadn't known that these applications would become mandatory for everyone residing in the US. And when he found out and confronted EB that the software might not only be unconstitutional, but could lead to tyranny, EB only laughed—and then almost fired him.

"You're shortsighted and naive," EB had told him. EB was a realist—or so he thought—and in an ever changing and progressing world, so must government be realistic to meet the immediate needs of its people. And as was learned from the First Pandemic, strict and swift directives from authorities were critical for social control to prevent loss of life and minimize damage. Since the Second Pandemic was exponentially more destructive, so also the response needed to be exponentially more forceful.

"No judge is going to prevent the government from mandating our software under some notion that it's unconstitutional," EB had told Bobby. "The Constitution is a living document. As such, it must be adapted to the times. The future isn't known and so a stagnant, binding Constitution that can't easily be changed will end up, as during the Second Pandemic, being more of a hindrance than a help. The reality in our modern, interconnected, ever changing, unpredictable, and technologically advancing world is that governments must be flexible to act and issue immediate social regulations—even if such rules would be oppressive or even unconstitutional in normal times. The whole is greater than the sum of its parts, and so just like a computer is just a conglomerate of parts and pieces, so, too, is society. If a part breaks or a circuit is blown, weeks or months of deliberations, meetings, and debates is not only unproductive, and ruinous, but absurd. Instead, the clear rational course of action is for a competent technician to be called to fix the broken computer expeditiously. What business could survive with broken computers or a nonfunctioning network for weeks or months? Only when all components are working correctly as they were precisely engineered to do will a computer system be useful. Otherwise, it's just a box full of wires and widgets."

As a technologist, maybe *the* technologist of the age, EB always seemed to use some kind of technological illustration to explain life and the universe. That's because everything really was technological to EB. Existence as it was known could be simplified down to parts and pieces, zeros and ones, atomic and subatomic particles all marvelously interacting together in harmony in what he called "the cosmos." And the cosmos, or universe, is one giant, extremely advanced technological system that evolved and is continuing to evolve as each of its countless parts and pieces, all perfectly connected, correctly interact.

EB wasn't certain whether there was a Creator that initiated the fabrication of the universe, but was pretty sure there wasn't. But even if there was, that was irrelevant to him and should be to everyone else. If a Creator did exist, then that "God"—like any sophisticated technologist—drafted the design, flipped the switch, and then let the machine function as engineered. "Think of it as 3D printing," he liked to explain, "and the start button was the Big Bang." EB once believed in a more personal, emotional, and immanent God, but that was long ago as a child when he also believed in Santa Clause and superheroes. But after his many years of study and learning from some of the brightest minds on the planet, EB had grown up and graduated with honors from such "superstitious nonsense" as he called it.

"The great realization of our times," EB continually reminded Bobby, "is that mankind has no limits, and through rigorous scientific effort, can collectively determine its own future. And since science applied is technology, it should be self-evident that technology controls the times. Consequently, for progress to continue in the US and the world, it is critical that the Constitution be adapted to what technology determines it should be—not the other way around. The pandemics are a perfect illustration that dramatic life changes happen unexpectedly and faster than constitutional change."

With such logic, EB wasn't the least bit ashamed to say that a technocratic elite should be the *de jure* leaders of society. "They are the *de facto* rulers regardless of whether the ruled masses elected them. In any area of life, whether government, law, media, science, education, the economy—even church and religion—technology determines how social structures function. Technology determines how fast and in what level of detail—or not—information is communicated within an industry or between industries. Technology controls everything, from how kids learn in school to how the country would respond to an EMP or nuclear attack. We technologists have evolved to be far more than Plato's philosopher kings. Like it or not, we have become the real power, priests, and parliament of the present age. We are the new masters of the universe.

"A Constitution from over two hundred years ago at one point might have been genius and necessary, but it's run its course, just as the electric engine has replaced the polluting, cumbersome, soon to be completely banned gas combustion engine," EB argued. "If the Constitution can't be quickly overhauled for the times, then there needs to be a new Constitution, or better, a fresh idea for a new social order altogether. A technological order, as demonstrated when we took swift action during and after the pandemics, is inescapable."

It was this kind of thinking that most disturbed Bobby. Just like oppressive systems of the past, EB was elevating a certain class—the technological intelligentsia—to priestly status who should hold all the keys of the kingdom. And like priestly classes of the past, they had their own secret languages and codes that insulated them from the masses and gave them power to control. Because the everyday man or woman was ignorant, unable to understand their geek-speak, they need not be consulted.

The pandemics, especially the Second Pandemic, were perfect examples. While some of the mitigating efforts of the elite were publicly announced and initiated, most were unseen and necessarily conducted behind the scenes because of the speed needed to effect action, or alternatively so as not to create panic, or worse, rebellion. Whether public or in secret, all were done according to how the science leaders directed, not according to the laws the people's representatives had established.

"Whether you or the masses approve or not, this was the reality," EB had explained to Bobby regarding the Second Pandemic, or P2. "Any other course of action wouldn't have been effective. The choice was to act immediately according to science or lose hundreds of millions if not billions of lives. P2 made it crystal clear and put beyond any debate that the Constitution cannot save America; only the scientific elite can."

EB had no problem acknowledging that the draconian controls exerted during each of the pandemics weren't pleasant, but insisted they were absolutely necessary and even an inevitable part of the ebb and flow of human progress. Negatively, many people had their lives turned upside down—economically, socially, culturally—or worse, ended, because of the ravages of COVID during P1 and P2. But positively, and much more important, society was finally awakened to the deep truth that it could reset itself and reform itself to a new way of life that would catapult society and humanity as a whole to its next evolutionary level.

"As the seasons have taught man for all time, death brings life," EB would say. "And never before had the world come together in such haste to collectively fight a common enemy as during the scourge of the pandemics. Yes, there were petty disagreements among nations over PPE supplies, vaccine distribution methods, and proper regulations to expunge the virus. But overall, the world cooperated on an unprecedented level, and demonstrated that, with effective global science-based leadership, any foe can be defeated when the world is united.

"This victory secured over the pandemics occurred because for the first time in history, on a global level, humanity was sufficiently interconnected, technologically. On the most basic level, the medical technologists who consisted of virologists, epidemiologists, and other specialists in medicine were able to quickly address the pandemics through international health agencies, specifically the World Health Organization, and coordinate and communicate instantly across oceans and over mountains. Quarantines, lockdowns, as well as business and school closures were all the result of medical and social technologists applying their specialized scientific knowledge, and then disseminating this information internationally at the speed of light.

"Then, beyond the diagnosis of the disease and implementation of the social containment models, the technologists also led in determining the best ways to protect societies from the ravages of P1 and P2. In the First Pandemic, technologists brought to light the need for masks, technologists rapidly diffused understanding of how basic hand washing, social distancing, and self-isolation could stem the spread of the virus, and of course—and maybe most importantly of all—the mRNA treatment was a technological grand slam, a revolution in vaccine development that has now forever changed humanity."

Like most scientists, EB knew that, technically, mRNA concoctions were not vaccines since they didn't eradicate the virus or prevent its spread. But the scientific community had decided it was time to change the definition of what a vaccine is since mRNA shots at least became a somewhat effective treatment to lessen the symptoms caused by the disease. But much more important to the technological elite, the mRNA technology was the first step in mass social genetic engineering. For EB, this alone made mandating the concoctions a wild success even though they were initially experimental and without any long-term testing.

"Yes, many criticized the mRNA vaccines initially and resisted them in P1. But that was because people were thinking about themselves, thinking individually instead of socially. There will always be casualties during great technological leaps forward. And so it was with the vaccine. But the injury they brought and the lives lost were insignificant compared to the long-term benefits of being able to insert engineered DNA-level instructions into the human body. The door had to be opened, and accepted—and should've been welcomed by the masses for the potential of transforming the human species by modifying its code. Of course, any technology is a risk, but the greater risk is stagnancy and hesitation. Only if the leading technologists take these big risks will there be big rewards down the road for the health and welfare of all."

And while EB went to great lengths to evangelize the nations as to the extraordinary potential of his and his colleagues' technologies, he liked to keep quiet the extraordinary financial rewards he and his comrades reaped from the pandemics. During the First Pandemic, the global financial system nearly collapsed, which would have wiped out the massive profits that had accrued to the scientific elite. Consequently, after P1, they convinced the financial technologists to flood the planet with freshly printed money, in all currencies, in order to keep the world's economies from crashing.

On the highest level, central bank boards used their monetary wizardry to create enough money to sustain their nations' economies during the catastrophic tumble in markets and jobs due to the rapid spread of the virus. Such foresight, they argued, would soften the devastating economic effects of the lockdowns, business closures, travel restrictions, and many other constraints—restrictions and emergency measures governments had convinced their citizens they had no choice but to take.

Consequently, trillions of dollars were conjured out of thin air and injected into the system by the fast-moving Federal Reserve monetary scientists in the US. Around the world, other central bank directors did the same and the planet was awash with new FIAT money magically created by the press of a button.

They all knew that what they really were doing was kicking the can down the road, but it was the only option in a hybrid world where money and power was still decentralized among nearly two hundred nation-states.

"Of course, the money would go back into the pockets of the productive," EB boasted. "Where else should it go? To the unproductive hordes? Enough was distributed to families, small businesses, nonprofit organizations, and corporations to keep the essential ones from collapsing. That was important. But more important is that we who are building the global technological and social infrastructure receive the stimulus so we can continue to shift power away from the inefficient and ignorant to the efficient and enlightened."

It was EB who brought Bobby to understand that the windfall from the pandemic years was by design, making those years eBeja's and EB's best ever for achieving massive profits and increased influence. EB had benefited nicely during the First Pandemic, but it was P2 and his patented Lockdown® software and network that made him one of the biggest Big Tech winners on the planet.

"I'm proud of this and what we in Big Tech have done. In the Second Pandemic, we basically saved humanity. Big Tech should absolutely be rewarded! Think about it—any sector that is based on and thereby dependent on science should be considered a part of Big Tech, or the technology sector. I know I'm defining it more broadly than most, but in order for the planet to move into its next phase of evolution, technology needs to take its rightful place. Here's the key: Big Tech not only includes the various fields of computer science, but must include any industry that is data driven. So not only would the medical, healthcare, and the pharmaceutical industries now be included, but virtually every industry should be seen as a subset of Big Tech. As such, those who design, engineer, and deploy the systems that enabled these sectors to function and flourish are inescapably the true lords of society, with we stakeholders of the infrastructure that manage, deliver, and control the data, its kings."

Subsuming everything under the Big Tech umbrella was part of the problem to Bobby. For this new ruling class was not like the kings of old, seeking to only amass wealth for themselves through the labor of a slave class. This they certainly strived for. But on top of that these elitists believed that their accumulation of power was the only way to truly protect themselves, their fortunes, and their plan to reset, remake and renew the world. "The planet can only be saved and perfected in an interconnected, globalized world," EB would often preach.

Though they were not able to fully accomplish this in the First Pandemic, by the Second Pandemic they had learned that only when there is an existential danger will the nations of the world abdicate their sovereignty. The First Pandemic set the stage to unite the world against the virus, enabling extraordinary amounts of labor and capital to be deployed against this global enemy. But it was during P2, when there was a truly great cost in human life, that desperate humanity accepted the belief that only under the command and control of the technologists, an existential pandemic threat could be overcome. The fear and devastation that P2 brought was enough to shift the mindset of nations around the world to capitulate to the idea that the sole hope for survival was a worldwide collective effort against the disease.

"And just as we succeeded in stopping COVID, can we not

do the same if we collectively fight the persistent enemies of poverty, ignorance, inequality, and war?" EB would ask. "We have proven from the resulting health, social, and financial success over the pandemics that the scientific community is really the only community capable of understanding the depth and complexity of human society, its needs and workable solutions that can be deployed. So, in this regard, it's also really the only sector that can be trusted to rule. If you like what the computer revolution has done for your life, let us engineer the entire world!"

EB often used the term "engineer" since it didn't smack of the autocratic control that he so despised, at least when others tried to practice it over him. For him, harmful dictatorships emerge only when the technological illiterate take control. Therefore, dictatorships aren't inherently evil but are only such when they are unscientific.

"Science is based on fact, on the absolute laws of the physical, material universe, not ideological, religious, or some other unprovable, concocted notion. This is why the vast majorities around the world have finally awakened and united together in support of centralized technocratic governance. Only this way will the planet and its communities be unencumbered by the slow democratic processes, uncontrollable decentralized nations, and chaotic individual rights. Post pandemic, the world finally sees that to save the planet, the technocratic elite needs the freedom and flexibility to lead and do whatever necessary to reset our technologically based systems to permanently establish a worldwide technocracy. How could any other type of person lead a community if he or she doesn't understand that a community— any community—is really a technological construct, a living machine with a specific task in relation to the global whole? How could a non-technocrat effectively organize it and manage it if they don't truly understand the science of people—the bits and bytes of their social programs—as well as the underlying complex code that determines what people really are and how they act?

"As every technocrat knows, the laws of the universe must be followed perfectly for technology to work. Since communities are technological constructs, so, too, must they also be designed and engineered to these same universal laws. Think of a computer. It is designed by engineering experts, assembled by expert technicians, and managed by hardware and software experts. Likewise, so should social policy be overseen by expert technologists. Remember the initial failure of categorizing businesses or organizations as 'essential' or 'non-essential' in P1? Such a catastrophe would have never occurred if the technologists instead of the sociologists and politicians were in charge. Acting on old models of old ideas from the ignorant, corporate distinctions were made blindly. There had been no testing and modeling, under real-world laboratory conditions, of deeming only some businesses essential. On the contrary, it was a knee-jerk reaction by mostly the uneducated and shallow to appear smart and in control during a crisis.

"In reality, the politicians were trying to appease and economically pander to their big donors, powerful constituent groups, and their party's base. How else could golf courses in Arizona be essential and open, but in California be deemed non-essential and closed by state edict? Or in Delaware, where 'essential' florists could deliver bouquets, but 'non-essential' restaurants were barred from delivering pizzas? If proper analysis had been done and if the politicians had paid attention to what the leading technologists, like myself and Marley, were saying, the refining down to 'essential' and 'non-essential' would never have taken place on a corporate or organizational level, but only on the much more reasonable *individual* level. Like a computer network, each part and component would have been analyzed relative to the proper functioning of the whole."

But people are not computers, Bobby had wanted to tell EB even though he knew EB wouldn't listen. Such a comment could also cost him his job, so he was very careful what to say and not to say when around EB, who he could see through his Pod system was just about finished in his eloquent lauding of Marley.

"And so just as Jacob had been a leader and savior during the pandemic," EB continued from the elaborate stage, "he has also been a leader in overcoming the greatest enemy of all—the mindset that death itself is inevitable. Because of his tireless efforts and marvelous mind, we now know that is not the case. Death is no longer inescapable. This was Jacob's true cause, the real reason he woke up each morning and spent his days laboring. It is his epitaph. So we are not here today to mourn or cry. That would imply Jacob is gone and no longer with us. No, let us celebrate this giant of a man—the giant whose intellectual power, creative force, and tireless dedication to the eternality of humanity has impacted all of us, and no doubt will continue to influence and shape us for centuries, even millennia, to come. Let us look at our time together on this cold and foggy Friday morning, not as the end of Jacob Marley, for it is not. But the beginning, the beginning of the next leg of his everlasting journey."

Again, the applause boomed, this time continuing and continuing as all eyes remained hypnotically fixed on EB.

CHAPTER 3

Along with the clapping and cheering, music started to play. Not the usual funeral dirge, but a soft electronic deep house style melody providing background to EB's sacred words.

"We have finally overcome the grave!" EB said, raising his voice a bit to marvelously blend with the digitized music and its beat.

"Because of Jacob, the grave as we have known it has been replaced with virtual life, digital continuation, re-created existence. No more do we sit silently as in days past, crying in pain and misery for the passing of our loved ones. Never again!"

Immediately the crowd, now swaying to the music, shouted "Never!" back to him.

"Instead, we celebrate, we make merry. Admirers around the world, now is not the time to grieve—now is the time to party!" he said, raising both hands in glory above his head. And with that, the event's DJ transitioned flawlessly to a rapturous EDM carol, an upbeat techno-mix suitable for this historic party, bringing the audience to their feet. Pod attendees throughout the world were also now bobbing their heads to the beat, with not a few rising up and dancing in front of their desks or in their living rooms or the clubs or schools or wherever they were connected in.

EB himself started to rock back and forth a little, in sync with the pulse, and then stepped back, yielding to the audience as he could see that the party spirit had taken over. The rest of the elites attending personally joined him moving or rocking on some level to the rhythm. Some were a little uncomfortable, but most were not, having already embraced the new format. Though it was cold and foggy, EB had insisted that the ceremony be conducted outdoors for this very reason; he knew Marley would be pleased. EB was a little upset, though, that it wasn't quite perfect since the fog and thick dark clouds above hid the sun. But at least it wasn't raining so the round elevated stage as well as the hundreds of seats surrounding it could remain uncovered and stay dry throughout the celebration.

New settings are required for new formats. And new settings emerge from new mindsets. EB was ecstatic that humanity had taken the great leap forward to the new technological mindset—his mindset—ever since the pandemics. The pain, suffering, and especially the loss brought on by the Second Pandemic genuinely turned out to be great gain—maybe the single greatest advancement ever for the planet. Pre-pandemic man had been stuck in the old order of beliefs. But following the global scourge, the lesson was learned and it seemed everyone's mindset had been changed to understand how critical science and technology were to the salvation of mankind. Yes, for a few right-wing nuts the new technological order emerging was being twisted into another one of their plethora of conspiracies. But for the vast majority, especially among the masses outside of the US, the virus had activated the fundamental transformation of social order that brought them to where they were today. Even funerals were now transformed.

Of course, it wasn't just the virus that did this. *I did this, and Marley did this*, EB thought as the music and celebration continued to reverberate through the cemetery, although that term had been for the most part canceled, in large part thanks to EB. The new and socially correct name was now *formetery*, representing the new understanding that death was simply a next step, a fresh formation of an individual, not a termination. Under the new mindset, the word "funeral" was no longer appropriate either since it represented all the old, sad, and depressing ideas about dying. Its replacement, *funerbration*, much better described how a person's progress on their transmigrational journey should be viewed as a celebration. And that is exactly what they were doing now for Marley, whose huge mausoleum just behind the stage was also pulsing to the cadence under the beat of celebratory neon lights.

Marley's massive tomb was quite a wonder, just as both he and EB had planned it to be. Unlike the decrepit mausoleums of the past, Marley's was a palace fit for a king because Marley was a king, a technological and financial monarch of the modern age whose life was to be continued via this first-of-kind ultra-modern showcase. It also served as a marvelous advertisement for this part of EB's corporate empire.

"People of the world, humanity is taking another leap forward today," EB bellowed over the pulsing, hypnotic music. "Because of Jacob Marley's genius and love for all people everywhere, and because of his foresight into the needs of our world, I bring you his and my promise that we will no longer neglect our planet by adhering to the archaic past where our planet's needs are taken for granted. No more are the days when Mother Earth is used to bury bodies six feet under in wooden boxes. No more will the remains of these temples be embalmed like mummies and stored away in the good soil of the planet to sit idle and decay away. The man we celebrate today, Jacob Marley, abhorred such backward and unscientific thinking. And so it's for him that today I'm announcing life and death. Life because there is now a better way, the new way of life that will enable you to never lose your loved ones. Life because you will be able to see them whenever you want, speak with them whenever you have need, and spend time with them as much as you desire. Life because Elevation has arrived!"

Again the attendees, both virtual and actual, erupted in applause and jubilation, cheering him wildly as the music continued to fill the foggy air. The anticipation was thick enough to cut with a knife, just as EB liked it to be. He always made his new product releases more than just an announcement. For him, they needed to be huge events, moments of history, larger than life, just as he saw himself.

"But where there is life," EB continued over the cheering and music, "there must be death. But the death I bring you today is that, finally, once and for all, we are bringing the body-burying industry to its long-needed end. People of the planet, we have put death to death! Right now, starting here at Bay Global Formetery, you will be the first to witness the end of death. As you all know, tens of thousands of bodies used to occupy sacred real estate here at Bay Global, buried deep beneath the dirt so that family and friends could never be with them. But all that changes today. The bodies are gone, the buried are buried no more. Life has overcome death and the grave, and as you will see, Elevation has triumphed!

"In the days of ancient Egypt," EB continued as he paced the stage, "the pyramid stood as a monument to life, a declaration that life could continue, a perfect technological structure that radiated hope that the grave was only a gateway to everlasting life. But what is life? What if you could sit with your departed grandmother, laugh with her, joke with her, and listen to her life stories, full of wisdom and wonder? What if, while interacting with her, all her actions and emotions were indistinguishable from how they were before she passed away? And even more, what if her most glaring flaws and degenerations were all eliminated? Should we not conclude that this beautiful loved one of yours has evolved to a new plane, a stage beyond us, the next level where we all want to be where there is no longer corruption?"

The crowds were silent now and the music softened as EB leaned in toward those who were actually in the audience. For those connected through the Pod, it was as if he were leaning right into their face.

"With Elevation," he explained, now in a hushed tone, perfectly choreographed to the faded melodies, "afflictions and faults such as mental illnesses, unbridled anger and rage, and cruelty are erased. When Elevated, it's as if you are born again, but even more alive with a heightened and advanced level of emotional consciousness. 'But how is this possible?' you ask. Technology. Technology Marley and I have created—the only one of its kind.

"Members of the new order, Marley and I spent our lives over the last decades to bring you technologies that will enhance and better your life. But now we bring you a technology that is so groundbreaking, so innovative that it may well be mankind's next evolutionary leap. Today I give you a technology that actually gives back life—elevated life—so that you are no longer slaves to death. And this new, elevated life will reside not underground in a coffin among the dead, but above ground among the living in the peaceful dwelling of a home, like this extraordinary pyramid home of Jacob Marley," EB said as he whisked around and pointed to the illuminated polyhedron.

Marley's sarcophagus was truly extraordinary. Towering exactly 47.9 feet in height, the monstrosity sat on its own quarter acre of lushly flowered gardens, mature cypress trees, and perfectly manicured lawn. To ensure absolute security, EB had surrounded it with a state-of-the-art invisible electromagnetic fence with a single entry gate that required a well-guarded passcode to enter. Pyramid in shape, the spectacular mausoleum was completely surfaced in reflective, solar energy–producing glass except for the wide single front door, which was crafted in pure twenty-four-carat gold. Modeled in some ways after the great pyramid of Giza, the middle of each wall was oriented exactly north, south, east, and west, and its height was exactly one-tenth of Pharaoh Khufu's resting place in Egypt. What was drastically different from its ancient predecessor, however, was what was found in its interior.

Starting with the entryway, and flowing throughout the rest of Marley's resting place was sophisticated mood lighting, so refined that it could almost be felt. Another creation of EB and Marley— before he passed—the emotional illumination reflected the mood not of the entrant, but of Marley himself. The secret to expressing Marley's emotional state of mind came from the living process the two had developed using a very tiny concoction of obscure and previously thought useless elements of the human body. These material components, unique trace elements that made up less than 1 percent of the body, were the only parts of the body that would actually be housed in one of these structures. This was because they were the only elements needed to reconstitute a person into his next phase of existence, or *Elevation*—the seemingly magical state of renewed life.

Because less than 1 percent of the human body was needed for Elevation, the remaining 99-plus percent of the body's substances—consisting of oxygen, carbon, hydrogen, nitrogen, calcium, and phosphorus—were salvaged by EB's company and harvested for numerous commercial and industrial needs, creating a whole new multitrillion-dollar industry of body parts recycling for eBeja.

Once inside Marley's pyramid, one would know immediately from the lighting what mood Marley was in. Much more a house than a tomb, the entryway led to an open Living Room, a full three-dimensional projection space where the interactions took place. Marley's Living Room was set up to look exactly like the living area of his previous penthouse home with the main furniture having been moved to the mausoleum, along with the most important pieces of his rich collection of art, sculptures, and artifacts.

In the center of the mood-lit room was the portal area. Marley had decided he wanted the portal to be overlaid with his favorite Persian rug, a one-of-a-kind gift from the late king of Saudi Arabia. The masterpiece of fine Vase Carpets of the Safavid period, most certainly a Kerman, was decorated with beautifully colored sickle-leaves, vine scrolls, and palmettes. With the rug now valued at over fifty million dollars, Marley had left instructions for it to be roped off so none of his few visitors would accidentally walk on it.

But the rug's value was only a fraction of the value of the technology that lay beneath it. The portal area was hidden under the floor and was activated when a guest would enter. Once the advanced AI-driven solid light hologram system was triggered, Marley would appear in the portal area on top of his beloved rug. From there, he could move around the Living Room at his leisure to interact with the visitors as an advanced, fully interactive, fully expressive tactile conglomerate of light and sound, somehow energized and animated by his trace elements.

Astoundingly true-to-life, the new Marley in every respect and quality was flawless. His mannerisms, expressions, and attitudes were perfect. Within the confines of his Living Room, he would walk around, sit in his chairs, admire his art and collectibles, all while conversing with his visitors. Marley would even would talk to himself, as Marley always had. It was extraordinary. The Elevated Marley knew everything Marley had known while alive, acted exactly as Marley did, but was now an even better version of Marley since he was void of his previous annoying habits and foibles.

Even Marley's morbid humor was intact, which had been perfectly on display a day earlier. It started when a couple of the engineers began arguing over the light levels of the Living Room. Marley, animated and walking about with EB at the time, suddenly erupted at the engineers with a horrid, almost deafening howl. He began berating one in particular for the slow progress he was making and the money that had been wasted because of his sluggishness. Through a special interconnection of his pyramid with eBeja, Marley's database was able to stay up to date on all the company's activity and, most importantly, its financials. This was important to EB who wanted to ensure that everything Marley knew before he passed, he would also know in his Elevated state.

True to form and shouting at the top of his lungs, Marley cursed the engineer and screamed, "I'm going to tear through you like butter!" and then in a move unexpected from a forty-eight-year-old man, darted straight at the poor technician. Forgetting for a moment that they were in a sarcophagus instead of the office, the technician covered his head with his arms and ducked as if to protect himself from the charging Marley. *Whoosh!* Marley passed right through him. The engineer felt a mild electric shock, but nothing more than a light jolt like when touching a nine-volt battery with the tongue. Marley then twirled around and started laughing hysterically. "Get it?" he convulsed. EB lost it himself and buckled over in laughter, something that hadn't happened since his early days in San Francisco when he was just getting started as a technologist.

"It won't be long now," EB informed his captive audience now at the very edge of the stage, "before every person, if they choose to give their loved ones the gift of full spectrum

Elevation, will be able to spend quality time, share the most precious moments, and interact with them in a beautiful setting like this pyramid home. Very soon, we will be launching Elevation Centers in formeteries all across the country and world so the dead can be brought back to life, turning the sorrow of the nations to joy!"

Even though Elevation was cost prohibitive to the masses, EB was absolutely confident that expansion to the general market could happen sooner rather than later, but only if the rich and powerful of the planet bought into it. And all indications were that they couldn't wait to jump in. Already, numerous wealthy elites from all countries around the world had indicated they were ready to pre-purchase their own custom-designed mausoleums for their own and their family members' Elevations. These commitments alone would create a tremendous windfall for EB, enabling him to lower the high price of Elevation and speed up the mass rollout of the product. And once the masses could enjoy this new revolutionary level of contact and interaction with departed loved ones, EB's profits would be elevated even further into the stratosphere.

"Global citizens, long speeches aren't needed anymore, nor are they desired. Actions are life, not words. This has always been one of my and Marley's mottos. So what better way to show you the glory of Elevation and celebrate Marley's Elevation than with actions—his actions, his life. Enlightened people of the planet, please welcome my partner, my comrade in arms, one of the most intelligent, enlightened, and gifted men of history—the one and only and newly Elevated Jacob Marley!"

Instantly, Marley manifested next to him, smiling from ear to ear, and took a bow as the audience again erupted in jubilation. The music volume was again increased matching the heights of the people's enthusiasm and everyone spontaneously started waving their arms, dancing and shouting praise for their reconstituted hero. Pre-distributed red and white confetti was thrown into the air by all, creating what looked like a bloody snowstorm surrounding Marley's platform. "Speech, speech!" the crowd started to yell in unison. Marley glanced at EB, who gave him a go-ahead thumbs-up, and then, turning back to the audience with arms raised, shouted "thank you, thank you!" in his true voice, amazingly amplified.

"I really didn't expect to give a speech. What an honor. Thank you! Your eyes are showing you that I'm here, your ears hear my voice, all your senses tell you that Jacob Marley is right here in front of you," he bellowed, patting his chest with both hands as if to affirm his corporality. "Well, citizens, I am here!" Again, the crowd, both the ones there in body and those connected remotely, cheered and applauded wildly.

"I'm overwhelmed with your support and commitment to our new way, the world's new way of life instead of death. Death has for so long been a brutal sting to those left behind, a painful separation and unbearable parting. But no more!" he said, waving clasped hands over his head in victory.

Then, unseen before except to the few who had graced the inside of his mausoleum, Marley took a step and another and another, walking to the edge of the stage. The audience went silent as he started to jog its perimeter, smiling and waving in unprecedented realism. He couldn't go beyond the edge—the technology wouldn't allow it. But it was far enough for the people to realize that a great next step had been taken. What Marley demonstrated was that EB and his company had finally perfected the procedure to harvest the complete brain, every one of its 86 billion neurons and 125 trillion synapses—the full connectome— and then, in conjunction with the trace elements, animate it with perfect emotional precision, holographically. The possibilities seemed limitless, as did EB's future profits.

CHAPTER 4

Bobby, like many of the world's Podded participants, was on his feet, not jubilant, but aghast—not at all accustomed to the new "progressive" way of celebrating death. To him, it felt more like a company rally than a funeral.

He had known something big was coming but had no idea it would be this dramatic, or disturbing. Now all the late nights at the office made sense. He had worked his tail off to help prepare for Marley's Elevation, but had no idea his funerbration would be the place for the company's big reveal. But unsettling as the whole affair was, it made sense—at least EB sense. Always going large and looking for any advantage over the competition, EB never pulled back from a big opportunity. What better way to announce this giant revolution than through the company's virtual-reality Pod-connected world while onstage with the resurrected Marley?

Maybe EB was right and death should be redefined, and I should really embrace this modern view. Bobby reasoned that if humanity had come this far technologically and the psyche of a person could now be fully uploaded, and then projected in a living-room-sized space, it wouldn't be long until there really were synthetic-intelligence, android-type life forms that lived forever. Contrary to all Bobby had learned growing up, and instinctually thought today, seeing Marley leisurely jog around, interact with EB, and express genuine emotion had him confused. Not a technologist, it wasn't possible for him to comprehend how all of this was scientifically possible. Had EB discovered a way to bypass death? But if so, that would mean death was purely a material occurrence, and not a spiritual state. Reconciling what he was seeing with his basic Christian beliefs was quite difficult. Regardless, he liked the challenge.

Having grown up in a fairly conservative Presbyterian home and neighborhood, Bobby couldn't remember a time where he didn't believe the basic doctrines of the church. Death was not supposed to be a normal process of the planet and man, but was a consequence of an action—a divine judgment on humanity that came as a result of the first man and woman's criminal rebellion against their Creator. Such a view of death was just accepted, and never really questioned by his siblings, friends, and fellow churchgoers. Even at the small Christian college where Bobby earned his BA and MBA in accounting, there hadn't been a real debate that death might be simply a biological malady, like leprosy, that could eventually be eradicated.

Perhaps there were debates about it and he just hadn't noticed. His family never had a lot of money, and so the funds his parents spent for his education meant a lot to him. They knew he was a high IQ math whiz and sacrificed a great deal of their time and energy to help the young prodigy go to Martin Samson College, the "Harvard" of Christian colleges. Known for its math program on the undergraduate level, and even more reputable for its master's-level accounting degree, graduates were aggressively recruited by some of the largest and most prestigious companies in the country. So Bobby focused like a laser on his specialty, keeping his eye on the prize instead of going to hear campus speakers or delving into doctrinal questions. He did take the required minimum courses in Bible, History of Christianity, and some straightforward "Christian Life" classes. But for him, time not in class was time in the library studying, and if extra time permitted, being with his sweetheart.

His parents, who had been married for thirty years now, had always told him, "Don't jump into marriage; it's for a lifetime." But when Bobby first caught a glimpse of Olivia in the small church he attended one snowy November Sunday during his junior year, he knew. No second thoughts or hesitation, as if receiving a divine word from heaven. He just knew she would be his wife. He couldn't explain it to anyone, nor did he feel the need. Of course his parents were shocked when during Christmas break he broke the news to them that he had met the girl he would grow old with. After all, the wonder kid was only sixteen and she, though the same age, was still a junior in high school. They gave him every excuse they could think of to slow down, get to know her better, make sure the feeling was mutual, and even tried the old "feelings come and go, but a spouse is always there" line.

He was glad they did spend the entire holiday trying to convince him that he simply had a crush and it very likely could fade once the warm fuzzies wore off. They did that because they cared. They also didn't want him to get distracted from the program they both had worked so hard to get him accepted into, and paid so much money for. But after three weeks of testing his resolve, they relented, seeing that Bobby was serious and actually was taking it slow.

Occasionally overhearing him on the communicator with her, they later told him that they were genuinely touched with how kind and honorable in his words he was to her, and how he would spend hour upon hour chatting with her about deep and substantive issues relating to marriage, relationships, family, and, of course, sex. They weren't eavesdropping, and would have rather not heard anything. But Bobby wasn't a secretive person and so would speak openly regardless of who was in the room with him. Bobby actually wanted them to hear and see his conversations, and understand that this was his true first love. He wanted to show her off to the world, and for everyone to know how blessed he felt and what a gift he believed Olivia was. For him, there weren't enough hours in the day for their long and many conversations, emails, and VR chats.

"Thank God for unlimited VR talk time," they reminded him since they were also paying for his VR connector and all his other bills while he was in college. But after receiving all A's during the first semester he was together with Olivia, they were confident that their investment in his future was being well managed and wouldn't be squandered by a distracting crush. They did ask Bobby to promise to wait at least until he finished his undergraduate program and she finished high school before getting married. This had been their plan all along, and so one year later, during Christmas break of his senior year, he proposed, and she accepted, making Christmas a doubly special time for them.

The love birds honored Bobby's parents' request and weren't married until after they both graduated, both with honors, in a beautiful summer wedding at the church where they met. The honeymoon would have to wait, however, since funds and time were limited. Separated now financially from their parents, the couple had decided they both would work as much as they could during the summer to save money for a nicer and larger space to live than the couples' dorm reserved for married grad students. Bobby had been accepted into the graduate program, so they knew that they would have at least two more years at the school. But that wasn't going to stop them from starting a family, so a place of their own, with space for kids, was important to them. Plus, it was against school rules to have babies in the dorms.

They did find a cute little house to rent right next to the campus just as Bobby started his master's accounting program, and having timed it perfectly, had their first child, Martha, before he finished his first year. By the time he graduated, again on the honor roll and with a specialization in multinational corporate accounting, Olivia had given birth again. They both had always wanted a big family, having come from larger families themselves, and so saw this as only the beginning of their conception venture. Of course, it really wasn't up to them, but together they prayed for God's blessing and a quiver full of little arrows to fill their house. They were convinced that with the fantastic job offer Bobby already had, a big family wouldn't be a financial difficulty at all—until they moved to the Bay Area.

The sticker shock of San Francisco's outrageous cost of living quickly changed their minds. They knew that housing would be expensive, but it was all the other expenses, from electricity to food as well as connectivity fees and other bills, that made adding additional children to their tribe much more difficult than anticipated. But even those expenses would have been manageable if it weren't for the exorbitant local and state taxes Bobby would have to pay.

Just after Bobby and his family moved to San Francisco to be with eBeja, California amended its constitution and officially became the People's Republic of California. The "new" socialist California took nearly 50 percent of their income in state, local, sales, VAT, and all other taxes. There were no exemptions or loopholes. And this was on top of an already outrageous federal income tax. Yes, all Bobby's and his family's healthcare was covered, but since Obamacare decades earlier, the quality of healthcare had diminished so substantially over the years that it was hardly used. Most people went around it and used black market doctors and health providers, which had to be paid for outside the monolithic, now consolidated, single-payer Medicare system.

But it wasn't healthcare that was sucking all the state and local taxes; it was housing. A major part of the new "Golden State's golden transformation to socialism," as they touted it, was the socialization of all housing. Just as all healthcare had been finally centralized in government so all could have "affordable" healthcare, so in the PRC was all housing subsumed under government rent and price controls. This became a huge hurdle for the Cratchits, as California's new policy toward large families became very, very unfriendly, crippling their ability to be allotted an affordable space big enough to accommodate the number of children they wanted to have.

Suddenly, a voice drew him out of his thoughts. "You can sit down now; it's over." It was Anna again, still virtually next to him, looking amazing, at least for a digital persona.

"Oh, yes, of course," Bobby replied, as he pulled his mind away from his own family and focused again on his corporate one and its event at hand.

Quickly seating himself, he realized he was the last one to sit down in his own VR Pod space, and was a bit embarrassed. Marley had finished his speech and the audience had quieted and reclined again after their long ovation. *At least the recording will show that I stayed standing longer than anyone else! It could be ammunition with EB if he ever questions my loyalty to the Elevation project.*

Waving goodbye to everyone, with many doing the same to him, Marley vanished as abruptly as he had appeared. "You are all witnesses that we have crossed over and are now in a new era where passing away is not the end of life, but the beginning. Immortality has come!" EB authoritatively said.

"Go now in the peace of knowing that Marley is with us forever, and of course, the same can be true for all of you. Global citizens, what progress we've made! So, even as you leave, continue this celebration in your hearts and minds. To keep the soiree going, we've scheduled several future times of conversation and interaction with our esteemed genius as well. All information can be found on the eBeja memorial page on the company site." The audience once again vigorously applauded.

"So, until our next gathering with the great Jacob Marley, good afternoon." And with that, EB dismissed the global audience with the date and time of the next interaction with Marley flashing in a bright three-dimensional holographic message in the center of the stage where the other holograph had just been. Bobby was certain he would not be a part of that interaction, unless EB made him. EB made him do a lot of things he would have preferred not to do. But such was the cost of doing business, or in Bobby's case, doing EB's business, which was very, very big business.

A countdown clock appeared in the upper right corner of his vision, alerting Pod connectees that their event was about to end. The clock blinked in red digits . . . *10* . . . *9* . . . *8* . . . which also seemed to be a countdown of EB's departure in his S-92 medium-lift twin-engine Sikorsky from the event. *6* . . . *5* . . . *4.* The lifelike 3D image of EB's luxury 'copter departing from the helipad next to Marley's mausoleum whisking him away to his next appointment began to fade. *3* . . . *2* . . . *1* . . . Bobby's helmet went dark.

STAVE 2

SEVEN YEARS LATER

CHAPTER 5

This year was special in San Francisco. Not so much because of an earth-changing event that occurred here, although there had been one of those. Or because the planet's high-tech hub had introduced another technology that further connected, enhanced, or extended people's lives. Certainly, there had also been a number of these unleashed upon the world from this now semi-autonomous city-state.

No, this particular year was special because at this special time of the year—a time of laughter, goodwill, and tradition for a significant many—it was snowing. Rare as a blood-red Mountain Star ruby, this snowfall at sea level in San Francisco came as part of a once-in-forty-year storm and cold spell that also brought with it fierce winds, fog, rain, and temperatures in the twenties. This wasn't a blizzard—the city likely had never experienced one. But it felt like one with the flurries being whipped about by the unusually swift gusts mixed with the cold wetness of the accompanying rain creating a miserable meteorological amalgamation.

Such woeful weather, however, didn't deter the city from its customary and surprisingly unhindered display of the season that celebrated the birth of Christ. For the faithful, the sleety snow—bothersome as it was—was a welcome and wondrous addition to the celebration. Slowed traffic and uncomfortable walks were a small price to pay for a once-in-a-lifetime white Christmas. And, ironically, the rotten weather ended up having the opposite effect of what would be expected. The San Francisco Ballet's majestic performance of *The Nutcracker* was better attended than ever, as was the city's Dickens Fair where the squeezing, wrenching, grasping, scraping, clutching, covetous old sinner Scrooge and his ghosts were on full display and a delight to all. For many of the city's quiet, content, more reserved, and humble, it really was the most wonderful time of the year.

But not so for EB. He had come to despise this time of year as buffoonery, a most silly season that exemplified a leap into the past's superstitions instead of the future's science. At least there was an economic silver lining—or, for EB, a golden one. As with many businesses with a significant retail component, Christmas consumerism brought wondrous end-of-year profits. "Only for my wallet is this the most wonderful time of the year!" EB grumbled to himself, amused with the irony that the holiday representing giving became the best time of getting for him and eBeja.

But there was no positive way to spin the dark clouds under which his great city was besieged. From his top-floor office, the storm looked even worse than from street level as icy rain battered his windows, creating an extremely annoying lashing sound, like a whip on a man's back. And worse, the sleet completely obstructed his marvelous 360-degree city-light and bay views.

Situated on the outskirts of the Embarcadero area, the eBeja Tower and Green was the city's newest high-rise office complex and park located on the famed Telegraph Hill. EB purchased the little mountain from the city in a deal that not only no one thought possible, but that was opposed by virtually everyone. So outrageous was the idea of commercially developing Telegraph Hill, the city thought it was a prank when EB submitted a plan to bring the park and tower into the twenty-first century.

The proposal was no joke, however, and called for carving out a 1.5-acre section of the 4.47-acre park for the building of a new structure, the eBeja Tower, and also completely redesigning the surrounding green area. The stunning and elaborate plan for The Green, as it would be called, included a complete overhaul of the park, a new concert area, a people's garden that would be the hydroponic envy of the world, and a full-acre climate-controlled rain forest arboretum-zoo showcasing a diverse selection of the Amazon's plant, bird, and fish species "in order to help educate on how important the Amazon Forest is to the well-being of the planet," his plan stated.

While all of that looked nice on paper, the only reason the city didn't just toss the audacious proposal in the trash was that in addition to footing all the costs for construction and development of this green paradise, EB would pay the city directly an enormous $13 billion in cash, more than the entire GDP of the Bahamas. The total cost of the project would run north of $25 billion, five times what Apple's UFO-looking campus cost, and almost twice the cost of the world's second most expensive commercial project, the Abraj Al-Bait complex of seven towers in Mecca, Saudi Arabia. The Masjid al-Haram mosque that surrounds the Kaaba in Mecca, Saudi Arabia, is the most expensive and valuable edifice ever constructed, with a final price tag of $100 billion. EB wouldn't go that high, although for him educating the world on how to save the planet was far more important than what was being taught at the Masjid al-Haram— and more profitable. "Religion is where the real money is," EB liked to remind people.

Initially, as tempting as the multibillion-dollar windfall was to the city, they passed on the deal, citing impossible obstacles to overcome, including citywide opposition of nearly every civic and nonprofit organization, all the major building and trade associations, the unions of the area, and even national groups, both political and educational. All voiced opposition to transferring the famed hill into private company hands. That was until the SwarmTroopers swooped in, led by their founder, CEO, Chairman of the Board, and Supreme Commander Narud Esminet.

Esminet was a close friend of EB's as well as a friendly corporate competitor. The two had come to know each other when EB first moved to San Francisco, meeting him at a political function. Esminet was much more politically savvy and connected than EB was at the time, and for whatever reason, took a great interest in EB, taking him under his wing. As a result, EB ended up spending a great deal of time with the older, more sophisticated Esminet, often being invited to his eight-acre estate in Atherton for dinner, as well as excursions on his enormous 530-foot Lürssen mega-yacht, *Abyss*. The two grew close and EB came to depend on Narud and his extraordinary worldly wisdom for advice.

After being rejected by the city, it was Narud that EB looked to for help. This was the first time that EB had gone directly to Narud for this kind of assistance. Narud had given him years of incredible business counsel, but never in all that time did EB want to actually ask Narud for something beyond his advice. EB had exhausted every avenue he knew of to get the proposal approved, however, and was finally told that, in no uncertain terms, the city was against it, as was a very powerful national coalition, and so he should drop it. Such all-encompassing rejection made EB all the more determined, and so he finally went to Narud who, within weeks, made it happen. He didn't know how he did it, or who he met with to so quickly change the hostility and opposition that had everyone fuming against EB, but once Narud stepped in, like magic, the city approved the deal and the eBeja Tower and Green was built.

One of the reasons Narud so willingly intervened was because the new eBeja complex was also a memorial and tribute to Marley. EB's sole executor, sole trustee, sole administrator, sole beneficiary and heir, Marley was the only one EB had truly trusted and so had been the key to EB's success and formation under Narud. After Marley's horrible and sudden death seven years previous, EB had not been the same. And even after seven years of frequent visits and interactions with Marley at his pyramid mausoleum, EB only sank deeper into a state of detachment and bitterness.

He never told Narud of his feelings, and instead would boast to Narud of their many ventures and conquests together, stories he thought would please Narud. To the world, Marley's Elevation was the beginning of the end of death, something to celebrate. But the world had never known Marley as EB had. He was the brother EB never had growing up, and though he was still there in the mausoleum, EB resented that he wasn't with him in the office, on their trips, in meetings and negotiations and takeovers. For EB, Marley's departure was also the departure of his own soul. Narud could see this and knew that a constant reminder of Marley would feed the deep pain, anger, and scorching ambition of EB like nothing else could. Erecting one of the tallest towers in the city bearing their names would be that fuel needed to keep the consuming fire continuously burning in EB's mind.

The plaza and company name, eBeja, was conceived as a contraction of EB, or more precisely, Ebenezer, the given name his mother crowned him with that appeared on his birth certificate—which he had hated since childhood—and Jacob, or Jake, as EB sometimes called him. The name also had a double meaning, one that honored the Bejas people group as an example of the company itself and the type of people he and Marley were in their own minds.

Bejas were a legendary people inhabiting Sudan, Eritrea, and most significantly for EB, Egypt. They had driven, passionate, and courageous personalities and so were considered men who were movers and shakers of their community. As conquerors, Bejas made big things happen, and were very competitive, having a strong sense of honor and fairness. But since "all's fair in love and war," and business is war, they, like EB, were always out to win by any means and at any cost for the greater good. To act in any other way would be unfair, ultimately, to humanity and the planet. The "e" at the beginning of the name stood for "electronic," the essence of all his ventures. It was also his and Marley's nod to the early companies of the first days of the tech explosion such as eBay and eTrade.

It was Narud who first introduced EB to the Bejas and helped him gain the appreciation for the nearly forgotten people. Not only the Bejas, but there were many groups, cultures, and ideas to which Narud opened EB's eyes. Narud thought differently than other people, and therefore acted differently, not in a way that put EB, or anyone for that matter, off. On the contrary, his thinking was extraordinary and soaring, always fixed on the big picture and humanity's plight, and always laser focused on the inseparable connection between business and politics, between money and social change, between cognition and culture.

On a personal level, like EB, Narud was single, uninterested in romantic relationships of any kind, and, maybe because of that, humorless. There was never any meaningless chatter or callous joking between them. In fact, EB had never seen Narud smile. That didn't bother him, though—EB didn't like to smile either. So, instead of lavish parties and unbridled carousing as was so typical among the high-tech elite, their times together were always filled with deep discussions, topical explorations, and even strategizing about remaking the world. History had given them a responsibility, they believed. They were part of the inevitable genetic and intellectual advancement of humanity, randomly ordained by chance to their high place, and so were rewarded accordingly. But with such ability and power, according to Narud, came a duty, one owed to all of humanity.

The corollary was also true, however: humanity owed them as well. In the dispensation of their gifts, Narud taught him that they must always achieve their ends, using any means or method necessary for success. That was not a license for anything goes, but rather an invitation to use great craftiness and shrewdness. By doing such, they would be rewarded. The greater their craftiness, the greater their reward. In doing this, their leadership shouldn't be too overbearing, but also never weak. Softness, accommodation, and submission were the worst forms of weakness. Thus, in firm, unmoving, never-bending confidence, it was essential that they recognize they were the chosen ones, that the roll of the cosmic dice had come up double sixes for them, and that, like it or not, they were mankind's royal flush. "Put yourself first," Narud would say, "and not only will you benefit humanity, but they will benefit you."

All these years after first encountering Narud, EB still hadn't met anyone like him. He was clearly a step above the rest—even above the incredibly smart and talented of Silicon Valley. But beyond his encyclopedic knowledge and unmatchable intellect, there was an emanation about him. Not an aura in the new-age sense of the word, but a real presence that was persuasive, magnetic, captivating, and enlightening. Part of that appeal was Narud's heritage—EB thought he came from an Indian or Pakistani background, but he couldn't be sure. He once asked Narud about it, and to his surprise, all Narud would say is that he was "from the East" and to leave it at that.

His appearance was also part of his magnetism. Always dressed in solid black, which contrasted beautifully with his pure white hair, the slender five-foot-two dynamo looked more like a priest than a technology titan. Wherever he went, he commanded the space. Whether at a meeting of engineers or elite bankers, Narud overwhelmed and somehow brought everyone to see things his way, small as he was. Unlike EB, he did this with few words and a quiet, whispering voice. Just as he had never been seen smiling, neither had he ever been known to raise his voice or become angry, especially with EB, something that always made EB feel inferior.

So, as much as he admired Narud, EB felt a struggle with him, as a son might feel with his father. It certainly was partly because of their business rivalry since, in a way, their companies were competing against each other. But EB knew the real tension was deeper and more profound than who could build the biggest business. When he thought about it, he found there was a desperate, uncontrollable, and deeply unwanted compulsion to please Narud and be more like him. He hated that there was anyone other than himself that occupied so much of his thought life, but down inside, Narud and his words constantly spoke to him, guided him, and, without his permission, had become his reference point as a needed life compass in the tumultuous ocean of high tech. Difficult as it was to acknowledge, EB's global financial and social successes, especially Elevation, were because of Narud.

eBeja had grown exponentially—almost miraculously it seemed—since they introduced the new Elevation technology and service seven years ago at Marley's funeral. But after pulling away all the hype and peeling back the optics, it was because Narud had been there from the beginning, guiding him to see where exactly to focus his own genius. Not that he just gave EB the formulations or algorithms that brought about their new life business. He didn't—not directly. Rather, it was as if Narud knew them but instead of handing them to EB, he guided him down a path to uncover the secret that would lead him to this unimaginable success. He would quiz EB relentlessly, forcing EB's mind to process until it ached from the difficulty and intensity of the challenges Narud gave him. *He must know some secret or undiscovered law of physics*, EB had continually thought.

Then there was that phrase that Narud said over and over to him: "Closing the vault of death opens the vault of life." Finally, one day, it clicked and everything seemed to fall together. It was an epiphany that EB immediately shared with Marley, who also instantly grasped the mystery. The two knew they had just been handed the world's most valuable winning lottery ticket, and it wasn't long before the two titans figured out the key to Elevation—and, most importantly to them, how to monetize it. Their success was rapid, hitting the trillion-dollar valuation mark only three years later, crushing the time it took previous trillion-dollar-mark giants.

Alphabet/Google took twenty-one years to reach the milestone, but had since, following the conclusion of the Ukraine/Russia/India/NATO or URIN War as World War III came to be known, declared bankruptcy. This was due to the breakup of their advertising monopoly on top of massive fines and a plethora of lawsuits against them regarding illegal data collection, advertising swindles, decades-long anticompetitive conduct that violated antitrust laws, and extreme censorship. Virtually every Western country had come together and banned them and all subsidiaries from any business activity on- or offline.

Tesla took eighteen years to hit a trillion, and was still thriving as it expanded into electric air cars and space vehicles for the general public, an industry EB had longed desired to penetrate. Facebook had rocketed to the trillion-dollar club, taking only seventeen years, but following the URIN war had collapsed due to their advertising empire also being dismantled as Google's was, along with China, Russia, and EU bans on the rebranded Meta flop. Sinking like a MySpace ship, Facebook/Meta was rapidly replaced by eBeja's Pod social network and VR system.

Microsoft, Amazon, and Apple also had been part of the club at one time, but all fell out of favor with consumers, and in the face of an army of smaller, privacy-focused startups, were now only second- or third-rate players in the consumer-tech and retail markets.

After the fall of these giants, Narud's SwarmTroopers stormed the world and held the record for fastest to the mountaintop, achieving a trillion-dollar worth in eight short years. They were able to do this mainly by securing virtually every government contract in their field, on a global level. No one knew how Narud achieved such domination in such record time, but then again no one really knew how Narud did anything. He had powers no one else did, and regardless of the government, corporation, organization, political party, or person, he had the ability to make whatever he wanted to happen, just as he did with the eBeja Tower, and just as he did with Elevation.

Although EB enjoyed the esteem and glory for Elevation, it was Narud who really deserved the credit for eBeja's meteoric rise. Not only had he given EB the mysterious trace elements key to Elevation, but Narud was the one who introduced EB to his incredible government connections, giving eBeja the exclusive contract to obtain the elements as well as sole contractor status, alongside SwarmTroopers, for their data services. And after doing all that for EB, he refused to take any money, stock, or options in eBeja or any of its subsidiaries. EB wondered how many other groups or corporations behind which Narud was the real brains and power. Unless Narud would share such information, EB knew he'd never know.

As influential and effective as Narud was, part of his persona was not to take credit publicly, but to remain in the shadows and out of the limelight. Rarely was an article written, a hologram broadcast, or a reference made to him in public. He was the invisible man, even though he had more wealth than could be imagined. But money didn't move him; power did. And EB was the focus of his efforts in this regard. "What you become and where you end up is my reward," was what he had told EB. Sadly, Marley's enjoyment of their success was short lived as he wasn't able to handle such immediate fame and fortune—a combination that directly led to the tragedy that came upon him only months after eBeja hit the trillion-dollar valuation jackpot.

So the cold reality and what disturbed EB most was that it was really Narud—Father Esminet as Marley sometimes had called him—who had provided him with what made him who he was. It was unspoken between the two, but EB owed Narud everything, even his very life. But though he was bitter about most everything else in his outwardly magnificent career, EB wasn't in this. He was scared, even terrified, that Narud owned him, but not bitter. Instead it became what motivated him, and even though he had to wrestle with it daily, compelled him to strive to be like Narud, and if possible better and bigger since he believed that was also what Narud wanted.

Purchasing Telegraph Hill was one way to show Narud, and the Silicon Valley elite, that he was following in his footsteps and was proud to be a Narud disciple. He never vocalized this hidden admiration and compulsive emulation to anyone, not even Marley, and especially not to Narud, though he was convinced Narud knew. He had made a few proclamations about Narud and his influence, but in public it was always to draw the attention back to himself, which he continually tried to convince himself was where the spotlight should be. He hated this incessant, fiery mind battle, but in the end decided his actions were his declarations, and in a city of obelisks, there was no better way to show respect for Narud, while simultaneously exalting himself, than by erecting a vertical electronic planet-saving superstructure modeled after Narud's famed SwarmTrooper Tower that, like Narud's Tower, would be a beacon for the new world order they had been plotting to build.

CHAPTER 6

"Would any of you mind if I turn the heat up a little?" Bobby asked the employees clustered in cubicles outside of his office.

"I would love that!" one of his young assistants quickly responded as she rubbed her hands together. Most of the rest just gave Bobby a slight nod of approval or a thumbs-up, but nothing that could later be officially confirmed as an affirmative.

The issue wasn't that it was a little too cool on their floor. In fact it was freezing, at least compared to normal. The problem was the cold spell that was icing the city was so unexpected, even for Christmas Eve, that they didn't have time to make proper requests for temperature adjustments. Unlike most other office constructs, eBeja's building was an environmental masterpiece for energy conservation and internal climate control. So, in order to change the very carefully monitored and controlled internal temperature, an elaborate series of forms needed to be filled out, approvals had to be given, and analyses conducted to determine any detrimental or unexpected consequences, both financially and environmentally, for the adjustment.

Using China's Shanghai Tower as its inspiration for such eco-conscious controls, EB incorporated forty-seven different sustainable technologies, including renewable energy sources, extensive landscaping to help keep the building at an optimal temperature, and a unique flame shape, which helped improve the building's wind resistance. Wind speed and frequency was greater on Telegraph Hill than in the financial district where most of the other high-rise buildings were forested, but EB took advantage of that. In another design first, he had the all-solar energy-producing surface glass engineered so it appeared to flicker, like a wild campfire flame, when gusts exceeding 15 mph hit the structure. The effect was especially elegant at night when the building's lights were on.

The fire-like form of the building also nicely facilitated a spiraling parapet starting at its top that collected rainwater used for heating and air-conditioning systems. The building's close proximity to the bay made it cost effective to add wind turbines below the parapet to generate on-site power. EB was proud that these efforts reduced what its total energy consumption would have been without them by 18 percent. Additionally, its carbon footprint was cut by an estimated 37,000 metric tons yearly and the eco-friendly materials used there saved him over $30 million in material costs, earning the structure the coveted American LEED Platinum certification.

EB treasured the LEED accolade, especially since it made him appear to be more green minded than his competitors, an extremely important reputational advantage to have in San Francisco. And advantage was everything in the cutthroat world of big business in which he moved. All the important companies were fully committed to eradicating anthropogenic climate change, but reality dictates that sustainability cannot come at the expense of profits. *How does one change the world without money?* An early lesson Narud ingrained in him along with its corollary—*the one with the most money gets to choose how to change the world.* So the main battle was in appearance, reputation, and perception, areas where EB's expertise was unsurpassed.

Part of the green optics jihad was internal as well. EB needed his 180,000-plus full-time employees located in 72 locations across 31 countries to be on board and be his and his company's enthusiastic green ambassadors. Having one of the most environmentally friendly buildings in the country helped. Financial incentives to employees for participating was an even better way to motivate green evangelism. One of the ways he did this was to set up strict temperature parameters for all his offices to save on energy costs, reduce fossil fuel use, and so on. Most offices did the best they could to adhere to the standards, but since EB wasn't at all his locations personally, none were as rigid as the HQ in San Francisco from where EB ruled his empire on a day-to-day basis. Also, because the other offices were not, and in many cases could not be, environmentally retrofitted, sometimes it wasn't possible to keep the faith, especially in some of their third-world and Asia locations.

But at the flagship campus in San Francisco, there was no excuse. One of the key inspirations EB borrowed from the Shanghai Tower was to use Danish engineering solutions company Danfoss to develop a marvelous money-saving water control valve system that made heating, ventilation, and AC more efficient. Efficiency was synonymous with profits for eBeja, so the more efficient the better. And the Danfoss system was, like the Danes from which it came, as efficient as technologically possible. Using 3,900 water control valves, the system automatically secured control and ensured the right balance of water flow in the miles-long piping throughout the building. This not only reduced wastage, but provided a practical advantage so that any floor could get the temperature desired quickly, regardless of temperatures throughout the rest of the building— as long as those temperatures were within company policy guidelines and processed through the long approval chain.

This freak, once-in-forty-year freeze wasn't in the policy handbook, though. And since Christmastime in San Francisco is usually very mild, all the temperature system controls were preset accordingly. Good green soldiers that they were, employees wore heavy coats and sometimes even gloves over the last few days since the inside of the building felt almost as cold as it was outside. EB had sent a memo to the entire building when the forecast for the frost was first announced, stating in no uncertain terms that the temperature controls were not to be touched. A spike in the energy needs for temperature adjustment would blow his consumption targets for the month, even with the Danfoss system. In fact, because everyone else in the Bay Area was suddenly desperate for heat, electricity costs had spiked to historic highs. "Grin and bear it," EB had stated in his memo. "The last thing we should do is abandon our commitment to the environmental standards we've set, especially in difficult times. During this rare low-pressure anomaly, let's show the city and world that eBeja is not just about great products and great service, but great sacrifice for the planet." The memo concluded with a list of stiff sanctions for any violators.

But tonight was Christmas Eve, and Bobby thought that surely in the spirit of the season, it should be all right if he turned the heat up just a bit to get through these last hours of the evening, especially since the cold front had unexpectedly turned polar in the last several hours. Light had turned to darkness outside, and with all-in dedication to EB, most of the workers were still at their desk toiling away. A very few somehow managed to slip away to enjoy Christmas Eve festivities with friends or family, but most didn't dare. Monitored by an elaborate company-wide tool EB named CommuNEST® to provide a "Nest of Safety and Security for Our Community," every employee and executive under EB was tracked to the minute that they were at their desk, on their computer, or anywhere on the campus. All calls, whether company related or personal, were also scanned as was any conversation or other communication.

Using a full-spectrum entity analytics system combined with a whole campus video surveillance network, CommuNEST enabled EB to detect and record not just regular movements and communications, but the actions of like and related entities across the entire company. Once in the system, the massive AI platform would cross-reference, analyze, and actually make decisions based on the data collected about company events, employees, tangible assets of the company, transactions, and relationships. These measures were not only necessary to ensure the highest levels of fealty and productivity, but also provided fortress-like security for the corporation, protecting it from both domestic and foreign competitor spying and sabotage. It was also very good at keeping people from leaving a few minutes early.

The unspoken rule for all employees was that leaving before 8:00 p.m. on any day except a company holiday—and Christmas Eve was certainly not one of those—earned the violator a demerit. That regulation wasn't formally written anywhere as it would have violated San Francisco's strict labor laws. But it was nevertheless rigorously enforced by company security and management via CommuNEST.

And here, on this silent and freezing night, all was calm in the company, it seemed, and all bright with eBeja having surpassed their annual financial goals. But 8:00 p.m. was still ninety minutes away and Bobby, together with the rest of his crew, were turning into icicles. Would the company really penalize an entire floor for turning up the heat just a tad so they couldn't see their breath? A quote by G. K. Chesterton came to Bobby's mind: "I believe in getting into hot water; it keeps you clean." *And warm!* Bobby thought. With that, he logged in to the code-protected eBeja Tower temperature control system.

CHAPTER 7

He hadn't even punched in the second number of the lengthy passcode only a few in the building had before a unique triple buzz rattled his imbedded Personal Protection Chip, or PPC communication app. It was EB.

Bobby instantly stopped tapping in the code because of the shock, and through his preprogrammed thought sequence, opened the connection.

"Yes, EB?" He said into the air, which his subcutaneous intercom picked up perfectly.

"What are you doing?" EB asked. Only Bobby could hear him in the cochlea-implanted speaker all PPC communication users were required by regulation to have.

"Well, there's only an hour and a half left until the pause, and the entire floor is freezing, so I thought—"

"You thought what? That you'd break the rules? That you'd destroy our perfect environmental score with only a week left in the year? That you'd cost the company who knows how much for a few extra degrees of warmth? That you'd cause a scandal that my enemies could exploit to ruin me? Tell me what you thought, Bobby!"

"None of that, sir. It's Christmas Eve and in the spirit of goodwill and grace I thought a little heat for the floor would be a great gift for the troops. 'Tis the season."

"Hexagas nonsense! 'Tis the season to work!"

EB's shortening for sulfur hexafluoride to "hexagas" was his way of demeaning and degrading, just as sulfur hexaflouride can severely pollute and degrade the atmosphere, being 22,200 times more potent than carbon dioxide. Bobby was amused whenever he used the term since eBeja was one of the world's largest users of the gas as an insulator at its electronics production plants in other countries.

"Come up to my office. Now!" EB barked.

Other than the senior vice presidents and company executives, no one other than Bobby had clearance to access the thirty-sixth floor, EB's full-floor lair. Security badges had gone out of style and use a few years ago when PPCs were introduced as part of the CommuNEST solution. The Personal Protection Chips were tiny grain-sized data chips that were injected into the hand or wrist area and provided a constant interface with the CommuNEST AI system for monitoring and analysis. Like many of the employees, Bobby hadn't wanted one but reluctantly agreed since it could be easily removed at any time—at least that's what they told him. It was also compulsory for employment.

To guard employee privacy, there was an accompanying wristband to the PPC that could be worn when off campus to block it from operating, but only off campus. Again, that's what all the employees were told, though they didn't have a way to verify it. What was certain was that the wristbands were useless when on the property, making not only every movement trackable, but also all vital signs, emotional waves, and brain pulses, which were digitized and stored in CommuNEST. Corporate policy also disallowed the wristbands to be worn if an employee needed to be away from the building for company business, convincing most that the wristbands probably did work.

The elevator located in the center of the twisting flame-shaped tower automatically scanned Bobby's PPC and admitted him without any button pressing, knowing exactly where to take him. Occupying the entire top floor, which was the tip of the flame,

EB's office had only one known entry and exit point: the elevator. To access his chamber, one had to have the code and be given personal authorization by EB himself. Without it, the elevator's last stop was the floor beneath EB's where his executive staff were officed. The executive team consisted of ten senior vice presidents whose offices covered half the floor, with windows facing mostly to the east and north, and the executive officers—the Chief Financial Officer, Chief Marketing and Sales Officer, Chief Technology Officer, and Chief Operations Officer—with spectacular views of the Golden Gate Bridge, Sausalito, and the downtown financial district.

Arriving in an instant to the top floor, Bobby entered the uncomfortably warm room with EB's cold presence staring at him from its center, seated behind his extraordinary Amazon rain forest–cut mahogany desk. EB was a collector of incredibly valuable and old artifacts, which he liked to display across his desk instead of pens, papers, and files. Bobby had heard that some of them were so valuable that museum curators would visit to examine them. A big history buff himself, he had always wanted to ask EB what they were, but was never given the time, or courtesy, for an inquiry. And he didn't dare try to initiate a conversation himself. Bobby also noticed that there was the usual martini glass on his desk, half empty, infused with his customary double garlic–stuffed olives on a toothpick that leaned on the shapely glass's side.

"You're an example for this company, Bobby, one of the most important cogs in this great wheel of progress that is propelling us into the future. Do you believe that?"

"Thank you, sir. Yes, sir."

"But you are not irreplaceable! Do you believe that?"

"I know that for a fact, sir."

"Then why the hexagas would you risk your tremendous

position, your immensely coveted status, frankly, why would you risk everything for a few final minutes of comfort? Did you join this company to be comfortable?"

"It was only my floor, sir, and since the entire floor is dedicated to serve the company needs of you and the executives, I had planned to mention that this was a Christmas gift from you. I think the staff would've been touched and it would have increased the admiration and appreciation they have for you. Everyone knows how important LEED's Platinum certification is, so I would have never done it if I thought it would affect that."

"There you go thinking again. First of all, I don't need you to help me build my reputation or appreciation among the staff. Secondly, how do you know that the huge jump in energy use from your heat-seeking escapade wouldn't impact my certification?"

"Well, sir, I crunched the numbers and—"

"You crunched some numbers? And that gives you the authority to violate company policy, set an example of rebellion instead of obedience, and potentially open the door for negative publicity that could—and think about this—tank our stock going into the last days of the year?"

"I wouldn't dream of doing anything I thought would truly have a negative impact on this company, or the environment."

"But you did, or were about to if I hadn't stopped you! Don't you see, if everyone fudges just a little and thinks 'my little use of fossil fuel, my little purchase of a plastic bottle of water, my occasionally using a plastic bag for my groceries won't harm anything'—that's the problem! Taken in aggregate, they harm everything. This is why we're in the mess we're in!"

Bobby nodded, not necessarily in agreement but to indicate he was listening carefully to what he knew would be a long speech now that EB had ascended his soapbox. Quietly and slowly, while focused attentively on EB, Bobby unzipped his North Face coat, having started to drip in sweat, not only in fear of EB, but because the room was a sauna.

"And what do you really know about the environment, young Bobby? How many tons of carbon dioxide have you kept from being emitted? And have you paid a single penny to offset your own carbon footprint? As our numbers guy, you know we've paid millions, and have committed to using credits to offset the entirety of our emissions in the US."

Bobby wanted to respond that he wasn't paid enough to offset his nonexistent footprint, and that EB hadn't paid a penny to offset the real pollution that was being spewed by his factories, plants, and refineries in other countries. But as he had learned long ago, most of EB's questions were rhetorical. EB would let Bobby know when he was ready to crush his opinions. In these homilies, he always at some point gave an opportunity for Bobby to share a few ideas or counter thoughts, only to shoot them down, regardless of their merit, and then finalize the discussion by personally berating Bobby.

"We've had this talk before," EB continued after taking a sip of his martini. "I understand that you haven't spent the time or had the level of training on this as I have, but it should be clear to you by now that climate change is the biggest threat to US and global security that modern humans have ever faced. Concentrations of carbon dioxide currently in the atmosphere have not been equaled for millions of years."

Bobby continued to stand at attention in front of EB's massive Brazil-sourced desk, listening intently, while managing to slip his parka off without breaking eye contact.

"If we continue on our current path, Bobby, we will inevitably face the collapse of everything that gives us our security. We've made progress over the years, but not enough. Not enough to compromise a little because of some sentiment you feel about a two-thousand-year-old story of Magi following a star. You do know that stars don't move, don't you? Focus on the now: food production, access to fresh water, habitable ambient temperature, and ocean food chains—all will fall apart if everyone doesn't get in line and consistently, day in and day out, with military-like discipline, do their part.

"Carbon dioxide is the killer," EB continued as he stood up from his rain forest–harvested podium and walked to the window, unable to see anything but the foggy darkness and the harsh sleety snow shooting through it in a fusillade against the window protecting him. The usual surrounding jungle of lit buildings were mere phantoms, coming and going like vapor.

"Look at the snow and rain whipping this city. You don't like it and wanted to turn up the heat to mitigate its effects on you, on our employees, and on the company. But what do you think is causing this? Make no mistake, this anomalous bitter cold storm is because people like you don't think before they act. Most of our energy still comes from fossil fuels that generate CO2, the most dangerous and prevalent greenhouse gas—still at the highest levels ever recorded. Angering the earth has consequences, consequences like this," he said pointing to the storm. "It's really not that complicated."

EB then paused as he continued to look through the glass into the dark, cold, bleak, biting weather. "Well? Is this too complicated for you to grasp?"

Bobby knew it was now his turn, and that he needed to respond thoughtfully. In an argument, EB didn't respect truckling. "No, sir, it's not too complicated. But a question that I have on this is why during the Ice Age, when there weren't any factories or oil refineries or any human-generated carbon dioxide emissions, why CO2 levels were ten times higher than they are today?"

EB abruptly turned from the window. Bobby had his attention.

"It seems to me quite clear that many, many factors impact climate—such as volcanoes, wind oscillations, ocean cycles, the tilt of the earth's axis, and maybe most significantly, solar activity. Scientific studies I've seen say CO2 is just one factor, and not at all the control switch of the climate."

"Scientists you've read?" EB barked, raising his thick eyebrows at Bobby in unbelief at his faithlessness. "Hexagas horse manure! Give me a reputable scientist's name or some notable study that demonstrates man-emitted CO2 today isn't creating the climate emergency in which we find ourselves!"

"Yes, sir. One that comes to mind is a former University of Pennsylvania geologist, Dr. Robert Giegengack, who taught that, in no uncertain terms, CO2 is not the villain that it has been portrayed. According to his data, which has yet to be refuted, CO2 levels today are among the lowest in Earth's history. There's also University of London Professor Emeritus Philip Stott. If I remember his quote correctly, he said that 'the very idea that we can manage climate change predictably by understanding and manipulating at the margins one politically selected factor—CO2—is as misguided as it gets. Its scientific nonsense.'" He did remember it accurately, word for word as usual.

"But probably the most convincing was the more than thirty-one-thousand scientists and experts who decades ago signed a statement in 2008—a reaffirmation of the original 1998 Global Warming Petition—that rejected the idea. The effort was led by Professor Frederick Seitz, a former president of the US National Academy of Sciences, and has been affirmed numerous times since, with many more scientists and experts joining the declaration. Here's the exact language of the petition they all agreed upon:

There is no convincing scientific evidence that human release of carbon dioxide, methane, or other greenhouse gasses is causing or will, in the foreseeable future, cause catastrophic heating of the earth's atmosphere and disruption of the earth's climate. Moreover, there is substantial scientific evidence that increases in atmospheric carbon dioxide produce many beneficial effects upon the natural plant and animal environments of the earth.

EB's face started to turn red and Bobby wondered if he shouldn't have just agreed that ninety more minutes of cold wouldn't kill him or the staff, though it might devastate the planet.

"Hexagas buffoonery! You cherry-pick your quotes and evidence, as do all second-rate minds. For years now, it's been a foregone fact that the scientific consensus—and I'm one of the 97 percent who have contributed to this science-based unanimity—is that anthropogenic climate change is and will be catastrophic to the planet, and to its inhabitants. This statistic comes directly from the global entity tasked with studying *all* the facts—the United Nations Intergovernmental Panel on Climate Change. End of story."

"Of course, sir, that's what I've heard and read as well. But if there's such a clear consensus, why would a UN IPCC lead author, Dr. Richard Tol, say that this 97 percent figure is essentially, and I quote again, 'pulled from thin air' and quote 'is not based on any credible research whatsoever'? And what about the thirty-one thousand eminent scientists I just mentioned from the Oregon Statement? That doesn't sound like consensus to me."

Before EB could answer, Bobby swallowed his fear and

mentioned one more point he thought it important for EB consider.

"With all respect, sir, since when does a majority of scientific agreement on a matter guarantee that a minority hypothesis isn't scientifically true? Wasn't Copernicus in the extreme minority in his day claiming that the sun was at the center of the solar system and the earth was one of the planets revolving around it? Or Galileo, Kepler, even Newton? Weren't they all scorned by the so-called scientific establishment of their day that had staked their reputations, salaries, and social status on widely rejected theories, such as a geocentric model of the universe?"

"Comparing the scientists of Copernicus's time to today's science community is ridiculous," EB shot back. "As is the fact we are spending my valuable time, which means my money, on this absurd conversation."

Bobby used all his face muscle power to refrain from grinning since it was EB who had chosen the topic and initiated the discussion.

"All those who agree about climate change would also agree with you that Copernicus helped change science forever," EB continued. "But he did it by being scientific. That's what multiple studies published in peer-reviewed scientific journals show—that 97 percent or more of actively publishing climate scientists agree climate-warming trends over the past century are extremely likely due to human activities. They've come to this conclusion by being scientific. Additionally, in case you had missed this as you've missed so much else, most of the leading scientific organizations worldwide have issued public statements endorsing this position."

Wanting to quit before getting EB too riled up on this, Bobby again nodded that he heard the point and began to turn toward the elevator door giving him the all important last word.

"Well? No response, Bobby? Maybe you are able to learn something that will change your Neanderthal worldview, after all."

Realizing his beatdown wasn't over yet, Bobby readied for what he was really hoping would be the final round. "Yes, I definitely learn from you," Bobby said as EB's left eye squinted at him. That was EB's tell that he didn't want any sucking up, which was what Bobby just did.

"But I also learned from an article by Princeton Professor Emeritus of Physics William Happer that he didn't see a whole lot of difference between the consensus on climate change and the consensus on witches."

"Witches? What consensus is there on witches except that their outfits make great Halloween costumes?" EB retorted, shaking his head in pity at his ignorant assistant.

"At the witch trials in Salem, the judges were educated at Harvard and their view of witches and witchcraft was supposedly 100 percent science. The way Happer put it, 'The one or two people who said there were no witches were immediately hung. Not much has changed.' They were following the science, EB, or at least they thought they were. Are you certain we're not making the same error today? And isn't the danger of bad, non-scientific decisions being made and implemented exacerbated when the process is centralized in a top-down governmental body, whether a global one like the UN or nationally like in the federal government? Isn't that the essence of anti-science, when a centralized political body gets to decide what is or isn't science?" Bobby quickly added to recover from his flattery.

EB stared coldly at Bobby, not because he had convinced him of anything. He hadn't, not even a smidgeon. He never would in his N1 status. But EB respected his uncanny memory for quotes and statistics and things, as well as his boldness to say what his memory dictated to him. And that made him think, though he'd never admit it to anyone. And that's also why he kept Bobby and his unorthodox ideas around. Angry as he might make EB, and foolish as the ideas were in today's modern scientific world, Bobby's photographic memory had the highest level of accuracy he'd ever seen. His IQ was off the charts as well. This was one of the reasons he had hired him in the first place, to make sure all his numbers and financials and accounts were perfect. But his gift also seemed to compel Bobby to respond to him, making the awkward lad the only one who would dare disagree with him. And it frustrated EB that he always did it respectfully. He really would've liked a little more of a brawl. Nevertheless, the choirboy was as talented with numbers as he was spouting off quotations, and so made EB gobs of money. That was even more a reason to keep the poor lost soul on the payroll.

Recognizing that the stare was EB's way of dismissing him, Bobby once again nodded as if to thank him for the privilege of the conversation and time in his office. He actually was thankful. Cold and cutting as EB was, and as emotionally difficult as it was to be his punching bag, there was something about EB that went beyond his intellect and technological acumen that made him thankful for his boss. He hadn't put his finger on it yet, but there was something about him beyond him just being the provider of his paycheck, small as it was. Or maybe not. It was Christmas Eve and he was probably confusing that with his feelings of appreciation for the holiday excitement he felt knowing that he would be with his family shortly.

With his mind now off EB and on his family, Bobby turned toward the door to exit. But before he could get on the elevator, EB's communicator alerted EB. Checking the caller ID only EB could see in the upper right of his vision, EB raised his hand abruptly to stop Bobby's departure. Apparently, he wanted him to stay in his office during the call.

CHAPTER 8

"Merry Christmas, Uncle!" a very cheerful voice greeted him. EB stared down at his desk as though Bobby were not there, knowing he couldn't hear. But he wanted Bobby to catch this conversation that he knew would irk him, so he subtly directed his communication implant to broadcast on his office speaker system.

"More like hexagas hogwash!" was EB's quick reply to his nephew Frederick who inevitably called him every Christmas Eve at just about this time.

"Hogwash? Why would you say that, Uncle EB? You don't really mean it, do you?"

"I do. Please tell me what's so merry about a time of year when extreme amounts of dirty, deadly pollutants are spewed into the air so as to produce distracting toys to be put under dead trees on a random day only to be forgotten and forsaken after a few days?" he said glancing up without moving his head to make sure Bobby was taking in the lesson.

"Oh, come on, Uncle," returned the nephew still full of joy and cheer. "Why so dismal? What reason have you to be so disapproving of gift giving, when its simply to show appreciation for a friendship, or to see a child light up with excitement, or to show another the love the holiday represents? You certainly have plenty of toys yourself."

EB wasn't expecting that one. "Hexagas! I don't know what toys you think I own, but I assure you, I haven't wasted my time playing in years. And neither should you in a world that's still awash with fascists and is failing in the fight against climate deniers because, even after all the progress made, it's still full of superstitions and sentimental notions like the one you're clinging to—namely, that around the twenty fifth of December every year, somehow, magically, everyone decides to love one another. Love? The greatest hexagas of all!"

"Don't be bitter, Uncle!" said the nephew.

"And don't you presume to know my inner state," returned EB with a scowl. "This isn't bitterness you're hearing. It's what you call love, but true love that isn't an emotional buzzing feeling or an elevated heart rate. It's straight-up fact; it's refusing to pretend there is some place in the way beyond where harps are playing, angels are dancing, and all is well. And it's rejecting that there is such a grand place that we should carve out a day from productive labor and instead replace money-producing work with nonsensical spending and erecting of cut trees that no longer help the earth breathe, but instead become waste on which it chokes.

"It's you that should be bitter, Fred, for what else should anyone be who places all their hope in a huckster's holiday that perpetuates the very myth that brought upon us all this misery? Yes, you heard me correctly—all the misery. It is this myth you're clinging to that has tricked humanity into believing that we don't have to save ourselves by unifying together as one species and remake the planet—because it'll all be burned up someday anyway!" EB was now indignant.

"If I could work my will," he continued, now hastily pacing, head still down, "every ignorant idiot who goes about with 'Merry Christmas' on his lips should be caged in a glass chamber full of sulfur hexafluoride and gassed, and then after a long, torturous death, be forever denied Elevation and instead be wrapped in a colorful paper-wrapped box topped with a giant bow and sunk in the sea. Or, better yet, send it as a gift to me. Now that's a

Christmas present I'd sit on Santa's lap to get!"

"Uncle!" pleaded the nephew.

"Nephew!" the uncle shot back sternly. "Keep your superstitions in your own way, and let me keep the facts of reality in mine."

"Facts?" his nephew returned, his voice raised a bit. "Christmas is a fact, dear uncle, because Christ is a fact."

"Well then, enjoy your facts and I'll enjoy mine. At least my facts show tangible results and are not so heavenly minded as to do no good . . . or I should more accurately say do great harm on the earth"—EB paused for dramatic affect—"and to the earth!"

"A man of your learning can't be so misinformed," Fred gently replied, "as to deny that Christ's words—not man's opinion of what Christ said or might be, but His real words as faithfully recorded by His students, followers, and messengers—have had an extraordinary impact for good on earth. More so, I'd bet, than any other's. How do His directives to love your enemies, to serve others instead of take advantage of them, to refrain from stealing and lying, to honor mother and father, to go out of your way to protect your neighbor's property, to be faithful to your spouse and not cheat, and to honor the Creator who gave us life produce anything but good?

"Where is the great harm that you speak of in the countless orphanages that were built in the name of Christ Jesus over the centuries across the continents, or the myriad hospitals where the sick could be healed, with the soup kitchens for the downtrodden and outcasts in this city as well as all the others around the country, all established without the least concern for financial gain or profit?

"Under what name were the original schools and universities established throughout this land with such a zeal for knowledge and learning because of the clarity, purpose, and hope that the name of Jesus gave to the educators, in this life and the life to come? And what better way is there to protect the planet's environment than for a person to be mindful that the earth is an engineered masterpiece, given as a gift to humanity, full of the most beautiful and extraordinary examples of the Creator's life, diversity, creativity, and love?"

Unable to restrain himself, Bobby involuntarily clenched his fist and with forearm raised, let loose a vigorous fist pump and an uncontrolled "Amen!" Becoming immediately aware of the impropriety, he adjusted the pumping arm toward the one over which his parka was still draped and feigned adjusting it to a more comfortable position.

"Impressed?" EB immediately rebuked, moving toward Bobby and pointing his bony finger directly at his face. "So will be your lovely wife and family be when you lose your job and are downgraded back to N2!"

After putting Bobby in his place, EB said, "Thank you for the eloquent sermon, Frederick. Billy Graham would be proud. Oh, but I forgot, he's gone, dead in the ground, and if it wasn't for his own Elevation, which his supporters paid dearly for, I might add, he would probably have been forgotten by now. Chew on those facts!"

"Oh, Uncle, don't be frustrated or angry. I called to invite you to the game tomorrow if you don't have other plans. The 49ers are playing a Christmas Day home game tomorrow evening for the first time in decades—I believe 1993 was the last time. My wife won a fifty-yard-line luxury suite in her company Christmas lottery. The suite holds up to twenty-seven people. We have thirteen couples coming and would love for you to join us. There will be a ton of catered food—nothing fancy since most everyone will have already eaten Christmas dinner with their families, but there will be plenty: burgers, beer brats, barbecue ribs, fries, chips, salads, and lots to drink. It will be incredible fun, a great way to finish the day! What do you say, Uncle?"

"I'd rather watch demons tackling devils in hell," he said grimacing.

"Oh please. We're all going to go a couple hours early after time with family and just hang out in the suite, play some Christmas music while we watch the teams warm up. And we're doing a fun gift exchange—just little gifts to add to the merriment!"

"I do have other plans, but even if I didn't, Fred, I'd make some to avoid such an unproductive and low-class waste of my priceless time. Can you think of anything more degrading than watching grown men gallop up and down a field like dogs chasing a ball?"

"Come on, Uncle EB! It's harmless fun, and sport is good for the soul."

"I've already told you. Watching a game and partying in a luxury suite to make merry and celebrate this meaningless holiday—watching two speeding BART trains at rush hour collide would be more merry to me! I've got to go, Fred, good day!" EB said, getting ready to disconnect.

"Wait, Uncle, please. I'm not looking for anything here, and would never try to take advantage of you in any way. I'd simply like to spend time with my uncle, with family."

"Hexagas! Family? The worst of our planet's wars all started as intra- or inter-family fights. Look, I'm going to disconnect now."

"Well, I've tried, and know, Uncle, that I will continue to try as your disdain for the season in no way has spilled over on me. I truly wish you a Merry Christmas and Happy New Year!"

And with that, EB said no more and disconnected his communication implant.

"You were pretty excited about my nephew Fred's little diatribe, were you, Bobby? Seems it got you all worked up like you were at a back-country tent revival."

"Sir, I would've left but thought you wanted me to wait here for something," Bobby replied.

"No, I wanted you to stay and to hear how foolish and delusional my nephew and his ideas are. Does he remind you of anyone?"

Bobby wasn't sure if he wanted him to answer or not. But it became irrelevant as EB cut him off before he could say anything. "Reluctantly, tomorrow is an optional personal day."

"A holiday, sir, only once a year," Bobby said softly.

"No, it is not a holiday. That word is a modern construction of 'holy day,' and tomorrow is not holy, but simply a day, a Wednesday just like any other with twenty-four hours, fourteen hundred and forty minutes, some of it lit, the other part dark when the earth turns away from the sun. If it is holy to you personally, that is your prerogative, but it seems to me to be a poor excuse to pick a man's pocket. Nevertheless, some of us will be here in great spirits doing something truly productive and profitable to save the planet. I suppose you'll be taking a personal day all day tomorrow?"

"Well, sir, I—"

"Just be here early on Thursday. Not a minute late, you hear me? I have a very important Pod meeting with Singapore on Friday and there is still much with their year-end figures I'll need you to go over with me."

"Of course. Yes, thank you, EB," Bobby said, bowing his head a little as he whisked around and scampered out of the office before EB could come up with some other insult, invective, or vituperation.

CHAPTER 9

EB really did have other plans, though they were not set in stone. Narud had invited him to his office at the SwarmTrooper Tower on his way home, not for any kind of Christmas Eve affair but at EB's request, to give EB some counsel. It wasn't eight o'clock yet, but unlike his employees, EB was always on the clock. The idea of "quitting time" offended him since it bred a mentality that divided life into employment work and then everything else. But this wasn't reality. Work needs didn't just stop at 5:00 p.m. or 8:00 p.m. and then start again at some set time the next morning, especially the work eBeja was doing.

EB led by example and had spent his life on this never slowing treadmill. But the results spoke for themselves. Although there were numerous factors contributing to EB's enormous wealth and success, he attributed his continuous, tireless, endless laboring as one of the most important. Widely known throughout the company, his workaholism was successfully imitated by those who were part of eBeja. It had become an unwritten standard for his staff to spend long days, even nights, at the office dutifully sacrificing their own personal time, their extracurricular activities, and even their families for the company's contribution to the greater good. Though he didn't smile much, if there was anything that made him grin, this was it. "A person's loyalties cannot be divided, and there is always a first loyalty," EB taught them, emphasizing to his employees that eBeja—which was really just EB now that fleshly Marley was gone—was to be their first priority. In everything.

This is why he introduced the term *pause* to replace *quitting time*. Once his underlings understood that he was allowing them to pause their work for a temporary rest, to see their family if need be, and sleep, their productivity level would skyrocket. But consistent, every-day, legally enforced quitting times were backward and were a leftover from a time when children were required to slave in coal mines or factories. Important as labor laws were at that time, those days were long gone. In the techno-era, advancement was moving forward at the speed of electricity, not shovels, and to keep up, a new work ethic and mindset was required.

So EB would continue to be the role model and not pause this evening, but push himself as he did every day. He had been doing this since arriving in San Francisco, regularly reminding his staff of this, and that he hadn't taken a vacation since then either. And while he considered himself blessed by the universe with incredible genetic structure giving him almost superhuman health and stamina to live this way, over the last year he had started to feel less energy and a little more tired than usual. And this was what he wanted to talk to Narud about. Since Narud was quite a bit older than he and had an uncanny ability to hone in on EB's exact needs, he knew the sage would have some wise words for him, as he had on everything in EB's life.

Frustrated, EB would've already driven to the SwarmTrooper Tower and been absorbing Narud's counsel if he hadn't been interrupted by Bobby's do-goodism and Fred's conscience-pacifying call. But hopefully the time with the two Christmas-loving serfs hadn't been a total waste. *Maybe they'll think about some of the things I said*, thought EB. *Those were the best gifts I could give them!* He congratulated himself as he donned his heavy overcoat and top hat and headed to the ground floor of his building for a quick stop at the Philz Coffee cafe for a well-needed espresso.

EB didn't usually grace the lower floors of the building since he could go directly from his office pinnacle to the garage in the express elevator, but he wanted a little jolt before the meeting and had decided to have a driver take him to Narud's Tower instead of driving himself. Plus, he would be able to spend a minute admiring the murals while waiting for his customized blend of espresso to be made.

One of the city's requirements for EB to be able to demolish the Coit Tower and replace it with his flame-emulating eBeja Tower was that all the art and murals had to be preserved and made available to the public just as they were in Coit. Not an easy task, the flame's architectural team had figured out how to keep the first and second floors of the Coit Tower intact and built the new eBeja Tower's grand three-story-high entry foyer around it. Surrounded with fountains, gardens, other shops—like Philz— and lots of commercially leased space, the new Coit gallery was a hit.

eBeja's mural-filled grand entry was an enormous step up from the run-down, almost dungeon-like feel of the old Coit exhibit. To welcome the public, EB had a fifteen-foot statue erected of Earl Warren to replace the previous twelve-foot one of Christopher Columbus. The Columbus statue had stood in the center of the parking roundabout in front of the old Coit Tower from 1957 until city officials removed America's discoverer in 2015 because, as Recreation and Parks Director Phil Ginsburg squawked at the time, Columbus "had become an upsetting symbol of oppression and racism." EB didn't care that the accusations were demonstrably false, and contrived to be used as propaganda to promote the progressivists' race revolution to overthrow the Constitution. Sometimes a little deception is needed to create the chaos necessary for revolutionary change, and there was no question in EB's mind that the current order under the Constitution needed to be abolished, just like the Coit structure, and brought into modern times.

Warren much more accurately represented where his and San Francisco's values were now in the technological age. Not perfectly, but much more than Columbus. Most famous as Chief Justice of the Supreme Court, Warren had also been the governor of California from 1943 to 1953. Most notably for EB, he was governor after the conclusion of what EB liked to call *The Second Great Imperial Struggle*, or World War II. Most didn't understand that WWII was, in its essence, a fight to end the nation-state system once and for all so humanity could ascend to a unified international social order that would be embodied in a United Nations.

A Republican, though in name only, Warren was dedicated to this dream, and at the San Francisco Conference, or United Nations Conference on International Organization as it was formally called, was chosen to give the opening welcome speech in April of 1945. It was from this speech that EB personally chose the words that would be engraved on the marble base of his idol: "We recognize that our future is linked with a world future in which the term 'good neighbor' has become a global consideration." Also engraved on the plaque was a reminder that the globalist-minded Warren was: "A statesman and judge, locally educated at University of California, Berkeley who served dutifully as Grand Master of the Freemasons for the state of California." This last line was included at the urging of Narud, who himself had served as California's Grand Master, as well as Sovereign Grand Inspector General of the Supreme Council in California's Ancient and Accepted Scottish Rite of Freemasonry as a thirty-third-degree Mason.

In addition to the preserved murals and new statue, the famed views of the old tower, which some considered the most optimal of the bay and the surrounding counties, were also retained, and significantly improved. The twentieth floor of the eBeja Tower, which put it at the exact same height for viewing as the old tower, was dedicated to the public and was a dramatic expansion and improvement over the utterly outdated early-twentieth-century view deck. Complete with a gourmet restaurant, extended skywalk platforms to feel like you were walking on air over two hundred feet up, a covered deck that encircled the building, and a virtual reality arcade, the new panorama porch dwarfed its outdated predecessor. An elevator exclusively for the public to enjoy the 360-degree views was also added.

All these upgrades and improvements made eBeja a top tourist destination, only adding to eBeja's prestige—and profits. With all the new frills, EB was able to substantially increase the fee charged to access to the view floor and amenities, much to the outrage of the usual city complainers. But the protestors didn't succeed in their efforts to make the view deck affordable. In fact, due to the dramatic increase in visitor numbers, the added shopping, expanded rain forest park, and overall draw the tower had become, this little Coit part of his business turned a profit sooner than projected and became one more moneymaking addition to his empire.

"Triple three blend espresso!"

Hearing the barista's call, EB pulled himself away from his favorite mural, *Power* by Frederick Law Olmsted Jr. He loved the imagery of the raised fist of determination rising out of a blazing fire, a flame that reminded him of the building itself, as well as his own journey. Whenever he had to descend to the main floor, he would make it a point to meditate on the mural. It seemed to strengthen him, inspire him, and reinforce his mission and purpose. Funny, though, today, as he gazed on it, he had a different feeling, like a burning dread had come over him instead of the usual motivation and power.

"What took you so long?" EB barked at the young woman who had alone taken his order, ground the beans, and prepared the drink.

"Sorry about that, sir. We're a little short staffed since its Christmas Eve," she gently replied with a big smile that infuriated EB.

"Hexagas nonsense! I have an extremely important appointment, much, much more important than anything you're doing. Now you've made me late." She hadn't, but EB's mission was accomplished as her smile withered away into humiliation.

Power, EB thought as he grabbed his liquid boost and headed out the front door where his driver would meet him. *It's the only thing that changes people to be more productive.*

CHAPTER 10

"SwarmTrooper Tower, sir?" his driver confirmed through the implanted intercom from his bulletproof glass separated cockpit.

"Yes, and take the Embarcadero. It will be faster," he ordered, also wanting to avoid the Christmas lights and decorations that polluted the streets of the more direct route.

EB would have driven himself to Narud's lair for the meeting, but still had more work to do on the new partnership he and Narud were going to discuss in addition to EB's personal matters. EB was convinced that this particular agreement between their two companies, something to do with combining the two companies' data, would be the most significant of the numerous other joint ventures they'd launched over the years. And though he knew the numbers for his data empire backward and forward, he wanted to review the details one last time to ensure nothing was missed. But even if such a rarity occurred and there was something he overlooked, Narud would catch it.

In all the years of doing business together, EB had never seen Narud make a mistake. His obsession with perfection and details was another trait EB gleaned from him, though he still had not arrived at Narud's level. But as of late, he felt closer than ever. It might be that this was why Narud wanted to embark on this new partnership now. Maybe he was finally at the level of perfection Narud had been waiting for. He certainly thought he had arrived, except for that little flaw he just couldn't seem to shake: his love for sleep, the little he had each night. Of course Narud had somehow overcome the sleep burden, like everything else. This amazed EB. He just couldn't understand how someone of Narud's age could do as much as he did with as much energy and power as he always had, and never tire or sleep.

Not deterred, EB was determined to conquer that foe someday as well, but in the meantime he would crunch the numbers for the umpteenth time from his Mercedes office as they made the ten-minute drive across town. Rolling in a VIP Rolls-Royce Edition S-Class with a 32-valve Turbo V8 engine, this mobile masterpiece had been extended nearly three feet to accommodate a mini version of the AI system in the eBeja building. And instead of the usual two posh extra-wide all-leather reclining seats, along with their accompanying LCD flat-screen TVs, his had a single 360-degree swiveling adjustable Shell Cordovan leather office chair. Located more in the center of the chassis than in the rear where seats were usually placed, his chair was surrounded by three extra large embedded computer screens, as well as a security monitor on the front panel where he could keep track of his building and staff. He encased it all in the same beautiful deep brown illegally harvested mahogany from which his office desk was made.

EB liked to drink, and imbibe other substances, but only in the late night after leaving the office. For him, intoxication was all part of the cycle of the day that provided a mental deviation from the norm, a creative interlude or energy extension so he could be more productive. Not many could effectively manage such a life, but he was convinced he had been genetically gifted as one of the few that could, and so embraced it wholeheartedly. Of course, he would not in any way ever reveal to others his secret, nor encourage anyone to journey into the wonders of ancient and modern medicine as he did. The simple truth was that the masses of the lower tiers could not handle it as he could. Consequently, alcohol and all other recreational drugs—except caffeine, of course—were banned at all eBeja properties and locations, including their fleet of limos, planes, and helicopters. Even in this company Mercedes of his, EB enforced the ban replacing the typical fancy bar usually loaded with top-shelf spirits at the head of the passenger space with a small server array that gave his roving office the connectivity and capacity for full control of his empire when on the road. He completed his high-tech chariot with a laser printer, a 3D printer, and PlayStation 8 full emersion reality gaming system for when he felt the need to maim and slaughter.

"The front entrance as usual, sir?" asked the driver as they pulled in front of the monstrous tower.

"No, drop me off in the rear under the Transit Park overpass so I don't have to step out into this god-awful sleet storm or whatever the hexagas it is that's coming down on us," he corrected his dim driver, not wanting Narud to see him looking wet and windblown.

The SwarmTrooper Transit Center and Park, like the tower that shared its newest corporate owner's name, had become a city landmark and architectural wonder. Spanning four blocks and literally traversing multiple streets, the public transit center connected nineteen transit networks from the Bay Area, state of California, and the nation, including the new Bay Drone air transportation service. Several stories high, the STTCP resembled more of a fashion mall than a transport hub. EB's favorite part of the complex was the richly vegetated top floor of the center that was once public, but now a privately owned, by-invitation-only park that Narud procured as part of the pact the city made with him when he purchased the tower and its plaza outright from the previous owners.

A beautiful oasis surrounded by high-rises on all sides, the park he renamed to market his company name boasted more than five acres of lushly landscaped area, punctuated with an amphitheater, jogging/walking trail, and fifteen unique ecosystems filled with some 650 trees and nearly 18,000 plants. To a great extent, this man-made Garden of Eden was the model EB had used for his rain forest park on Telegraph Hill, except for the new reptile mini-zoo that Narud added showcasing his world-class private collection of some of the planet's most poisonous ophidians. If the weather hadn't been so atrocious, EB would have taken a few extra minutes to roam the garden and admire Narud's snakes.

That would have to wait. He was behind anyway and needed to get to Narud's office as soon as possible so as not to lose any more time with him. Exiting his car, EB gasped as he realized that, though he had successfully avoided Christmas on the drive there, he had completely forgotten that the transit center would be festively decorated and populated with joyful, happy, smiling merrymakers. *Hexagas!* he thought. *It's like a green and red plague of trees, bells, wreaths, and caroling. I would've thought Narud would've put an end to this pandemic of idiocy.* He made a note to himself to ask Narud about this once he escaped from this clamoring Christmas zoo.

To avoid walking directly to the SwarmTrooper Tower from the transit center and defeat his purpose of staying dry, he'd take the escalator up from the Grand Hall and then use the skywalk that connected the tower to the hub. To get there, though, he'd have to rumble around and through all the little shops of festive knickknacks and food booths set up in the center's Grand Hall for the Holiday Market that had for years now been an annual tradition. Only this year, there were more present than ever inside the Hall, even though it was Christmas Eve. Usually, the Holiday Market extended outside to the tower's plaza area, but due to the outrageous cold, wet, and dreary weather, all activities and decor were moved inside, creating a close and overly congested market.

Can't these cockroaches just use Amazon or have their meals in their own homes? he thought as he nearly sprinted toward the ascending staircase that would elevate him to sanity. Not a long walk, it nevertheless seemed to take forever as he fought his way through the hordes of laughing families, bouncing kids, and fun-seeking teens. The final obstacle before the escalator's on-ramp was a group of boys—none older than thirteen or fourteen—a multicultural rainbow of Asian, Black, White and Latino carolers all dressed in perfect little suits and bow ties. In a harmony that soared through the center, and tortured EB's ears, the juvenile choir serenaded the swarm of merrymakers with the Christmas classic "O Holy Night."

"O Holy Night! / The stars are brightly shining / It is the night of the dear Savior's birth!" they sang.

EB couldn't stand it, such an assault on his senses that he had no choice to hear or not to hear.

"Holy night hexagas!" EB yelled at them brazenly as he skirted past them. "Not everyone wants to hear your irksome jingles! You know, some of us are quite offended by your dear savior's birth!"

Stunned at EB's outburst, the boys looked to their director for guidance, as they continued to sing, but more softly now. Ignoring EB's spasm, the director pushed up on the air in front of him with both hands, calling upon his choir to not relent, but keep caroling with elevated voices.

EB didn't have time to waste on such vermin, and so again in disgust, he leaned over the railing of the escalator he had stepped on and shouted down upon them. "Hypocrites, all of you. Hexagas hypocrites!"

"Fall on your knees / Oh hear the angel voices / Oh night divine / Oh night when Christ was born," the chorus continued, back to its initial glory and volume, causing EB to cover his ears as he continued to curse them on his upward ride out of the Grand Hall.

In the daytime, the center was suffused with natural light through its numerous light columns, with the 120-foot-tall Grand Hall part of the center brilliantly lit via the largest skylight. But with the sun having gone to sleep and the angry stormy night on a rampage lashing the city, the Hall's main illumination became the holiday's refulgence, especially the creatively lit trees dressed with the most imaginative crafts and ornaments.

Looking up the escalator as he was lifted away from the beaming boys, his eyes were drawn to the large darkened skylight directly above him. Nearly black in contrast to the Hall, it was not a quiet darkness that the dome window shielded from entry, but a monstrous murkiness of fury haunted with ghouls of fog, gray cloud ghosts, and hellish hail-like poundings. It was as if the elements were all conspiring together in utter disdain and rioting against the Grand Hall and the lighthearted conviviality it was hosting. Though the elements were rebuffed by the window, the darkness prevailed and poured down on EB, giving him another dose of dread, this time accompanied by a freezing cold chill that made the hair on his arms stand paralyzed in fear. Disoriented from the dousing, EB looked away from the skylight, glancing down again at the young singers he had just excoriated, unable to shake off the unexpected terror.

"Hexagas choruses!" he muttered to himself as he squeezed the moving handrail as tight as he could while the folding stairs moved him away from the gala.

Arriving at his destination, he had no sooner stepped off the escalator than was again assaulted. This time by an unduly jolly voice coming from an overly fed Santa Claus of a man standing next to a suspended red kettle with a slit in the top, behind which stood two elderly women gently ringing bells, buttoned up to their chins to fight the piercing, searching, biting cold.

"Merry Christmas, sir. May I trouble you for a moment of your time?" said the shivering, but dry, overcoat-bundled charity worker.

"You want me to *give* you my time? Yes, that is troubling. My time is not free. People pay me handsomely for my time!" the CEO replied bitterly.

"Yes, sir, and I know your time is very valuable but we're not looking for anything for ourselves but are taking up a special fund to help the city's poor and destitute with meals during this holiday season."

"Poor and destitute? This is San Francisco! There are no truly poor, nor any destitute, except the ones that want to be that way," Ebenezer said with a scowl.

"Sir, I can see you are a well-established man, and one of great means," the gentleman replied as the sisters stopped their bells. "Tragically, there are many not as fortunate as you who are in desperate need of food, medical and financial help to pay basic bills, especially during this extra cold winter we're having, and shelter. And you've seen the myriad of homeless on our streets. Some have become targets and are regularly assaulted; others are criminals assaulting pedestrians, stealing with impunity from local shops and injecting drugs openly."

"Are there no prisons?" asked EB

"Yes, sir, plenty of prisons, filled to capacity—over capacity— to the point that the authorities are releasing criminals back on the streets because there is no more space to house them. We have several programs to help the homeless that are not on the streets by choice, but because they've lost their jobs or been the victim of a crime."

"Does the city not have a welfare department?" demanded EB. "Are not the city shelters still in operation?"

"They are, though I wish I could say they were not," the gentleman replied. "These homeless shelters—the women's shelters and many of the other taxpayer-funded homes—have become worse than the problem they're trying to solve. Exorbitant amounts of money have been thrown at these shelters and services, only to be squandered away, wasted, embezzled, or even used to facilitate the very problem itself. Are you aware that the city pays the homeless and addicts a monthly stipend, and will even help an addict buy the paraphernalia needed to inject their poison, only feeding their addiction and compounding their many problems? It's not an exaggeration to say the system is run not like a charity, but like a corrupt cartel where a paycheck trumps pity and progress is measured in terms of dollars received and spent, instead of by whether a life is truly helped and changed."

"They pay them with food stamps and provide them with other needed funds. Are you really saying that our expansive government welfare system is not helping, and may even be doing more harm than good?" EB asked.

"Government-based welfare and charity seldom works and has a gross history of abuse and failure," the jolly man replied with a frown.

"And you have a better solution?" EB said in frustration as he checked his watch.

"Giving those in need a plate of food at feeding time makes them like animals in a zoo. Charity must be based on love, given by people who genuinely care about them as real people. It has to be individually focused and based on their unique needs, not a socialistic project based on broad-brush, one-size-fits-all, mechanistic programs that dehumanize them.

"Our efforts are based on compassion," the happy Santa continued, "which in essence means to 'suffer with.' We have individuals and families all over California, and nationwide, for that matter, that have opened their homes to deserted children, battered women, trafficked families, and demoralized nomadic men. Their home-sponsors care for them, work with them, and welcome them as part of the family. And for the men, especially, our members either employ them directly or help them secure employment in the community. Productive, helpful, rewarding work is especially important for men. Overall, our objective is to elevate them all to the high status that they really are, individually crafted creatures delicately, carefully, and lovingly designed in the image of their magnificent Creator."

"More likely randomly arranged amalgamations of matter somehow clawing their way out of a prebiotic soup due to the accidental roll of the cosmic dice in an ever-expanding space-time continuum," snarled Ebenezer.

"What hope is there in that?" inquired the man humbly. "If you are correct, then what meaning is there for our existence? It leaves humanity trapped in a horrible prison of purposeless pain and despair!"

"You're starting to understand," replied EB.

"Well, one of the blessings of free speech—we can agree to disagree. But I'm sure we can both agree that those less fortunate and in dire circumstances need our help. What shall I put you down for?"

"Nothing!" EB replied.

"You wish to be anonymous?"

"I wish to be left alone," said EB, again checking his watch. "Since you ask me what I wish, that is my answer. Listen, I don't do this Christmas thing and won't playact as though one day is more merry or sacred than others, and I certainly can't afford to make those who have chosen to be idle merry either. Do you know how much I pay in taxes every year? More, I'm sure, than every merrymaker in this Hall tonight combined pays, and much of it goes to build the welfare programs you so easily discount and dismiss. Our social system is the only way we'll ever put a dent in poverty, overcome disease, educate the ignorant, and, if we rid the world of religious zealots like you, we might even abolish war. Yes, the welfare state has cost and will continue to cost much, but so be it. Those who are badly off rarely change, so let them have their welfare checks and food stamps, let them stay in the shelters or, if need be, let them sleep on the streets in tents if that's what they want to do. But keep them away from me!"

"Many don't want to be on food stamps or sleep on the streets; and many would rather die than go to the shelters."

"If they would rather die," said EB, "they had better do it, and decrease the planet's surplus population!"

"There have been many despots in the last century that have said the same," observed the gentleman, bells quieted.

"It's not my business," EB returned. "It's enough for a man to understand his own business, and not to interfere with other people's. Life is survival of the fittest. Leave the unfit to the bureaucrats. What do you think taxes are for? Now I must go. Some of us are trying to be productive instead of wasting time and energy perpetuating myths about a virgin giving birth or angelic visitations."

Seeing clearly that it would be useless to pursue his point, the man bowed slightly and thanked EB for his time and again wished him a Merry Christmas as he scurried off to his appointment with Narud.

"We need to pray for that soul," the gentleman said to the two ladies who had long since ceased ringing their bells, and instead stood quietly next to him during the entire conversation.

"It's what we've been doing since you approached him," one

responded with a twinkle in her eye.

CHAPTER 11

Even though EB would have disapproved, when the large red digital numbers of the wall clock hit exactly 8:00 p.m., the entire staff in virtually perfect unison logged out on the CommuNEST system. All except for Bobby. He hadn't finished the prep work EB had ordered him to do yet, and so would toil a little longer. *As usual*, he thought, *I'll be the last one out of this building. And on Christmas Eve!*

He felt ashamed that he hadn't stood up to EB a little more firmly and insisted on leaving at eight. Olivia had dropped Timmy at the company day care center earlier in the day so she could do some last-minute Christmas shopping downtown, an area she seldom frequented. It would be a wonderful break for her, and Bobby was glad to accommodate so she could have some well-deserved time to herself. Her more than full-time job of caring for their five children could at times be more demanding than Bobby's, he felt. But at least she didn't have an EB to contend with. He was deeply thankful for that.

"Hello, Jenny?" Bobby said through the company communicator channel. "It looks like I'll be running a little late again. I'm so sorry for this, but EB has an important meeting day after tomorrow and I won't be in tomorrow, with it being Christmas and all and—"

"Don't give it a second thought," Jenny reassured him. "You know I love little Timmy and would spend the whole night with him if I could. We're having so much fun down here playing and doing Christmas crafts that I didn't even realize it was eight o'clock. Oh, by the way, Timmy has a surprise for you when you get here. Get done what you need to. I'll see you then."

Not wanting to keep Jenny at the day care center any longer than was necessary, for the next twenty minutes Bobby poured himself into the last set of the annual numbers he needed to analyze. Everything looked good and he was confident EB's Pod connection with Singapore would go perfectly. After cleaning up his desk and packing up his shoulder bag, he logged out of CommuNEST. 8:25 p.m. *Good*, Bobby thought. *EB will see that I did stay late to finish.* The constant war of always trying to please EB grated on his soul, but he suppressed the frustration, especially tonight.

As soon as Bobby stepped foot into the day care center, Timmy let out a howl. "Daddy!" he yelled and laughed at the same time in delight, clapping his little hands. He would have run to give his dad a big hug, but his braced legs and wheelchair-bound body prevented such a move.

Born with Osteogenesis Imperfecta Type 3/4, or brittle bone disease, Tim's genetic condition caused his body to under-produce collagen, a main part of connective tissue that connects and supports the whole body, including the bones. The disease not only stunted Tim's growth, so he was quite small in stature, but also caused his teeth to break off, his legs to bow, and made his little chest barrel in shape. As the name implied, Tim's bones broke so easily that he had already experienced over fifty bone fractures in his short seven years of life, and nearly as many surgeries.

Tragically, Tim was in immediate need of another major surgery, but Bobby's insurance limit covering Tim had been reached last year and Bobby had already drained his savings for Timmy's recent hospital and care bills. This was another reason Bobby worked late whenever he was needed, and always did whatever EB asked of him. He had to keep his job, no matter what, just to keep up with Timmy's ongoing treatments and medication. Bobby's finances were so tight that every penny was accounted for just to cover the basics his family needed to live and eat and keep little Timmy alive. Any interruption or reduction in his pay would be catastrophic, something Bobby couldn't bear even thinking about.

Tim, of course, was too young to understand all this and how fragile and expensive his life was right now. Bobby was glad for that, but knew a day would come—if Timmy survived that long—when Timmy would start to comprehend the financial toll he took on the family. Bobby, and his entire family, were committed to find a solution for Timmy before that day came. But for now, he didn't comprehend that, nor how delicate his life really was. Instead, he saw himself as most young boys do—with eternal optimism, hopeful in each day. The Cratchits were exceedingly thankful for this, that right now they had been blessed with the most gentle, caring, and thoughtful of souls, who was also a fighter that never gave up no matter how much pain or difficulty he had.

"There's my little Timmy!" Bobby shot back as he rushed over to Tim and knelt in front of his suitable, but older model electric wheelchair.

"Have you been having fun with Jenny?"

"Oh yes, Papa, they have so many fun toys and computer games here to play with and I made this for you!" Tim said as he handed his dad a beautiful, watercolor masterpiece.

"What's this?" Bobby asked.

"It's the story of Christmas, when Jesus was born," Tim replied.

Bobby examined the 8 ½ x 11 sheet that, in surprising realism for a seven-year-old, portrayed Jesus in a manger with a big yellow star above the structure surrounded by a few slightly out of proportion animals, very colorful wise men, and in the center of the picture, Mary, Joseph, and another figure that Bobby couldn't interpret.

"Who's this?" Bobby asked, pointing to the small figure just to the side of baby Jesus lying on what looked like a bed of hay.

"That's the little drummer boy. See his drum here," Timmy said, pointing to a little brown circle. "He's playing a song for Jesus. That's all he had was a drum. But he played it for Jesus. That's like me. I don't have any money so I made this picture for you and Jesus."

"I'm sure He loves it," Bobby said, trying to hold back a tear. "And you know He loves you because you're His child, not because of anything you do, right, Timmy?"

"I know. I just wanted to give Jesus a Christmas present," Timmy said, smiling. Can we go see Mommy now?"

"Of course. Jenny, thank you again for staying late," Bobby said as he mentally commanded $100 to be instantly transferred to her account, even though he really couldn't afford it. Within a fraction of a second, a little chime alerted her what had happened.

"Merry Christmas, Jenny. You're always so helpful to us with Tim. Just a little Christmas cheer Olivia and I hope you'll spend to have an even merrier holiday season."

Jenny knew that times were tough for Bobby and Olivia, with all of Timmy's needs. Olivia had shared in more detail with Jenny their situation, making the gift all the sweeter. "Merry Christmas to you too." She smiled back.

"I'm taking the rest of the week off, so I won't see you until next year," she said as Bobby wheeled Tim out of the high-tech kinder care. "So Happy New Year! And Happy New Year to you, too, Timmy!"

"Happy New Year, Jenny," Timmy said, waving as his father

wheeled him briskly to the garage elevator. Olivia had left their electric minivan there for Bobby and grabbed a Lyft ride to Union Square where Bobby would drive with Tim to meet her. This would give them some time together in the Square. It would also give Timmy an opportunity to see the giant, elaborately decorated and beautifully lit tree in the Square's center before their forty-five-minute drive home to their assigned sector in Pittsburg.

Christmas Eve traffic at this hour was very minimal, especially because of the storm, so it only took them a few minutes to be guided via the van's autopilot system to the SFMTA Union Square Garage. Parking was free after 5:00 p.m. for the revelers willing to endure the cold. *A nice gift from the city,* thought Bobby. Leaving Tim's chair in the van, he bundled himself and Tim with coats and gloves and then boosted little Timmy onto his shoulder for the short walk from the handicap-designated parking space to the plaza.

"Hurry, Daddy, hurry!" urged Tim as he held himself steady with Bobby's head while bouncing up and down. "We're going to see the Christmas tree?"

"Of course, and would you like to see the ice skaters too?"

"Yay!" Timmy screamed so loudly with excitement that his little voice echoed through the garage, startling a few other holiday enthusiasts.

"There she is, Tim!" Bobby said, pointing to Olivia who had received Bobby's brain-sent text regarding their ETA. As they embarked up the stairs just outside the garage to the plaza, Bobby noticed that instead of the driving, punishing sleet that had assaulted the windows of EB's office, there were delicate snowflakes dancing in a soft wind, finishing their spins and leaps with a melting bow on their concrete stage. *A perfect Christmas Eve for Timmy,* Bobby thought, but then couldn't stop the one that followed. *I hope it's not his last.*

Flushing that last unwelcomed thought out of his mind, he grabbed his young wife and embraced her, with Tim joining the hug and kiss from his shoulder-high perch. Bobby loved Olivia, deeply and truly, with a love that he couldn't explain, but knew was a gift from above. He had never experienced anything like it before he met his pretty, blondish brown–haired companion. And she was genuinely that, a companion and friend, someone he loved to be around even after their many years together. They seldom had a cross word between them, though there were many issues and ideas in which they didn't fully agree. But because of the respect they had for each other, each wanted to listen to the other knowing they would learn something or grow in their understanding of their other half.

Their relationship was indeed rare, like rubies, to the point that many of their friends, and even some of Bobby's coworkers, had commented on it. How, after their years together, so many kids, and such difficulty with Timmy, could they still be like newlyweds? "We have God's love for each other—it's as simple as that," Bobby would tell whoever inquired. If probed further, he'd explain that from the beginning of their relationship, they'd determined to focus on how they could serve each other above and over themselves. "Wanting her best and always thinking how I can meet or help her needs comes before my own," he'd share. But even that didn't get to the heart of it. "It's not something you can work up in yourself, though. It's a spiritual change that is like a resurrection—a recurring, every-day resurrection. Jesus said He is the resurrection and the life, and that's what this is—His resurrection power in both of us that enables us to see each other as He does, instead of how we otherwise would see each other in all our depravity, full of flaws."

The way he would describe that continuous resurrection love

power was that when he thought of Olivia, he wanted to be kind to her no matter what, he couldn't help but be patient with her, he was never jealous because he trusted her completely, he wanted to share everything with her, including his deepest needs and struggles—of which there were many—and if she did something hurtful or wrong to him, instead of resenting her or becoming bitter, the love power that worked in him enabled him to overlook it, forgive it, or do whatever he could to help fix it. And that was a major part of it. Unlike other husbands he spent time with, he didn't feel the need to be right all the time. And neither did she. They both were dedicated to humility, esteeming each other—including their respective opinions, dreams, and goals—above themselves.

"That can't be done if someone is seeking their own will, desires, or way first. The culture today says 'look out for number one, make the most of yourself, love yourself . . . self, self, self.' It's exactly the opposite in our marriage. I look out for her first and she looks out for me; I lay down my life for her and serve her, focusing on her and the children, and she does the same. There's so much truth in the saying, 'to live you must first die.' So this is our mentality—again, a mindset that we can't achieve on our own, but a determination to depend daily on God to resurrect this love in us. And He does."

It wasn't a fake act or some religious show they were performing. This was how they truly were with each other. They didn't always feel this love power, and sometimes they didn't live it. But whether times were wonderful or extremely stressful, which lately seemed to have increased exponentially for both of them with the financial difficulties, Timmy's condition, and Bobby's daily lashings from EB, they focused instead on the infinite One who had no stress, no worries, and no lack, who truly infused their souls with the confidence and power to overcome any obstacle.

"Did EB keep you there late again?" Olivia inquired. "He does know it's Christmas Eve, doesn't he?"

"He definitely knows, but you know EB: work first, play later," Bobby replied as he took her hand while securing Timmy with the other. "But it doesn't matter what EB thinks. We're together now, and even though it will be a little late when we get home, all of us will have a wonderful Christmas Eve together."

"He did give you the full day off tomorrow, didn't he?" Olivia stopped in a moment of fear that EB had come up with some meeting, plan, emergency, or any of the many other excuses he often made to keep Bobby away from his family.

"All day! And my communicator is off, and I put my PPC bracelet on as soon as we pulled out of eBeja's garage. So no interruptions or disturbances!" Bobby said proudly while together they walked past the Derby Monument, through the sparkling, white-lighted palm tree–lined square to its center to see this year's coniferous marvel. Little Timmy could hardly contain his excitement as he gazed up at the eighty-five-foot-tall tree.

"The sign here says it has more than thirty thousand lights and around eleven hundred decorations," Olivia said. "And look at the size of the star on top. It's a beautiful reminder of the real star that led the Magi to the manger."

"Like the star you painted today," Bobby said to Timmy.

"Painted?" Olivia asked.

"Oh yes, Timmy painted a masterpiece with Jenny this evening. Suitable for framing! It's in the car, hon."

"Daddy, why did God use a star to show them where Jesus was?" little Tim inquired.

"That's a great question, Timmy," his father replied, impressed with the depth of his simple question. "We don't know all the reasons, but the Bible records that these Magi were astronomers of their day, and believed that the God who created the whole universe also set the stars into place to give His people here on earth signs."

"But why?" Tim probed.

"Well, think how big the universe is and how many stars there are. If God created all of the stars and spread out the whole universe, what does that tell you about God?"

"He's got more power than Superman!" Tim said.

"Exactly. Infinite power. That's why we call Him 'the Almighty,'" Bobby responded, laughing with admiration at Tim's answer.

"What does 'im-fin-it' mean?" Tim asked, trying to sound out the word.

"It's 'in-finite' with an 'n,'" Bobby instructed. "Infinite means limitless power, without end. It means God has all the power that is possible to have. To be God, He would have to. If there was anything anywhere that God did not have power over, then He wouldn't be God. One of the requirements of being God is to have total power, in every way, at all times."

"Wow, so that means God can do anything!" Timmy observed.

"Yes, nothing is too difficult for Him. One way God shows us this omnipotence is by creating the huge universe, full of galaxies and planets and solar systems that are scattered over billions and billions of miles all around us."

"Om rip o pants," Timmy muttered in an effort to learn a new word, causing Olivia to laugh out loud.

"Yes, He could rip your pants, you little munchkin," Olivia said as she kissed his cheek in delight. "The word is om-nip-o-tence."

"Om rip o tans," Tim tried again, and then kept whispering to himself as his father continued the lesson.

"Yes, omnipotence, which means total power over all," Bobby continued. "Whatever or whoever has all the power is God. Now we could never discover this on our own, so God told us about Himself, and the people that He told wrote it down. He told us He has all this power so we could know that all that exists—the universe, the stars and the earth, and all that's in the earth—didn't just happen by accident, but that there is a Being that created it."

"So that's why God used a star," Tim said in epiphany. "Because anyone could make a big light or sign, but only God could make a star appear at the right time, at the right place, so the wise men could find Jesus!"

"Yes! This is how the wise men knew that something incredible was happening, something from God to help them and the whole world."

"Do you think God will show us a star to help us—to help me?" Tim asked with a little bit of sadness.

Bobby and Olivia paused at Tim's inquiry, not wanting to say anything that would give little Timmy false hope. For a moment, all three looked up at the giant tree's star in silence as the snow fell on them lightly.

"God has all power. Right, my, little man?" Olivia said, putting her gentle hands on his questioning face after wiping a tear away from her own. "Well, if He has all power, that means nothing is too hard for Him to do. And if nothing is too difficult for God, then if He makes a promise, that means He has the power to keep that promise. So nothing can stop Him from keeping His promises, right?"

"Uh-huh." Timmy nodded.

"And what do you know about how God feels about you?"

"That He loves me," Timmy said.

"Correct, more than anyone. More than your daddy loves you, more than I love you—although I can't fathom how that's possible. He has more love for you than all the world's love put together," she said, looking in his eyes. "And He has told us, has had it written down for us so we'll never forget, that He is the Great Healer."

"You showed me this in the Bible, Mommy, how Jesus always healed sick people like me."

"Yes, and what else does God's Word teach us about Jesus? That He's the same yesterday, today, and forever. So, if God is always the same—healing all who came to Him, having all power and loving you with the greatest love possible—what do you think the Great Healer will do for you since He has promised to heal any who come to Him confidently, fully trusting in Him?"

"God always keeps His promises," Tim answered.

"Always, because God cannot lie."

"So maybe this star is for me," Timmy said, looking up again at the glowing orb.

"Not maybe, Son," Bobby jumped in. "You have His promise. We have His promise. And so together we will not doubt Him but trust Him that He'll send a star to you just like He did for the Magi."

Timmy smiled, still looking up. "I believe He will."

After another minute of quiet, he said, "Let's go see the ice skaters!" And so they found their way to the open-air rink where old and young alike were carving eights or falling down. Regardless of their ability, all were enjoying a genuinely cold night on cold ice under the cold, dark clouds that, for some reason, withheld their wrath on this little spot in the city, and instead sprinkled them with gentle flurries instead of the fury that had been unleashed on the rest of the bay.

CHAPTER 12

"It's always enlightening to see you, EB," said the aged tech giant as he motioned for him to have a seat in one of the two stiff metal chairs situated in front of his office fireplace. "You're a supernova in our American galaxy of ussselesssss, endlesssss intellectual debris and empty mindsssss." Narud's soft voice was punctuated with long s's wherever a word ended in "s" or had double s's in the middle, giving his quiet, steady tone a near continual hissing sound. The fire also hissed, and cracked and popped, sending sparks flying up the flume, slightly echoing against the bare floors, walls, and ceilings in his sparsely furnished, otherwise cold office. EB had always wondered why Narud had a fireplace in his office, especially a wood-burning one. Not that it mattered; in fact, it made him want one for his office, a big one like the one he had in his penthouse.

Narud differed from EB not only in his penchant for minimalism, but in how he managed his firm. Unlike EB, Narud had never implemented a full-spectrum monitoring system or elaborate PPE tracking protocol for his employees and executives. Rather, he organized them and trained them more like a special forces military unit than a product-producing enterprise, depending on their internal discipline as soldiers, not external control systems, to flawlessly execute his commands.

As Supreme Commander, the internal company title that all staff were expected to use when addressing him, Narud's authority was absolute. The rest of the world acknowledged him in typical corporate fashion as CEO and Chairman of the Board, which is how he was addressed in rare articles or reports about him or when titles were used under his name in video or holograms. Inside the confines of his tower, however, using those plebian terms was forbidden and grounds for dismissal. "Sssuch idiociesss are beneath me and do not begin to accurately communicate my real purpossse, power, and persssona," he had told EB. Neither did normal business attire. So Narud always wore an all-black uniform and black ankle boots that gave him a warrior priest–like aura. Combined with his blinding white hair, Narud commanded with a five-star general's respect and fear, far greater and more powerful than what any security or Big Brother system could impose.

Uniforms were not only important to Narud, but essential to company discipline. Just as generals in wartime are never seen in public without their uniform, so also Narud had never appeared in public without his full black regalia. "Uniforms remind, reflect, and reinforce," Narud would say to his troopers. "They remind you that you are part of a greater whole, an essential element of something greater than yourself and have a duty to uphold what your uniform exemplifies. The uniform also brings reflection that the war is raging, and you are in it, not observing it. These uniforms you proudly wear reinforce that while the competition wears jeans and T-shirts, degrading themselves and portraying slackness, an arrogant laziness and self-centered purposelessness, you are exalted, elevated as the best in your field. Disciplined, energetic, always active and engaged, your uniform trumpets to the world that your purpose is unwavering, and so you will be victorious in conquering your foes of the competition."

As Supreme Commander, Narud's pure black war attire was unique in the company. All his other executives and staff had differences in their uniforms that distinguished them in two basic classes. The executives of the company, including his numerous vice presidents, were required to wear dark metal gray suits, with matching boots of the same style and brand as Narud's. Jet black collarless shirts were worn under the suit jacket, which was not a typical semi-formal-type jacket, but were custom designed to look more like lightweight bomber jackets. Also collarless like the shirts, the jackets only zipped up three-fourths of the way leaving an open "U" revealing the blackness of the undershirt. Special long metal-gray overcoats were required outside the tower, even in pleasant weather, as were matching pullover hats that were more like helmets.

Non-executive staff, whether manager or first-day employee, had a completely different uniform color. The style was the same from the boots to the overcoat and helmet, but instead of being gray, their pants and jackets were brilliant white with a black stripe running down each side of their jackets. Their shirts were also all black and were completely covered by the collarless white jacket that, unlike the executives', zipped all the way up, creating a one-inch white rim surrounding the neck. No skin was revealed except for the laborer's face, part of the neck, and hands.

Both the men and women SwarmTroopers wore the same uniforms, with no distinctions because of sex, since there was no distinction with Narud's expectations of them. Narud's discipline was ruthless, but even-handed. Women weren't treated with any less respect, nor were they given any advantage or allowance. Narud mocked the "lukewarm feminists and leftists," as he called them, who tried to achieve the true egalitarianism he had incorporated, but could not because they refused to be fully and consistently equal. As such, they were charlatans and "obvious compromisers" as they hypocritically incorporated contradictory policies such as maternity leave, sex-based quotas, and dumbed-down physical qualifications where strength and stamina were required in the job.

This didn't mean Narud didn't train the women to use their feminine guiles when needed. He understood better than most the uncontrollable desires most men have, and how these lusts could be manipulated and exploited for his advantage. In fact, he had incorporated an entire training module for hand-selected women of his company to learn the crafts of seduction and honey traps. He lost count of how many victories he had achieved against the unsuspecting competition through this unconventional warfare.

Narud also had a module like this for men. Since more and more companies were promoting women to positions of authority and influence, Narud created a special unit in his army that would target these women of power, seducing them through romance, affirmation, and false pretenses. Much of Narud's success over the years came through piercing the naive establishment's facade that women and men were equal in their dispositions and desires. He also had achieved countless victories exploiting the differences in men's and women's methodologies of handling power and authority. In a bewildered culture that couldn't even define what a man or woman was, but yet at the same time tried desperately to retain so-called "feminine" and "masculine" traits, Narud could twist, turn, and subjugate just about anyone he targeted.

And so while he taught his commerce forces of both sexes to exploit their enemy's naivety, inherent contradictions, inconsistencies, and blatant hypocrisies, he didn't tolerate even a smidgen in his own ranks. Women and men were barred from wearing makeup of any kind. "Clown masks," Narud called the use of cosmetics. "An attempt to hide the evolutionary blessed decay into ugliness, which is denial of the natural self." They were an attempt to "pretend to be what a person is not—an inauthentic falsification of beauty that springs from deep self-loathing and insecurities, a charlatanism used by clowns, prostitutes, and cross-dressing transvestite sissies."

Long hair was also not permitted for either sex, since short, close-shaved hair was more practical, efficient, and easier to manage. Decorating the body, whether with colored or longer nails, jewelry, or any other adornments for beautification, was likewise barred as a petty and hollow self-indulgence and an indication of non-egalitarian weakness that distracted from the war at hand. "Can you imagine Seal Team warriors in the heat of the battle ducking behind a wall to adjust their makeup to look pretty or to check to make sure they didn't break a nail? War is constant, and so must be the soldier," he taught.

Like the Troopers, Narud's building was also designed for his total war. A rising single cylindrical missile-like structure, the SwarmTrooper Tower stood at over 1,270 feet, 200 feet higher than the previous version of the tower. And although its new height made it the tallest building west of the Mississippi and the fifth-tallest building in the country, surpassing the Empire State Building in New York, Narud did not heighten the tower only for bragging rights. It was strategic and numerological as well, with the 1 + 2 + 7 numerals adding up to 10, which then would be cubed since there were three numbers, equaling 1,000, which to Narud, indicated perfection and the mandate to usher in a millennial empire.

Many of the same features of the old tower had been retained, although remodeled and improved, making the old structure incomparable to Narud's citadel. The idea of a billboard-like display encompassing the top floors was retained, but now occupied ten full floors with triple the original number of LED lights per panel. "The Crown," as Narud called it, was a much more advanced 360-degree electric diadem that now projected stunning holographic still or moving images that could be seen up to forty miles away. Narud utilized it not only to project artwork and scenes from the city, sometimes live, sometimes produced, as allowed by the city, but had arranged that the panels would also display color patterns that corresponded to different times of the day, temperatures, and weather events, giving the city an always visible clock, forecast, and thermometer. What the city officials didn't know, however, was that all the images, art, scenes, colors, and patterns he displayed were carefully chosen and meticulously arranged according to the ancient psycho-spiritual craft in which Narud was also a supreme commander.

His new tower also kept the same base structure with each elevation above the twenty-sixth floor, curving and tapering away from the street, creating a narrow, slender top finished with the ten-story sculptural display crown completing the missile look. The building's curvature reduced the apparent height and massing of the building when viewed by pedestrians immediately below, and with Narud's extension, gave the impression when viewing from below that the tower continued infinitely into the heavens. From above the building, it looked like an ICBM aimed at heaven.

The crown was not only an architectural feature, designed as an unenclosed latticework of structure continuing the expression of metal wrapping the occupied floors of the tower below, but was a declaration of Narud's power. Whereas the previous tower had an uneventful flat top, Narud added four metal spikes or horns at each rounded corner of the tower's roof to serve as elevator and stair outlets for rooftop access, each piercing exactly sixty-six feet and six inches above the roof into the sky. At the tip of each metallic spire sat an encased spotlight that could either be lit in colors to match the tower's *coronas* display, or project a solid light beam into the atmosphere as far as the eye could see.

Like many of the other skyscrapers of the city, many of which had been added in the last decade, the inside of the SwarmTrooper's space in the tower was highly technological. Unlike all the others, it was minimalist, reflecting a cyber-military theme. Tenants on the bottom floors designed their offices as desired, but from the twenty-sixth floor, where the building's tapering curvature began, to the tower's top, all the floors were SwarmTrooper offices with Narud's signature fortress-type look and feel. As with their uniforms, the colors of all floors were consistent with only whites, blacks, and grays being allowed. Other colors were only seen on the plethora of monitors, screens, and display panels scattered throughout the floors on desks, walls, above doorways, or on the projection flooring of the structure.

And just as a military base has the highest possible security, so, too, did the tower. Access to the tower's non-commercial upper space was strictly off limits to outsiders unless cleared by Narud's private security force for very specific purposes. All floors were compartmentalized, with impenetrable sliding steel doors separating each section of a floor. If there was any disturbance or security event, the problem could quickly be isolated by locking down the area where it was occurring.

To further security, all executives were armed as well. Standard firearms were laughable to Narud, so he armed his executive soldiers with electromagnetic-directed energy weapons embedded into their watches. These illegal weapons built by Narud's firm were ideal for defense as they utilized electromagnetic radiation to deliver heat, mechanical, or electrical energy to a target. Depending on the setting, the invisible projection could cause mild pain, inflict permanent damage, or even kill. They also were excellent offensive weapons that the Swarm force used to sabotage competitors' electronic equipment and technology as needed.

As a whole, the SwarmTrooper floors were divided into thirds, the bottom third being dedicated to the hardware division of the company, the middle to the software side, and the top third was the skunk works black ops section where their top-secret projects—such as their weapons—were engineered, tested, and developed. At the zenith of the tower, Narud's executives occupied the top floors, except for the very top floor just under the ten-story unoccupied crown. This watchtower encompassing the entire top floor was about a quarter in part Narud's office, with the rest of it serving as his personal and highly secretive laboratory, lair, and temple's inner sanctum. It was in this office portion that EB was trying to make himself comfortable on the hard, cold, uncushioned chair in which Narud had directed him to sit.

"It's even more enlightening to be with you, Narud," EB said. "I'm glad you have this fire going; it's like Siberia out there, and almost as cold in here. And these metal chairs certainly aren't helping. What's going on with this weather?"

"The weather always tells a story," said Narud. "It reminds us that our task goes beyond the acquisition of wealth, or the attainment of power, or conquering the superstitions of the masses. Possess all of that, but fail to control the climate, and we have gained nothing."

"We're certainly making progress in that, but clearly not enough to prevent such an anomaly like this super storm," EB postulated.

"Anomaly? This is no anomaly. This is the earth speaking to us, telling us of its pain, its anger, its growing impatience with its occupants, punishing us because of our inaction. Why is it that we seek to save this unfeeling master?"

"Because our survival depends on it. The survival of our species, our lives, and, of course, our money," EB replied, realizing there would be no small talk before class began at Narud University.

"Not survival," continued Narud in his hissing hypnotic whisper voice. "Weak men think in terms of surviving. Strong men in terms of thriving. Surviving is defensive, thriving offensive. The survival mindset means there is a greater force than you, oppressing you, and that you are a slave. It therefore negates thriving."

"Evolutionarily speaking, then, survival of the fittest is thriving?" asked EB.

"The road of humanity is the long road of progress, from prebiotic slop to Homo sapiens man. Among mankind, there are those who survive and then there are the very few who have propelled themselves beyond survival. The key is to reject the old and embrace the new. Isn't this the essence of technology? Always searching, seeking, experimenting until the new emerges that replaces the obsolete old? And for what purpose?"

"Efficiency, of course," EB answered.

"And what is efficiency except another way of becoming more dominant? Electronic communication is more efficient than the pony express. But to what end? Electronic communication gives us greater dominance over our time, over who we interact with, over relationships. But what is essential for you to see, EB, is that we must focus our efforts in domination over that which we do not currently have full control."

"The climate," said EB nodding.

"We relegated the pony express to the history books, and the technologists who did so, who brought telecommunication into existence, who mastered the atomic elements so that words and ideas can be electronically transmitted instantaneously through the air, are now masters of the universe. But they will not always be so. They will soon fall to the technologists who control the climate. Global communication is a means for uniting the world, but controlling the planet's climate is controlling the world."

"And this new partnership between our companies will facilitate this?" asked EB.

"The reason you are losing energy and becoming more tired than before is not because of your age. Look at me—how old do you think I am?"

"I've often wondered, but didn't think it very respectful to ask. Candidly, I've tried to look it up, but no one seems to know. I couldn't find it anywhere," EB said, glad that Narud hadn't forgotten to address his personal need.

"And you won't find it. It's irrelevant. All you need to understand is that I'm ageless here," Narud said, pointing to the side of his brain. "What's up here has been around since the beginning, and is the wisdom that made the mighty men of old great warriors, epic builders and masons, giants of their day, masters under the Masters.

"This body looks old," he continued, still monotonous, patting his chest with both hands, "but that is only for convenience. Do you understand what I'm saying, EB?"

"I think so."

"No, you must truly grasp this, or all our work, our friendship, our future together is in vain."

"Well, then, here's what I see. I need to have the right mindset, to understand what it is that great men of the past have believed. How they thought of themselves and the world around them, which is what made them what they were. That their perceptions were accurate and absolute in terms of how reality is, so just like with technology, thought-engineering done according to the laws of the universe will bring success and progress."

"You're getting there, EB. But go deeper. Why is having the right mindset so important? What is the end goal? Your lethargy is because you're losing sight of the *telios*. If you live only for the now, you've capitulated, given up, and submitted yourself to the proposition that the future is beyond your control. That is defeat. You must take the future, and you do this by making the rules, not following them. That is the key to understanding what those of old and new have that generates power and energy. The world's future is in your hands, and you must dominate it today to control it tomorrow."

"Yes, you are right. I have been so focused on eBeja, and building my own little empire, that I've lost sight of why I'm doing all this, the end goal, or *telios*, as you call it. Of course, it's to save the planet, which I really believe and have spent my adult life—at least while here in San Francisco—trying to accomplish. But that's not really the final, final objective, is it?"

"Very good, EB. Then what is the final objective, the end goal?"

"Not just to save the planet, but to dominate it. Control it."

"If you control the planet, you'll have saved it. But saving the planet doesn't necessarily mean you control it. And if you don't, if we don't, it means someone else does," Narud said, softly leaning in to EB to make certain he understood the gravity of the moment.

"I'm feeling my energy return as we speak," EB noticed.

"The earth is ours and the fullness therein. But we must take it. No one will hand it to us. And this partnership I want us to have—this next-level partnership, for we have been partners now for years in our exploits and ambitions—this next-level partnership will do that, make us the head and not the tail."

"What level of partnership are you wanting, Narud?" EB asked. "Are you proposing our companies work together on specific tasks or am I hearing you say that we should possibly merge?"

"Defining the structure now is not important. Action will determine the structure. Look at our companies. What does each have that the other needs?"

"Well—" EB tried to answer but was cut off.

"Your company is about people and relationships. Your flagship products, the Elevation and Pod technologies, have brought people to love and admire your company because you have connected them in ways never thought possible and reunited them with their lost ones. You have canceled death and brought them together in virtual life. The people of the world see you as a savior and therefore are in your hand. You now control virtually the entire planet's social media. Like you or not, you have become the leader that the world has been looking for," said Narud as he stood up and walked to his desk where he pressed a button on the large control board built into its side. Pointing to a detailed 3D chart that was projected from somewhere in the office and appeared just off to the side of where the two had been sitting, Narud drew EB's attention to the column that listed all the companies and services of eBeja. Elevation was at the top of the list.

EB twisted his chair about forty-five degrees to see the holographic screen more clearly, and then stood up himself as he was starting to sweat from the fire's heat. "Elevation was really your idea, Narud. It wouldn't exist apart from you."

"Your company is people. My company is data," Narud continued, ignoring EB's flattery. "As you know, SwarmTroopers has marshaled the world's corporate data—that great swarm of government, commercial, financial, and organizational information—into our backup systems, server arrays, information clouds at our land-, sea-, and space-based data storage facilities. I have been given a power, EB, so that everything I touch succeeds, as long as it is for the purpose of the mighty ancients. SwarmTroopers has become the uncontested leader in its field, the universally recognized premier data management and organization system, moving and protecting the world's most confidential, secret, and important digital information flawlessly, with unheard-of cost efficiencies and reliability. This is because of my technology. But my real success is due to my and my forefathers' unconventional methodologies."

"You do have a very unique, in a way terrifying, sales force," EB noted cautiously.

"They are much more than a sales force, and intimidation is only one of my methods—and certainly not the most important. Much more relevant to my skyrocketing success has been the company's vast espionage network, high-level penetrations, irresistible shakedowns, focused blackmailing, and innumerable bribes that have secured our victory over all the major large corporations, nonprofits, and governments of the world.

"Our methods have been especially successful with governments. Once infiltrated inside, we have been able to force votes to go our way so our legislation becomes law. Our mass penetrations into the leading agencies around the globe have enabled us to execute mandates on the corporate world that compelled their data into our hands. By my last calculation, we have control of or have direct access to more than 91 percent of the world's corporate and government transactional, informational, and financial data—non-confidential as well as confidential. So, my son, combined with your massive store of the world's personal, relational, and social data from Pod, Elevation, and your other ventures, together our companies literally have full-spectrum informational control on nearly every organization and human being on the planet—96 percent, I'm estimating, and that's probably low by a point or so."

"Yes, we've discussed this before, although your numbers

have increased marvelously since then," EB noted.

"What we haven't discussed before is using my newest technology in conjunction with this data, to bring us to the final solution."

"New technology?"

"I've given you bits and pieces because I didn't want to give you the full story until it had been perfected. But now we've perfected it. It's called *Cosmosology*."

"Related to cosmology, I imagine?"

"Everything is related to cosmology, because the universe is everything. But *Cosmosology* is the merging of space and planetary geoengineering so as to control all aspects of the climate, especially weather, on the earth from space. We have perfected the science, and within a matter of months—not years, but months—can surreptitiously deploy our systems in countries throughout the world that will give us full global power over the climate. We'll use our control of their critical data—their military, financial, corporate trade, and any other government data needed—to ensure their compliance. Simultaneously, we'll be positioning our connection hubs and satellites in space."

"Incredible." EB was in awe. "Scientists have been working on geoengineering projects for decades, and have made astounding advancements. But I had no idea the technology had reached this level."

"Current geoengineering hasn't even come close to this level and is nothing compared to what we have. Just as Elevation is far beyond what previous holographic technologies could do, and goes even further beyond what are perceived as the limits of physics—almost in a spiritual way—so, too, this system gives us full planet control beyond what today's laws of physics deem possible."

EB's energy was not only returning, but surging with the news.

"So how do our combined data and technologies interface with this?"

"Once the full-planet *Cosmosology* system is in place, climate and weather control can be used based on the data we have to shape every country on the planet as we see fit. And not just countries, but counties, cities, towns, and even neighborhoods with our micro-climate adjustment capabilities."

"Absolutely amazing. This could end the climate emergency that's going to destroy us!" EB emphasized.

"Exactly. Under our climate governance, we will be able to once and for all halt destructive climate change and end the climate emergency our planet is now experiencing. But then what? What do we do after that? What is the final, final solution?"

"Well, I imagine—" EB said slowly.

"Perfect it!" Narud interrupted. "MASGER is what we call the *Cosmosology* system we've engineered and it is not just to end the climate emergency, but to gain control of the planet so we can finally perfect it, and ourselves."

"MASGER? What does it mean?" EB asked in delight.

"It is what it stands for: Managed Atmosphere by Space and Geo Engineering Regulation. But look it up in Hebrew if you really want to know its true meaning."

"I will," EB lied. He knew he wouldn't bother himself with such subtleties.

"Since years back, even millennia, our brothers and sisters sought to bring about the unification of our planet under a single authority using other methods, means, and manipulations. But none have yet succeeded. All have failed," Narud recalled.

"The Great Reset," EB interjected.

"Yes, the Great Reset was one of the most recent attempts, and was a big step forward for us. But even before that, all the way back to our beginnings in the modern age, this has been the objective. The Great Revolution, or French Revolution, was the spark that ignited the flame that later burst into the blaze of International Revolutionary Socialism, the historic movement that nearly conquered the world. Through both its expressions, Eastern and Western revolutionary socialism, the world came under its spell."

"Yes, but the world still remains horribly divided, especially between these two streams of Eastern and Western revolutionary socialism," EB pointed out.

"Revolution has been with man since his beginning, and should be understood to be his first major step of progress. Determined to shake off the shackles with which heaven had bound him, the first human rebelled. He refused to accept there being any limitations or constraints that would hinder his autonomy or his knowledge. But the first man was weak and retreated from the revolution he started, reverting back to subservience, obsequiousness, and slavish obedience to an imagined creator.

"Not too long afterward, however, another stepped up who was the real first man, the first true revolutionary who dedicated himself to throw off the shackles of superstition, reject the idea that mankind would never have true autonomy, but be forever dependent on the divine and dictates from above to survive, let alone thrive. This new man recognized that decrees from on high do not liberate, but choke, strangle, and deny man of unbridled freedom. It wasn't a heavenly being or beings that would save us, but a united humanity, dedicated to build a better world together that would bring about true liberty, harmony, and fraternity. This man was a mighty man, a hunter, the world's first conqueror. He was also a builder and set about to right the world, bring it together as one, so the name of *humanity* was elevated above all and into the heavens. And so the war began, he and his powerful revolutionaries against the weak reactionaries who sought to conserve superstition and religion. This is the war that continues to this day.

"The modern expression of this war to abolish tradition, religion, and a vertical theocentric focus for man and society," Narud continued, "is through International Socialism. But the campaign for International Socialism has been stalled now for more than a century as the movement split into an Eastern expression, as can be seen in China, Russia, Iran, and North Korea, and the Western version, which dominates most of Europe, Canada, and the rest of the Western aligned nations. Eastern revolutionary thought is based on the belief that in order to advance the revolution to its next phase, violent confrontation and ultimately armed conflict or war is necessary. Only through violence, force, and bloodshed can the human condition be sufficiently changed for progress to be achieved. To our Eastern comrades, revolution is necessarily and therefore will always be violent.

"Our Western revolutionary comrades reject the notion that violence is necessary, and instead postulate—as Western Democratic Socialists, Fabians, or whatever name they want to call themselves—that nonviolent persuasion and use of the democratic processes, such as the ballot box, courts, schools, media, and other cultural structures and institutions, are more effective tools to construct the universal global socialist order. So the difference, my son, is not the end goal or objective, but only the means. Both agree that, in the end, private property, family, decentralized authority, religious superstitions and all its constraints must be smashed and obliterated. This concept has been encapsulated in many slogans over the years such as 'from each according to their ability, to each according to their need' or, more recently, 'you will have nothing and love it.' But they all say the same thing.

"Therefore, EB, it's absolutely critical that you understand the global struggle of the last hundred and fifty years has been a family fight, so to speak, over which side of the family—Eastern- or Western-style international socialism—will control the levers of global power. But for the first time in centuries, due to efforts I'm involved in that you don't yet know about, both sides have come together and forged a global Forum that sits above the governments, corporations, and institutions of the world."

"A Forum? Which Forum is this?"

"You'll find out soon enough. Suffice it to say the group is the elite of elites, the leaders of leaders, the world's most powerful and influential finally together at the same table. Through its efforts, the entire world family is united for the first time since the Great Tower of old was erected by the first revolutionary, my true father, in Babylon. My son, we, the true stakeholders of the planet, are ready to build out the global world order. It will happen in our generation—it's happening now. Under the banner of global governance, the institutions are finally now in place and the mindset is there for all nations to lay down their divisive sovereignty claims and be united. But to finalize this unified planetary authority, the world's population must first be harnessed."

"And this is what MASGER will do?" EB said, trying to follow.

"No, there is another step that is in play right now that is necessary to yoke the masses and in all respects subjugate humanity so that no rebellion can rise to undo the centralization of nations under the Forum's global authority. Again, I can't give you all the details right now, EB, except that it is our technology to store and control the world's data that will make this final step possible."

"And after that step, then MASGER is deployed?"

"Exactly. Here's what's important for you to know right now. Once the masses are collared, there will be an internal *bataille finale*, a final struggle among the Forum leaders as to who will be at the top, the king of kings, so to speak. MASGER is how the throne becomes ours!"

"I understand there's information you can't give me right now, but it seems to me everything hinges on this 'collaring' of the masses. If that doesn't occur, then the rest of the plan falls apart?"

"Correct, EB."

"Well, I see a problem. While many other countries, really all the other countries of the world, will likely acquiesce to authoritarian control on some level or another, I would think the population of this country, the land of the free and home of the brave, would not so easily be shackled. It's in our nature to live free or die."

"You make an important point, EB. There has been no single nation or notion that has prevented the culmination of the global revolution more than America and the mindset that has made it the thorn in our side that it is. We have made great strides in canceling the opposition, capturing the election process, and creating a decrepit culture needed for its implosion. But somehow, in a way that's still a mystery to me and the elders, this country will not fold. The Constitution is a part of the problem, as the vast majority of the populace still believe it and adhere to it. Over the decades, and really since we were able to force the union of diverse states through our war of aggression, and subject them to centralized federal government control, we have made astounding progress in gutting the Constitution of its decentralizing, authority-limiting system of checks and balances. But in spite of all that, it is still a mighty foe that continues to endure all our efforts to destroy it.

"But beyond the Constitution," Narud continued as he paced his office, "is the Judeo-Christian fanaticism that keeps this nation sick, so much so that a large majority continually and incessantly reject the intellectual vaccines we have offered to heal them of their nonsensical superstitions. The real belief that there is a Creator, a God, who has all power, is everywhere present, and knows all there is to know and could be known, is the great crutch of American society that must be broken. But if this was all, if it was only a matter of dispelling the idea of 'God' from the minds of the Americans, especially children, we'd be finished. It is this book they cling to, their Bible, that they have full confidence in as the revealed, perfect, inerrant Word of that Being that is the problem. Couple that with the propaganda the book puts forward that this infinite God has appointed His own governor, His own government, His own Sovereign Ruler who exercises His all-encompassing authority and power over heaven and earth, even power over death itself, from some faraway place—the very powerful notion of a ruler in exile—and you have an undefeatable foe."

"Oh yes, I understand, Narud. I grew up with some of that humbug myself. But it just doesn't seem that powerful to me," said EB.

"Don't underestimate them, EB! It is soul penetrating, uncompromising belief and intellectually irrefutable confidence that moves mountains. They won't change or bend, because they see their mission as divinely sanctioned, and so are willing to lay down their lives, even unto death, to prevent us from obtaining our objectives. They are the vanguard of the reactionaries and are the only real obstacle left to us fulfilling our destiny, to us building our tower and city—to us becoming gods."

"And the plan you have to subjugate the world's populations, it will be potent enough to defeat them?" EB asked.

"Our plan—The Plan—gives the Forum the power to take dominion over this country once and for all, and thereafter the world. Not even the true believers will be able to resist. Those who will be the most resistant are a very small number among the opposition, just as in our camp there is only a small number pulling the strings. The vast majority of the reactionaries are only fellow travelers of this faith in a Jewish savior. So yes, while they are a potent and formidable force, most of them are naive and oftentimes seek to gain the favor of the very companies, organizations, and people they are at war with—like SwarmTroopers or eBeja.

"You see, many of them have become proud, arrogant, and self-seeking, trying to make a name for themselves, setting up mega ministries in their own names that are full of corruption, manipulation, and pastor or papal worship. They speak loudly, but carry a soft stick, and though they criticize us, condemn our ways, and call on us to change and follow their God, most deep down are afraid to separate from us. The very world they say should be abandoned in the name of morality, ethics, and holiness, they embrace, betraying the very cause to which they have pledged their fealty. They have become hypocritical stooges, useful idiots that we can manipulate for our purposes."

"Yes, seeing this greed and hypocrisy is one of the reasons I was convinced they are phony and delusional. So you believe that we can use this to our advantage?" EB asked.

"Without a doubt. It's already being done. For example, both you and I have vacuumed up their churches', synagogues' and nonprofit ministries' private donor, personnel, and confidential data without even a whimper of resistance. Even some of those groups they deem as the strongest, or most powerful in refuting our vision, their so-called apologists, defenders of the faith, and scholars, have come to us with checkbooks open, handing over all their most sensitive and secretive data to us with a smile and their money. I'm not talking about their digitized sermons, lectures, books, teachings, and other proselytizing nonsense, but their financial and relational data—data most of their donors and participants don't even know we have.

"But you see, EB, they love being associated with our global brands and prestige. So weak in their faith, they seek our approval, our compliments, and our help in their pathetic little crusades. And so they gladly bypass their own communities' data services—our competition—and instead hire us to store, manage, and protect it. Imagine, we are protecting their most precious information and data! They think our self-designed privacy policies and the laws of the land guard them, and that they could sue us if we mishandle or somehow release their data to the public. What they fail to realize is that we have no interest in releasing their data publicly or in any way mismanaging it. EB, they're clueless that we've already appropriated all their data for our purposes, in ways that are undetectable. The reality is, once that data is in our servers, its ours! Their centers of learning—their private schools, colleges, and universities—have done the same.

"Altogether, they're worse than harlots, who at least get paid. But these, these so-called lights of the world, salt of the earth—we are able to make them adulteresses who not only willingly give themselves to us, but even pay us enormous sums to facilitate their infidelities. And they are proud of it! Blind leading the blind, they have no idea that in the end we'll enslave them. You'd think they'd have learned the consequences for partaking of forbidden fruit. But alas, they truly are as sheep ready to be slaughtered. So this is one of the ways, EB, we're bringing about their destruction and the subjugation of this nation.

"We've also done the same with the reactionaries' nonreligious organizations, associations, and networks. They're lazy in many ways and are likewise paying us to store, manage, and move their data—the very data we have been and will continue to use to annihilate them. Even after the great Censorship Protocol was implemented publicly years ago by our people—and continues to this very day—they still skip along, happy-go-lucky, and though continuously complaining and grumbling in their media outlets, books, and structures about censorship and bias, they still use our systems, depend on our information channels and infrastructure, and clasp hands with our institutions. Even their homes, children, and most personal thoughts, through thought texts and messages, are being digitized, vacuumed up, sorted, and filed through our Internet of Things into our storage and management systems. Fools! It's a mystery how they have survived this long given their childlike ignorance to so willingly take the candy we offer them. My boy, they're also like cattle not realizing we have and control all of their data, finally, and so are ready to move in for the butchering."

"Music to my ears, Narud, and so even though I don't know what this so-called Plan is that will bring such an historic and final victory, I'm with you. I know you'll give me the specifics when it's time. For now, let me know what you need from me. We've spent our whole lives preparing, strategizing, and laboring for such a time as this!"

"I knew I could count on you, my son. Together, after the Plan is implemented and then MASGER is deployed, nothing will be impossible for us!"

"Everything seems to hang on the success of MASGER. Can you give me any more information on how it will be used to elevate us to lead this Forum you mentioned?"

"I can't say much, but I'll tell you this: by using MASGER to threaten, or as necessary, actually create droughts, hurricanes, super polar vortexes, incomprehensible heat waves, and flooding anywhere we choose, no one will oppose us. They will all capitulate and agree we are the rightful heirs to lead the final world order that will bring the planet to perfection."

"Narud, what if one of the elders of this Forum decides to defect, or marshals an army against us? The US still has the most powerful military in the world. Couldn't they just take us out—either conventionally or through a missile strike? Even a tactical nuke against wherever MASGER is based is possible if it's decided they don't want us at the top of the pyramid."

"No military or weapon system can stop us. How will they send forces if we can blind them with blizzards, torrential rain, and hurricane-speed winds? What army can withstand a flurry of monsoons or tornados brought upon their heads? How can a missile, whether conventional or nuclear, hit us if we can disable their radar systems with electrical storms? They cannot penetrate us because they will never know where we are. From the beginning, neither the US nor any military will be able to track our location. EB, we control the air through which their signals fly!"

"So the MASGER isn't based here, in your tower?"

"At the right time, you'll know the *where* and *how*. But for now, you only need to know the *what* and *why*. And the final part of the *what*, and possibly most important aspect of the system, is that MASGER gives us full control of the new energy sources, as well as significant leverage over the old. Wind, solar, hydro, electric, and nuclear energy, which have nearly overtaken the old coal and fossil fuel systems, are in our hands through MASGER. We will determine where and when wind farms are viable, we will determine how much sunlight is given in any particular location, and most profoundly, our system will determine who gets nuclear power, where, and how much.

"Remember the Fukushima nuclear disaster of 2011? In a moment, the Fukushima Daiichi Nuclear Power Plant in Ōkuma, Fukushima, Japan, was rendered useless with the leaking radiation posing an existential danger to the entire country. And what caused this? The Tōhoku earthquake and resulting tsunami that occurred on March 11 of that year. Our system gives us power not only to influence the earth's tectonic plates and thereby create earthquakes where we want, but to determine the exact date and time when we want, leading to deadly, nation-crippling tsunamis as needed. All energy, EB, will be under our direct control!"

"The unholy trinity of data, climate, and energy!" EB laughed.

"Exactly! Control of the data gives us the information we need to gain control of the masses and keep them enslaved once the Plan goes into effect. Then we use MASGER to have complete domination over the planet's climate and energy, and thereby the world, with our complete authority over the Forum. Remember, EB, the world elite have already united together in order to build a one-world tower, a single global system of governance. MASGER will be welcomed by the Forum elite. It's the royal flush that defeats all other hands and makes it easy for them to see that we have the final word in any matters of disagreement or dispute that might rise among us."

"We'll be unstoppable!"

"Yes, but we mustn't become arrogant, EB. There will be great struggle and loss of life to implement the Plan. The most fierce opposition to all this will be these reactionary Christians, conservatives, libertarians, and constitutionalists. But I assure you, EB, the Plan will subject them and all their power centers, or exterminate them if they resist."

"How many casualties and deaths do you estimate will result in this final Plan to complete the revolution?"

"Even if 75 percent of the planet's population is eliminated, our cause is just and is the only hope for humanity. We could bring about human perfection with only 25 percent of humanity remaining if need be. The casualty rate shouldn't be that high, however. But make no mistake, it will be massive. In every war, collateral damage is inescapable. It's the cost of doing business, my son."

"Of course. Saving mankind is the only business that matters, at whatever the cost. It's the old sinking lifeboat dilemma—those that want to rock the boat must be thrown over," EB agreed, feeling the power and anticipation exploding through him like a bomb. "With MASGER, there's no question we'll be the new masters of the universe, ascending to unimaginable heights raising our seat of power even above the stars of heaven! I've believed my whole adult life that collective humanity was the only hope for us, but never thought I would sit with you enthroned over the masses, able to save the ignorant superstitious hordes from themselves. If history has ordained us to succeed where so many of our fathers and mothers before us have failed, we must embrace the calling—I must embrace the calling—to ascend above the tops of the clouds of the masses so they see us for what we are: the most high over them, even their gods!" EB concluded.

"Yessss, my sssson," Narud whispered quietly as he slithered up next to EB and put his hand on his shoulder. "That is the true definition of progressss."

CHAPTER 13

EB's head was still spinning in euphoria after the short trip back to Telegraph Hill. Narud had done it again, taking him beyond where he had ever imagined, and giving him new immeasurable hope in the heights of power the two were about to attain. So exhilarated was EB that he not only gave his driver a $500 tip, but as he exited his limo, he returned the driver's "thank you, EB, and Merry Christmas" with a "Merry Christmas" of his own. He was a bit stunned he had said it, but if there ever was a reason to be full of good cheer, this was it. Narud had picked him, over all the other tech wizards and big data titans—not just in the Bay Area, but in the entire world—to be his partner in this venture to finally and really save the planet.

Yes, it is a Merry Christmas, he thought to himself as he caught himself grinning ever so slightly. *After all, the word 'Christ' comes from the Greek* Christos, *which means "anointed one." Well, it seems to me I've just been anointed by the Supreme Commander himself to be his right-hand man to save and deliver humanity. First, from death through Elevation technology and now through MASGER to usher mankind into the promised land.*

"Who's your messiah now?" he shouted out loud to an empty street as gave a mental command through his PPC to the building's security system.

EB would have had his driver drop him off directly at his home, but today he had driven to the office as he did every December 24. Even though he knew he would be meeting with Narud until this late hour, he had decided to have his driver take him back and forth to the SwarmTrooper Tower so he could not only do some work on the drive, but also to keep his tradition of finishing his day with his customary Christmas Eve drive back to his penthouse. It wasn't that the drive home was far; it wasn't. He could walk it in twenty minutes if he really wanted to. Rather, it was because by this time of night, the streets of San Francisco would be cleared of nearly everyone, except the swarms of homeless, of course. Practically the whole city would be at home or some establishment celebrating the holiday in one form or another. And that made the city a ghost town of vacant roadways where he could take his magnificent Nevera for a tear.

Having just upgraded it to the newest model, EB's Automobili Rimac electric hypercar had arrived only a few weeks ago from Croatia, where the company's headquarters and manufacturing plant was located. The fully electronic wonder vehicle had dazzled sports car enthusiasts since first being produced in small numbers in the early 2020s, making ownership of one a privilege only for the wealthiest of the elite. EB, of course, had no trouble securing this latest edition, and even had it semi-customized, making it a true one-of-a-kind Nevera. The $24.5 million price tag with customizations might have seemed steep even to the uber-wealthy for a production car, low as the production numbers were, but for EB it was worth every penny. With its newly invented magnum grip tires and six internal electric motors, the beast generated 2,612 horsepower, making it the first production car to launch from zero to sixty in under one second—0.94 seconds, to be exact—a number its inventor, Mate Rimac, and his engineers personally assured EB was accurate.

Tonight he would test that out, unofficially, of course, on a few of his favorite tar stretches in the downtown without any fear of reprisal. Just as nearly all the people were at home and the city shut down for the big day tomorrow, so, too, were most of the police off duty or hunkered down at the stations. The horrid weather only exacerbated the city's deserted status and lack of patrol officers, adding to EB's excitement since it would make his ride an even more intoxicating, albeit dangerous, rip. Though his Nevera could reach a top speed of 330 mph, the real value to EB was its physics-redefining electric vehicle technology that enabled him to preserve the environment while destroying speed limits.

There's my pride and joy, EB thought after the building allowed him to enter his highly secured fortress-like private parking area where his stunning Nevera awaited him. When designing the eBeja Tower, EB insisted on having his own private parking garage for moments such as this. His own personal garage at home was much larger since it was filled with his antique and sports car collection. But this private space under the tower, which accommodated up to four automobiles, was where he liked to keep his Nevera, the favorite of all his vehicles. Having it stored at the office enabled him to shoot down to the garage during the day just to admire it, or sit in it and listen to its remarkable audio system. It was also convenient to have it close by when important clients or prospects were in the building. Having owned at least one Nevera of every previous model, EB had become somewhat of a legend among San Francisco's super-rich car aficionados. He knew that dangling the possibility of seeing and sitting in this newest, one-of-a-kind Nevera would entice some of the fattest of the Bay Area cats and generate new deals and opportunities just as his previous ones had.

Part of the sizzle was that EB had also tied the Nevera into the latest upgrade of his "whole life" PPC. An incredible innovation in and of itself, the newest PPC was another first, using brain waves to issue instructions that the chip then executed, like having the Nevera door unlock and actually open for him, awaiting him like a princess for her prince. The keyless feature was an option with all new Neveras, but having the key encoded into his PPC chip was one of the customizations EB had specially engineered. By thinking a unique thought with a trigger word, the doors would unlock, his door would open, and the racing machine would start. No more keys to lose or buttons to press. To make his ride an even greater boast, and more efficient, he had other programs encoded into his chipped wrist such as turning the sound system on or off at will, adjusting the internal climate and temperature, and even activating its self-driving mode so he could have his gunmetal-gray electric storm roll itself in and pick him up if need be.

After disengaging it from the electric charging port, EB slid into his luxurious leather driver's seat, mentally adjusted the volume a little, and then eagerly opened the center console storage bay. Another customization, EB had not only a little area refrigerated so he could keep snacks and bottled water, but there was a one-of-a-kind mixing system that could, on command from his PPC, mix just about any drink that suited him. Preparing for his solo rally race home, he decided to have another martini, extra dirty, that his mixologist car would perfectly make—but without the olive itself. Once dispensed into the single-serving mini-sports-bottle-like container, EB took a large sip, and reclined back in his F1-like chair as the music pounded. This was his usual routine when getting ready to drive any of his sports cars. Tonight, though, he'd add one other element to enhance the ride.

Popping open another compartment, this one hidden under his steering panel, he took out a small gold electrically sealed box that resembled a fancy business card holder. Inside were at least forty very small square sheets of what looked like plain paper. There was nothing written on the paper, but undetectable to the eye was that each little piece was laced with an exact 50-microgram dose of lysergic acid dimethylamine. Another gift from Narud, EB had begun microdosing LSD just before he came up with the Elevation technology. At first hesitant to try it, Narud's consistent prodding gave him the confidence to at least see what it was all about. He was assured that there would be no addiction, hallucinations, or any negative psychological or physiological effects. Rather, he was promised, he would chemically enhance his mind to a completely new level and experience greater energy, problem-solving capacity, and focus. It only took one microdose to convince him. The enhancement it gave him was astounding, especially in his creativity, a creativity that he was certain helped spawn Elevation.

Marley had noticed the difference immediately and asked him what had changed. EB was hesitant to share his newfound power with Marley, not because he didn't want Marley to advance, but because of Marley's own addiction issues, especially with recreational drugs. Prior to Marley meeting EB, Marley had acquired a fierce cocaine habit. Not that EB really cared; he didn't. *To each his own* was EB's philosophy on fleshly indulgences, but not when it came to productivity. EB knew the two could go places together, so he helped Marley curtail his habit to some extent and made him promise that his chemical romances wouldn't interfere with their work. Marley continued to party hard at night and on weekends all through their time together as entrepreneurial partners. But true to his word, Marley always kept it out of the office. EB didn't know if giving him the secret of microdosing LSD would help or harm him, but finally decided that it wasn't up to him and so he shared all Narud had taught him on the magic results of taking tiny mind-enhancing LSD doses each morning.

Since that first experience, EB had taken microdoses with his orange juice and wheat flax religiously every morning to start the day. But what EB rarely did was do what he was about to do tonight. *If ever there was a night for a last hurrah, this is it*, EB decided. For how better to celebrate all that was about to come his way with his new partnership with Narud than by adding a little chemical-induced elevation to the evening? So, licking his finger to secure one of the tiny sheets, EB lifted it to his tongue where it quickly dissolved. After its disappearance, he took another large gulp to finish his martini and then leaned back again, waiting for the synthetic acceleration.

The LSD usually started elevating EB within forty minutes or so, but on this night, he didn't want to wait that long. After about twenty five minutes of listening to some of his old-time favorites—an eclectic mix including the Rolling Stones' *Sympathy for the Devil* and Beethoven's celebration of revolution in his *Symphony No. 3*—EB revved his engine several times in rhythmic sync with the pounding music. The glory of Beethoven filled his cockpit in a quality that nearly exactly mimicked the sound of the Third Symphony's first public performance at Theater an der Wien in Vienna on April 7, 1805. So enrapturing was the music that EB nearly abandoned his drive to listen to its full forty-five minutes. But a sudden unwelcome thought of Marley's fate seven years ago unexpectedly interrupted his private concert.

EB quickly shook away the Marley memory, changed the music to the next song, and again revved his engine. A slight tingle in his brain and down the back of his neck signaled that, for better or worse, the moment had come and his pre-Christmas Grand Prix was about to begin. He mentally commanded the system to open the reinforced steel garage door, inched out to the edge of the street, and looked both ways even though he knew the street would be void of traffic. Seeing nothing but whipping rain, sleet, and wind, he flipped on his wipers and yelled over the ripping Guns N' Roses tune now playing, "This ride's for you, Marley!" He then slammed the acceleration pedal to the floor, peeling out into a hard left turn, and rocketed like a missile down the drenched, slippery, storm-engulfed track of destiny.

EB liked the damp, dreary, frigid snow-rain battering against his road rocket—as long as there wasn't any hail that would dent the pristine finish. With the music still blasting, EB was in automotive heaven. The handling of the vehicle on the icy roads was extraordinary. He couldn't go as fast as he had planned, but the added difficulty of navigating what he envisioned as his own personal Red Bull Ring in such dreadful weather made the ritual all the more rewarding. Like the F1 track in Austria, his route home had a few tight right turns and hills he would ascend and descend in a blaze, with no police to worry about or contend with.

Flying down the road, EB felt power flowing not only through his rocket's transmission, but through his veins as well. His mental acuity was at its peak with his mind's eyes seeing and understanding on the level that was fitting for a technology king. The world made sense, as did his place and his coming mission. This was how it was supposed to be, he felt. History was in the making, and had selected him to be the razor's edge. *Incredible*, he thought. *The time has come for the next great leap of mankind, a great reset that will finally usher humanity into a global harmony, order, and peace. And I am the head of it all.* With that, there was even a fraction of a moment where he felt a slight spark of gratitude. But who or what would he thank? After all, this gloriously thrilling new ride, his vast fortunes, global fame, and most of all, the coming ascension to incomprehensible global power with Narud was ultimately just a cosmic accident, but one he took advantage of with hard work and flawless choices. "Thank you, EB! The world is yours," EB shouted in defiance as a new tune had started. Randomly selected by his car, it was not the power music he had been listening to, but his old chill favorite *Saving My Love* by Chris Malinchak, which magically enveloped him as it reverberated through his one-man concert hall of a ship that was blasting him toward his destination.

As the dreamy song came to an end, concluding with raindrop-like sounds melodically slowing, the last note, which normally extends for a few final seconds and then drops off, started instead to increase in volume. EB nodded, thinking his AI automobile was composing just for him. But instead of coming to a crescendo, the loudness just increased and increased to the point that it sounded like an unbearable screech, as when scanning a radio for a signal. The screech then morphed and compounded into a scream, a horrible bloodcurdling scream like that of a mother whose baby just died in her arms. So unbearable was the noise, EB immediately mentally commanded the forward signal to his sound system, thinking one of the tracks had corrupted. But nothing changed and the scream just continued, relentlessly, without mercy. EB frantically issued mental, then verbal, commands again and again, trying every combination he could conceive. Having no effect, he finally resorted to manually twisting the volume button and then, still with no change, pressing the off switch.

Still nothing. Just that soul-piercing, brain-assaulting scream.

EB had heard that hallucinations were possible when microdosing, although extremely rare. He had never had one before in all his years of medicating himself. But there was a first time for everything, he thought, and so he tried to gather his thoughts and pull himself together as the stabbing shrill tore at his soul and shattered his ears. Instinctively, he jerked his car to the side of the road and parked, thinking that he had overloaded his system and just needed to calm himself and reduce the adrenaline rush. *That must be what's happening*, he speculated. *The combination of the acid and the adrenaline was too much for my system.*

Parked, he still couldn't stop the scream that was either

erupting from his speakers, or just manifesting in his mind—or both. Not wanting to soak himself in the rain, he hesitated from opening the door. But his need to try to get some air and walk this off was too great. So, pushing his door hard against the fierce wind that now felt like a hurricane, he managed to open it only to bring a flood of icy sleet into his cockpit.

Sliding out of his seat onto the deserted road, he quickly shut the door to minimize its water intake, but then noticed that the scream, which he thought also might be in his head, was muffled. It wasn't his imagination at all, but was blaring only from the car speakers. Even though the painfully deafening cry was muffled, he could still hear it continuing and continuing, unabated, and seemingly increasing in intensity and fervency.

What am I going to do now? he thought to himself as he started pacing beside his car, disgusted that his race had been aborted. He knew that he would at some point need to man up, get back into his Nevera, and endure the grating noise obviously produced by some electrical malfunction. "Hexagas! For what I paid for this thing . . . and not even a month . . . hexagas hell," he cursed out loud into the desolate building-lined stormy canyon where he was stranded.

Gathering his strength, now freezing, soaking, and cursing, EB took a leap toward his shrieking machine to rapidly open the door and brave the doom that awaited him, when out of the corner of his eye, he spotted some movement across the street. Halting his step, he turned and tried to make out through the sheet of vertical water what the commotion was in the alley across from him. To his horror, there in the garbage-filled and tent-lined back street was a gang of some sort. A group of young thugs, it appeared, whaling on some poor soul of a man. Kicking, punching, then kicking and stomping again, the assailants were relentlessly beating the man who could barely lift his arms to thwart their blows. He could see one of the bangers was rifling through his jacket and pants, obviously looking for some loot to reward their efforts. EB knew he needed to get away immediately, or he might be next. But for some reason, with the scream still blaring in its muffled state behind him, he couldn't move and could only stand frozen, watching the hoodlums annihilate their poor victim.

"Hey!" EB found himself yelling, in unbelief that he would dare confront the half dozen street pirates. "Hey you!"

Suddenly they all stopped, with each bending up from their crouching, punching, or kicking positions, and simultaneously turned and stared directly at him. Sensing he now needed to just bolt and get away as fast as he could, EB reached for the door handle, but once again uncontrollably stopped. Surprisingly, the gang didn't charge him or make a move. Instead, as if in a choreographed curtain call, all the hooligans looked straight at him and eerily bowed to him, with their leader yelling back to him through the rain after they completed their genuflection, "Thank you!"

EB was stunned, as well as terrified. *What was that about? Why didn't they attack me? They could clearly see that compared to that sorry sap from whom they had probably scored maybe a couple hundred dollars, I was their jackpot.* EB regularly carried several thousand dollars on his person, and had even more in his car, which itself—even if sold for scraps—would have set the gang members up for life. Not waiting to see why they bowed to him instead of brutalizing him, EB shook his head and forced himself to climb back into his audio torture chamber. But when he opened the door, there was silence. The screams had stopped and the next song on his list of driving tunes had started to play. "Hexagas horrors!" EB muttered as he grabbed the little gold box of microdoses. "Self memo: You, EB, will never combine LSD, adrenaline, alcohol, and rainy weather again. Ever!"

Sitting in the newly formed lake on his leather driving seat, EB slowly pulled away from the curb. He didn't want to look at the gang again, but couldn't help it. So, trying to appear as though he were just looking over his shoulder to check for nonexistent oncoming traffic, he turned his head slightly just enough so he could get a final glimpse of them. The last thing he wanted now was to look too obviously at them, insult them, and provoke a chase. But from the brief glance, he saw that again they bowed, in unison, almost hypnotically, with extremely serious expressions on their faces. Still shaken, EB quickly twisted his head back so he directly faced the road and gunned it, squealing the tires in his escape.

CHAPTER 14

The sight of The Needle, as his residence building with a long, pointed top was called, and his hidden garage entry on the east side of this luxury abode never looked as good to EB as it did tonight. For the first time since he could remember, he was glad to be home. A concept long forgotten by EB, "home" as a place of rest and repose was as foreign to him as the notion that coal could ever produce clean power.

Waiting open, the sliding garage door had already sensed his approach through its infrared signal system that was tied into all sixteen collector vehicles and three motorcycles he kept there. Exhausted, EB whipped into the underground car grotto thinking he'd go straight to bed and skip wiping off the water and sleet that covered his new Nevera. Doing so was a cardinal sin in his book, but the toll the screams had taken on his psyche, combined with the adrenaline, vodka, and microdose had wiped him out. All he could think about was his magnificent 6000 calico-pocketed spring Majesty Vispring bed. Costing several hundred thousand dollars, tonight its perfect weight distribution system customized exactly to EB's size and weight would be worth every penny, especially since the mattress contained some of the softest materials in the world: British fleece wool, Shetland wool silk, cashmere, and European horsetail. The Nevera would have to forgive him and stay wet until morning.

As he exited his vehicle already half asleep in anticipation of the warmth of his goose down comforter, and just before the garage closed behind him, a horrible barking startled him out of his flustered and altered state of consciousness. Turning toward the noise, he was shocked to see an unleashed cocker spaniel come running through the last gap of the closing garage doors, then slide uncontrollably on his wet epoxied showroom floor directly toward him.

"Hexagas hounds! What the—" And before he could finish his sentence, the soaking wet spaniel skid on his zero-traction claws right into the side of EB's prized 1967 all-original Ferrari 275 GTB/4S NART Spider. After recovering from the collision, the cream-colored canine shook wildly, splashing his shed wetness all over the immaculately preserved sports car's driver's-side door. With a 300-horsepower 3.3 L V-12 engine, it was one of only ten to have been produced and was one of EB's most prized possessions. Since purchasing it, he had babied his little Spider, rarely taking it out on even the nicest of days, so as not to risk it being marked, dinged, or scratched even the slightest. But here, in his impenetrable vehicle fortress, this little mutt had collided with it and then soaked it with who knows what kind of sleety rainwater mixture, possibly undoing all the meticulous care he'd given it over the years.

Furious, EB yelled out at the dog and charged toward it, thinking a second shaking might be coming. He could hear the pup's master outside the now closed garage door also yelling what must have been the dog's name while pounding on the outside of the door. Amidst all the commotion, the cocker, apparently named Louie, just sat down, seemingly confused, and looked up with his big brown eyes and smiled, panting, at the unfamiliar man running madly toward him.

Not missing a step, EB, who had played a little soccer in his youth at school, pulled back his kicking leg and, in what would have been a magnificent goal-scoring strike, booted the poor creature completely off the ground and back into the door through which he had charged. Louie released a horrid yelping cry as EB's foot connected to its ribs, and then another as it crashed against the hard steel door. The animal crumbled to the smooth concrete floor and just lay there, motionless.

"Hey, what's going on in there!" the dog's owner screamed at the top of her lungs. But EB could barely hear her since the door shut out almost all outside noise, road or otherwise. "Louie, Louie! Hey, open this door! Whoever you are, open this door right now!" the pooch's owner continued to shout to an ignoring EB.

Seeing that he had solved the problem and prevented any further assault on his baby Spider, EB, standing over the whimpering animal, gave a mental command for the door to open.

"Get your dog out of here!" EB barked. "Don't you know there are leash laws in the city? I should sue you. Look what your mutt did to my car," he continued as he pointed to the wet chassis.

"What did you do to my dog?" the owner shouted back at EB as she gathered up Louie in her arms. "Louie, Louie, you'll be all right. Hey, mister, what's your problem?"

Oblivious to the stranger and her question, EB quickly commanded his entry barrier to close and knelt down next to the Spider as the garage door slid shut, barely missing the stranger and her whining pet, shutting them out of EB's world.

"You'd think it was Halloween with all the crazies out there tonight! Unbelievable!" EB muttered to himself as he wiped off the few drops with a fresh Meguiar's Supreme Shine microfiber towel stored on the shelf next to the vehicle. "But at least it's finally quiet, and my bed awaits me!" Still rattled a little, but satisfied that the evening's nightmare was over and he would soon be enjoying a nightcap and then his plush mattress, he walked back over to his Nevera to give it a final, loving look before ascending to his penthouse.

Encompassing the entire top floor of The Needle, EB's palatial condominium was more like a mansion in the sky than an apartment. As one of the incentives offered with the ninety-nine-year lease of his $110 million sky estate, a direct express elevator from his private garage to his top floor penthouse was included, enabling him to go up and down to his palace at will, without having the inconvenience of meeting other residents of the tower. Tonight he was especially glad for that feature since he was in no mood for any more encounters with humans or animals. *Same thing, really*, he thought.

As with all of his high-tech devices, gadgets, and accessories, EB's penthouse was completely interconnected with every networkable possession he owned via his PPC. Whereas the rest of his staff's chips were only for corporate security, and unbeknownst to them, personal time monitoring, his had a much wider protection sphere, ensuring his complete control, not only over his company, but all his global assets. Access to his elevator was no exception. Again using a unique thought pattern and trigger word, EB could have had his elevator waiting open for him even before he parked if he wanted. But because of tonight's mayhem, he had forgotten to send the signal and now had to wait.

Standing in front of the elevator, EB monitored the elevator's status on an elaborate panel screen that showed exactly where the transporter was located in its shaft. The touch screen also served as a backup security system to access his home in case his PPC ever malfunctioned. *Forty-three, forty-two, forty-one*, EB mentally counted down the floors it passed, staring at the screen as if that would help speed it up. Thirty-eight, thirty-seven, thirty-six . . . Once again, EB began to envision himself with a hot, stiff drink—make it a double—in his hand as he reclined in bed.

"Let's go!" EB chided the Mitsubishi-designed SkyLyft super-vator, which usually took only seventeen seconds to travel from his penthouse to the garage. "What's taking you so long? Hurry up!"

But at his command, instead of any acceleration, there was a static blip and then a series of sparks and some kind of electric eruption on the screen. The descending numbers began twisting and contorting, finally shaping into what looked like a very bad digital rendition of a hideous and marred zombie-like face. EB rubbed his eyes and then looked closer. The face became clearer and less pixilated. As it contorted, EB could see that it was a face he recognized, though marred with scars, sores, decay, and extreme weathering. EB gasped in unbelief. It was Marley's face!

EB wiped his eyes, and then, again and again, cursed himself that his microdose trip still wasn't over. But when he finally removed his fists from his eyes, the face not only hadn't been wiped away, but now extended out as a full three-dimensional head, with bulging, staring eyes less than a foot away from his own. Strangely, the head had a wild mess of hair, curiously stirred, as though he had just come in from the storm; and, though the dark eyes were wide open and piercing him, they were perfectly motionless. That, and the cranium's livid color, made it horrible; but its horror seemed to be in spite of the massacred, melted face and beyond its control, rather than a part of its own expression.

Still hearing remnants of the screams from earlier in his head like a fading ringing people sometimes have in their ear, the appearance of Marley's face made those screams come alive again. Together, the two knocked EB to the ground where, languishing, he rapidly tried to scoot himself backward, away from the assault on his senses. But his eyes couldn't stop staring at his old partner's head since his own head was paralyzed, refusing to turn to the right or left so he could avoid the glowing orb. Marley's head would not relent, however, and continued to approach him even as he scooted himself backward on his backside across the blemish-free garage floor. Then, just as Marley was about to descend upon him, he stopped his futile attempt to escape, and leaning back on his arms, just shut his eyes tightly, bracing for impact.

But the collision never came, only a sudden silence of the screams in his head. Still terrified, EB cracked open one of his eyes expecting to see Marley's gross complexion right there in front of him. Instead, there was nothing but a lifeless garage full of his toys.

"Hexagas hallucinations!" EB gasped as he picked himself up, again wiping his eyes as if they had been the source of his encounter. He then spun around surveying the four corners of the garage to see if maybe Marley's head had gone elsewhere, but the only thing out of place was a little puddle of canine blood still pooled on the floor area next to the door.

Cautiously, he approached the elevator monitor, poking it with his finger to make sure it was just the touch screen it had always been. Seeing and feeling that it had returned to normal, EB issued a command for the panel to show the elevator's location, revealing it descending again exactly from the point it was just before Marley's interruption. Within seconds, it arrived and the door opened, providing what EB hoped would be his escape from these very ridiculous and unwelcomed mind tricks. *Fitting,* he thought, *for such a night as this.*

The inside of the elevator was lined with a series of eight security monitors, two on each of its upper walls, that covered all the main areas of his 7,400-square-foot top-floor mansion. Checking each carefully as he ascended, EB wanted to make sure there wasn't another surprise waiting for him. Although this elaborate security had been in place since he'd leased the top floor four years previous, he hadn't ever really needed it or had any incidents requiring its sophistication, even though over the last decade the city had almost fully bifurcated into safe and unsafe zones. EB didn't complain, however, as he was a strong supporter and advocate of city policy being more and more lenient with criminal activity.

Shortages in police power, due mainly to a fierce backlash against the police and a deliberate effort by city officials and their radical power base to defund them, as well as policies put into place to not enforce laws prohibiting smaller crimes like shoplifting, minor assaults, and open city-funded drug use, together led to an unprecedented explosion in violence and crime. The diminution of the very idea of "crime" and recategorization as "sickness" also contributed to the mayhem. EB agreed with the logic, and understood that in order for there to be any significant advancement in the human condition, there must be periods of transitional upheaval. Society itself, more specifically the old Judeo-Christian order with its simplistic and archaic views of "evil" and "good," was really to be blamed for the condition of its citizens. And the oppressive policies of the past that condemned alternative lifestyles, groups, or certain actions were really the crimes that needed to be addressed. Science was demonstrating that what the fundamentalists used to deem "a sin" was really a medical condition, or in some cases just an unfounded bias against sexual, financial, or social freedom that could really be healthy, happy, and holistic lifestyles.

But transitioning from the old order to a new, a more enlightened society would not come without the inevitable violence, disorder, and crises that accompany the necessary destruction of the past during the transition. Criminals in most cases were just the victims of the old order's unjust and unfair biases over decades of oppression and stigmatization. Man is not inherently *depraved*, with a soiled, evil soul that resulted from some rebellion or wicked act by the first humans as taught in the old system. On the contrary, having graduated from preschool superstitions of angry gods and visiting spirits, the world had finally come to realize that man is born intrinsically good and is only really *deprived* and corrupted by his environment—whether family, friends, or society as a whole. So, instead of waiting for some mythical divine intervention required to transform man or woman from a degeneracy that's on the inside, and thereby society in the same manner, a collective effort by humanity, from humanity, and for humanity to educate, legislate, and manipulate the elements scientifically and technologically was needed to reconstruct and perfect man and his communities from the outside. Science had discovered the error of the notion that "it's not what goes into a person that defiles them, but what comes out of the heart." Modern knowledge now understood it was the influences from the outside of a person that made them what they were on the inside.

With this revolutionary enlightenment of thought, the world had finally and irreversibly made the leap to see that criminality needs constructive and, at times, coercive encouragement, not condemnation. Who were those who were stealing from the local mart but the poor who had been marginalized through unjust and discriminatory housing, labor, or lifestyle laws? Why were gangs of youth forming and rampaging except that the old system gave them no hope, no real opportunities, and no education to understand the true and glorious upward path of Diversity, Inclusivity, and Equity—"the path to DIE" as EB called it—on which humanity must traverse to advance?

Nevertheless, as much as EB supported the criminals' transition to sainthood through these policies, he knew that in the short term he could only help them if he himself was safe from their social puberty-caused violence. It was only a matter of time before his neighborhood would be affected, which was an important reason why he chose to live in The Needle. Second to none in protection around the outside of the building, the internal security was also marketed as impenetrable.

Except for little dogs, EB thought sarcastically, making a note to himself that he would have a word with the building's security superintendent on how such an elaborate security system could allow such a penetration into his citadel.

But important as it was, it wasn't the fortress-like protection that was most critical to EB in his move to The Needle. Nor was it all the amenities, the great status that came from living at the city's premier address, or the pleasure he derived from his luxurious penthouse accouterments and spectacular views. For EB, living in The Needle was fundamentally a statement of his purpose and work in life, work that was precisely represented by the name "The Needle" itself, as well as brilliantly showcased through the building's actual resemblance to its profound name.

Awarded as the Best Structural Engineering and Best Geotechnical Engineering building in its class, The Needle stood as the peak in high-rise construction for safety and innovation. The building rested on fifty-four seven-foot-diameter concrete piles socketed into bedrock located over 250 feet below the ground. The syringe shape of the building was achieved through the fabrication of a high-strength steel exoskeleton structural system, which functioned like a giant shock absorber, providing the most advanced levels of safety in seismic construction. Its roof, which rose over nine hundred feet above sea level, was rounded and mostly controlled by EB as part of the penthouse. He didn't own it outright because no one owned any residential property outright anymore, but also because maintenance, security, and engineering needed to have access to it, making about a third of it part of the building's common area. But the remaining two-thirds was closed off and iron fenced for EB's sole use. To accommodate his taste, EB had an infinity edge pool, a large flower, fruit, and vegetable garden, a sports court, a net-enclosed golf driving range, and a small observatory built on his section. In the center of the roof, the part of the area EB controlled, stood a giant one-hundred-foot-tall steel antenna spike that pierced into the clouds, giving the structure its upward-pointing needle appearance.

EB actually hated needle injections into his own body and had never used them for his own enhancements. He couldn't stand the instant pain from the prick that, no matter how much preparation was made, always shocked his senses. But non-needle-infused chemical enhancements had become an essential part of EB's everyday life, and in his own estimation, had contributed immensely to his scientific creativity, second only in influence to Narud's inspiration. EB would not be who he was today if it wasn't for the betterment his microdosing gave him. And though averse to needles, what better way to symbolically represent his own dependence on regular infusions than with a needle.

Beyond a symbol of his own benefiting, needles also stood as one of the most significant instruments of science in all of history, enabling man to advance through the intermingling of exterior substances with his interior systems. Whether used in experiments, in treating infections or diseases, inserting Personal Protection Chips, or facilitating the transhumanization of the species, the needle was a marvelous symbol of modern medicine, science, and the technology that was transforming mankind into its next stage of evolutionary development.

Living in such a metaphor for his life had not gone unnoticed by his peers and the press at large. "Living His Work: Global

Leader Leases Needle Penthouse" and "Inject This: EB Lives and Moves The Needle to the Highest Levels" were a few of the headlines that promoted EB's whole life approach to technology and the transformation of the species.

"I live, eat, breathe, work, think, and on occasion dream technology twenty-four seven," EB told one reporter. "Man is in a unique place today to integrate himself with technology, advance himself genetically, fine-tune himself medicinally, and unite together socially. Isn't this the only real attainable goal we can all get behind and support? Who doesn't want this?" EB rarely gave interviews since they inherently couldn't convey the complexity of what his life's work was about. But on the rare occasion when he did, he made sure that the reporter did no ad-libbing or editorializing. "Print only my words and all my words or there will be no words," was how he summarized it for them.

The reason for his being so particular was that, as Narud had taught him, "only small portions of our work can be revealed at a time. The public must be spoon-fed into the transformation and transition of their transhumanization. Progress takes time. In the 1940s, computers weighed thirty tons, occupied nearly two thousand square feet of space, and could calculate roughly five thousand instructions per second. Today, our internal communicators can process nearly thirty billion per second. Soon, we won't be able to accurately calculate the number of instructions that are being processed each second and will only measure in nanoseconds. This is what will enable artificial intelligence to be integrated with human intelligence, birthing the next level of human evolution—a transhuman intelligence. It will be—and really now is—a living thing, self-organizing, bringing us into singularity, a collective whole. Understand, having invented the gods, we are about to become them."

CHAPTER 15

After his lightning-fast trip to the top, EB stepped with relief into his penthouse's grand entry foyer that itself was as large as some of the one-bedroom apartments in which his single lower-level workers lived. Soaring with fifteen-foot ceilings throughout, EB's palatial penthouse of four bedrooms, a rec room, office, and five-and-a-half baths was no ordinary luxury estate. It certainly had all the features and advantages of a nine-figure abode, but as the domicile of the most celebrated tech titan on the planet, these digs went to another level, especially technologically. EB didn't just have a smart home. Rather, through his own customizations and additions, he had what he was convinced was the world's smartest home.

The key to his pad's brilliance was his digital butler, Genius®. A whole home artificial intelligence system he'd first developed for himself, Genius was so effective and revolutionary in its abilities that EB trademarked a dumbed-down version, which eBeja could mass-produce and peddle as another profoundly profitable product. Designed as a whole house detection and analysis system, the nearly conscious Genius was engineered using the technology core EB had incorporated into Marley's pyramid, combined with his Pod network intelligence and his company's CommuNEST security and monitoring platform. As such, Genius was permanently integrated with EB's PPC and therefore could at all times sense all his emotions and thoughts, including his moods, appetite level and could even cross-reference any of his communications with the database of information Genius had on EB in order to have all his needs fulfilled upon arriving home. Tonight, however, something was wrong.

"Genius!" EB spoke aloud after a few moments, standing helplessly in his cold, dark foyer. Out of habit, he reached instinctively, albeit blindly, to set his briefcase on his Minotti quincy. As he stretched his arm downward, an icy gust seemed to flow up his arm sleeve from the honed limestone foyer floor, giving him a horrible shiver. "Genius, lights on, heat on, mood setting six!" he commanded out loud several times, fearful that Marley's demonic head might appear again.

It wasn't pitch black in his palace, since the floor-to-ceiling window walls were trying to provide some illumination by ushering in the outlines from the thick cloud cover, faint glow of the rolling fog, and slight reflections of the punishing ice rain. But such shade only produced unrecognizable silhouettes, exactly what EB did not want to see on this night. Usually an awe-inspiring rainbow of flickers from the buildings below and the stars or moonlight above pouring through his glass walls, tonight's light was darkness—a gray, gloomy dullness of shadow-filled blackness. Though darkness was cheap, and EB liked that about it, he needed light on this night, not just to maneuver his way around his home, but to interrupt any further surprises and bring a settling to his terrorized soul.

"This has never happened before, and should never happen," EB continued to himself. "Genius, all systems reset! Now!" Again, nothing. *Did the whole building's power just go down? Must've just happened. The elevator worked fine. Probably the storm*, he thought to console himself.

Fortunately, he had a few old-style flashlights stored in various locations, though he had never used them and didn't know if they even had batteries. After inching his way to the nearest closet and rummaging with his hands, he finally found one. Amazingly, the batteries still had a charge and so like a camper navigating a forest, he followed the flashlight's beam down the long lamp- and sculpture-filled hallway from the closet, then through the dining area adorned with an exquisite Lolli e Memmoli large-cut crystal chandelier that beautifully reflected the shaft of light on his round .999 pure brushed platinum ten-person Henge dining table and its magnificent mahogany chairs. Making his way around the never-used slab, EB finally made it to the back of the condo where his multipurpose network utility room was located. Having learned long ago of the necessity for redundancy in any network system, EB had insisted on a basic power backup system, separate from the building's main electrical grid. Possibly just a product of his paranoia, EB was now pleased with himself that he had contended for an old-school Tesla battery-powered emergency setup.

EB hoped he remembered how the thing worked, having never had to use it before. But even if he didn't, he'd figure it out. After all, systems and networks were his wheelhouse. "Voila!" EB exclaimed as a few emergency lights throughout his place lit up, dimly lighting the condo. "Better than nothing."

The scattered floor lights didn't illuminate the penthouse the way he had thought they would when he contracted for the system, an oversight he would correct soon enough. But they were sufficient for the remainder of the night. After all, it was late, and after a quick bite to eat, he'd go straight into bed. He'd normally stay up a few more hours, working, writing, ciphering, and plotting. Tonight, especially, he had thought as he was racing, but before the screams, that he'd spend the late hours mulling over the incredible partnership Narud had proposed, and even start drafting the integration plans of his systems with MASGER. But what was supposed to be an evening of victorious meeting, racing, planning, and plotting—what should have been one of the greatest nights of his life so far—had turned out differently and been spoiled.

"Hexagas hallucinations!" he muttered to himself again, unable to shake the image of Marley's distorted, grotesque face with its piercing eyes staring a hole through him from only inches away. He was frightened that with Genius out of commission, his automated security system might also have malfunctioned. Not taking any chances, EB made his way back to the elevator and, after realizing that his PPC connectivity to the elevator had been cut off as well, tried pressing the call button on its control pad. No response. But that didn't really matter—he certainly wasn't going anywhere else tonight. And just to make certain he didn't have any unwanted visitors, he initiated the manual lock to prevent any access or movement both from the garage or from there in his condo.

His front door already had the highest level of security, allowing access only to EB through biometric scans of his retina and fingerprint. The door itself was 4.5 inches thick of 14-gauge galvanized steel, with twelve security cylinders around the full perimeter of the door, making it virtually impossible to penetrate once the cylinders were engaged. Achieving the highest FE15 rating under US State Department Standard SD-STD-01.01 for security, EB's fortress entry was also UL 8 Equivalent under the FB6 Ballistic Standard so it could withstand fire from any rifle or laser weapon including automatic weapons that, thanks to very strict gun control laws, he knew the citizens of San Francisco couldn't own. Then again, it wouldn't be the law-abiding citizen coming after him, but criminals. And criminals by definition weren't going to abide by the law, especially the laws prohibiting gun possession.

EB tried to open his main door, but all twelve bolts had

automatically engaged when the power failed, preventing any possibility of him exiting this way until power was restored. When he'd moved in four years earlier, he had added two drop-down three-inch-thick-by-six-inch-wide galvanized steel barrier bars that covered the full width of the door. These pull-down bars had no electronic connections at all, providing an extra layer of safety for times like tonight when systems were down or electricity out. So, even though his stronghold's door had fully locked itself, again out of an abundance of caution together with the fear that stalked him, EB dropped the bars into their slots.

Still not convinced he was safe, he took a final walk through all the rooms of his home inspecting closets, behind doors, under beds, and in any nook, cabinet, or cranny where an invader might hide. Finding nothing, he found his way to the kitchen and, still quivering, reluctantly grabbed some leftover General Tsao's chicken, egg fried rice, and pot stickers from his manual refrigerator, though without power, was still cold inside. That's about all he had in that seldom-used icebox, except for a few beers, a carton of milk, and several decaying vegetables. Not that EB didn't eat well. He did, like the king that he was. But Genius, whom he often also called his digital wife, took care of all his eating and nutritional needs.

Connected to all his favorite stores and shops, Genius monitored EB's minute-by-minute activity determining exactly what his caloric intake should be, and precisely what nutritional value the food needed to be to keep him at his peak. All the food, beverages, and snacks were auto-purchased as needed and delivered to the delivery bay on the building's first floor. EB had his own commercial-size refrigerator located in the building's residents' warehouse to store items until needed. In addition to all its other abilities, Genius had also been programmed as a world-class chef, and in EB's fully automated kitchen, would prepare his meals according to EB's exact moods, appetites, and micro-nutritional needs. The meals were always perfect and there were never any leftovers, since any remaining food had lost its peak nutritional value and had to be discarded. Occasionally, though, EB would bypass Chef Genius and bring a meal in on his way home, as he had done the day before with the Chinese food. In this instance, he was glad he did or he would have gone to bed as hungry as he was upset and scared.

Making his way to his living room area to eat, he plopped down on his couch, disoriented from the commingling of the fear that gripped him and a corresponding rage that was now swelling up inside him. *How could such a momentous day be ending so badly?* he wondered, banging his chicken and dumpling plate down on his Minotti coffee table, along with his bottle of Peroni that splashed all over the table's gorgeous surface. A not-so-small amount also made it to the matching couch, his pant leg, and the floor. Again cursing that the universe was against him since leaving the meeting with Narud, he found his way to his bedroom and frustratingly changed out of his wet pants and the rest of his priestly black outfit and Chucks and into a pair of sweats and a T-shirt. Due to the permeating chill that had also overtaken him, he then covered himself with his charcoal gray Derek Rose Duke Piped cashmere robe. EB was not one to stay in a rage for long at all, however. The fact that he was almost always steadily angry helped. For him, rage was a step toward not being in control, while anger was one of his secret tools for always keeping the upper hand. Not crossing the line was a discipline he had acquired over years of practice. He wasn't going to slip now.

Taking a deep breath, EB calmed himself as much as he could and then wolfed down what remained of his cold dinner as he gazed out his window wall at the gloom hanging over the city. Normally, he had unobstructed views sweeping west from the

Pacific Ocean and Farallon Islands, north across the Golden Gate Bridge to Marin County, east across the Bay Bridge to Mt. Diablo, and south to Silicon Valley. But nothing was normal since he had left the SwarmTrooper Tower. Strangely, that was the only building he could see through the stormy darkness. Not completely, but enough to make out its imposing outline thrusting through a sea of dreadful black clouds that buried the rest of the inferior buildings and structures below it. Strangely tonight, it was pulsing with an eerie red glow.

At least they have power, EB thought. Which reminded him that he needed to check if the whole building was without power, or if this was Genius's fault.

"Bernard, is that you?" EB inquired after calling down to the concierge through his PPC communication system, fully networked into the entire building's intercom.

"Good evening, Mr. EB. How may I assist you?" Bernard replied.

"Excellent. I thought my PPC might be completely shut down. Look, my power is off up here. Is the rest of the building's power off or is it just me?"

"No, sir, the building's power is on and I've had no other calls from residents to inform me of an outage. I'd say it could be the storm, but frankly, sir, I don't know how it's possible that you don't have power when the rest of the building does. Why don't I call the building superintendent for you?"

"Yes, please do that and just see if he can get it fixed. I'm going to bed and don't want to be disturbed. I'll count on the power being restored by the morning."

"Absolutely, sir. Very strange. I mean, I just don't see how . . . anyway, I'll make sure it's taken care of."

EB knew that Bernard was just being proper, but that neither he nor the superintendent could fix his Genius. Not only was it out of their league, but they had no idea that it even existed. Under his breath, he cursed the engineer who had installed Genius and promised it would work flawlessly for him. He had no idea that Genius could somehow disable all his electricity, or even itself be disabled. His penthouse was inseparably tied into the building's grid and could no more be separated from it than his water could be separated from the building's supply.

Nothing tonight is making sense, he thought as he washed down the final bite of Tsao's chicken with his beer, bewildered and frustrated. But tomorrow he would get it fixed, regardless of what day it was. The thought of rousing his engineer away from his home and family on Christmas Day to fix Genius, and inconvenience him the way he had been inconvenienced, helped calm his nerves and gave him more than a little bit of comfort.

Finished with his leftovers, EB instinctively tried again to give Genius mental commands. Realizing his folly, he grabbed his backup remote control to his Sony 64K Full 3D Holographic theater TV wall and platform. *Maybe I can bypass Genius,* he thought. But after pressing the on button a few times with no response, he cursed himself, Genius, and the night and threw the remote across the room into one of his Minotti chairs.

I'll bet the fireplace works, though, he thought since it ran on natural gas instead of electricity. Knowing mental commands were futile at this point, he found its remote and pressed the flame button, which instantly caused a monstrous blaze to erupt in the ten-foot, marble-encased rectangular opening.

"Now that's better!" EB exclaimed, pleased that at least his living room ewas now moderately lit from the inferno's flames, which would also start to warm it up. This was the first time EB had sat in his living room with only a fire and no electric lighting. Overpowering the annoying two emergency floor lights, the fire created a very calming and subdued environment, something EB rarely experienced at home—or anywhere, for that matter. In fact, he couldn't recall a time since before Marley's death that he had just sat, doing nothing. Of course, it wasn't his choice tonight, as he would rather be working to increase his fortune on Narud's Plan than be trapped in inactivity.

But the warmth of the fire gradually wrapped around him like a blanket, helping him forget his monetary ambitions for the moment and quieting the spontaneous shakes he had from both the chilly room and shivery encounters. The lack of the usual ambient noise, whether from his Holovision system or music playing or the verbal feedback Genius was always giving, also helped him to relax. He still had not completely rid himself of the awful screams that continued to distantly reverberate in the deep recesses of his mind, but they seemed to be fading, as was the ire.

Taking in the moment, EB noticed how the writhing flames reflected off his magnificent art collection, making his sculptures and paintings scattered throughout the living room dance and sway. His tall six-foot-by-three-foot *Cathedral* painting by Jackson Pollack especially captured the glow and shadowy movement. EB had acquired the piece from the Dallas Museum of Art in exchange for outfitting the city of Dallas with his Pod system. Financially, it wasn't the best deal for EB, but aesthetically EB had coveted the evolutionary masterpiece from the first time he had laid eyes on it. To him, it represented perfectly his repulsion for the cathedrals of man as nothingness, with the scattered drippings perfectly exemplifying their religious nonsense.

The shattering of religion was not the real essence of the work, however. More than an obliteration of traditional faith-based cathedrals, the masterpiece extolled the church of a godless material universe. Randomly splattered into existence, *Cathedral* wonderfully portrayed the universe's "active painting" of stars, galaxies, and the earth, indiscriminately spread out on the arbitrarily concocted canvas of the space-time continuum. Like the universe, Pollock sought to produce his paint dribbles with the same chaotic chance flinging in which humanity, and thereby he himself, had come into existence. "When I am in my painting, I'm not aware of what I'm doing," Pollock had affirmed.

Pollock's painting wasn't his favorite, however. That honor belonged to Norwegian Edvard Munch's seminal *The Scream*. The version EB owned was the pastel version of 1893, considered the second most valuable of Munch's renditions. The first and original version was the one he painted and exhibited in 1893, still on display at the collection of the National Gallery of Norway in Oslo. This was the version that had the barely visible pencil inscription in Norwegian: *Kan kun være malet af en gal Mand!* Translated to English, the revealing message said, "could only have been painted by a madman."

Only a handful of his elite associates were aware that he was the owner of Munch's pastel gem, a treasure given to him as a gift by Narud, who himself somehow acquired it in an undisclosed manner from the Munch Museum in Oslo. Needless to say, EB was overwhelmed that Narud would give him such an amazing objet d'art. When he inquired why Narud would bestow such a treasure to him and what significance it had in their relationship, Narud only responded, "Someday you will understand." To this day he still didn't understand, but frankly hadn't given it much more thought until now since it was in his possession, graced his living area wall, and added another ten figures to his net worth.

Staring at it under the fire's glow, EB was astounded how tonight more than any other time it seemed to come alive, jerking back and forth as the fireplace's flames made the screaming object contort and writhe as it shrieked. *Perhaps the significance is in the blood-red sky*, EB thought, remembering that Munch's inspiration for the sunset portrayed in the painting was likely the volcano on the Krakatoa Island in Indonesia that had erupted in 1883. The massive explosion left a lasting impact not only in Indonesia, but on the rest of the world, even as far as places in the Northern Hemisphere. The effects from the volcanic ash were visible in the skies during Munch's life in Norway, turning normal sunsets bloody red. EB loved that part of the painting, but even more now as the picture prophetically, it seemed, foretold of a coming eruption that would change the world.

The horrified look on the screaming entity had always symbolized for EB the disposition of man if he did not address and rectify the climate apocalypse that would destroy the earth and all of humanity with it. But as he gazed at it under the animating influence of the fire, he saw a different meaning since he and Narud were now working together through MESGAR to not just save the planet, but to annihilate the weak, backward, unenlightened superstitious climate deniers.

That look will be the fascists' scream, the earth haters' horror and terror as their theistic delusions are exterminated and they are finally subjugated— either by persuasion, or more likely, by force, he thought. *They will scream indeed, when we rule them, so they can never turn the clock back again. This must be at least a part of what Narud meant.* Now warmed from the fire, such a thought kindled EB's revolutionary fervor, melting away the fear the earlier screams had caused.

There was one more piece to this puzzle, however. As magnificent as the piece was in and of itself, there was more to the pastel than just the iconic image, its colors and portrayal of the human condition. Like the message that Munch had scratched onto his original, this version also had an inscription, but one that no one else besides him and Narud knew existed. Unlike the other sentence that was ever so lightly written on the top left corner of the painting, the message on EB's version was located in the great blue and black swirls on its right side. And, also unlike the original, this message was not a series of words, but a meme of numbers, letters, and symbols. Unnoticeable, unless examined under a combination of black light and X-ray, the code was in three cryptic segments:

$$\Delta X3\mu 天 \quad ¿»ø \quad ¶=\infty 1$$

Narud had explained that even he didn't know their full meaning, but knew they were essential keys to success in saving the planet and would be understood in time. Until tonight, EB had always thought they were simply puzzles that Narud wanted EB to decipher to be a more successful and wealthy businessman, or possibly just an exercise given by his mentor to test his acumen. In his stressed, confused, and microdosed state of mind, however, under the strange glow of the fire, he had an epiphany.

The symbolic revelation was not simply an added element of the artist, nor one of Narud's many motivational tools, but was specifically for this exact time. He couldn't explain how he knew this, but after tonight's conversation with Narud and the events that followed, he knew it was a harbinger regarding their partnership, the new technology and the historic leap it would facilitate. He was seeing it clearly, as if the fire's light was outlining the symbols right before his eyes and revealing their purpose. These together were the map, each segment a coded formula he needed to follow in order to realize their objectives of the coming global order that would save mankind.

Having uncovered the first level of the secret, EB's thoughts were no longer plagued by the earlier terrors of the evening. In fact, he was starting to feel exhilarated again, as he had in Narud's office, drunk with anticipation. Even the exhaustion had dissipated as EB meditated on the mission he was about to undertake with his mentor. Basking in the fire's glow, he began planning and plotting the next steps he and Narud would need to take to combine their companies so they could implement MESGAR across the globe as quickly as possible.

The icy rain still thumped his wall of windows like ten thousand little fists relentlessly pounding in an effort to get in. Through them, he could still see the red pulse of Narud's tower, occasionally disappearing when the sleet's reinforcements arrived, then reappearing after their retreat in defeat against the panes. The intermittent red brought a level of peace on top of his renewed enthusiasm, though not contentment. Better would be that he was finally gaining back control and power, not only of his thoughts, but his emotions and wits as well.

He was still a bit confused, however, as to how the combination of the microdose with all the other elements of the evening, both internal and external, had assaulted him earlier. But EB decided he didn't care and it didn't matter in light of the bigger picture unfolding in front of him. Chemistry was chemistry and the dose would soon wear off and with it, the mirages it conjured. The future was what mattered and what he would focus on. He mustn't get distracted or deterred. Like a red pulsing siren, the phantasmal tower was not only calming him, but alerting him, warning him, reminding him that the emergency was now, and needed his full attention.

Even though all his staff and associates would be celebrating Christmas tomorrow, EB decided then he would go back to the office as early as possible. He didn't know how long his Genius would be impaired and the power with it, so a full day at the office where he wouldn't have distractions and could work on the plan would be ideal. *Time for bed, and a sound sleep so I will be fully refreshed and clear minded in the morning.*

Collecting his empty Joseon plate from the beer-splattered coffee table, he strolled back to the kitchen where he would leave it soiled in the sink until morning. He never washed his own dishes and wasn't about to start. But at the exact moment he stepped onto the cold venetian kitchen tile, the piercing shrill of his whole house alarm erupted in a caterwaul so deafening, EB dropped his imported hand-painted porcelain plate, shattering it, in order to shield his ears. Pressing them as hard as he could to suppress the siren's agonizing blare, he glanced at the monitor posted above the sink to see what the security system would show him. Apparently running off the backup power, the monitor flashed the live video feed from the various cameras, which were also on backup power.

There was nothing outside the front door or at the private elevator port, he observed, nor in the garage, where all appeared quiet. The four cameras covering his two-thousand-plus-square-foot patio that surrounded his unit were also desolate. He could see the whole patio perfectly, even though the patio floodlights didn't come on since the night vision technology of his cameras made day and night indistinguishable. He waited for his roof cameras videos, which, like the others, revealed nothing out of the ordinary.

Out of habit, he immediately tried to command Genius to shut off the alarm, again forgetting the system was down and his wife/butler/slave was out of commission. Turning his thoughts to his communicator implant, he tried to reconnect with management again.

"Bernard, are you there? Hello?" But nothing, only a dead silence. He tried a few times with the same result, then switched his thoughts to contact the emergency numbers for the building's security as well as his own company's security. He may as well have sent signals to a wall.

"The backup!" he said to himself, remembering that he had installed a manual communication link that ran off the backup power. Still covering his ears, he ran to the utility room where it was housed.

"Hello? Is anyone there?" he yelled into the wall-mounted communicator after pressing the necessary connection buttons. Nothing, only the hiss of electrical impulses. *Impossible!* he thought since part of the purpose of the giant antenna on his part of the roof was to give him uninterruptible and error-proof call service, along with communication capabilities and network capacity even AT&T didn't have. Regardless, his screen just flashed "No Signal" each time he tried to make the calls, not only to the concierge, but the building superintendent, both security outfits again, and then finally, out of desperation, to the police.

"Hexagas!" he yelled, exasperated, as all lines were completely dead. Next to the com system was the panel that gave manual control of his security system. Frantically, he again pressed buttons to turn off the alarm.

"What's my damn code?" He hadn't ever used the manual controls before, except for the one time when the engineer was showing him how to use it and helped him set up his manual code, a passcode he had long forgotten. He punched in his birthday, Marley's birthday, his sister's birthday, every birthday he could think of, except Narud's. He didn't know his. He did them backward, then tried every other number combination he thought might be a possible code to stop the maddening sirens. Again nothing.

He continued relentlessly, and then finally heard the confirmation tone, barely, that indicated the system had been turned off. 042270 had been the code. *Of course!* he thought. *The date of the first Earth Day last century and inauguration of humanity's effort to save the planet. How could I have forgotten?* Relieved, he waited for the excruciating alerts to cease. But they didn't. Even after thirty seconds, then a minute, then two, they continued their merciless clamor. Furious, and also starting to feel that horrid fear return, he gave the com system one more try to connect to his building's palace guard. Amazingly, there was a click, as if he had made a connection, which was followed not by a human voice, but an archaic busy signal.

"Busy? When does a company have a busy signal? Those have been out of use for years!"

He continued to press the buttons on the panel with one hand thinking somehow he might override the system and get a connection, while ridiculously covering only one ear with the other hand. Again, nothing but a *beep beep beep* busy signal. After a few cycles, the busy signal itself began increasing in volume with each beep, quickly rising almost to the unbearable level of the wailing siren, both on his internal implanted speaker as well as on all his external home speakers. Worse than the earlier screams in his car, these inharmoniously persistent beepings and alarm blarings were then joined by a screeching feedback, like when a microphone is too close to its amplifier. Next to enter was the doorbell, which jumped in with its own continuous ringing, and then finally all the rest of his electronic signals, alerts, and buzzings, which sounded off in full volume.

Befuddled as to how to escape the soul-ripping pandemonium in what he felt was now a technological prison of his own making, EB dashed around from room to room seeking some relief. But the noise echoed through them all, through all the intercoms, all the other speakers he had wired into the system, and most painfully, in his head through his internal speaker array, continuing to get louder and louder. Despondent, he moved back into the living room and sat helplessly in his big leather chair next to the fire, bent over due to the pain, and pressed his hands as tightly as possible over his ears. But they only barely deflected the noise, a noise so devastating, EB was certain that it would shatter his eardrums causing an air embolism in his lungs, which would then travel to his heart and finally kill him. But just as he thought his eardrums were about to explode, as well as his sanity, all the alarms, sirens, signals, and bells stopped at once, together, as suddenly as they had started.

Well, there it is—I've lost my hearing, EB thought as his ears and head throbbed in pain. Hoping he was wrong, he grabbed the nearest object, a decorative poker that was useless for his gas-produced fire, and tapped it on the marble hearth. The little tings from the tapping were music to his ears, albeit painful tunes. Glad he wasn't deaf, he became infuriated at his Genius engineers, security personnel, and maintenance staff for their negligence. *Surely they could have prevented this.* EB's ear pain started to subside a bit, but not the cold fury that was rapidly overtaking his body and soul. Scooting his chair closer to the fire in an effort to get warm again and calm himself, he became hot with rage and began planning their demise. All of them, together—the whole lot of incompetent imbeciles—would pay dearly for their carelessness and negligence. But before he could even get to the next thought of how he might destroy them, his private elevator began to hum as if it were ascending from the garage.

Impossible, he thought. He checked around him and the power was still most certainly off, with only the dim emergency lights and fire partially illuminating the quieted room. But the humming of the super-vator was unmistakable, like a quiet jet or high-speed train approaching. EB wanted to get up and go check on it, but realized he had already done all he could to lock it up. Terror gripped the middle-aged mogul as he just stared at the elevator door and dug his fingers into the finely leathered chair arms.

As it continued to rise, moving closer and closer, another

sound became discernable—a crying or wailing accompanied by rapid clankings, like chains being dragged then whipped against steel. He couldn't make it out exactly, but as the elevator advanced, it sounded like a chained-up wild animal furiously thrashing about in its cage. The roars and screeches were monstrous, unlike anything he'd heard, whether from a real animal or by a Hollywood special effect.

EB wanted to run, but where? His front door was sealed shut and there was no other exit but through that very elevator. *The roof!* he thought. The access door was just past the elevator shaft and if he moved now, he'd have just enough time to get up to safety before the hyper-speed transporter arrived.

"Hexagas hogwash!" he said to himself. "What am I thinking? It is physically impossible that the elevator is moving when there is no electricity. Nor is it possible that its door can open. The laws of physics, the laws of the universe won't allow it! You are not going anywhere, EB, but are going to stay right here by your fire until this microdose-induced flashback illusion ceases. Even better, just ignore all this nonsense and go to bed."

And just as the last word passed from his mouth, the elevator door locks unlatched, and the door crashed open. The elevator wasn't there, only a deep, dark hole extending downward sixty-six floors with a box in it rising at an extraordinary pace. As much as he wanted to, ignoring the wild clamor that was coming up toward him was impossible. As with earlier in the evening, there were screams, horrible mind-altering screams, only this time they were accompanied by unbearable yowls of pain, desperation, and terrible sorrow. The whipping and pounding against the steel walls of the elevator, the scraping and clashing of the chains and metals, combined with the wailings, echoed up the shaft and spilled over into EB's lair, again flooding his palace in unbearable noise. Only this time it was the sound of misery.

The excruciating cacophony increased in volume and intensity at the same rapidity as the elevator's speed, becoming so loud that again he thought his hearing would be annihilated and he would perish. Like a bullhorn pressed right to his face, it was so intolerable that he knew he must evacuate the living room and try to get to the roof. He tried to raise himself up, but his legs wouldn't obey his mind. He tried and tried, exerting himself with all his strength to stand, but couldn't move a muscle no matter how hard he tried. Refusing to accept he was paralyzed, he continued to try to free himself from the captivity of his chair, as well as the terror he was trying desperately to will away.

As he struggled and wrestled and exerted, he was jolted by another assailant, the familiar security system siren that started erupting again, but this time accompanied by the emergency lights and all the buttons on the control panels throughout the house, which together began flashing, like a Christmas tree. Then, on this most unsilent and unholy night, the horrid chorus crescendoed to its climax as the elevator reached its destination.

EB shut his eyes instinctively, believing that somehow if he couldn't see what was coming, the nightmare would just go away. But crashing his fantasy, the steel cage slammed to a stop, doors open, with its occupant standing in its center. Opening one eye, EB saw a man of sorts, half there, half invisible, with human legs, a torso, and arms flailing about swatting at something. He had to see it more clearly, so he opened his other eye bringing into focus a swarm of horrible electrified demon-like creatures that swirled around the man in the elevator, and through him, in a black smoke and with fire. The creatures looked like distorted birds, with lizard-like heads and piranha-like mouths, full of razor-sharp jagged teeth. Circling around the ephemeral man, they screamed in his ears, beat him with what looked like radiated fists, or fanatically tore at him, pulling the flesh off his face and body with their hideous claws. The poor man's meat poured through their little demonic hands like water, but then in a gust, rushed back to re-form his gruesome construction, only to be mauled again.

Jaw gaping, EB couldn't believe his senses. At first he couldn't clearly see who or what it was as it raged about so furiously when it exited the elevator. But once through the portal, he could see clearly it was indeed the same face he had seen before. No question, it was Marley—the rotted, decayed, and horribly disfigured Marley that he saw in his garage. Now in full body, he was clothed in the black priestly pants and collared shirt he always wore, all shrouded in the winter overcoat he had lived in when it was cold. But unlike the past where his fashion was always impeccable, spotless, without a crease or wrinkle, tonight his clothes were horribly torn, tattered, and soiled. Exposed through the tears and rips were sores and wounds, some so large they were leaking a black gas-like liquid that evaporated before it could hit the floor. Also erupting from the phantasm was a debilitating choking stench, like that of a rotting dead animal.

Holding his ragged outfit and melting body together were thick networking cables and wires of all sorts, wrapped around his torso and held together with an enormous flashing digital lock system. The wires and cables pulsed with electricity and data EB could actually see flowing in the air, extending outward from his body, like tails. Forming the links to these illuminated chains were large, heavy objects that clashed and slammed together as Marley convulsed, swatted at, and fought against the ghostly vultures surrounding and attacking him. Among the objects were steel bank deposit boxes, servers with lights pulsing, mirrors, glowing monitors playing videos of Marley's wild and wicked moments in life, giant virtual crypto coins linked together with bricks of silver, gold, and platinum, and at the end of the tails, large bags of pills and white powder bound to knots of needles, spoons, and filthy, well-used, residue-tarred glass pipes.

An extraordinary visual, Ebenezer just couldn't believe what he was seeing in front of him. Still paralyzed, he couldn't move either toward it to examine it, or away from it to flee its gruesome presence. So, with all the intellectual power he could muster, he focused his scientific mind to scrutinize, falsify, and debunk the phantom through and through as it moved toward him. And though he felt the chilling influence of its death-cold eyes, and could see the Hugo Boss label on its filthy, torn shirt, he was still incredulous, and fought against his senses.

This must be a prank! he concluded. *That's what all of this is—an elaborate hoax, a personal punking using my own holographic technology against me.*

"Hey!" shouted EB finally, yelling above the electronic racket and roar, caustic and cold as ever. "Enough is enough! Who's doing this? Charlie, is this your idea?" Charlie was his Chief Technology Officer and Engineer who had also helped develop Genius. Ever the prankster, Charlie never missed an opportunity to use his technological prowess to play tricks on people, especially the executive staff. EB hated his playful manner and constant joking, but tolerated him because there wasn't a better or more creative technologist out there—except for EB, of course.

Immediately, all the alarms, sirens, and digital chaos went quiet.

"You don't recognize me?" the apparition inquired in his familiar voice, still swatting away at the punishing devils as they relentlessly assaulted him.

"Well done, Charlie," EB replied, still quaking, but convinced he had persuaded Charlie to turn the volume off. "I have to hand it to you—I don't know how you pulled this one off, but it's your best one yet. But it's time to knock it off. I'll have you know that if you don't end this charade right now, you'll be the one punked right out of a job!"

"You don't believe in me," the ghost observed.

"OK, I'll play along," EB said in apprehensive frustration, still unable to shake the terror that had seized his soul. "Sure, Jacob, I believe in you. I resurrected you, don't you remember? I built you the world's most elaborate mausoleum, didn't I? And together we created the very Elevation technology that enables you to be here right now, didn't we?"

"I am not a ghost in your machine," it retorted. "You know that what is now before you is not possible to produce technologically."

"I know no such thing!" EB replied angrily. "Charlie, the game is over. Stop now or you'll never work in this city again!"

And then, after a brief moment of silence, Marley opened his mouth wide—so wide and distorted EB could have himself climbed inside—and let out a most disturbing frightful cry and shook its data-pulsing electronic chain with such a dismal and appalling noise, scaring even the cloud of demonic entities around him, that EB shrank back into his chair, pulling his knees to his chest to hide himself.

"What do you want with me?" EB stuttered from under his arms.

"Much," Marley replied, raising an arm in his classic manner.

"So you are Marley? How can that be?" the disoriented EB asked, unable to deny that the specter's voice disturbed the very marrow in his bones.

"Why do you deny your senses? Is not our company, your life, even all of science built upon the reliability of the senses?" Marley asked, having moved right to the edge of EB's chair where the tech giant huddled in the fetal position.

"Well, um, not necessarily," EB answered, peering up over his arms. "Even a little thing can affect and distort them. A slight disorder of the stomach can distort perception. If you're not a sophisticated hoax of my engineer, you may be an undigested nugget of chicken, a blot of hot mustard, a bit of carrot from my leftover egg fried rice, a fragment of an underdone potsticker."

Pleased with himself, EB uncoiled himself and sat back up in his oversized chair, but still curled up like a baby, to continue the lecture.

"The scientific method is what makes science: Observe a phenomenon that is in question, then collect all related data and formulate a hypothesis based on the observation. Third, test the hypothesis under strict scientific conditions, meaning conduct accurate experiments to determine whether the hypothesis agrees with or contradicts what is already proven in the real world. And finally, determine the results of the experiment. If the data found in the analysis is consistent with the hypothesis, it is accepted. If not, then it must be rejected. This is called falsification. If I can show from my carefully controlled experiment that my hypothesis is false, that hypothesis is not science."

"And are you not now in a real penthouse, by a real fire, in the real world talking with me?" Marley asked.

"Yes, my home is real, that fire in the fireplace is real and beyond dispute. But that I am talking to you may very well be a trick, whether of my own mind produced from psychedelic substances I ingested earlier, or by a prankster like Charlie. It seems I have been seeing mirages this entire evening, and so no, I don't believe you are the real Jacob Marley. An Elevation? Possibly. But the real Marley is dead and gone, extinguished into nothingness."

"Have your microdoses ever caused you to perceive your old partner, ravaged by death and sin, standing before you in eternal agony? Is your mind able to turn your Nevera's audio system into a graveyard of wails and howls? Can a hallucination dismantle Genius?" Marley quizzed.

EB was stunned the apparition knew the details of his evening. *No one could know, not even Charlie, all that has happened to me tonight . . . unless, of course, he caused them to happen*, EB thought while Marley's cold, dead eyes bore into his soul. *But how could that be? Charlie doesn't have access to my garage, let alone my Nevera—he doesn't even know I have one. And he certainly doesn't have any idea that I microdose.*

"Perhaps you are an Elevation that is somehow tapping into my mind, reading my thoughts to know all this information about me," EB charged, having finally dismissed that Charlie, or anyone, for that matter, could orchestrate his whole evening as a ruse. "And if you are an Elevation, then you are only a projection, a highly advanced virtual holographic environment. Yes, there's an element to it even we don't understand that causes the Elevated person to display a seeming life of its own, but this is likely artificial intelligence having surpassed its programmer."

"You, its inventor, know Elevation technology doesn't read minds," Marley groaned. "And how, with all its complex systems, could it be installed in your home here, undetected, in only a day? Was your security system not working yesterday? Who could penetrate it behind your back to engineer it? And where would all the elements of the configuration be hiding? Go look, search your house, and see if there is a single component anywhere."

After a few moments of cogitation, EB reluctantly conceded. "You are correct. That would be illogical," EB replied becoming more petrified of the inevitable conclusion toward which the conversation was heading.

"So I am not a technological manifestation. You have proven to yourself that I cannot be a hoax. All that is left is that I'm either a hallucination brought about by an undigested nugget of Tsao's chicken, or I am real. Would you agree, EB?"

"Well, I still don't believe you are the real spirit of Jacob Marley. To agree to that would be to acknowledge that there is another dimension beyond the material universe, that there are two contents, two realities: matter and spirit. And even more troubling, if you are really Marley, then death is not eradication into nothingness."

"Look at me, EEEEEEEE.BEEEEE," the phantom screamed. "Do I look like nothingness?"

"Perhaps you are just an undiscovered amalgamation of matter in a form we do not yet understand."

"What are the properties of matter, EB? Do not the laws of physics, upon which you have built your life, refute the very notion that I can be here? For seven years I've been in the grave, and now I emerge first revealing my head to you out of a control panel, and now all of me, in my eternal chains surrounded by living darkness that perpetually tortures me, rising in an elevator that has no electricity?"

"Well then, you are most definitely a hallucination, so vivid, so lifelike, that even now I am unable to free myself from it. But similar to dreams we think are real until we wake up, likewise this bad trip will soon end. It must!"

"Your Genius system objectively and truly is not working, though it should. Your electricity alone is shut off while everyone else's in the building is on. Are you able to hallucinate these realities? If you are so convinced this is a hallucination, go now and jump from your balcony and fly like a bird sixty-six floors down. Certainly you won't be hurt if this is a hallucination," the ghost prodded.

With that, Marley waved his decayed arm, causing the floor-to-ceiling sliding glass doors to his patio to fly open, allowing the cold wind and sleety rain to pour in.

"Go!" the ghost commanded. "Run and leap out into the night if this is only a delusion of your corrupt and evil mind!"

"I will not!" EB shot back. "You are the hallucination, not the nine hundred feet between here and the street."

There was silence as their eyes were locked. Then, this time using one hand to pry open his monstrous mouth, while shaking his chain in the other, Marley released another long, unbearable shriek, so ear shattering, so mind jarring, so full of soul-crushing dark power that EB lurched out of his chair and fell on his knees before the ghoul. In desperation, he leaned forward reaching for Marley's pant legs, only to witness his hands pass right through them, causing him to fall to the cold floor on his face. Staying there crumbled in his homaging position, he cried out to the ghost.

"Please!" he said. "Dreadful apparition, why do you trouble me?"

"Man of a twisted, worldly, unbelieving mind!" replied the entity. "Am I a hallucination or not?"

"You are not," said EB shaking like a diamondback's rattle. "You cannot be, for what hallucination can demonstrate such acuity while saturating all my senses with such conviction and fear? I dread that you yourself could kill me if you so desired. Hallucinations cannot kill."

"Indeed, I could kill you, and there is One greater than me that can not only kill your body, but your soul. It is that One you should fear most," the phantom warned as the patio doors slid closed.

"I don't understand what you're saying, Jacob. But please, why have you come to me?"

"I have come so that you won't end up as I am, shackled as I am," the apparition replied.

"Why, Jacob? Why are you chained like this?" EB implored,

still on his knees before his partner.

"I wear this chain that I forged in life," replied Marley, holding up the twisted fiber-optic wrapping still electronically pulsing with zeros and ones connecting all its appendages. "I made it link by link, algorithm by algorithm, and system by system; I integrated myself freely into it, and of my own free choice I made it a part of me. It's familiar to you, isn't it?"

EB trembled more and more.

"Don't you know," pursued his former partner, "the weight, length, and power of the massive cable you bear yourself? It was full, as heavy and as long as these, seven Christmas Eves ago. You have relentlessly labored on it since. And tonight, fashioned its most diabolical link of all. If only you could see your chain's enormity!"

EB patted around his legs and behind him, expecting to be buried in twisted, linked, and connected metals and transistors, but found nothing, and could see nothing but Marley's melting, rotting, semi-transparent flesh dissolving and then resolving itself.

"Please, Jacob, don't you have something positive for me?"

"I do not."

"For old times' sake, something just a little comforting that would give me just a drop of relief?"

"I have none to give. What you want comes from the other side of the great chasm, for those who themselves gave comfort and spent themselves to give others relief. There's so much more I want to tell you, EB, that you need to hear. But I have been severely limited, and am permitted to divulge very little. I can be here for only a momentary visit, and then I will be forced back to my eternal cell with these horrid, harassing beasts that never leave me alone or allow any peace; my prison, where I cannot rest, where day and night I stare in pain and regret at the jagged, infested walls lined with the same destroying distractions you see here fixed to my fetters, all with faces surrounding them, weeping. Children's faces, mother's faces, father's faces, all weeping!"

"You're not making sense, my old partner," EB responded, pressing himself up off his knees, feeling a little embarrassed. "You do look exhausted."

"Exhausted does not begin to describe my current condition, and what I have endured for the last seven years," said the ghost. "No rest, no peace. Incessant exhaustion, unceasing torture of remorse, and the knowledge that this agony will never end for me. Never!"

"Surely some relief will come soon. Nothing lasts forever," EB stated as a matter of fact.

Hearing this, the specter released another ear-shattering set of screeches, like the wailing of a thousand dogs simultaneously crying in pain.

"Oh, captive of captivity! You who is bound and deluded," cried the phantom. "You truly are ignorant of the vanity of it all. Nothing lasts forever that is composed of protons, neutrons, and electrons, but it is the spirit that occupies the molecular tent that is eternal. You incessantly labor knowing your days are numbered, that you are a vapor—here today, gone tomorrow—but for what are you working, striving, cheating, and lying? You do it for your decaying, dying self. You justify your means by an end that you ascribe with nobility, and yet you only do this to pacify your conscience that is screaming at you, day and night, moment by every ticking moment, hounding you of your hypocrisy, arrogance, and your guilt. Do you really believe ignobility can bring about that which is noble? Are you so disconnected that you think employing evil means will bring about a good end?"

"Our work was very important for the advancement of humanity," EB inserted. "That is most definitely a noble goal."

"What really is true advancement when the sentence of death is on us all? We were trapped in our own delusion of self-importance, self-centeredness, and self-aggrandizement and used that as an excuse. 'Beat the system,' we said to each other, determined to die with the most toys, foolishly thinking this is winning. Winning? It is enslaving! That's what it was and is. Using this short life for our own pleasure and well-being at the expense of others, to have others commend us, pat us on the back, admire us. 'Take, take, take!' we chanted, knowing we wouldn't bring one dollar with us to the grave. But we blocked that reality out, didn't want to think about it, pushing it off for another day while we deceived ourselves that we were 'helping people,' as if that's the mantra that would exculpate us from our many crimes and wipe the slate clean."

"But we did help many, many people, all over the world. And so what if we profited by it? That's the American dream! Our tremendous profits were proof of all the good we did. If people didn't benefit from our products, services, and inventions, they wouldn't have bought them!" EB retorted defensively.

"What does it profit you, EB, to gain the whole world but lose your soul?" the apparition shot back, piercing him again with those icy black eyes.

The earlier conversation with Narud flashed before his eyes accompanied by a flash of fear deep down, as if he were being cut in two. Trying to ignore it, EB attempted to steer the discussion back to Marley.

"What's happened to you, ol' Jake? Don't you remember all the adventures we had making our fortunes? Yes, we did wrong on occasion and weren't perfect. But who is? At least you lived life to the fullest, Jacob, and achieved great success because of it.

No one was better at business than you!"

"Business!" cried the ghost, wringing its hands and shaking its head. "Mankind was my business. The welfare of those created in the image of our Creator was my business; charity, mercy, speaking the truth, and benevolence were all my business. The vast networks we built, the innovations we introduced into the market, technologies we supplied were but a drop of water in the comprehensive ocean of what should have been my business!"

Marley held up his chain at arm's length for EB to observe, as if to make him understand the cause of all his unrelenting grief, and then with the strength and vigor that had complemented his acumen before his death, forcefully flung it in misery to crash loudly upon the ground again.

"Why did I never walk the streets where humanity lives, the hood where desperate calls for help always filled the air? Why did I turn away from those who asked for just a few pennies for the day's food, or a few dollars to those who gave up their lives in service of others? Instead, I poured my fortunes into the sea of selfishness, lavishing myself with things—meaningless, rusting, perishing things."

EB was utterly dismayed to hear the specter going on at this rate, and quaked even more uncontrollably. Again trying to hide this, EB blurted out whatever came into his mind.

"You had many fine possessions, Jake," he groveled. "World-class collections of properties, art, and the women—no one could compete with you in getting the girls."

"My own lusts drove me, which were never satisfied. Women were objects for my pleasure, destroying the marriage I once had. Instead of seeing my wife as my companion and confidante, my helper and lover, I threw away the greatest gift God gave me for momentarily pleasurable, but unfulfilling nights of base passion, pouring fuel on a sex addiction fire that, in the end, incinerated me."

"I disagree. Your wife was the real ball and chain, a constant nag that kept you down. Don't you remember all her manipulations and schemes to keep you away from your business, to keep you away from me?" EB tried to correct him.

"She was trying to save me!" the ghost shouted. "From myself, and from you! But I wouldn't let her because I was blinded by my own selfish ambition and determination to earn your approval. When she died, that is when I truly died."

"It's when you came alive! Only then were you free, my brother. Don't you remember? It was only after she was gone that we broke through and discovered Elevation! We would never have become two of the richest men in the world with her in the picture. I never told you this, Jake, but I admired you. After losing her, you were free; you did what you wanted and lived a life full of the richest pleasures and parties, unbridled glory with endless girls and glamor. You were a celebrity, Jacob, and lived the life I secretly wanted, but could never have."

"Celebrity?" the phantom gasped. "I was a catastrophe! All that glamor and fame only expedited my demise, energized my desires, and fed my addictions—the very addictions that you said nothing about, and never reached out to address."

"This I do regret. But you always handled them so well, especially the drugs, never letting them affect your work."

"They destroyed my work, and my life, just as yours are destroying you!"

"Marley, it wasn't your fault! You couldn't have known that she . . . what was her name? Oh yes, Hillary Dee you called her. You couldn't have possibly known Hillary Dee's plan."

"What I knew was that I only wanted an arrangement where I paid her for my own pleasure, but now I see it all clearly. She gave me what I deserved."

"She was a twisted, tatted, conniving whore, Jacob. She took advantage of you and she is rotting in prison, locked up now for what she did to you."

"For two years I used her only for her body, her phony compliments, to show her off like a trophy, all the while pretending our wild, unattached sex was freedom, when it really was the worst form of bondage destroying my soul. It was all about me trying to live as though I really was the god the world made me out to be. And what master of the universe should be denied any pleasure, any luxury, any desire he demands? Don't you see, EB? This is why she murdered me that dreadful night on the *Clinton.*"

"I don't see." EB cringed, recalling the shocking events that occurred on his yacht, which he had named after his favorite president.

"She came to know my weaknesses, and resented me because of them. I wasn't God. I was a codependent, shallow egomaniac that was deceiving myself and the world. But not her. She saw through my masquerade and became determined to show the world who this celebrity god really was," Marley mourned, pounding his chest. "That's why she laced the speedball with a lethal dose of ketamine. Her last words to me as she knelt over me under the ocean sky were, 'Imagine that, a Silicon Valley god slain by a slave of the streets. Who's saving the planet now, you pathetic imbecile! I win, you lose!' Understand, EB, the earth is better off without those who choose to live selfishly instead of love selflessly."

Struck by its words, EB stared at the ground as he wiped large amounts of perspiration from his forehead.

"Listen to me!" cried the ghost. "My time is nearly gone."

"I hear you," said EB. "At least I want to hear you, Jacob. Your words are like a hammer, and I am the nail."

"I am here tonight to tell you that you have yet a door of hope to escape the same chains that now bind me."

"You were always such a good friend to me," said EB. "I wish I would have told you that before."

"Then receive my words as words from a friend. You will be visited," resumed the ghost, "by three messengers, spirits from beyond the material plane."

EB's countenance fell and the fear that had become so familiar to him over the course of the evening again gripped him at such a prospect.

"Is that the door of hope you mentioned, Jacob?" he inquired, his voice faltering in despondency.

"It is."

"Look, Jake, you have given me much to think about tonight, and I am forever in your debt. But hasn't this gone far enough? Let's leave it at that, call it a night, and forget these other spirits," pleaded EB.

"Without their visits," said Marley's ghost, "there's no hope left for you to avoid the same verdict of justice that was given to me. My guilt is fixed for all eternity and there is no appeal before the Great Judge for reversal, no path or course of action to reduce the punishment, find leniency, or rid myself of these everlasting manacles. Why I was given these moments to come to you is a mystery, only understood by the All Knowing One. But this I can assure you. I will not return again to give you another chance."

"As much as I like seeing you, there is some comfort knowing you won't be back," EB said.

"Expect the first at 1:00 a.m., not a minute sooner or later."

"What? That's less than ninety minutes away," EB complained, checking his Patek Philippe Grandmaster Chime watch, which surprisingly had continued to keep perfect time. "Well, if there's nothing I can do to stop this nightmare and more apparitions must inevitably come, why not just have them all show up at once, do what they need to do, and be done with it?"

"The second spirit will follow at its foreordained time, as will the third," the departed spirit of Marley said, ignoring EB's appeal.

"What does that mean . . . foreordained time? Are you saying this insanity could go on for the whole night, or even for days or weeks?"

"Our time is up, EB, and you will never see me again—I hope. For your own sake, EB, encode this night into your brilliant brain so you'll never forget what has happened here!"

With these words, the specter gathered all the electronic chains he could—which were only a few of the load he dragged—under his right arm. With his left, he continued to swat at the ferocious ghouls that had plagued him during his entire visit. Jerking upright into a stiff rigidity, like a soldier coming to attention, the phantom then elevated off the floor and started to glide backward away from EB. And with each inch he moved, the massive glass sliding doors to EB's patio opened a little, so that when the phantom reached the threshold, the doors were once again wide open.

The apparition beckoned EB to approach, which he did. When they were within a couple yards of each other, Marley's ghost held up its hand, warning him not to come any closer. EB stopped immediately as a new chorus of chaotic, incoherent outbursts of lamentation and regret, painful, inexpressibly sorrowful, and self-accusatory wailings, rushed in to the living room, carried in by the storm's foggy wind and icy rain.

The specter, after listening for a moment, lifted its melting face to heaven and joined in the desperately mournful atonal requiem as it floated up over the balcony's railing and out into the bleak, tempestuous night. It moved through the punishing storm slowly until it was suddenly sucked into some kind of twisting vortex, like a horizontal tornado, that sped the ghost away from the building.

EB curiously followed it out, right up to the rail, only to see a swarm of restless, grieving phantoms, male and female, also being swept up into the fog-filled sleety cyclone. Every one of them wore chains like Marley's ghost but with its own unique dangles, with quite a number of them linked together with common bonds. None were free.

EB recognized many of them—celebrities, Hollywood producers, and revered politicians of their day. Among the screaming horde were elite generals, esteemed professors, black-robed judges, and numerous bankers, investors, and financiers admired and worshipped by the world. He could see famous lawyers he had manipulated cases with, social media titans he had advised, and to his great surprise, not a few technologists and engineers he had worked with, a few he even admired.

One in particular stood out to him, a former president while he was young, tall, and lanky, who along with the money boxes and safes, mirrors and drug paraphernalia had a giant iron hammer and steel sickle attached to the chains that bound his bony, grayish body. This one's cries seemed to rise above the multitude with which he was swirling, though not in sorrow, but rebellion and defiance, hopelessly waving a bloody, gory fist above his head.

Together, they all were being thrashed around and around, unable to escape the syphoning whirlwind that was carrying them across the city to a very particular end point—a hole that seemed to glow red. It was difficult to see as it faded in and out with the passing clouds, fog, and sleet. EB gripped his banister and leaned over as far as he could, straining to observe where they were being transported with such force, all the time shrieking, bawling, and howling. Just as he was about to give up trying to peer through the impenetrable darkness, by then completely soaked due to his curiosity, the clouds parted slightly, giving him a glimpse of their destiny. To EB's dismay, the red they were all being vacuumed into was Narud's illuminated tower top where, once inside, they and their spirit voices faded together into silence.

Drenched from both the pouring rain above and sweat coming from within, EB quickly returned to his living room, which also had taken in a significant amount of the storm's water. Splashing through the puddles in his bare feet, he pulled the normally electronically controlled doors shut. The room was still lit from the fireplace's blaze, and by it, EB examined the elevator by which Marley's ghost had entered. Its door was also shut tight, and the manual lock was in place as he had locked it with his own hands earlier. Its control pad radiated blue, with its button lit. EB hesitantly pressed the call button, and with a soothing hum, the car began to rocket up the shaft from the garage.

"Genius. Are you back?" he said out loud. "All power on, mode one." Without a moment's delay, all the lights in every room of his penthouse illuminated to full power, blinding his eyes a little. Shaking his head, he tried to say "Hexagas!" but stopped himself at the first syllable. Instead, he slowly shuffled himself out of the living room, down the hall to the master bedroom, and, after having his eye and thumbprint scanned, he mentally transmitted the code word to the control panel. Immediately his bedroom door silently slid open. Drained of every microgram of energy, EB gave one final command, this time out loud, as he made his way to his ultra-plush double king bed in the center of the room.

"Genius, night mode." The lights, including the emergency ones, obeyed his order, as did the fireplace, and his penthouse went completely dark. Not able to utter another word, think another thought, or engage in any other activity at all, EB fell onto his bed, without undressing, and instantly was asleep.

STAVE 3

SPIRIT ONE

CHAPTER 16

"It is now 12:00 a.m. Time to wake up, EB. The time is now 12:00 a.m." Just as when a mother calls her child from down the street to come for dinner, the words were heard, but ignored as EB continued to dream.

"Wake up, EB—12:00 a.m. Time to get up," the gentle woman's voice continued, this time rousing him out of a deep sleep.

"What? Where am I?" EB called out into the darkness of his room. Looking out of bed, he couldn't distinguish where the floor-to-ceiling transparent window wall ended and the opaque ceilings of his chamber began. He liked it that way and had specifically designed his bedroom to be pitch black when in Night Mode. The thick blackout curtains ensured this, as did the seal around his door that prevented any light from the rest of the house from seeping in.

"It is now 12:00 a.m.," the voice started again.

"Genius, shut up!" EB yelled out, quelling the seductive alarm.

In the silence, he endeavored to pierce the darkness with his ferret eyes, but couldn't see a thing, not the edge of his bed or even his hand in front of him clinging to his comforter. He wasn't completely awake yet, and so in the confusion that often accompanies the first minutes between slumber and being fully cognizant, he said the first thing that came to mind.

"Genius, open the curtains." With a swish, the large drapes covering the full wall directly in front of him parted, revealing the cityscape, still stormy and miserable.

Wait a minute, EB thought as he had finally fully emerged from dormancy. *It's only 12:00 a.m.? I just went to bed a few minutes ago. How can this be?*

EB felt as though he had been sleeping for hours—even a whole day—and was not only wide awake, but completely recharged and physically refreshed. Being in such a state, free from the total physical exhaustion that had nearly crushed him earlier, was gratifying, but also alarming.

That must have been the deepest REM sleep ever, he thought, trying to make sense of his drastic transformation. *But what about all that happened before going to sleep?*

He scrambled out of bed to the window after suddenly recalling the images of all those entities being pulled by that dark tornado into the SwarmTrooper Tower. He could see the rain was still beating against the window, but was prevented from hearing its patter by the soundproof glass that ensured his solitude. Accompanying the downpour, clouds and fog swirled over the city unrepentantly, smothering all the lights below him—except for that red glow, still the only visible structure from his vantage point, pulsing from a dim to a bright red between the passing billows of darkness. This time, however, there was something in the middle of the red projection. It was difficult to make out, and EB stared for several minutes until there was a clear break in the clouds and fog. There at the center of the bloody beacon was an eye, staring right at him. EB knew it was only a projection, part of the art or images that rotated through the billboard. But tonight? *Why would it be part of tonight's display?* he wondered. It reminded him of the Eye of Sauron. His invigoration was soon overcome with apprehension as the crimson-surrounded evil eye of Barad-dûr penetrated him, causing the memories of the previous hours to strike at his spirit again.

EB immediately ran back to his bed and slid under the covers as the ruddy glow filled his room. Not wanting to fall back into the earlier terror, EB determined to figure out the meaning of it all and so thought, and thought, and continued to think it over and over and over. *Perhaps this had all just been a dream. I hadn't even considered that*, EB mused. He had dismissed the possibility of it all being an elaborate high-tech hoax. Not even his top engineer, as good as he was in his field, could have pulled that off. And although his little dose of LSD could have been bad and produced such wild hallucinations, at least he knew he wasn't malingering or in any way feigning it. For him, the screams, ghosts, and terror were more real than the bed he was hunkered in. All his senses, trained and refined as they were as a revered scientist, told him the events had been real, as real as the conversation he'd had with Narud or the missionary at the tower plaza.

He knew he wasn't a schizophrenic and didn't have any psychotic conditions. He regularly underwent full physical and psychological testing by his physician and psychiatrist, two of the best in California, if not the world. No, it could not have been a hallucination from any physical abnormality or condition. The only possibility was that the microdose gave him a very, very bad trip. But he knew the science there as well: there had never been a case to his knowledge of such a tiny amount of LSD causing such dramatic, prolonged, and realistic hallucinations. Physiologically, it would be impossible for the trace amount of the chemical to interact in such a way as to generate a delusion such as Marley, the demons, and all the exterior events that accompanied their visitation.

EB grabbed his ePad, another huge market eBeja had come to dominate, knocking out Apple, Microsoft, and the other many players in the pad space, to use instead of his PPC and its internal projection system. Though his implanted chip and brain-screen were more convenient, he liked to stay up to speed on his company's latest releases of the ePad and so occasionally used it as a mobile control panel for his fully interconnected life. Plus, in some ways he liked being old school, like with his music, car collection, and parsing his data or watching video on an ePad.

Scrolling through the different areas he could control with it—his company, his employees, his ventures, his relationships—he arrived at the section for his penthouse. Here he could see the minute-by-minute logs of Genius, to know for certain if Genius had really been off, and if all the other systems in his house were down as he had experienced. After a few more swipes, he reached the section showing the time he arrived back home. There it was. He entered his garage, the log revealed, and then after an unusually long period of twelve minutes, the log showed the elevator taking him up to his penthouse.

That is exactly in line with the trespassing mutt and then Marley's head accosting me, EB calculated. There was no delay or issue with Genius or the electric power in his penthouse, the log documented. The elevator arrived at his private entrance exactly twenty-three seconds later, slightly longer than usual. But right at that point, the log showed an electrical interruption of some sort. Trying to probe deeper into its cause, the records revealed only that all the power had been immediately cut off, including the power source for Genius.

He then clicked the video button next to that section of data, and up came the several squares showing video from the four different angles his garage cameras recorded. Playing them back in sync, all the recorded events were just as the log documented, exactly as he remembered: there he was roaring into the garage, then kicking the dog, after that summoning the elevator—and then, that's when he fell back because of Marley's head coming through the panel. He could see himself scooting back as fast as he could away from something, but that something wasn't visible. Marley's head wasn't on camera at all. Then all the video went dead and there was nothing else recorded from that point on, not only in his garage, but in his elevator and penthouse, until Genius and the electricity came back on after Marley's visitation.

A hallucination cannot cause a power outage, EB surmised, *but the cameras didn't record Marley. They caught everything else perfectly, except Marley's head.*

Then, switching to a different section of the program, EB called up the entire building's data. Swiping to the section showing all the building's power usage, the log showed that while his power was off, all the rest of the building's electricity was on. Not believing what he was seeing, EB went deeper, examining each floor, then each unit. Not a single one had lost power last night. Even the roof had full uninterrupted power all day and evening.

"How the hexagas?" EB muttered out loud.

The building's electrical supply was metered unit by unit, but was designed with multiple redundancies so that no home or office would ever be without power unless the entire building was without power. And even then, there were several backup systems that could generate full power for the entire building for hours if need be. None of that happened earlier, according to the records, making it impossible, scientifically speaking, for the events to have happened. But there it was, not just in his mind, but logged and documented. His penthouse didn't have power, Genius really did shut down, but the building did have uninterrupted electricity.

Dumbfounded, EB didn't want to believe the data, but knew he had to follow the science. No drug-induced hallucination—no hallucination of any kind from any source—could create this anomaly. And it certainly couldn't have been orchestrated by any person or group, being technically and logistically impossible. And even if it were possible, an Elevation-level hologram of Marley's head would have shown up on the video. All the data proved incontrovertibly that he hadn't dreamed it, or imagined it, or in any way concocted it in his mind. As much as he wanted it to be, it wasn't just his perception. What he had experienced was supported by documented, external reality. But how could that be? It defied the laws of physics, the laws of science as he knew them. The more he thought, the more perplexed he was; and the more he endeavored not to think, the more he thought.

If Marley's ghost really did visit him, and this is what bothered him most, then that meant the nightmare wasn't over. What had he said? "Expect the first at 1:00 a.m., not a minute sooner or later."

"Genius, exactly what time is it now?" EB inquired of his artificial genie.

"The time is now 12:33 a.m.," Genius replied.

In what felt like only a minute or two, EB had spent more than thirty minutes ruminating. If Marley's prophecy was true, he had less than half an hour to prepare for the next round in the ring with his destiny. He wasn't about to go back to sleep; he couldn't even if he wanted to. So he decided to prove once and for all whether this was all just a product of his imagination, a perceptual fiction all generated by an obscene, unwanted, and involuntary combination of synaptic firings . . . or that there really was a dimension beyond the material, external to himself, that, unfortunately, he was in subjection to.

Was there a way to set up some parameters so whatever happened in the next short while could be tested? How could he demonstrate scientifically that he was or wasn't imagining these disturbing visits from beyond? EB put his computer brain to work to come up with a controlled test or tests that would satisfy him and his peers. He had started to think how the world would perceive him if what was happening to him was real. Would they reject him and call him an unstable fanatic? Would he be relegated from his high stature among elites down to what they scorned and disdained most: a common man of irrationalities with nonsensical superstitious crutches? Would the media say he'd gone mad? Might he be committed to an insane asylum? And what would Narud think? This disturbed him most. What would become of his venture with Narud, the ultimate fulfillment of all he'd worked for and dreamed about? No, he wouldn't allow whatever was plaguing him to come between him and his mentor. And he certainly wouldn't sacrifice his life for some illusion, delusion, or degeneration.

The first proof would be through an attempt to record whatever might come. Since the many cameras around the home had gone dark after the power shut off, he didn't have any footage from Marley's visit to his living room. So, just in case everything went dark again, he would set up several hidden battery-operated infrared cameras around his room that were much more sophisticated than his garage and home security cameras. He had a closet full of top-of-the-line gadgets, including four high-resolution full 16K military-grade night-vision cameras that recorded in both video and holographic mode simultaneously. They also were equipped with electromagnetic field meters, which would register any electromagnetic radiation or magnetic field disruptions as well as thermal imaging scanners to record temperature variations.

Tech wizard that he was, he could easily get the cameras set up, tested, and preset to start recording at exactly 12:59 a.m. They would not only record locally onto the micro disk in each camera, but he tied them in to his corporate security system so they would livestream through his network and be preserved for later viewing in his corporate cloud, as long as the power didn't go down again. Additionally, so there would be no question of its authenticity, he programmed them for a live simulcast via a couple of his social media accounts.

The next verification he thought of would be to have someone there with him to corroborate whatever happened, just in case the cameras didn't work or capture the whole event as the garage cameras had failed to do. A real person with him would also be able to vouch for the experience even if connectivity or the electricity was disrupted. If there were no network issues or interruptions, there might be hundreds of thousands, if not millions, that would witness the events live on social media. But this wasn't the best evidence since the viewers were virtual and there could be claims that whatever happened was staged. Having another person there with him in his room to be an eyewitness to whatever happened would help substantiate the video, especially if that person was a neutral third party. The only person he could think of who could make it up to his place in time was the building night manager, Bernard, whom he had spoken to earlier.

Confident his communication network was also restored, EB willed the quick dial command to reach the front desk manager.

"Hello," a voice said into his head.

"Yes, this is EB. Is this—" and he was cut off.

"—and Merry Christmas. You've reached the voicemail for the on-duty manager. Your needs are our top concern. Please leave a brief message and your attempt to connect with us will be returned as soon as possible. As always—"

EB mentally disconnected and cut the message short. He tried again and again, but with no human answering. It looked like he wouldn't be able to have a witness with him, after all. The recordings and live holographic stream would have to do.

The only other authentication he could cobble together before the hour struck was to acquire some kind of physical evidence of any entity that might invade his space. The question was—how could he gather such a specimen? Marley had been ethereal—there, but not there. He could see right through his grotesque presence at times and wasn't able to touch him, yet he somehow was outfitted with discernable clothing and chains that rattled, clanked, and exploded against the ground. He could smell his putrid decaying corpse and yet not a stain of his dripping flesh or a mark from all his clamoring about was left behind. This was all very perplexing to EB, whose materialism negated the possibility of another dimension not composed of tangible particles.

Perhaps the spirits Marley said were coming were different, and had clothing from which he could take a clip, or hair that could be cut. Deciding that he would only be able to determine how to acquire his last piece of evidence once the entities arrived, EB made some preparations so as not to leave anything to chance. First, he took a small pair of scissors from his bathroom and tucked them away in his robe pocket. He added a couple of ziplock plastic bags he had on hand to store any objects he obtained. And finally he put a couple of cotton swabs in with the scissors in case there was some kind of liquid, secretion, or plasma he could later test.

"Genius, time!" he commanded after getting everything in place and ready for what he hoped was an event that wouldn't happen.

"The time is now 12:53 a.m.," the system responded.

EB decided to turn out all the lights again and close the curtains, mainly to cut out the red glow from SwarmTrooper Tower that saturated his room. As much as he had prepared, in his mind he found it ridiculous that he had gone to such levels to arrange for something that wasn't going to happen, and chided himself for getting caught up in the very superstitious nonsense to which he had dedicated his life to refuting.

What's happening to me? he thought, annoyed at himself and the whole evening, but also still unable to shake the impending feeling of doom that enveloped him. Pulling his covers up over his legs as he sat up against his headboard, he determined with all his strength to ride out the next few minutes as the scientist he was. The more he thought about it, the more he convinced himself that there must be a purely rational explanation for all that had transpired. He would not be a coward or succumb to senseless fears. He had set up a few tests—not perfect, but sufficient to at least begin a serious and rigorous inquiry, if such was even required at all.

"Genius, display time," he called out.

A three-dimensional hologram of the time appeared above his floor, between the foot of his bed and the closed window curtains. "12:57" were the large numbers on display as Genius announced the time. EB subconsciously gripped his blanket in his fists while forcing a stoic calmness on his face no one could see.

"12:58," Genius chimed.

"Two minutes," EB said out loud.

"12:59."

"One minute until nothing," EB again spoke out into his empty room.

"The time is now 1:00 a.m.," Genius finally said.

"So here we are," said EB, triumphantly, "and nothing!"

He spoke just as the hologram morphed into a large "1:00."

"Genius, display off," EB commanded, feeling relieved. But just as the display disappeared, brilliant white light flashed through the room and the large window drapes whipped open, faster than Genius could've ever done it. Utterly startled, EB nearly jumped out of his bed from the shock of the instantaneous, perfectly timed events. With his back still against his headboard trembling, he noticed something on the other side of his windows, emanating the blinding light that now filled his quarters. He put his hand to his brow to shield his eyes, and tried to see what it was that was shining like a star through his window. Finally catching an angle where his hand blocked just enough of the light, he caught a glimpse of a visitor, just as Marley had promised.

It was a strange figure—awesome in its splendor, but at the same time unintimidating and welcoming, like a child. But it was definitely not a child. The being was small, like a seven- or eight-year-old, and evenly proportioned, except for its arms, which were long, like the gray aliens portrayed by Hollywood. Different from the grays, however, this entity's arms were quite muscular, emanating physical strength. It also didn't have a praying mantis–shaped head like the grays.

That was all EB could see against the bright light. Then, in a blink, the being appeared next to his bed, having either teleported or moved through the window so quickly EB couldn't see it. Immediately, the light surrounding its luminescent body dimmed so that EB didn't have to squint any more or use his hand to shelter his eyes. Once his pupils dilated back to normal, he found himself face-to-face with the unearthly entity who, standing upright, was about the height of his elevated mattress.

The being's features were much clearer to him now, and he could see that, along with its muscular body, it had long white hair, if it was hair at all. It flowed like water and yet radiated pure white light, like the hottest white fire. It wasn't feminine, but majestic, accenting the being's power. To EB, the entity looked like a miniature Viking, but without the beard, armor, scars, or wrinkles. In fact, there wasn't a wrinkle on its perfect face, which was so smooth, EB couldn't tell whether it was made of skin or some other coating. The being's outfit was also white and fire-like, matching its hair—it consisted of a long tunic of pure light over a skintight uniform of some kind; and around the entity's waist was bound a lustrous belt, with a sheen of astounding, glistening beauty—more beautiful than anything EB had seen in his luxury-filled life.

But the strangest thing about the creature was the clear jet of white fire that sprang from the crown of its head. The beam of white fire pulsed hotter, then cooler, as it shot up as a single flame through the ceiling. EB imagined it was seen shooting from his building through the clouds into the heavens throughout the whole city by anyone that happened to be outside at that unforgivable hour. The very strange part was that, as it pulsed, the being's body would alternately disappear into the fire light, leaving only the beam, then reappear in its complete form. Surrounding the beam were what looked like giant electrons doing a chaotic but orderly dance around the creature's body. Its hands and feet also radiated with the same hot white fire, revealing their shape only when the fire subsided.

After what must have been a full five minutes of just staring at the creature, EB glanced around the room to see if the cameras were on as planned. They were, each with their little red light on indicating that all that he was seeing would be streaming to audiences around the world, and recorded for all to see when this experience ended. *At least people won't think I've gone insane*, he thought to himself as the invader stood silently, scanning him with its white-light eyes. Satisfied that he had not lost his faculties, and that the recordings would vindicate him, he mustered enough strength to break the ice.

"Are you the spirit that Marley said would come to me?" EB

finally asked.

"I am." The voice was powerful but gentle. Singularly low in volume with almost an echo, as if, instead of being so close beside him, it was at a distance.

"Who, and what, are you?" EB demanded.

"I am the spirit of the past."

"Long past?" inquired EB.

"No. Your past."

"My past? What concern could you have with my past?"

"Your welfare!" said the spirit plainly, sending a chill up and down EB's spine.

Reflexively, EB's mind immediately rejected such a concern, and began to enumerate back to himself his many assets, associations, and accolades, which by any standard would be considered welfare extraordinaire. Wheels turning, EB then, naturally, started to calculate how to monetize this encounter, realizing that this discovery of whatever it was could be a new and very profitable venture that would add even more to his fortune.

Perhaps this creature is a living quantum entity, an emissary of a wholly different race sent to bring our two civilizations together, he thought. EB had never fully dismissed the possibility of other life forms existing elsewhere in the universe. Rather, by his calculations, there was a strong likelihood of there being multiple species, even myriads of exobiological examples scattered through the billions of galaxies. The issue was proof. Where was the real, incontrovertible evidence? Not fuzzy videos of flying disks or unverifiable abduction experiences, but real proof that could stand up to the rules of evidence, whether in a laboratory or courtroom. If this is what this being was, and he was recording it all, he knew he'd hit another mother lode.

EB's entrepreneurial instincts and scientific acumen were

telling him a new theory may be in the making here, one that would not only explain the night's events, but possibly the meaning of the universe as well. He again quickly scanned the room for the little red lights ensuring the cameras were capturing all of this for later exploitation.

The entity must have heard him thinking and immediately interrupted his grandiose hypothecating.

"Your thoughts prove your need. Restoration is at hand, so pay attention!"

It put out its strong hand as it spoke, and clasped him firmly but gently by the arm. EB was astounded by its strength—a strength far beyond any human. Though the creature's clasp on his arm did not hurt at all, it was viselike, a hold that couldn't be undone by anything he could do.

EB was himself in marvelous physical shape, with regular exercise and working out almost a religion to him. What greater goal could he have for himself than perfecting himself? And that meant perfecting his body. To him, there was no real distinction between his muscles and his emotions, his bone structure and his mind. He was a unity of matter, period. And so this ghostly grip intrigued him as much as it frightened him. How could such a small, gentle creature have such enormous power? So strong was the hold, it felt as if his arm were fusing with the entity's hand, like two pieces of titanium being smelted into one, becoming perfectly united, yet still somehow remaining separate.

But there was something more. There was also a comfort in this unity, a calming he had never felt before, as if for the first time in his adult life he was not alone. He had never really thought about that before, being alone, since he really wasn't alone, except for the few hours at his apartment most nights to sleep. Otherwise, from wake up to head down, he was surrounded by his staff, admirers, social media followers, the press, employees, and the hordes of people always wanting something from him. But in this instance, in the moment where for the first time in a very long time he felt that he wasn't alone, came the realization that he was alone, and had always been alone.

"Get up! Walk with me!" the spirit said, pointing toward the window.

EB wasn't expecting that, a directive that he must go somewhere with the being, and outside of the purview of his cameras. That certainly wasn't going to work. At least with Marley's ghost he wasn't forced to go anywhere. And though he was exceedingly, almost recklessly adventurous, and though the doom that had clouded his soul and fears that accompanied it were subsiding and being replaced with ambition, he was in no mood to leave his warm bed. But the grasp of the entity could not be resisted and its gentle power compelled him—not by pulling him against his will, but through realization that going with the electron-surrounded being was in his best interests.

Resolved that his cameras had recorded enough for some level of proof, he rose and moved with the spirit toward the window, still wrapped in his robe with the same leisurely clothing underneath he had put on earlier.

"I am a mortal," EB remonstrated, gripped with the reality of where they were going. "Have you heard of gravity? A cage from which I wish I could free myself, but cannot, and so will fall to my death if we go out there!"

"Put your hand here," said the spirit, laying EB's hand directly in the center of the being's torso, where the heart would be if it had one. "Keep it there and you will be truly Elevated!"

As the words were spoken, they passed through the unopened windows and lifted above the city below. EB closed his eyes in terror expecting the dive to commence imminently. He could feel that he was outside in the cold, wet air, but had no sense of the fall that should be a scientific certainty. EB slightly opened one eye in a squint to peek at what he thought would be a series of windows vertically rushing by him, but instead found himself standing securely on a suburban road, lined with flowering dogwood and red maple trees. The city had completely vanished, not a speck of it to be seen anywhere. The darkness, fog, noise, and claustrophobia of the urban jungle had vanished with it, and in its place a crisp, clean, and bright day with snow on the ground and the sound of children laughing and playing in a field beyond them.

"Are you kidding me?" EB blurted out, holding his hands above his head in wonderment, having been released from the spirit's grasp. "This is my old school! I spent my elementary and high school years right here, playing baseball and soccer in that field. I was a boy here!"

EB gazed giddily at the surroundings, spinning to see this familiar but long forgotten world. He was conscious of a thousand smells floating in the air, each one connected with a thousand thoughts, and hopes, and dreams, and cares long, long forgotten. He must have spent twenty minutes reveling there, staring, admiring and reminiscing.

"How are you doing this? Some alien technology, I'm guessing."

"Am I so alien to you?" the spirit replied. "Look closely."

EB complied and continued his survey of their landing area. "This is incredible!" he said, still in astonishment. Then, shaking his head, he leaned over, packed a hand full of snow into a snowball, and after a terrific windup, threw it at a tree about sixty feet away. Splat, right in the center of the trunk. "Steee-rike!" he yelled, proud that he still had his wicked pitching arm that his grade school peers had assured him would land him in the Major Leagues.

"Your lip is trembling," said the spirit. "And what is that glistening on your cheek?"

"What? Stop clowning around. It's nothing at all. Must be a splash of melted snow from the snowball," EB replied, collecting himself. *Keep it real, EB. Don't let yourself get sucked in and get emotional. You've probably been put in a trance or something. This alien is messing with your mind.*

"Did you say something?" inquired the entity.

"Not really, just a little overwhelmed with how real everything seems. Lead on, alien. Let's get this dream over with."

"I'm not an alien as you are imagining, though I have been alien to you," the spirit said again, taking hold of EB's arm.

"Yes, lead on. Please."

"Don't you know the way?"

After one final 360-degree look around, he nodded, thinking he might as well enjoy the dream, or whatever he was experiencing.

"Know it? I know Papa Wycliffe's like the back of my hand and could walk it blindfolded—that is if it's really as it was. You know how dreams are. Ever see the movie *Inception?*"

"Have you ever seen the movie *Dead Man Walking?*" replied the entity.

EB felt as though a dagger had just struck his heart, real as real could be. So he put his head down and vigorously walked forward, trying to stay just in front of the spirit so he wouldn't have to look at it.

CHAPTER 17

As EB and the spirit of the past traversed the winding path on which they had appeared, EB quickly forgot his guide's wounding remark and became absorbed in his surroundings. He easily recognized every gate and post and tree, with all its astounding detail, looking exactly as he remembered it from long ago. Memories began to flood his brain of the many days of playing, learning, and exploring on the 3,200-acre campus of the Northeast's most elite private school, Wycliffe's Preparatory Academy.

Founded in 1894, the all-boys boarding school was one of the most exclusive, and beautiful, in the country. Situated on a lush plain that backed up to, and gradually ascended, a forested hill, the school resembled a king's regal estate more than an elite academy for boys. It was filled with trees of all kinds, numerous open-lawn areas, and just about every species of shrub, bush, and flower that would grow in the Northeast. Its grounds were a showcase of flora, always immaculately manicured except for this time of the year when all were blanketed with a thin sheet of glistening white frozen water.

Unique among preparatory schools, St. Wycliffe's had two separate but connecting campuses, one for the grade school and the other, much larger, one for the high school. Both campuses were full time boarding, meaning that all of the students were required to live there during the academic year and were only allowed to leave during holidays or summer break. Many never left at all, though, choosing rather to study and prepare themselves so as to keep pace with their very competitive peers.

So high was the demand to attend St. Wycliffe's that, once accepted, most students spent their entire childhood and teen years there, attending both the elementary and high school. But this was only possible if they maintained the required high grade-point average, adhered to the school's rigorous standards, and endured its legendary military-like discipline. Not everyone made it, and the school maintained its elite status and reputation by never playing favorites. Though many very wealthy, influential, and famous families sent their children there, all understood that the school's motto, "achieve or leave," was applied indiscriminately based solely on performance.

Some parents, for whatever reason—whether because they wanted to ensure their child made it through the program, or because they were uncaring parents not wanting their children to interrupt their extravagant lives—simply paid the tuition and left their children in the full-time custody of the school. For these fortunate unfortunates, St. Wycliffe's became all the family they really ever knew, earning it the nickname "Papa Wycliffe's."

EB hadn't been one of these "academic orphans," as some of the teachers called them, but neither was he one of the students who was regularly visited by his family during the year, or who spent summer breaks away from campus. As one of the "lifers" who started first grade there and stayed through the end of high school, he did leave the campus to be with his family, which consisted of his father and sister, but only once each year during the Christmas break.

"There, that's Papa Wycliffe's main campus area," EB said enthusiastically to the spirit, pointing ahead. As the two rounded a turn, the main buildings of the school came into view, all exuding the same Ivy League–like, small-town glory he remembered. Closest to them was the high school cafeteria, then just past it was the shared library, and in the distance in the middle of this learning town, up a small hill, was the tall joint campus church steeple that could be seen from anywhere on the grounds.

Sandwiched between the library and the chapel stood a massive, much more modern-looking anomaly, the Isaac Newton Science & Technology Center, the only contemporary style of construction on the campus. Composed of four connecting buildings in the shape of a cross, each of the sections of the INSTC was dedicated to one of the four STEM areas in which the school focused: science, technology, engineering, and mathematics. EB had spent an extraordinary amount of time in these buildings, and had always credited them as the halls where he was given the foundational tools for his success.

Of Wycliffe's 224 faculty and staff of EB's day, over 40 percent of those taught in INSTC, all of whom were of the highest caliber. Of these gifted science teachers, not a few were there who had tired of the university rat race, or retired from top-tier schools, giving Wycliffe's their talent instead of other, much better-paying organizations. They almost always took huge pay cuts to teach the world's most gifted and brightest in the sciences compared to what they could have received from large corporations, government entities, or research organizations. But they did it for the results they achieved with their students, in the sciences. Wycliffe's did have an excellent liberal arts program of social sciences and humanities, but that's not why parents sent their children there and spent nearly $200,000 per year in tuition, regardless of the grade level. It was for the science, and the school's famed immersion program, which started its pupils on a rigorous course of math, science, and even engineering from the day they started first grade.

Sports, entertainment, and extracurricular activities all existed and were encouraged at Wycliffe's, but never emphasized, nor given the esteem as in other, lesser schools. They were always just that—extracurricular, like recess in other schools. The heroes on campus, whether in first grade or seniors in high school, were those who won the science fairs, or placed in international mathematics competitions. The Student Hall trophy case had exactly zero trophies for sports, but hundreds for math, science, technology, and engineering contests, including twenty-four first-place winners of the renowned Science Talent Search, the nation's oldest and most prestigious science competition for high school seniors.

Besides the extraordinary faculty, one of the other reasons for Wycliffe's incredible track record was its sophisticated and advanced array of science laboratories, the most elaborate of any prep school in the country. Such a combination ensured that the high school graduates were regularly recruited to all the major science and technology universities, including MIT, CalTech, Stanford, Berkeley, Georgia Tech, and Carnegie Mellon. So many of the graduates made it to the top tech and Ivy League schools, far more than other famous preparatory schools, that a quip circulated among both the students and their parents: "If you want to run with the elite, go to Phillips Exeter. If you want to run over the elite, go to Wycliffe's."

"Hey there, watch where you're going!" EB shouted with a rare laugh as several bundled-up boys pedaling hard on their bikes came whipping by him and his ethereal companion on the snow-cleared path. Like EB, they were laughing, and also delightfully shouting directions to each other as they zipped down and around the school's walkways. EB had also loved to bike on these paths, in both summer and winter. And since there were no cars and very few other students in this area of the campus, as well as lots of turns and jumps, it became known as Wycliffe's own Daytona. What he didn't love was that he almost always had raced it alone.

"These are but shadows of the things that have been," said the spirit. "They have no consciousness of us and can't hear you or see you."

As they meandered around the school's buildings, a few more students appeared, and a teacher or two, as well as a groundskeeper and that old cafeteria mom whose cooking he remembered was deliciously good. He could name them all as they had been his classmates, his instructors, mentors, and those he admired from afar as a youth. It was like a reunion for him, a joyful family reunion that brought a happiness he hadn't felt in years.

But why? Why was this making him so happy, and feel an internal lightness he had forgotten even existed? Here they were, acquaintances of old, none of whom he was still in touch with or even aware of where they now were in life. But he was so glad to see them, and hear their calls to one another wishing a Merry Christmas, or calling for Happy Holidays as they headed to cars to leave for the week, or toward the town that was built around the school where most of the teachers and workers lived.

Unfortunately, like him, some of the students either spent their Christmas holiday on campus, or were there right up until the last minute before Christmas Day itself, waiting for parents or guardians to fetch them. Boarding for all students was required, which meant that some of the unlucky students whose parents were too far away, or too busy, or just disinterested, inevitably would only receive a call to exchange Merry Christmases, if any message at all.

Hit by this arrow of memory, EB's mood shifted. What good was all this merriment anyway? How did it ever do him any good, or make him any close friends, or give him the respect of his peers? When did a Merry Christmas do anything but cost him in productive work and diminish his fortune as he paid employees to do nothing?

"The school is emptying fast for the holiday, but is not quite deserted," said the spirit.

"Yes, I know. Every year some of the kids get left here over the Christmas week. For whatever reason, they don't get to join their parents or family—one of the downfalls of growing up with a workaholic's silver spoon in your mouth."

"Like the solitary child, neglected by his classmates, who is in there," the being said, pointing up the hill to the chapel.

EB had hoped the spirit was not aware of this and quickly turned his face away as he simultaneously squinted his wetting eyes and mustered all his internal strength to hold inside him the involuntary convulsions of a sob. Once again, he was disgusted with himself for allowing such emotions. Since when did he ever even remotely care about such things? Why was he letting a dream elicit these useless feelings?

This dream and its conductor were beginning to grate on his soul. So what if he had been a loner as a boy, without real friends or close companions? Hadn't this actually strengthened him? He had always concluded that he was shunned, picked on, and bullied because the other students were jealous of his acumen and talents. Where were they now? And even if they managed to become something or someone, they couldn't touch what he had, who he was, what he'd become and contributed to the world! He'd wager his fortune that none of them—neither his classmates nor any graduates in the school's long history—had a net worth or status among the elites equal to his. And it was certain that none had the opportunity for global power that he and Narud were about to realize.

In his effort to bring himself back to his senses and reality, EB had not been paying attention to where he was walking with his annoying spirit guide and had become unconcerned with their trek. But then, jarring him from his mental boasts, a large and long structure emerged as if it was rising out of the ground just next to the ghost as they approached the campus hill's plateau. He lifted his head to see it in its fullness and realized that during his self-adulating they had walked all the way to Wycliffe's center point, the campus chapel. Made of polished white stone, the church was as bright as he remembered, shiny, as marble tends to be when the radiant sun glistens off its sheen. The crispness of the cold day and snow only added to its glowing majesty.

Entering the open front double wood doors, EB and the entity walked through the musty but welcoming foyer into the grand sanctuary. EB had spent much time there as a young elementary student, more so than he would now care to admit. At an early age, even before going to school, EB recalled that he had a sense of the eternal. But it wasn't until he was first introduced to the idea of a Great Benevolent Creator during his first year at the school that he would start using the word "God."

Established by Presbyterians in 1894, the school was founded under the motto "The beginning of knowledge is fear of the Lord," an adage from the book of Proverbs in the Bible. He never quite understood what that meant, but the school made certain that the students were regularly exposed to the teachings of the both the Old and New Testaments, not only in class, but via weekly attendance of a midweek chapel service that was required for all students. This wasn't a burden to EB; in fact, he ate it up in his early years at Wycliffe's. He loved going to the services on Wednesday afternoon, and then again on Sunday. He remembered that occasionally he would attend with friends, but like his bike riding and most other activities around campus, was mostly alone. Regardless of whether with others or by himself, he had been especially fond of the stories of men and women of faith that were told from the pulpit. These stories were always more than just history lessons of a time long ago. For him, they came alive when he heard them, as if specific to him and his needs right then.

He couldn't explain it back then, but felt as though God Himself was speaking to him through the sermons and teachings from the Bible. As he and the spirit stood in the high-ceilinged nave, he recalled several of the great Bible events he had internalized, such as the small and disrespected David coming to the rescue of not only his family, but his whole nation, by slaying the giant Goliath who wanted Israel destroyed. He remembered that, as a young boy, he had hoped he would be like a David.

Or the story of Noah, who also was alone in his time, an outcast who nobody listened to. Noah tried to tell the people of a coming disaster, a great judgment by the Judge of the universe for all the crimes against people and the environment of his day. Animals were subjected to all kinds of cruelty and violence, and people were relentlessly attacking, assaulting, and slaughtering each other. Committed to bring justice, the Creator brought the great flood that wiped out the riotous, murdering, and felonious world. But because Noah did what was right and had a heart to love and serve the Creator, God spared Noah and his family from the deluge. EB remembered that, as he sat in the pews, he prayed he would be like Noah and bring justice to what he was starting to understand was a similarly criminal and violent world.

Using a God-figure was a powerful tool to terrify young boys, EB thought as he reminisced, turning away from the spirit as if this would prevent the spirit from reading his mind. *Even I was manipulated by this religious hexagas! But at least a few seeds were sown and some motivation and commonsense lessons were given through these silly myths and ridiculous fairy tales. I guess in a way I will be like Noah and David bringing global justice by slaying the goliath of the vast conglomerate of climate change deniers with Narud.*

Reminding himself of his and Narud's destiny together made EB feel empowered. While Sunday school lessons had been fine as a young boy, he had long ago graduated from his grade school theism to rationalism and humanism, which, in his high school years, he came to believe was the only worldview that could adequately address and solve the world's major problems. Collective man was the answer, not some myth in the heavens. Only together as one world, socialistically, could the devastating issues of the world be successfully dealt with. And while markets and freedom and rights had their place, they all would have to be accurately defined, meticulously managed, and rigorously regulated through global governance. He grinned at the naivety of his younger years, but saw this moment as an epiphany. He indeed had come full circle.

Maybe this is what the electron entity is trying to show me? EB mused. Possibly, he thought, this was his mind's way of revealing to him that all his schooling was not just for him to become the great technologist and influencer that he was, but to give him vision how to use those talents and abilities to save the planet.

As he and the ghost walked down the church's center aisle, he felt like another Bible hero he hadn't thought of in many, many years: Moses. Here he was walking through the parted dry-wood pews, having escaped the bondage of religion, soon to emerge from the Red Sea of superstition on the other side, leading the world away from its false gods!

Reveling in this flash of inspiration, EB completed his journey and arrived at the front row, where the ghost halted their stroll. On that very first long, bare, and hard pew a lonely boy was reading from a book that seemed almost as big as the child. Scattered on the bench around him were several other classics, tomes that were well beyond his years at that point. EB had learned to read by the time he was three, he had been told, and where most kindergarten boys carried around action figures or toy robots, he would rather tote a book or computer wherever he went—although his toy robots were a close second. He'd built his first, very basic but fully functioning, robot arm when he was five.

The little man on the pew was on his knees, bent over and engrossed in the huge book, using his pointer finger to underline each sentence as he read it. EB had to lean over his childhood and forgotten former self to see what he was so engaged in. The letters were so small, he wondered how the boy could see them. Peering over his first-grade self, he saw that he was reading the Christmas story found in chapter two in the book of Luke, one of sixty-six books of that oversized Bible. His finger was underlining the part where an angel of the Lord stood before the shepherds:

And the glory of the Lord shone around them, and they were terrified. But the angel said to them, "Do not be afraid! For behold, I bring you good news of great joy that will be for all the people: Today in the city of David a Savior has been born to you. He is Christ the Lord! And this will be a sign to you: You will find a baby wrapped in swaddling cloths and lying in a manger."

And suddenly there appeared with the angel a great multitude of the heavenly host, praising God and saying: "Glory to God in the highest, and on earth peace to men on whom His favor rests!"

When the angels had left them and gone into heaven, the shepherds said to one another, "Let us go to Bethlehem and see this thing that has happened, which the Lord has made known to us."

So they hurried off and found Mary and Joseph and the Baby, who was lying in the manger. After they had seen the Child, they spread the message they had received about Him. And all who heard it were amazed at what the shepherds said to them. But Mary treasured up all these things and pondered them in her heart.

Right there, under the word "heart," young EB stopped his finger-guided reading and, lifting his head, whispered out into the empty chapel, "I wonder what Fran is thinking about right now?" Young EB often thought of his little sister, missing her the most of all while at the school. EB remembered how on that day there in the church, he had hoped he'd be able to go home that year to play with his baby sister. He had dreamed that she would grow up to be the perfect sibling he had always longed to have, someone who was his own flesh and blood that would understand him, and not judge him or bully him, but be a family member to have fun with, who would meet his friends and be his best friend.

After a few moments of hopeful thinking about his baby sister, the boy EB put his head back down, closed the giant Bible, and opened one of the other classics that were strewn about him on the pew. With just as much eagerness and curiosity, young EB dove into it and was translated into that author's world.

The illuminated spirit gently touched EB on the arm as he hovered over his younger self, and pointed for him to look over to the church windows. The church had beautiful, very old rainbow-colored stained glass portals lining the upper half of the tall chapel walls, each telling a story from the Bible. The ghost wasn't directing his eyes to these aesthetic panes, but to the plain ones below them that gave a clear view outside, also keeping the chapel lit during the day. There, outside the windows, EB gazed in awe as a parade of characters and figures went by.

"Look there, the one with the long robe and staff in hand. That must be Moses! I was just thinking of him!" EB laughed. "And behind him, do you see it, spirit? There's a great lion. That's

Aslan, and Peter is with him. Yes, yes, spirit, and there's the castle in the background, where Peter will be king! This is marvelous.

"And what's that? Incredible! There's the Wild Thing, with its horns and beard," EB continued in delight. "And Max—he was such a wild and naughty boy. Reminds me of me, a little." EB giggled. "And look, they've put a crown on his head and made Max king—king of the Wild Thing world. This is outrageous! Better than any movie. What a show! And who's next? Ah, there, the boy. He's standing with a really strange man, but you've got to love that outstanding top hat! And the suede overcoat! Of course, it's Willy Wonka and the boy is Charlie with his grandfather. He's won, spirit. Charlie had one of the golden tickets and won it all. He was honest and genuine, and so was rewarded with the grandest of grand prizes—Wonka's giant candy factory. What a story!"

To hear EB expending all the earnestness of his nature on these characters, in a most extraordinary voice between laughing and crying, and to see his heightened and excited face, would have been an earth-shattering surprise, if not inexcusable embarrassment, to his technology and finance colleagues in the Golden Gate City. EB wouldn't admit it out loud, and barely to himself, but he missed the bright, imaginative world of his earlier, simpler, and more hopeful life.

The images outside the window faded together with EB's exhilaration, leaving the tech titan hovering over a boy delightfully absorbed in his stories. "Poor kid!" he said to the ghost in pity for his former boy self. EB then sat down next to him on the pew and, leaning forward, put his hands over his face as if to hide it, and wept. After a few moments, EB stood up, his face now puffy and red, and reached into his sweatpants pocket, swishing around his wet hand for a tissue he knew wasn't there. "I wish . . ." he muttered. "Ah, it's too late. It's just too late."

"What is too late?" asked the entity.

"It's nothing, OK? Well, all right—earlier this evening at the transit center there were a group of boys singing Christmas carols. Hopeful, carefree boys. They actually were very talented! And there they were, instead of playing with their Xboxes or out causing trouble—there they were singing at the top of their lungs songs of joy, caught up in the moment, having fun, full of faith. And what did I do? I mocked and cursed them. That's what I did, like I do to anyone full of Christmas cheer. I should've given them something, you know? It's not as if I couldn't afford to help out a little. They were just schoolboys."

The spirit half smiled and waved his little powerful hands of fire, saying while he did so, "There is another Christmas you need to see!"

CHAPTER 18

EB didn't want to see anything else, especially another Christmas. As amusing as it was to be reminded of his childhood, those days were long gone, dead and buried. This had been a good lesson here at his old elementary, a lesson he'd take to heart to be more supportive of the younger generation, especially the ignorant ones still clinging to their immature dreams. After all, he was a champion of opportunity, employing tens of thousands of young men and women.

Yes, it was true he didn't do anything to charitably help the children of his community and the world, but wasn't that the job of the public school system, into which his sky-high state taxes were being poured? And if they weren't in school, was he not also paying another array of taxes and fees for social services to manage the more needy kids? Maybe there would be a way to bring grade-schoolers into employment, use them to make his company more productive and profitable. Now that was something to think about! Certainly a core value to extract from each according to their ability. But such progressive thinking would have to wait. It was time to return to bed and get his much-needed rest so tomorrow he could tackle the truly important matters of his future with Narud.

Just as he was about to deny the spirit's invitation and make his request to return home known to his host, the tall church sanctuary in which the tech titan and his mighty nuclear power plant of a host were standing began to shrink. All around him it began to compress downward, forcing the stained glass windows to be absorbed into pale white sterilized walls as if they were being sucked into a black hole. The steepled roof flattened out and then, as if a hydraulic press were pushing it down, it descended upon them. At the same time, the younger Ebenezer they had been watching grew larger, gained muscle mass, and developed sharper features—especially his eyes. Once full grown in size, a white coat swirled out of the commotion and covered him from his shoulders down to his shins.

The lighting also changed as the ceiling sprouted long, plastic-encased fluorescents. The windows through which EB had watched his childhood heroes evaporated, becoming whitewashed walls full of charts, diagrams, some shelves and a monitor here and there. Then the pulpit itself underwent a transformation, becoming a table, which then multiplied into table after table, with the pews turning into chairs and stools surrounding the newly birthed tables that filled the room. Last of all, the cross that had been at the front of the church behind the preacher's podium was sucked into the same black whirlpool that took the colored windows and, in its place, an overly large, round, and very plain clock materialized. It's second hand jaggedly jumped from dash to dash, with each jump bringing the ceiling a little further down toward them.

"Help, spirit!" EB yelled in panic as he covered his head with one arm and grabbed the ghost's tunic with the other, thinking they were going to be crushed under the structure's fall. But at about eight feet from the ground, it stopped as quickly as it had started, completing its architectural metamorphosis. EB lifted himself up from the protective crouch he had taken and, looking around, was astonished at where he now was.

"My tech lab!" EB exclaimed, noticing that his grown-up, teenage self was working at one of the tables that had manifested. The metal tables were covered with a combination electronic instruments, circuit boards, testing machines of various sorts, measuring tools, and wires. A spiderweb of cords connected to all the tables were carefully tied together at the bottom of each workbench and hidden under protective covers throughout the room, all routed to a bulky floor-to-ceiling IBM mainframe and an array of server racks in the corner of the laboratory.

The bulky mainframe setup was covered with lights that flickered—some green, some white, others red—and was decorated with strands of electric cords that hung from its inputs. Various measuring devices, storage sticks, and other integrated ornaments were connected to the big iron cabinet's metal trunk. Stationed on top of the machine was a pulsing IEEE 802.11b Direct Sequence Wi-Fi router, flickering like a star as it sent and received data through its invisible 2.4GHz band frequency. Scattered around the array were piles of computer wire, boxes of silicon wafers and electronic transformers, and several unopened packages of imported transistors and diodes. The dull hum of the mainframe and the surrounding electronic equipment filled the laboratory with machine-generated carols John Cage would most certainly have enjoyed. Completing the setting, the smell of burnt plastic and soldered metals filled the air, stimulating a most voracious creative appetite, one EB remembered well.

"Do you remember this day?" the spirit inquired.

EB did indeed as he gazed in wonder at his teenage self who, as at the church, was intently reading, alone, in the high-tech workshop. Inching as close to him as he could to observe what he was so engrossed in, EB saw the young Ebenezer again tracing his finger under a long, complicated equation he had written that seemed to go on for pages.

"Remember? This was the day I had one of my most incredible breakthroughs, ever!" EB said to the spirit, waving him to come see his formulation work. "The technology was so primitive then, but look here. This is when I came to really understand convolutional neural networks in my study of artificial neural networks. I had been poring over Wei Zhang's shift-invariant pattern models as applied to visual imagery analysis. The breakthrough was being able to formulate the shared-weight architecture of the convolution kernels or filters that slide along input features and provide translation-equivariant responses, which he called 'feature maps'!"

Spread out on the table around his workbook was a small library of other physics, computer engineering, and mathematics required reading textbooks for classes seniors at Wycliffe's were required to take to graduate. EB had read them all more than once, being the prodigy that he was. The school recognized his exceptional abilities by the time he was in second grade and quickly moved him up to the level where he would be challenged. Skipping several grades enabled him to enter his senior year at the age of twelve.

Closest to the young EB was a book not part of his school curriculum, however, but one that had become his new go-to manual for answers and inspiration: Carl Sagan's *Cosmos*. The teenager had it opened to the well-used and wrinkled first page, with the first line of the book's first chapter underlined, highlighted, and starred with comments he had written all around the page in the margins: *The cosmos is all that is or ever was or ever will be.* Above that sweeping opening dictum, in a blank space next to the title of the chapter, "The Shores of the Cosmic Ocean," was a quote that young EB had written from Albert Einstein, another mind he had come to worship:

Scientific research is based on the idea that everything that takes place is determined by laws of nature, and therefore this holds for the action of people. For this reason, a research scientist will hardly be inclined to believe that events could be influenced by a prayer, i.e., by a wish addressed to a Supernatural Being.

Absorbed, the younger EB didn't hear the door to the lab open, or the sound of a little girl delicately approaching him from behind. Hoping not to be detected, she snuck up on him on her tippy toes with a huge but mischievous smile. When within striking distance, the girl leaped at EB and wrapped her perfectly crafted little arms around his waist, pressing her cheek on his back. Young EB jumped in such fright that he let out a high-pitched scream as he quickly turned to see who had assailed him and interrupted his deep thinking.

"Hello, my brother!" the delightful child shouted. Fright turned to joy and EB let out another yell, but this time one of jubilation. Then, frantically, he bent down to give his younger sister a big welcoming hug. As he did so, she put her arms around his neck and started kissing his cheek between her laughs and giggles. "My dear, dear brother. I'm here to bring you home!" she beamed, now jumping in place while clapping her tiny hands. "Home, Brother, home, home!"

"Home, little Frances?" asked the teen still squatted down so he could be at eye level with his little sister whom he loved more than anyone in life.

"Yes!" said the child, full of glee. "Home forever. Forever and ever. Dad has changed—something's happened and he's super nice now. He's been so nice to me that he's even agreed that you should come home and be with us. We'll be a family again!"

"A family?" Young EB exhaled, shaking his head. "Oh, Frances, I want that—more than you know. But how? How can that be when Mom is gone?"

"Your mother's death took a great toll on your father," said the ghost quietly to EB who was in astonishment over the scene he had long ago put out of his mind.

"I didn't understand that then. All I knew was that since the first grade, I was boarded up here," EB retorted, waving his hand above his head in a roundabout motion to reference the school and the lab. To him, it had been a punishment. For what, he didn't have a clue. And so, as a boy, it weighed more and more on him that, for some reason, he was responsible for what had happened to his mother, what she did.

"But we can be a family—you, me, and Dad. He said it's OK now; he wants you home," Frances pleaded with him. "We can be a family now, this Christmas—through the entire break, all Christmas long. We'll have the best time, Brother. It really will be a Merry Christmas!"

"You've always been an amazing little woman, Fran," said the teen, standing up from her. Again, as only a child can, she leaped and clapped her hands, laughing and screaming in elation, trying to jump up to give him another hug. But being too little, she could only tiptoe and press her cheek to his belly and embrace his torso. Not waiting for him to bend down again, she grabbed his hand and in childish eagerness began to drag him past the cluttered tables, through the almost monotonous hum of the machines, and finally past the processing decoration whose lights incessantly and randomly flashed, to the door.

"She's such a tender blossom, whom a breath might have withered," said the glowing entity. "And what a heart! How could such perfection be a product of mindless forces and the winds of chance?"

EB could not contain his long-lost affection. "An incredible heart," sniffled EB. "Who can deny it? The most caring and thoughtful in the world! If all people were like her, perhaps I could believe it all wasn't just an accident and there really was a God of love."

CHAPTER 19

Saying those words brought an immediate anger to EB's soul. *God of love? Hexagas nonsense!* EB thought to himself as the healing memories of Frances triggered the mortifying thoughts of the other woman in his family life. *No God of love would have created such a treasure as Fran, and at the same time given me a mother that caused such grief.* EB couldn't stop his mind from stabbing him. While he blamed his father for abandoning him at the school and denying him of a normal childhood, deep down he knew it was his mother who had ultimately been the reason for his neglect and misery.

A woman of extraordinary intellect and beauty, EB's mother's genetic jackpot had been divided between EB and Frances. Fran certainly got her beauty and poise, a radiance that always preceded her. EB, on the other hand, while not ugly, didn't bring any swoons from the ladies for his appearance. Muscular, yet stringy with sharp features—such as his nose that was too long for his liking, or his pointy chin—EB had his father's build and carry. But his intellect came mostly from his mother.

With a PhD in molecular physics from Berkeley, EB's mother was a pioneer in her field, with an inborn capacity to think differently about the universe's foundational chemical properties. She utilized these talents mostly in her work on superstring theory, a conceptual framework in which the point-like particles of particle physics are replaced by one-dimensional objects called strings. And though a recipient of numerous awards and international recognition because of this work, accolades were never her objective. She researched because of a voracious curiosity about the cosmos that had encompassed her entire life since childhood. While her peers were busy publishing and groveling for advancement and approval, EB's mother was exploring and experimenting. This was one of the reasons she went to Berkeley first for her undergraduate and master's studies during the late 1970s and early 1980s, then her PhD. Of all the schools she had considered, Berkeley seemed to have the most open environment for experimentation and toleration, welcoming out-of-the-box ideas.

The student revolution of the 1960s had fascinated her, especially its emphasis on free thinking, free inquiry, free love— really, free everything. As a brilliant woman, she saw the revolution as a gift from the universe to her, giving her the academic opportunities that she thought she otherwise wouldn't have, together with the social liberty to live how she wanted.

Even so, she hadn't come to the school to become a radical. But slowly, like so many of her fellow students, she little by little became absorbed in the single social dogma of relativism that came to dominate the professorial pulpits. The 1960s freedom movement—of music, speech, love, and freedom from the shackles of the past moral and theological constraints—was still the spirit of the day among her fellow grad students. True liberty, said the movement, had no fences, and therefore had no limits. And though her long hours in the lab and research kept her from being fully swept up into the unrestrained hippie culture, her absorption into the seemingly unregulated subatomic quantum world led her to extrapolate, like her fellow counterculture coeds, that the underlying nature of the universe she theorized did translate into an absence of absolutes in virtually everything.

A love for classical music provided another practical guard to keep her from becoming a full-on relativist and beatnik. She admired the bohemian lifestyle to a point, but rejected their disdain for anything and everything that their dropout leaders deemed "imperialistic" or "bourgeois." To her, the beauty, symmetry, and harmony of Bach, Mozart, Handel, and Albinoni reflected the grandeur of the observable universe, even if its underlying nature was chaotic. Though this dualist perspective earned her the personal scorn of her radical peers and professors, even though they were awed at her acumen and astounded by her physics, it's what led EB's father to fall in love with her.

The two met at a choral concert at Stanford, where EB's father was attending business school, or B school, as they called it then. A whiz at finance and math, he didn't spend much time contemplating the stars in the universe, but rather how to become a star in the universe of investing, finance, and banking. His charisma was as powerful as his instinct for profitable investments, one trait EB did come to admire in him. During the concert, EB's dad couldn't help but notice her across the small auditorium. As with most guys that met her, he was first captured by her beauty. Elegantly dressed for the Baroque recital, she radiated what he thought was a dignity and almost royal-like decorum. So smitten was he that, after the program, he pushed through the small crowd, fumbling and stumbling over himself and others to meet her before she could leave. She also was impressed, especially with his boldness to approach her so randomly, and so agreed to a date—something she had thought she would not to do while working on her doctorate degree.

The two had a whirlwind Bay Area romance, full of outings to some of the finest restaurants on the planet—since both were foodies with hidden dreams of owning a fine-dining eatery someday—as well as to the many incredible view spots where they could quietly sit and watch the boats on the water. EB's father's attraction to her only grew from their first date to the point that, after only a few months together, he knew he wanted to marry her. The same couldn't be said of his mother. She really liked him and was impressed by not only his bravado and lightning-sharp wit, but with his practical ability to make money, and lots of it. But she didn't love him. Yet because of a deep insecurity that she would become so engrossed in her research, grow old, and never marry or have children, she succumbed to his aggressive pursuits and married him the year he graduated with his MBA.

She was still in the middle of her doctoral work, but because he had landed a fat cat job with a major investment and startup capital firm, she didn't feel that her long hours in the laboratory would in any way negatively affect their marriage. His new job was incredibly demanding, also requiring him to work long hours as well as do a great deal of traveling. But their time away from each other only fueled the passion they had for each other when together, making their first year of marriage absolute bliss.

It was after that first year that their troubles began. Her research in superstring theory was breaking new ground, and he was making deals that were setting profit records for his firm. On paper, all looked perfect. Their careers seemed anointed for greatness, and though among their peers they became more and more admired, their time together grew more and more fractured. They initially brushed it off, telling themselves that they would make more time for each other just after they leaped the next hurdle, overcame the next obstacle, figured out the next equation, or acquired the next investment asset. Soon their times together were reduced to "gotta run!" in the mornings and "are you awake?" at night when they were in town at the same time, or quick "checking in" phone calls while he was on the road or she was attending a conference. Neither had planned for such separation, but the winds of necessity mercilessly blew them in different directions.

She started to feel the pain of separation first. Not a physical pain, but the pain of loneliness. She wanted her husband there with her to explain to him the breakthroughs she was making, even if he didn't understand a word of it. Eventually, his ignorance of her field also became a point of separation, though she didn't want it to be. They still, on occasion, had incredible moments when together like the great fun of finding a new hole-in-the-wall bar with off-the-charts food, or quick getaways to a vineyard, or rare instances of laughing hysterically together watching *Cheers*. But she needed more, someone who could also understand what she was experiencing. Her experiments were opening her eyes to a whole new reality, a reality that he needed to be a part of. But he wasn't there, and when he was it was often superficial. Fun, engaging, pleasant—but superficial.

And it was in one of those moments of desperation for companionship when she slipped. She had just resolved a conundrum that had long eluded her, and needed to share. She called her husband, out of town again, who was receptive and even supportive of her breakthrough, but clearly didn't see the significance of what she had discovered. He tried, but just didn't have the capacity to grasp it. Her colleague and fellow researcher in the physics department, however, did.

He wasn't an attractive man at all, but was a typical geek—tall and lanky whose glasses were always a little crooked. But his mathematical IQ was off the charts. The more she observed his ciphering abilities and the breadth of his computational memory, the more admiration she had. There was no sexual or romantic attraction to him whatsoever, only a deep respect for his mind and dedication to their work. As such, he understood exactly what she was talking about anytime she needed a soul to hear one of her crazy hypotheses, or get her back on track when deviating from the science.

And so on that late night while her man was out of town signing deals, it happened. She had worked so hard on the puzzle she was absorbed in that she hadn't slept, except for an occasional nap on the lab cot, for three days. Her husband would be gone for nearly a week, so she thought it a good time to just immerse herself while he was away. Unexpectedly, she made the breakthrough, and her colleague was right there to share in the ecstasy. Initially, it was just a celebratory hug, but then became a longer embrace—something he had always dreamed of. She was tired, actually exhausted, and so her senses were dulled and fences down.

She was starving for a connection that was deeper than just passing minutes of hellos or "have a nice day." In that moment of his embrace, she felt that connection, that camaraderie of someone who fully agreed with her, had the same deep-soul beliefs she had. When their souls touched, she was unexpectedly overcome by an uncontrollable passion that was suddenly ignited in her. Her conscience screamed for her to stop, but the free-love spirit of the school pushed her on, assuring her that such a moment like this was ordained by the universe and should not only occur, but be wholeheartedly embraced. Confused, she couldn't help herself and suppressed the part of her that reeled in horror that she was about to break her vows and abandon her fidelity for a moment of pleasure that she knew deep down could not, and would not, last.

But by that moment, it was too late. Relativity overcame what she thought was an absolute, and for the rest of that night, the two doctoral candidates engaged in unbridled lust. When she awoke in her lab next to him the following morning, her heart sank and a deep regret enveloped her, unlike any she had ever experienced. She tried to chalk it up to a bourgeoisie emotion, a tie to old conservative mores that she shouldn't worry about. But the real guilt and shame only intensified. Days passed and the intensity grew. She tried as hard as she could to explain it away, rationalize it, and suppress it, only to find that, like the steadiness of the force of gravity of which she was an expert, it persisted. Something had been ruptured, a tragedy had just unfolded that was beyond her ability to repair. Yet somehow she had to deal with it. Her focus diminished the moment she had annihilated her innocence, and though she could speak the words, do the math, and continue her projects, the lightness of her being had been lost.

After weeks of wrestling whether to tell her husband of her adultery, she hardened herself in the decision that she would not. She knew it would utterly wreck him. From the moment they met, she knew that he loved her like no other with a perfect, selfless love. No matter what the occasion or where they were, he delighted in her. She knew that when he wasn't focused on his work, she was first and foremost on his mind, and that he was always thinking of ways to please her and make her happy. Even in her worst moments, he was kind to her, never speaking a demeaning word to her, nor would he ever in any way belittle her. He had the patience of Job with all her flaws and foibles, even laughing with her at them instead of condemning or castigating her. Always interested in what she had to say, he listened closely and tried to understand her theorems and postulates, even though they were a foreign language to him. And though he was a beast in the boardroom and annihilated his competition both within and outside of his company, with her he was selfless, abandoned, and vulnerable. She had no doubt that he would lay down his life for her.

Sadly, even though she desperately wanted it to be, she didn't have and never had that same love for him. She loved that he loved her so, and truly did melt by the way he looked at her, especially how he gazed into her eyes. He could have done that for hours, but she would always stop him after only a short duration. Not because she didn't enjoy it—she did more than words could describe. But she would turn away because she couldn't return the same look of unconditional perpetual love that poured from his soul. And she always felt guilty for that. Why wasn't her love like his? Was she so flawed that she would never love like that? Maybe that was partly why she made the choice to betray him, because of that guilt. It didn't make it right, but she argued with herself that for whatever reason she had committed such a grievous crime against her partner, she wasn't going to compound her treachery by ruining him.

But about a month and a half after her infidelity, the guilt, which wouldn't dissipate despite all her efforts, was unexpectedly compounded. She discovered she was pregnant. The minute she found out, her heart sunk under an overwhelming fear that the child was not from her husband, but was her colleague's. She didn't feel that way because she and her husband didn't have a healthy and regular sex life. They did. It was an amazing one, and they were very active at the time the baby was conceived. In fact, they had been more than active as one of the ways she was trying to make up for her indiscretion. Though he didn't know why, she went out of her way to plan romantic evenings when he was home, be extra playful when they were together, and do all she could to try to wash away the uncleanness she felt. He was completely oblivious to the reason for her extra efforts, and interpreted the increased attention, devotion, and lovemaking to a new level their relationship was achieving. For him, this only increased the love he had for her, and though he didn't think it possible, made his attraction and desire for her grow deeper and deeper. She could sense that, which only compounded the shame she felt. She wasn't acting or trying to trick him, but knew she wouldn't be like this if she hadn't done what she did.

But the pregnancy presented a completely new variable in the contorted mess. Should she tell her husband? Was she even certain it was not his? Though she felt it, her scientific training demanded that her hypothesis be tested. Genetic parental testing technology had just made a huge advance with the isolation of the first restriction enzyme, making Restriction Fragment Length Polymorphism (RFLP) analysis almost 100 percent reliable. She could get this done at the university—all she needed was a DNA sample from her husband. So, after easily gathering far more samples of hair, saliva, and mucus than needed, she had the test done and confirmed what her gut had already told her. The child was not her husband's.

Once she had the test results, the ultimate decision had to be made. She hadn't told either her husband or the baby's father, and so one option she weighed was just to abort the baby and be done with it. The politics of abortion had become more and more explosive around the country since the *Roe v. Wade* decision in 1973. In many ways, Berkeley had led the intellectual charge during the 1970s to make abortion legal across the country as a woman's right.

Though politically she agreed with this, personally she had great apprehension. As the baby was forming in her womb, she would talk to her child, dream about what the child would look like, and imagine a life they could have together. She tried, however, to push away those thoughts when in doubt about whether to keep the baby. But whether interacting with what was growing in her or shunning thoughts about her fetus, she couldn't deny that this was a baby inside her. Not just a glob of tissue or an extension of herself like an organ. She loved this baby, and with every passing day, the love only increased. She certainly didn't love her kidneys or feel so deeply about a cyst. There was no question that from the moment she knew she was pregnant, a spark of parental love ignited that couldn't be explained.

But were those simply emotions that would pass, possibly the sentiments necessary for the species' survival? Maybe this love she had was only just an excreted chemical compound in her brain that had evolved over the millions of years of human development as a protection mechanism to ensure that babies are guarded. After all, the human species wouldn't last long if babies were discarded when inconvenient. So, even though the feelings were restraining her from aborting the child, didn't prudence demand that she make a rational decision, a decision that would be best for all parties involved? And wouldn't such a decision also be what was best for humanity as a whole?

She felt like her analytical mind was at war with her nurturing heart. If she excluded her feelings, it seemed clear that if she had the baby, her marriage would fall apart and she would have to stop her research, at least for a time. She would most certainly lose her colleague as a fellow researcher and confidant. Together, those factors would potentially derail all the important work she was doing in molecular and particle physics—work that could be historically important to the whole human race. And was she even ready to be a mother? Even if her marriage stayed together, she wasn't ready to take on the twenty-four-seven chore of motherhood. And with all his travel, wheeling, and dealing, neither was her husband prepared to assume the mantle of fatherhood—or so she surmised. Intellectually and practically, aborting her baby seemed the logical way to go and the choice of fewest repercussions. But would this be what the baby would choose?

That thought haunted her every time she justified to herself eliminating the child. Babies don't want to die; they want to live. They are born crying for breath to live, crying for their mother to live, crying for care, protection, and nurturing—to live. How could she make arguments that taking an innocent life somehow was to the benefit of all? She didn't know what her husband would do or what he thought. And even if he wanted to get rid of the child, was that his decision? Hasn't any society that degrades innocent human life to the level of disposable trash eventually destroyed itself? When protection of the innocent is discarded, so, too, is justice. For isn't the very definition of justice to rescue the innocent from evil and preventable harm?

Back and forth she went, one moment convinced she should have an abortion, the next sobbing because she had, in a moment of weakness, succumbed to lust—which wasn't even that enjoyable in retrospect—putting her in this impossible crucible.

Everything changed, however, at about her twelfth week. She knew she would be showing very soon, and so had determined to make a decision that week. That same week also turned out to be the week she was presenting a paper before an international audience of leading astrophysicists. Though her work wasn't exactly in that field, much of what she had been working on regarding particle properties was directly applicable. And the astrophysics community had taken note. For her, this was one of the highlights of her doctoral program, like a championship college game where scouts for the pro teams fill the audience looking for their top draft pick. Also that week, her husband would know if a merger he had been working on for the last year would go through. If it did, it would be the biggest payday of their lives and earn him a promotion to be one of the company's vice presidents.

As she had anticipated, the presentation went flawlessly and she was flooded with messages, and even a few offers, regarding future opportunities and positions. Her life was taking off, but so was the life growing in her. Her husband also hit the ball out of the park with the merger going through, securing his promotion along with a huge bonus and salary increase. To bring another man's child into their home now would be catastrophic. Basking in the light of success and opportunity for both her and her man, she decided she couldn't delay any longer. It seemed the stars were all aligned that she should terminate the pregnancy. Though it broke her heart to think of doing it, she hoped the pain would go away sooner rather than later. But regardless, she was convinced that as long as the pain and shame went away eventually, all would turn out well for her and her husband, two up-and-coming Bay Area rock stars.

In her haste to finalize her solution, EB's mother decided on a clinic close to the university and made an appointment for Friday of their big week. She and her husband had decided to take the weekend off and go celebrate both of their achievements and she definitely didn't want there to be any possibility he would notice the little bump now just barely showing. So she booked a morning time for the operation so she would have time to recover, pack, and be ready to travel that afternoon.

Arriving at the clinic a little early, she was shocked by what greeted her. Though the right to abortion had been law for well over a decade, protests against the procedure had become commonplace, and were only increasing in fervency and number. She hadn't counted on there being many, if any, protestors at this clinic. This was Berkeley, after all, a leader in the abortion movement. But when she saw all the signs and banners that were being waved from the sidewalk, with slogans like "God is Pro Life," "Choose Life, Your Mom Did," and the one that really caught her attention, "Choose Adoption, Not Abortion," she almost drove away.

She hadn't even considered adoption, but maybe that was an option for her. As she parked her car, she continued to think about it and work out the pros and cons of adoption. She would have to tell her husband, of course, but if they put the child up for adoption, she would only be taken away from her work for a few weeks. She knew the school would have no problem giving her maternity leave. She could tell her colleague that she and her husband were pregnant, but they were giving it up for adoption. That way he'd not think first that it was his, and secondly, that she was going to leave him hanging in their research at this critical time. She sat in her car working through scenarios when it hit her—adoption wasn't an option at all. If she was going to go through the entire nine months with the baby, she would never be able to let it go. She could barely handle the thought now, but after nine months of loving the baby, nursing her infant, talking and singing to the child, and thinking of what a wonderful person it would grow up to be, her love would be uncontainable and inseparable.

With that, she exited her car, held her breath, and made a beeline through the gauntlet of protestors, signs, and shouts toward the front door of the clinic. As she walked through, she tried to tune out their comments and calls for her to stop what she was doing and accusations of being a baby-killing murderer. But one young voice caught her ear. She didn't know why, as it wasn't loud or condemning, but was a soft voice of a young woman like her who had somehow pushed up next to her.

"Your baby is special," the young protestor said right to her ear. "The most special thing that's ever happened in your life. And as much as you love your baby, your baby loves you!"

EB's mom stopped in her tracks and whipped around to see the face of the one that said those words. Once turned, she saw the young woman with a friendly smile on her face, just nodding. Other protestors, seeing she had stopped in her quest toward the door, pushed forward and squeezed out the young girl. EB's mother never saw her face again. What had stopped her was that, just that morning, as she was working up the courage to get to her appointment and get it over with, fighting the love and affection she had for the tiny human resting in her womb, she'd had the very thought that the woman had just spoken.

Your little baby loves you, truly loves you, was the whisper she heard in her head while looking at her belly in the mirror.

She quickly swept the thought away and then laughed to herself. *How could a twelve-week-old fetus have love?* she thought. But her quick mind answered her own question. *We are beings of love and feelings. It's innate in us, so of course my baby could have love—as certainly as it can have a heartbeat or experience pain.*

Hearing that young woman say the exact same thing as she had thought earlier, right to her ear, she couldn't go another step. She knew it was true. Although she fully realized that her husband loved her more than life itself, and regretted to no end that she didn't have the same for him, she did have that never-failing, impenetrable love for her baby. It was the only time in her life she experienced that, and it floored her to think that her baby had that for her. This child would complete the love circle she had always longed for. There was no formula or scientific quantification of it, only the total soul experience that one couldn't understand—or express—unless one had it. And she had it. No success or worldly accolades or paycheck could ever even come remotely close to its value, its beauty, its fulfillment. And with that, she turned back just before reaching that door of destiny, climbed back into her car, and drove back to her home, sobbing uncontrollably, but with a new sense of lightness, joy— and relief that she hadn't made another horrible mistake.

There was, however, one mistake she would make. Not wanting to destroy her husband, she decided to lie. When they went away that weekend, when they were in each other's arms, she put his hand on her stomach and asked him if he felt anything. He immediately understood and jumped out of their plush hotel bed and leapt for joy that they would have another member of their young family. After a few moments of jumping around the room in celebration, he fell down on the room's couch and wept with thankfulness. His sobbing broke her. Now there was no possibility of ever telling him that the child wasn't his. After seeing his reaction, she thought such a revelation would literally kill him. She had already killed her vows, and just barely escaped from killing her baby. She wasn't about to put a dagger in his heart after he had been so good to her, and she knew he would be the same to their baby.

And so EB was born, in the best hospital, surrounded by the best doctors and nurses, with what appeared on the surface to be the best parents. But as soon as he was born, something changed in his mother. She could see her colleague's face in the little child, the colleague she had come to despise because he didn't stop himself that night. She didn't either, but both were responsible, and he never took any responsibility. In fact, he never brought up that night again. They never talked about it, and he was clueless that he was the father of a little boy. Her hatred toward him grew and grew as did the uncontainable guilt she felt.

Sadly, her love for EB also turned to bitterness because of the reminder of that night and the reality of his true father. She tried with all her power to try to love EB, and desperately wanted to love him as she did when he was in her womb. But every time she looked at his tiny but extended nose, or his little piercing eyes, she resented him with the same disdain she had for her colleague who had taken advantage of her. Her husband was oblivious to the torture she was enduring, caught up in the bliss of having a new baby boy and their success so they could give him the world. She had never seen him so happy, and he often told her he was the luckiest man in the world with a wife like her and such a beautiful baby. He was so blinded by his love, he couldn't even see that EB didn't look anything like him, except for dark hair, which both he and EB's real father both had.

As much as she tried to contain the torturous pain, anger, hatred, and guilt, it only multiplied, exponentially. The utter contempt she felt toward her colleague would then trigger even more guilt. She wanted to forgive him, but couldn't—or wouldn't. Maybe if he would just approach her and say he was sorry and take some responsibility. But he never did, not once, and instead backed away from her, only communicating with the least number of words necessary for them to carry on their research. Older and further along in the doctoral program then her, within a year of EB's birth he had graduated and moved on, not telling her where he was going or what his plans were. She knew she would never see him again. She thought his departure might lessen the intensity of ill will she had toward him, but instead it magnified it. She was stuck in a lie, and once he left, it was clear that she would have to live wrapped up in that lie, alone, choking on the guilt.

As a scientist and researcher, she didn't have many friends since she spent so much time in the laboratory. Her colleague, before the incident, had been her only close friend. Once his friendship was gone and EB came along, she found herself feeling virtually alone. The couple had found a kind and experienced nanny to help out, who EB's mother got along with wonderfully. But that wasn't the same as a friendship, and there was no way she would risk talking to the nanny about her deep troubles, let alone confide in her the big secret since it might leak back to her husband. She also cut her hours down to be with the baby, which only increased her isolation. Her husband was amazing with the boy, always calling to check on him, bringing home whatever was needed, doing all the shopping so she could take care of him and not be burdened. But he was still away all day at work, and she was alone with a baby she was growing to hate as much as she hated his father.

With her hours at the university reduced, she fell behind on her research. She had been able to smooth over the decline in her performance for the first year, but once her colleague left, who had ended up doing the bulk of the work giving her the cover she needed, the university confronted her. The great promise she had once demonstrated, the international attention she had garnered, the admiration of colleagues she had earned all evaporated. And while she knew it wasn't EB's fault, she couldn't help but blame him for her demise. She became so angry and resentful, she sometimes even would say to baby EB that she wished she had gone through with the abortion. But every time she'd say it, or even think it, EB's loving eyes toward her would remind her that he wasn't the problem, and she'd break down in tears of confusion, turning her hatred onto herself.

Eventually, to cope with the pain and guilt, she turned to medication. First, antidepressants that were prescribed. But as those became less and less effective in altering her moods, she acquired a need for something more to relieve her anxiety, dull her pain, and give her a moment of pleasure in her dark world of hidden hatred and bitterness. Alcohol was the first additional crutch she used, then as that failed to deliver her, she turned to opioid painkillers, barbiturates, sleeping pills, and whatever designer street drug she could get her hands on. This went on for years, hidden mostly, yet still affecting not only her ability to mother EB, but be a good wife as well. Not knowing the extent of her pain and the addiction that followed, her husband became more and more frustrated of her frequent neglect of him, their home, and their child.

EB's father, as he was raised to believe, didn't give up on her though. His love for her never wavered, even during her worst binges or times of acting out. It was a horrible environment for EB, who as an exceptionally keen child seemed to understand there were deeper issues. He, like his legal father, loved his mother intensely, always wanting the best for her. It had always been that way with EB toward her, and there was nothing she could do that would change that. But unlike his father, he knew there was something underneath all her sadness, depression, and anger. His father would tell him that she was sick, that just as someone becomes ill due to natural causes, so, too, was her condition—just a disease that she had no control over. But EB knew that wasn't completely true. He was too young to explain it, and when he did try to probe that line of thought with his father, he was quickly shut down and told that he was just a little kid and didn't understand.

In what finally seemed to be a breakthrough for the family, EB's mother became pregnant when EB was five years old. EB was in a kindergarten program at the time, which provided some relief to his mother having to take care of him. Having a break from him did seem to help her. In a way, it hurt EB that his mother seemed a little happier when he was away, but his inner pain was outweighed by his joy of seeing his mother not as depressed and actually happy sometimes. His father saw it, too, and her elevated state helped the couple spend more quality time together as well, especially in bed.

The nine months of her pregnancy turned out to be the best time EB could remember so far in his short life. His mother stopped drinking completely and had been prescribed a moderate dose of amfebutamone, a bupropion antidepressant that had just recently been approved for market release. Though she still fought with the hatred toward EB that had calloused her heart, for the first time she was able to give him a little of the love he had so deeply craved, though she still had never told him to his face that she loved him. A far cry from the love normal mothers give their children, the little bit felt like a tidal wave of affection compared to the drought in which he had been living.

She also began to smile again, and her husband truly believed that she was on the railway of recovery. *Maybe we should just keep having children*, he thought, *if pregnancy brings such healing and peace.* One time he even jokingly suggested that to her, and to his surprise, she laughed and agreed. Such were the nine months, especially the last six, of her pregnancy. It was far from perfect, but compared to what had been for the previous five years, both EB and his father were overjoyed and couldn't wait to add another member to the family—and then maybe another and another.

The time came for her to have her baby, which her physicians were amazed was so healthy. She had done significant damage to her body over the five years of abusing it, but apparently not enough to affect the little girl that was coming. EB remembered well the evening she went into labor. He had completed a boring day in kindergarten, a grade level he thought useless since they were learning things he had mastered when he was two, and was at home. His father had just come home from work and they were sitting down for dinner when his mother started her contractions. They immediately rushed to the hospital where she soon went into labor.

But what they all were expecting to be a smooth delivery became exactly the opposite. As she went into labor, something happened. The physicians on hand didn't know exactly what occurred, but thought it might have had something to do with the combination of her depression and heavy drug abuse. Even though she had stopped using once pregnant, something was triggered when she went into labor. EB's father was in the delivery room when it happened. EB, who had been told to stay in the waiting area while she delivered, had secretly followed his mom and dad to the delivery room and hid outside the door. No one could have prepared him for what he was about to observe. He couldn't see it initially, but could hear everything—the doctors talking to her, his dad comforting her, and all the other chatter going on in the room. But his fun spying adventure was interrupted when he heard his mother in a panic tell his father to quickly come near to her.

"What's the matter, sweetheart?" his father said.

"I'm in pain—not just labor pain. My heart—I can't breathe," she said, grabbing his hand.

"Doctor, what's going on?" he yelled as he noticed her vitals suddenly going haywire. "Doctor, doctor! Please!"

The physician immediately began checking her and called to the nurse for something EB's dad didn't hear because his mother just then pulled him close.

"There's something I must tell you," young EB heard her say, but just barely, as he stood behind the door. He wanted to hear it, too, but knew he'd get in trouble if he went into the room. But his love for his mother overruled his fear of punishment and he burst through the doors just as she gasped, "Ebenezer is not your son. I'm so sorry. My colleague—it was a mistake. It destroyed me. I'm so, so sorry." At that moment she saw EB out of the corner of her eye and turned and looked at him with the saddest face he had ever seen, but said nothing. The doctor then called out for her to push while simultaneously yelling to a nurse that she was coding. It was mayhem, but somehow she sent EB's little sister into the attending physician's hands with one last push— one accompanied by a gasping, bloodcurdling scream. It was the last thing EB ever heard come out of her mouth.

EB's father stood over her lifeless body in unbelief as the steady single sound of the heart monitor and the wailing of his new daughter blared through the room. After a few minutes holding her hand, he collapsed to his knees and wept, crying to heaven for answers why the one he had loved so was taken from him. "Why, why?" he kept moaning. During those moments, Ebenezer—still standing back against the door—watched his father transform. He could never describe exactly what happened, only that, from then on, his dad was different. The inherent joy and life that he always carried with him and filled any room he occupied was gone. His bright and love-filled eyes went dark. And worst of all for the five year old EB, an anger rose up in him that couldn't be extinguished. EB saw that fury when, from the bedside, his kneeling father turned and stared at him with a coldness he had never shown before. He didn't say anything to EB, but only stared at him, making him feel like a complete stranger.

"Dad, what happened to Mommy? Is she dead?" the young Ebenezer asked, but without a response.

"Get him out of here," the doctor interjected. And a nurse quickly whisked the boy out of the delivery room.

From that time on, EB's father never looked at him the same way or treated him as he had those first five years. It seemed to EB that the only affection his father had and the only concern in his life after that day was toward his new little sister, whom he had named Frances. In fact, it was immediately after that horrible day of loss that his father told him that he would be going away in the fall to a new school, a boarding school where he would live and study. His father told him sternly that he was to devote himself to his studies and not expect to come home, except maybe for Christmas.

Young EB couldn't understand it all, for in his mind he

thought that all his father's anger, aloofness, and apathy was only due to the sadness of his mother dying. He had no idea that now, every time his father looked at him with his long, pointed nose, jagged facial features, and piercing eyes, he saw his wife's quirky colleague, the man with whom his beloved had betrayed him. EB had no idea that this was the reason his dad wouldn't hug or kiss him anymore, and could barely stand to be in the same room with him.

EB was overwhelmed with sadness as well, and being ignored and repulsed as he was by the only one who could really console him made his sorrow worse. His nanny, who by this time had moved in to take care of him and his little sister day and night, was the only one who gave him any comfort at all. But she was so busy with little Fran that she hardly had any time for him other than feeding him and making sure he stayed out of his father's way.

The coldness, neglect, and hostility went on for the months leading up to the day EB was sent away to Wycliffe's, which was also his birthday. His father not only didn't see him off to his new study home, but didn't even wish him a happy birthday before he departed. Only his nanny did as she was tasked with taking him to the airport to drop him in the care of the airline attendants, who, in turn, would turn him over to a school representative when they landed.

EB, for the first time, was away from family, alone, and in a completely foreign environment. There was no consoling parent there to hug him goodbye and reassure him he would do well at the school, or enjoy it. His nanny had tried to reassure him that his new life at Wycliffe's would be a great adventure, with lots of other boys his age that he could play with and study with. And while this appealed greatly to EB, who was being crushed at home, it didn't erase the deep sense of abandonment and rejection that had crashed down upon him after his mother's death. His father hadn't socialized much after his mother's death, and had pulled him out of the private kindergarten for which he had been paying a fortune. EB was so far ahead of his peers that his father didn't see a single reason to keep him there now that his mother, who had been the one insisting he attend if only for the social reasons, had passed away.

This left EB at home nearly all the time only with the nanny and Fran, with lots of time to himself in his room to brood in loneliness and pain. EB loved his little sister with the same love he had for his mother, but there was only so much time he could spend with an infant. And since his dad wouldn't play with him or spend any time with him, he tried to console himself that his school would make things better for him and give him the companionship he would never have at home. Doting over Fran was the only thing he and his dad had in common now, and sadly, was the only time they were together before his uprooting.

CHAPTER 20

"To be forgiven, you must forgive those that have caused harm to you," the illuminated spirit finally said.

"What? What are you talking about?" said EB, realizing the entity not only was aware of what he had been thinking, but knew the whole of his past.

"Fran's incredible heart. It was such a heart of love, made so through forgiveness," the entity pressed.

"Yes, *was*," EB sadly replied.

"She wasn't very old when she died," said the ghost.

"Another proof there is no true justice in the universe," EB replied, shaking his head. "She was only a young woman in her mid-twenties."

"And her child?"

"Yes, only one."

"Your nephew," emphasized the entity.

Uneasy in his mind and shaken, EB answered softly and briefly. "Yes." With his head down, EB had failed to notice that, at that very moment, the pair had left the school and its laboratory behind them and were now back in the busy thoroughfares of the big city, where shadowy pedestrians passed them, around them, and right through them; where shadowy trucks, taxis, and transport vehicles honked at each other as they battled for the lane, and all the rest of the strife and tumult of a real, bustling city enveloped them. It was made plain enough, by the lamppost decorations and festiveness of the shops, that here, too, the holiday season was in full swing with Christmas wreaths, bows, and stars, as well as lit menorahs for Hanukkah and candles for Kwanza. Together, the streets that evening were all lit up.

The spirit stopped at a certain office front door and asked EB if he knew it.

Still trying to shake away his familial tragedy upon tragedy, EB didn't immediately respond.

"A man is not just the sum of the experiences his environment imposes on him," the spirit said, sensing the pain that had resurrected in EB's heart.

"What?" EB replied to the unexpected comment. "Of course he is," he insisted.

"I'll show you," his guide gently assured him. "Do you know this place?"

"Know it?" said EB looking up at the lit sign of three small clouds over the door. "This is Cirro, where I had my first real job in the tech industry."

Without opening the door, they went in, gliding past the front security station and up a set of stairs to the large open work space filled with desks, some stand-up style, others normal where the worker sits, all with at least one monitor on top. At the back of the huge area, abuzz with talk of JavaScript, SQL, and LLVM complier technologies, was the sight of the elder of the group of young professionals sitting in his glass-encased office. Looked at as the bread and water of the company, the elder CEO was small in frame but a giant in energy, leadership, and entrepreneurial prowess.

"Look there, it's old Frankie P!" EB pointed out, relieved to be in an environment of more pleasant memories. "I haven't thought about him for years. This is fantastic; Frankie P is alive again!"

Old Frankie laid down his Montblanc pen and looked at his watch, which digitally informed him that the five o'clock hour had arrived. With a big smile, he rubbed his hands together, adjusted his fine Italian black sports coat, and called out in his high-pitched, attention-grabbing, rich, persuasive, jovial voice: "Yo! Ebenezer! Guy!"

EB's former self, now a young man with both an MBA from Wharton and an MIT doctoral degree in physics, statistics, and data science with postdoctoral work in AI, rose from his desk and briskly made his way to Frankie's cube, accompanied by his fellow datapreneur, Guy.

Only six months old, the San Francisco startup had hired EB as their number three employee with a 10 percent ownership stake to be its lead technologist. Cirro founder Frankie had invested all the startup capital for the company from his own fortune he had earned from his previous ventures, including AutoWorks, Green Socket, and iBoard, which was bought by Apple in its early days, and gave Steve Jobs the idea for the whole "i" product line. But to Frankie, all of those past successes paled in comparison to what Cirro was about to do: change the way data was stored, accessed, and transferred over the cloud.

Focused on giving smaller businesses the ability to leverage the latest in cloud technology using an alternative to costly DevOps teams and the big cloud vendors like AWS, Azure, and the Salesforce Platform, Cirro was positioned to be a giant killer. In contrast to these expensive, dictatorial, and complex behemoths controlling the clouds, Cirro's platform could be deployed quickly and inexpensively, providing complete automation of the ongoing maintenance and security processes. With small and medium-sized businesses making up nearly 90 percent of cloud business, Cirro was about to make the Big Cloud overlords obsolete.

"This was really the beginning of it all for me. We were such a great team!" EB said to the ghost, remembering the monumental turning point for his career when Cirro started to be hailed as the next big thing in data and cloud computing.

"Do you know what time it is and how much work there still is to do?" Frankie brusquely asked his two stars, trying to hide his smile. "I'm afraid we're going to have to cancel this evening's activities and pull another all-nighter. At least you and Guy will need to!"

EB moved up close to Frankie as he began to quiz the younger EB and Guy and waved for the ghost to come close as well.

"Frankie always had such a great sense of humor, which really motivated us. Watch this, spirit. This was one of his little jokes that always kept us in good spirits. It was amazing how he made us want to work hard for him," EB instructed the ghost just as young EB began his reply to Frankie.

"What?" EB's younger self burst out. "Of course we have a lot to do, but we always have a lot to do. Really, Frankie, it's almost 5:00 p.m. and the whole company has been really looking forward to tonight. Look, Guy and I will come back and—"

"Come back? You will do no such thing!" Frankie said sternly as he stared the young EB and Guy down. It seemed a full minute passed as Frankie just poker-stared at the two budding technologists. But just when they were about to fold and announce the bad news to the company, Frankie blinked. "Well, if you are sure that tonight's event will be of benefit to the company . . . then let's get this party started!" he said, bursting into a laugh.

Both EB and Guy busted up laughing with him, thankful that this was another one of his pranks and that Frankie wasn't going to push them to work through the night. In their enthusiasm, the two vivacious doctors fist-bumped each other and scrambled out of the office to the center of their wall-less work area to brief the team. The whole company had been looking forward to the big holiday party planned for that evening, a catered extravaganza

Frankie and his wife had planned not only to celebrate the holidays, but to thank the team for their incredibly hard and successful work over the last six months.

"Fellow workers and geniuses, may I have your attention," EB hollered. "Please, take your fingers off your keyboards and try to refrain from completing your latest lines of code. Thank you."

Immediately, everyone in the room, and in the other areas of the sprawling office watching EB's announcement on their monitors, quieted their chatter and halted all their work.

"Thank you," EB said, smiling. "As you all know, our work over the last six months has been nothing short of spectacular! Let's review what's happened in this short time. First, after only three months in operation, we achieved Bay Area Startup of the Year. Then the next month we made *Forbes* Top 10 Companies to Watch. And then just last week—and this may be the most significant of all . . . yes, wait for it—*Wired* magazine put us on their cover as the Next Big Thing in Tech! Google, Amazon, IBM, Microsoft, and all you Big Tech Cloud controllers—we have you in our sights!"

The company employees roared in approval, jumping out of their desk chairs, high-fiving each other and chanting, "Cirro, Cirro, Cirro." Motioning for quiet after allowing a few minutes of the employees' self-adulation, young EB continued.

"We'll have much more to say about this later this evening. But for now let's just say that six months ago, we were all trying to figure out how to pay the ridiculously high rents we all have living in this city. Some of you doubled up, others rented bed space in row house garages. And as you all know, Guy and I opted for our luxurious army cots in the back room. Thank you, Frankie, for not charging us rent for those!"

The room of young geniuses nodded and laughed as Frankie took a bow.

"But today . . . today! Thanks to the businesses that have lined up to implement our solution, our valuation has skyrocketed faster than even Facebook's did only a few years back. So now our most pressing problem seems to be that we're all trying to figure out which million-dollar flat we're going to buy!"

Again, wild cheers and chants, hollers and high fives.

"Fellow laborers," EB continued, now shouting over the top of their hurrahs. "Every single one of you is now a multimillionaire! Now let's go celebrate that together! The band is already playing, so all of you turn your systems off, shut down your mental processors, and get over to the Top of the Mark for what will undoubtedly be the greatest holiday party of your life!"

Young EB smiled as he looked over the young army of marketers, engineers, programmers, and project managers, all ecstatic and well deserving of not only the party, but the fortune that had befallen them. Before making his way back to his own desk, he glanced to the back of the room where Frankie's glass box was positioned, and nodded, not at Frankie—who was himself cheering and clapping with the group—but at Frankie's secretary, Belle.

Truth be told, everyone in the room wasn't awash in newfound wealth. There was one exception, Belle, who was the only one who didn't have company stock and options. But to young EB, she was the richest in the room, an elegant beauty who seemed to care nothing about money or success. During his six months at the company, EB had been watching her. Not just because she was drop-dead gorgeous to him, but because he saw that Belle found an unexplainable and euphoric pleasure in just serving, whether in assisting her boss and staying after hours to do so, or running menial errands for coders whose train of thought couldn't be interrupted. Whether just keeping the copy machine full of paper for the whole company or running back and forth from the printer across the street, Belle did whatever was needed of her with amazing enthusiasm, as if she was having the time of her life, which she actually was. Such an attitude brought everyone else into her bliss, especially when it was accompanied with her contagious, disarming smile that had no regard for reward.

Frankie's wife was equally a part of the success of the company, always at the office helping him in whatever way she could, at least until the early afternoon. Each day she left at around two o'clock to pick up their twin daughters from school. But during the four or five hours she was at the office, she put her twenty years of marketing and PR skills to work. As a PR phenom, she knew many people around the city and was probably better connected than Frankie. It was her idea to reserve the entire Top of the Mark restaurant that occupied the nineteenth floor of the Intercontinental Hotel for the big party.

Having the entire restaurant closed for a single group was almost unheard of. Top of the Mark had space for parties and private events, but almost never would close completely. It had happened only two times before. The first was when the president of the United States gave a speech there and had it closed for security reasons. The second time was a private event for the top executives of IHG Hotel and Resorts, the parent company of Intercontinental.

Somehow Frankie's wife made it happen for a third time so that the luxurious establishment with some of the best restaurant views in the city belonged to Cirro that night. Determined to make it a night of history, she had the entire restaurant decorated in the red and green colors of Cirro, which tied in nicely to Christmas. The holiday was only a few days away, and was of all holidays the one she and Frankie loved to celebrate most. She also had all the tables moved out of the elevated center area of the restaurant to provide a wonderful open space for Cumulus, one of the most popular bands in the world, and for the dancing that would undoubtedly extend into the early hours of the morning.

A connoisseur as much as she was a mover and shaker, she personally selected the menu for the evening, a royal feast fit for the new Cirro kings of data. Displayed buffet style so everyone could enjoy as much as they wanted, the salad and appetizer selections included the restaurant's best, among them artichoke velout, fava bean salad with mushroom carpaccio, and seared hokkaido scallops over roasted leeks with amarosa fingerling potatoes finished with white caviar.

For those wanting a more filling plate, poached striped bass was beautifully presented and an excellent option for the pescetarians of the company along with pasture-raised chicken roulade and maple-brined kurobuta pork chop in its natural juices festively garnished with balsamic glazed strawberries and apples. To top off the feast, and as a special Christmas offering, were several full-body ducks roasted and carved to preference with a pickled radicchio, fennel marmalade, and huckleberry sauce for topping.

Frankie, in his never-ending humor, added the ducks as a nod to one of his favorite Christmas television programs: *A Christmas Story*. He even had a large picture of Ralphie's face, complete with his large glasses and unforgettable smile, printed and displayed next to the table with the ducks as an advertisement for the party raffle, which of course featured an official Red Ryder, carbine action, 200-shot, range model air rifle, with a compass in the stock as well as a sundial that told time.

"Everyone wanted the Red Ryder," EB explained to the spirit, who had instantly teleported them from the office to the Top of the Mark to join the party. "And as funny as the ducks were as the main course, they actually tasted incredible. There were six of them, as I recall, and all were gone by the end of the evening."

"You all had such fun together, building the company and relationships," the fiery entity replied.

"We did, and Frankie made it that way. He was always so generous, even when we didn't know if we would make it as a company in those first couple months. He and his wife always brought catered meals in to us when we worked through the night, or would advance funds if needed for unexpected expenses. And the benefits! Wow, there was nothing like them at the time—full health, medical and dental; the game room for blowing off steam; and unlimited soda and water bottles! That was one of the reasons Guy and I slept there so much—it was better than going home to a tiny, run-down apartment for sure."

"But all this spending, all that excess use of electricity, and the plastic water bottles . . . it's so wasteful," the spirit interjected with a sarcasm EB missed. "This is why we're in the mess we're in!"

"Mess? This is why the company succeeded! Frankie had the power to render us happy or unhappy, to make our days of work light or burdensome; enjoyable or unbearable. If you could put a price on all the positive words he said to us and all the forgiving looks—in things so minor and insignificant that it would be impossible to add and calculate their sum—what then? The success he fostered and happiness he gave would far surpass the personal fortune he sank financially into Cirro."

Proud of his analysis, EB turned away from the ghost and found his way up the couple of wooden stairs to the center area of the restaurant where Cumulus was playing one of their big hits, and the employees were dancing away. Before long, EB was caught up in the partying and soon was acting like a man out of his wits. His whole heart and soul were back in that scene, and with his former self and the other employees he danced and laughed and sang, paying no attention to what he would have looked like if he could have been seen. Several times while partying, he forgot he was only an observer and tried to join conversations on the dance floor or at the buffet table. Being ignored, he laughed at himself for continually forgetting that his presence was only ethereal, but nevertheless swirled on to the next group or area to enjoy the company of his comrades.

His one final moment of lapse, however, was in an attempt to say something to the beautiful young woman who had been standing to the side of all the fun, like an overseer making sure nothing lacked at the party. She radiated in the city lights that flowed through the large view window where she was standing, and looked far better than EB had remembered. With the TransAmerica pyramid outside the window and below her in the background, she stood and twirled her hair with her fingers as she talked with his younger self. EB wanted to say something both to her and his younger self, and so bolted to the corner table area where they were conversing.

"Listen, both of you . . ." EB said, trying to tap his younger self on the shoulder but of course finding his hand to pass right through him. The two continued, uninterrupted, laughing and flirting as the band played. Again realizing his foolishness and the futility of his effort, EB sulked away back to the ghost.

"There was something you wanted to say to Belle?" the spirit inquired.

There was much that he wanted to say. For it was that night at the Christmas party—at least that's what Belle called it, Christmas being her favorite time of the year—that young EB had come to realize he didn't want to be with anyone but Belle. She never fully understood why someone as brilliant and now successful as EB would be interested in her, but she wasn't going to fight the all-encompassing and overwhelming attraction she had for him as well. Even his nerdy look and the little bit of relational awkwardness he still had were appealing to her. Not until they dated for several months did she learn that she was his first real relationship. He had been out with a girl here and there while in his master's and doctoral programs, but nothing more than just friendly dates. He had been so focused on school, he told her, that he didn't make time for girls. But when he saw Belle that first time in the office, his synapses exploded and he knew he wanted to get to know her. He just didn't know how to go about it.

It took EB months to work up the courage to ask her out for a date, and though he had overcome much of his social clumsiness and isolation habits of high school, he didn't have a clue how to approach a woman—let alone such a beautiful one as Belle. What he didn't know was how much she admired him all those months, and how attractive he was to her—long nose, pointy chin and all. When he finally did ask her if she wanted to go for a drink after work one day, she leapt at the chance, having prayed he would do so.

They immediately clicked and shared everything about themselves with each other, from their dreams, favorites, and peeves to their deepest secrets and fears. One thing EB told her that she found incredibly hard to believe was that he once was a bullied loner with no friends. At the company, ever since she had known him, he was exactly the opposite. He had transformed dramatically and was well liked by all, but also respected and even admired, making him the company's clear second in command under Frankie. EB was the captain, under General Frankie, that kept the ship afloat, organized, and always moving forward. Unlike at Wycliffe's, at Cirro and in the city's entrepreneurial community at large, everyone looked up to him as a new breed of innovator with vast knowledge, strong character, and a rare trait of being able to bring the widest assortment of people together to get things done. Whether solving an immensely difficult computational problem or smoothing the way for two prima donna engineers to work together, EB had the gift.

Their romance was storybook, especially after the holiday party. Though they had been dating for a couple of months before the party, it was there, surrounded by their friends and colleagues, overlooking the city with some of the finest food and music in the spirit of Christmas, that it all just seemed to come together. Within a year, they were engaged, having been deemed the Bay Area's perfect couple by their peers and the nosey tabloids of the city.

For EB, it was surprisingly easy being in such an amazing relationship. Since he hadn't had one before Belle, he had nothing to compare it to, nor any baggage that would tarnish what they had. The same was true for Belle. Though she had dated quite a bit in high school and college, she had only had one serious relationship previously with a boy she would have married if he hadn't died in a freak skydiving accident. Losing him had brought her to realize how precious life is and how quickly and unexpectedly it can be taken. From that point on, she cherished her friendships and family overall, living life with them to the fullest and never taking time with them for granted, especially with EB. He had never had the kind of love and attention Belle gave him before, the kind completely opposite from what his mother had given him. And while he relished her doting, affection, and concern for every aspect of his life, subconsciously he didn't know what to do, how to respond, or, most significantly, how to return such devotion and loyalty. If there was a crack in their relationship, this was it. But it was only a crack, EB would assure himself, failing to realize that, as with a windshield, if a crack spreads, eventually the whole window shatters.

"You had something important you wanted to say to her?" the spirit again asked after seeing EB was in deep thought about her.

"No, it's nothing," EB replied. "I just wanted to say hello, that's all." Time then seemed to accelerate before his eyes. Within seconds, all the employees, including himself and Belle, were gone; the band's roadies had packed up all their equipment; and the restaurant workers had finished removing the very little extra food and restored the dining tables back to their positions on the dance floor. The lights dimmed and only EB and the spirit remained.

"My time grows short," said the entity. "We must go, now!"

The spirit's command produced an immediate effect and again EB was conveyed to a new but familiar scene with his younger self. Only this time, he was several years older and though his face didn't show any of the harsh and rigid lines of aging—he was still in his prime—it had begun to wear with signs of stress and avarice. His once calm yet bright and enthusiastic demeanor had transformed to one of eagerness and greed, and there was a restless motion in his eyes—always moving to the left when conversing, never able to look at someone directly. Nor could he sit or stand still, but always had to be in motion, either pacing or checking his watch or phone, or motioning with his arms and hands. Rapacity had taken root, sprouting into a showman always seeking attention and admiration. And here, at a large table conveniently close to a well-stacked bar, he was surrounded by admirers, both men and women, hanging on his every word as they tightly held their glasses full of Christmas libations.

"Spirit, why bring me here?" EB asked once he recognized the familiar swanky surroundings.

"You don't remember this pivotal day?" the ghost replied, pointing him over to the table where his charismatic self was performing.

And like a bolt of lightning from the heavens, the memory of the evening struck him. He didn't want to be there, let alone listen to himself that Christmas Eve, wowing his inebriated followers at the table. The younger, rougher EB was also intoxicated, maybe even more so than the others, which only encouraged him to expound on his latest achievements and boast of his recent takedowns. There were more people around the table listening than there were chairs, many more. A number of patrons had come over from other tables, and still more from their barstools when they realized EB was in their midst. Having graced the cover of nearly every financial, technology, and business-oriented periodical by that time, EB had become a powerhouse figure in the city, a young billionaire mogul, a true shining star of material success.

It was rare for him to be out in the city like this, at a ritzy bar conversing and disclosing. But it was Christmas Eve, and though he had plans to be at Belle's for Christmas Eve dinner later, he had decided to go to Happy Hour to loosen up to get him through another boring meal with his fiancée. He figured there would be others like him at this establishment who, instead of participating in some meaningless ritual, would be having some fun and talking about important issues, like how the city had become the epicenter of the world's technological revolution— which they had ignited. And he was correct. The place was packed with young and old, all successful or wanting to be, geniuses from around the world. And while EB wasn't the only big name in the joint, he was certainly the biggest deal.

"Soon will come a day, and I mean very soon—not way off decades from now, but in a few short years you will all be able to go anywhere you want, attend any function, or be anyone you want . . . virtually," young EB preached to his inebriated congregation around the bar table. "We are very close to a virtual reality experience that will be indistinguishable from reality. I'm not talking about a Matrix-like prison, or a rule of Terminator machines over man, but a whole new experience where you could be anywhere—like right here at this table—but actually be at home in your Pod."

"You'll be able to eat and drink in your Pod helmet, and so could pour yourself a pint, and literally sit here with us, drink—even get drunk! Do whatever and not know that you aren't really here," EB continued, lifting his just-refilled glass to a toast and then chugging it all down.

And so he continued to prophecy about the future and what he would accomplish to better people's lives and the planet, drawing even more around him as newcomers entered the bar. And with each prognostication, he would lead the crowd in a toast, sometimes as they gave him a round of enthusiastic applause, and then downed another drink.

"It was as if I was God speaking to them," EB said to the spirit as he pointed to all the people leaning in to hear him. "I had them wrapped around my finger."

"Especially her," the ghost replied.

The woman the spirit had pointed to had been there since EB first arrived and found a place right next to him. Her name was Jenni Rene, a bland but fiery redhead who had recently come to work for EB in his new venture. After Cirro went public, EB, Guy, and of course Frankie all became billionaires. As with many newly public companies, new executives were brought in, and EB—by his own insistence—moved into a consulting position in Cirro, largely just a figurehead. This gave him the time he needed to start his own company with another Bay Area phenom with whom he had become close friends, who had also hit the jackpot in a computer venture: Jacob Marley. The two together became unstoppable and redefined the technology landscape.

EB didn't personally hire Jenni Rene, but once she caught his attention in their large and thoroughly modernist office complex, he couldn't take his eyes off her. It wasn't that he was interested in her; he wasn't. Nor was she exceptionally attractive. She was plain and freckled with an almost pouty look. Regardless, she had a way about her that did something to him—something very different than what he had with Belle. It was a visual fascination for sure, but also something more. Something deeper inside, which felt like a hook that had dug into his soul and was pulling him in.

This strange infatuation continued to increase over the months as the whole company worked hard and often stayed late trying to build another mega success. Jenni Rene was always there, and saw that EB was always looking at her. As it turned out, that was her goal all along, which is why she always wore the shortest skirt allowed to the office each day. She had a great body, especially her legs, and she knew it, and after all the months of trolling, had finally hooked EB with it. She also accentuated her ruddy face with the brightest red lipstick EB had ever seen and regularly flaunted very tight and accentuating shirts or, if in a loose blouse, deliberately made sure the top three buttons were undone.

Completely the opposite from Belle, Jenni Rene was also very aggressive and forward, unapologetically going after what she wanted. Normally, that assertive and overbearing style by a woman in business was a complete turn-off to EB. But when translated into her flirting with EB, oddly, he found it melted him. At one point, Marley even warned EB to watch out for her, knowing that though EB was true to Belle and had always been, he was still just a man and clearly Jenni Rene was after him. Self-assured EB disregarded his advice, however, thinking of her more as a type of red licorice for his eyes that was there to be enjoyed. For all the work EB was doing and all the time spent at the office, he deserved a little treat—but for his eyes only, he reasoned.

Since the eyes are the window to the soul, however, EB's visual fascination soon grew to an irrational obsession. A genius and mogul in science and business, EB was a novice with women and their guiles. Belle had been his only true love, and as such, kept EB from having any interest in other women, in and out of the office. Not because she was possessive or demanding, but because she trusted him, adored him, and made EB feel indestructible. He didn't even look at another woman in all their time together at Cirro. But that all changed after Cirro went public.

Thanks to EB convincing Frankie to allocate a generous number of company shares to her before they went public, Belle decided to quit Cirro after her payout, thinking it would be better for their relationship for her to focus on getting ready for their wedding and having a family. EB and Belle had worked together every day until that point, but once she had left, EB started to feel vulnerable. Not in building his business, but in interacting with women. Neither of the two had realized how much they depended on each other, and needed to be around each other. This was especially true for EB. But instead of asking Belle to come back and join him and help him in his new venture, he decided to explore his new freedom and build his new venture without her.

At first, it wasn't really an issue for EB. There was the usual banter around the company about this girl or that woman, but nothing that distracted or even remotely tempted EB away from Belle. Then pale Jenni Rene showed up. And it wasn't just her short skirts and open blouses that drew him in like a moth to a flame, but the way she always pompously, yet seductively talked to him. EB couldn't explain it, but he was entranced with her sharp, manipulating yet arousing words, regardless of what she was saying. And with Belle not around, EB could spend all the time he wanted looking, listening, and lusting after her.

Although he didn't fully expect it, her being at the bar didn't really surprise EB. He wasn't at all disappointed and thought this would be a good first time for them to interact outside of the office. Belle was at her apartment cooking dinner, and so there was no chance of her catching EB talking with Jenni Rene. And even if she did, he was only talking. There was nothing wrong with a little verbal flirtation, was there?

As he continued to stand in front of the long wooden bar table, waxing and drinking, he would look down at her and smile. No doubt she had deliberately positioned herself right next to him so when he looked down, he could see directly into her blouse. While at first he tried to guard his eyes from peering, the more he drank, the more difficult it was to control them. By the second hour of what was turning out to be a very happy hour for him, he stopped trying to leash his wandering eyes and just let them loose.

EB had picked up a few other habits since his big payday, including dabbling in drugs. At first it was just a little marijuana with Marley at his pad. When he and Jacob became partners, EB knew Jacob had a substance problem. But his work ethic, smarts, and just the way they were always on the same page together caused him to overlook what he thought was just a little foible. One night while the two of them were working late, Marley offered EB a hit off a joint he was smoking. He'd offered before, but EB had always refused. But this time, he had been fighting with Belle earlier and was stressed about their situation. He felt she was pressuring them to finalize what had become a five-year engagement and get married. Although he wanted that at some point, he didn't like it when she pressed him. So he inhaled to calm his nerves. From there, he and Marley began to enjoy getting high together more regularly, something Belle found out about and strongly disapproved of. But EB thought it not only relaxed him, but gave him a mental boost in the creative areas where he knew he was lacking. So, knowing Belle wouldn't tolerate it, he decided to hide it from her. And since they didn't live together, it was easy to do.

Not long after he started using weed, mostly in edible forms or vaping since as a scientist he knew very well the carcinogenic nature of smoking, he decided to try cocaine. Again, Marley was the instigator. He never pushed it on EB, but as they spent more and more evenings together working on their new venture, EB would become envious of Jake who seemed to have an endless supply of energy, not only throughout the day, but even late into the night. He finally accepted an offer from Marley finding that not only did it turn him into the Energizer Bunny, but gave him power that he didn't otherwise have. And even more exciting to him, it eviscerated, at least while he was high, some of the insecurities with which he had always struggled. Belle again noticed there was some kind of change, but decided not to ask specifically what the cause was. She chalked it up to the new business and all the stress, challenges, and difficulties associated with starting up a new tech enterprise.

From her position seated below him, Jenni Rene noticed EB's eyes enveloping her, and returned the gesture by tapping him on the leg when everyone else was clapping for him, or gently but discreetly rubbing her foot on his calf under the table. EB felt both moves, but having put down at least eight drinks by then, didn't think too much of it other than that it felt good and was probably just an accidental brush.

"I didn't realize it before, but Jenni Rene was deliberately doing that," EB said to the spirit, pointing to her clearly conscious efforts to seductively touch and rub on EB.

"Not only does alcohol dull the senses; it lowers inhibitions that keep you from foolish and harmful actions," the ghost replied.

"Don't I know that. Can't tell you how many times I've learned that the hard way!"

"I can," the entity pointed out as the younger EB excused himself from the table and made his way toward the men's room.

After finishing his business, young EB stumbled out only to see Jenni Rene standing just outside the bathroom door.

"Let me help you," Jenni Rene said to the inebriated EB as he almost lost his balance.

"No, no, I'm fine. Just a little tired," he replied as she wrapped her arm around his waist to hold him up.

"You've had quite a bit to drink, boss," she seductively said. "Are you sure you're OK? Here, let's walk it off." With his arm over her shoulder, she led him out the back door into the nearly pitch-black alley behind the bar and started walking with him while rubbing his chest. "Just a little walk and you'll be fine. Don't worry, I'll take care of you."

They continued down the alley away from the bar just far enough so no one who might come out the back way could see them.

"No, no! Stop!" the elder EB yelled, trying to get the attention of the two shadows strolling into the dark. Running after them, he put his arms out as if to tackle his younger self, but as with the shadows before, went right through him, tumbling to the ground in front of them. The two walked right over and through EB as he lay on the ground pleading with his younger self to go back to the bar.

"Spirit, can't you help him? Look what she's doing to him!"

"The past can't be changed. It's fixed as sure as your Cirro payout was fixed," the lighted being reminded him, igniting to a hot glow.

The two shadows then stopped, or more precisely Jenni Rene stopped them both and pressed him up against the alley wall.

"What are you doing?" young EB slurred.

"Here, this will give you some energy," she replied and pulled out a little vial from her purse filled with white powder.

"No, I didn't for need it now. Just, I be should getting back, for the bar," Ebenezer said incoherently.

But she pressed the vial up to his nose, from which he willingly took a big sniff. Then she did the same. She guided him a couple more times until she could see it was coursing through him, bringing him to life. When she saw that his eyes were focused, she started to unbutton his shirt and press herself up against him.

"Spirit, why make me watch this? I have regretted what happened here every day since," EB mourned as he looked down putting his head in his hands.

"A part of you died here in this alley. She's a destroyer, who feeds on men's souls. But you fed her yours—willingly. And so it is here that your life was forfeited and credibility shattered. For a man dedicated to fulfilling contracts and who expects business agreements to be honored to the letter, in this instance for a fleeting moment of pleasure, you broke your most sacred promise, a commitment more inviolable than any financial transaction conducted on earth," the ghost said.

"Shattered? I've engaged in many transactions and secured some of the most lucrative contracts on the planet after this event!" EB spouted, angry at the spirit's word. "And that occurred because people trust me, because my word is my bond. I have never violated or not fulfilled an agreement which was properly signed and executed."

"Except for your promise to Belle!" the entity said sharply.

"That's different," EB defended, but in a lower tone.

"You are correct. It is different because it rises to a level infinitely higher than that of your moneymaking, which deals only with things. Your betrothal wasn't some business dealing for you to profit by, a contract to manipulate for your own glory, or an arrangement that you get to decide when and how it is to be conducted, and at what cost. Your true veracity, fidelity, and loyalty are in your keeping your promise to this girl, who loved you, much more than in your honoring a scribble that enables you to accumulate more objects to feed your ego. Your engagement involved not a material possession, but the heart of another human. Her very life was in your hand."

Stunned, EB turned fully away from the sordid scene in the alley and begged the spirit to take him away from there. After many moments of enduring the debauched moans and grunts of his younger self's vile degeneracy, the entity obliged and transported them to their next destination. There, relieved to be away from the shameful sight and degrading sounds, he again found he wasn't alone, but stood in front of the beautiful young Belle whose eyes were filled with tears, sparkling in the light that radiated out of the ghost of Christmas past.

CHAPTER 21

"I guess it doesn't matter much to you at all," she said softly. "Probably not at all."

"It does matter," the younger, but tired EB rejoined. "I don't understand what the problem is. It seems we have this conversation so often now."

"The problem? You don't see that your work has consumed you, and that it has completely displaced me?"

"Please, Belle. My work has not replaced you or displaced you. You're the reason for my work."

"I've heard this before, and we've gone round and round on it. You say that I'm the reason for your work, but you're not around anymore to demonstrate that. And when you are around, you only want to talk about your work, global warming, and the ecological disaster that you think is imminent, or all the deals you've made, all the money you've accumulated, or how great your new company is."

"Well, that is all true. But regarding climate change, someone has got to do something about it."

"You see? I've been replaced with an idol."

"What nonsense are you talking about. What idol?"

"A golden one, or maybe its green. Your self-worship and exaltation believing that you have to be the one to save everything. You have a messiah complex, EB."

"If everyone who cares about this planet and its future just simply said, 'Oh, the other guy will do it,' or 'She'll take care of it, so I don't need to do anything,' where would that leave us? Nothing would get done. That's not a messiah complex; that's being responsible."

"And so it has to be you, twenty-four seven, that is responsible for it all? You don't speak tenderly to me anymore. You hardly take me out or spend time with me. For the love of God, we're engaged, EB! If I didn't know better, I'd think you'd cheated on me and have another woman you're hiding."

"I haven't cheated—there is no other woman," EB lied. "And the love of God has nothing to do with us. If there was such a divine being of love, I wouldn't have to worry about our planet like I do. And I wouldn't have to work so hard, start the companies I've built, or make the money needed to keep it all going."

"You don't see it. This is the new you, EB, the real you. You're using ecology as an excuse for your own self-aggrandizement, as a way to pacify your conscience that is screaming at you that you've changed, become uncontrollably greedy, obsessed with becoming rich, and caring more about the greatness of your bank accounts than the greatness of our relationship."

"There's nothing wrong with being wealthy! Who builds and donates to the charities that take care of the poor? Who pays the lion's share of the taxes that fund welfare services and brings justice to our communities and country? Who builds companies that create jobs so people can eat, live, have families, and enjoy life? It's me! And others that are wealthy. Those of us who have been gifted by the universe. You've never understood that about me, Belle. You think I'm greedy when I'm just market smart and able to outmaneuver other competitors to bring about a better product or service to the benefit of all. That's what free enterprise competition is all about."

"If only that were you, EB. What charities have you built or supported that don't feed back into your own goals and businesses? You're interested only in charities that make you richer, in pocket and reputation! And your concept of justice is the justice of sweet backroom deals, bribing officials, and undercutting fair competition through intimidation, blackmail, government bribes, and corporate espionage. Don't play the 'free market' card with me, EB. I'm no dummy. I've watched you over these years we've been together, and your market is anything but a free one. It's a black one, full of corruption, cronyism, and kickbacks!"

"You're so dramatic, and you're overexaggerating. Every company needs to use whatever means are at its disposal to maximize profits. That's the American way—shareholders come first. And shareholders are concerned about one thing: profit. No profit, no share value or dividends. As long as it's not illegal, it's fair."

"You mean as long as you don't get caught. There is such a thing as right and wrong, good and evil, that transcends laws and regulations that can be manipulated, distorted, and misinterpreted. I have a good mind to go to the authorities with all the dirt I have on you and your wonderful, planet-saving and -connecting companies. All the lying, cheating, corruption, and deception I've seen. You'd be in prison for ten lifetimes if it all came out. You pretend to be an upright free market capitalist in character and community, when in actuality—and you know what I'm saying is true—you're a criminal, a voracious socialist wolf in free enterprise clothing."

"You're treading on very thin ice, Belle!" EB shot back, shocked at her. Then, taking a seat beside her, he looked directly into her eyes. "I think it's you that has changed. You never used to be like this, worried about all these little things. You liked the lifestyle I've given you with all the travel, celebrity schmoozing, and corporate events, not to mention all the presents."

"That's because I was in love with you! But to my shame, love blinded me."

"*Was* in love with me?"

"Oh, EB, I would be in love with you if you were in love with me. But you're not. Your first love is your green empire, and it's turned you dirty brown. You love the regulations that have been legislated that protect you, give you the advantage that you and your big-money and technology pals have bought politically, swelling your net worth beyond the heavens."

"This is how the world works, Belle."

"Only a world that has bowed the knee to corruption and sold its soul for a fleeting paycheck. Such is not my world, at least not anymore. And it wasn't your world when we met! Our love then was pure, sweet, and perfect. It's only this selfless love we had, a sacrificing love where I put you before me, and you do the same, that can bring true happiness in marriage and life. Think about it, how happy we were when we were one in heart! But now we live in misery, endless fighting, wanting to be away from each other. It's because we are two, now, not one. Something changed in you, and whatever you did, it shattered our bond."

"Perhaps we are two now," EB agreed, remembering Jenni Rene in the alleyway, while also realizing for the first time that over the years Belle had seen and come to know too much about him—and could ruin him.

"And so I ask you, what does it profit you, EB, to gain the whole world but lose your soul, and me and true love with it? Tell me, if this great love had never been between us," said the sad girl, looking up at him through blurry eyes that had wet her cheeks, "would you pursue me now as you did before in our days together at Cirro?"

EB paused, though only for a second, but to Belle it was an eternity.

"I didn't think so."

Internally, he relented. Perhaps he had permanently broken their bond. If that was so, then it was true that she could no longer travel at his side down the path of glory he was determined to take. "Apparently, you're convinced of that," he said with a struggle.

"I wish I could believe that you would," she answered. "God knows how I want us to be as we were, when we worked together—not for money—but for the joy of doing something meaningful in the world, focused on the Golden Rule, not accumulating gold in order to rule. It's clear that you don't want that anymore, and even more clear that if today I was the penniless secretary as when we met, you wouldn't give me the time of day. So it is with a full heart for the love of the man you once were, but broken by what you've become, that I say goodbye, EB."

He motioned as if to reply, thinking he should perhaps stop her, beg for another chance. But realizing the choice at hand— her or his mission—he said nothing. And so they parted.

"Spirit!" said EB. "Enough! I can't relive any more of this! It's as if you delight in torturing me. Please, take me home."

"One shadow more!" exclaimed the entity.

"I'm serious, you goblin, no more!" cried EB, trying to escape his guide. "Enough is enough. I don't want to see anything else, not another second!"

But the relentless and incredibly powerful small entity stopped him in his first stride and submitted him by subduing both his arms behind his back, forcing him to observe what happened next.

During the struggle, they had transported to another scene and place—a driveway flanked on both sides by a large and beautiful tree-filled, snow-covered yard. The driveway was long and wound about in a "u" shape in front of a pillared front porch and then back out to a quiet suburban road. Next to the house they stood in front of, but not too close, was another house and then another, all down the road, each with a front yard, a driveway of some sort—some u-shaped, others straight—and a unique entryway. None were very large or luxurious—these weren't estates or McMansions—but nicely crafted three- or four-bedroom family homes, all brightly decorated with lights, some blue, some white, many green and red, most with displays of stars, reindeer, or crèches, and all full of children and comfort.

"Where are we?" EB barked, still trying in vain to free himself from the entity's iron grip. "I've never been here before."

But before he could finish his sentence, the two were inside the welcoming home, standing in the living room filled with the smell of fresh pine from both the local-cut Christmas tree filling a corner and the winter fire burning what must have been logs from the same forest.

In front of the warm blaze sat a beautiful young girl, so similar to the one he had just seen that EB thought she might be the same one, until he saw the girl's mother, now a radiant woman, sitting opposite her daughter. The noise in this room was a chorus of high-pitched laughs, shouts, screams of delight, and imitations, for there were other children there, probably the whole neighborhood, which were more than EB could or wanted to count in his agitated state of mind. Running to and fro, they were playing wildly with each other. But per the mother's instructions, they were also extremely careful not to spill over into the tree area where there were stacks of wrapped presents. The performance was uproarious beyond belief, but controlled, with the kids pretending to get knocked down or pushed a little only so they could sneak over near the presents and touch one, or move it a little to try and ascertain its contents.

The one-room town of little humans was clamorous and

hyperactive, but no one seemed to care. On the contrary, the mother and daughter laughed heartily at their tumbling, teasing, and trickery, enjoying it—so it seemed—as much as the children. So much so, the older daughter soon began to mingle herself in their play, only to be immediately grabbed, piled upon, and tagged most ruthlessly by the playful gang as they initiated her into their gaming.

"I'm home!" came the call from the front door, echoing thunderously into their play room; and without missing a beat, like an army responding to its captain's call to charge the enemy, the troops turned as a single unit and rushed the unsuspecting father, whose arms were filled with grocery bags and even more wrapped boxes, which could only hope to find room to park in the overflow area under the tree. Before he even had a chance to close the door behind him and free himself of his cargo, the defenseless carrier was overwhelmed with an onslaught of shouting and struggling, with some of the little warriors scaling him from the hall bench, which they converted to a ladder to pillage from the plastic sacks and despoil him of the colorful paper-wrapped parcels. Others wrapped themselves around his legs and rode them like a horse. Only the most agile made it all the way to his summit where they halted his march by hugging him around his neck. The ones who didn't make it in time to scale the giant reinforced the others, circling him with their little hands clasped, singing in irrepressible affection "Ring Around the Rosie."

After the long battle, which the father had lost before it even began, being forced immediately to the kitchen, the little army retreated with their spoils of candy canes and green or red foil-wrapped chocolate Christmas drops. Satisfied in their victory, and exhausted from the evening's nonstop action, the little fighters were divided up into two camps: the neighboring kids who were promptly bundled up by the daughter in their little coats, gloves, and hats and sent on their way, each with a bag of booty; and the smaller battalion that lived there at the home. Once their comrades were safely on their way, the members of the smaller squad were stripped out of their uniforms, dressed in their pajamas, and tucked into their bunks, all four of them.

After the groceries were put away and more wood added to the fire, the remaining three sat together on their puffy, pillowy couch in the golden silence that had finally descended onto the battlefield. EB watched this part more attentively than ever, as the master of the house, with his arm around his wife, and daughter leaning fondly on him, basked together in the soothing glow of the friendly, waving flames. EB couldn't help but think that there could have been another girl, different in look but as graceful and as full of promise, who might be resting on his lap, calling him father.

"Belle," said the husband, turning to his wife with a smile, "I saw an old friend of yours this afternoon."

"Who was it?"

"Guess!"

"Well, let's see. Was it in town?"

"Not our town; no, it was in the city."

"You drove all the way to San Francisco today? No wonder you were gone so long. That's more than ninety minutes away. Oh, I know," she added in the same breath, laughing as he laughed with her. "Ebenezer!"

"Yup! EB in the flesh. I went to the new complex on Telegraph Hill—well, apparently, it's EB's new mega complex. It's really incredible, Belle, completely different from the old museum and tower that used to be there. There are some incredible specialty shops there, and from what I was told, EB's company occupies all the top office floors."

"Was there a specialty shop there that possibly had something for me?" Belle asked, teasing her man, but only partly.

"Don't ask questions at Christmastime!" he teased her back, giving her a kiss on her forehead. "I'm not going to tell you what shops I went to, but while there I meandered over into the grand entry area where all the murals from the old tower are still on display. There's a coffee bar there, so I thought I'd grab a latte before the long drive home."

"Wait, you skipped the part about what you bought for me!" Belle again prodded, this time causing her almost-asleep daughter to giggle.

"OK, I bought a—" he started.

"No, don't tell me!" she interrupted, covering his mouth with her hand and causing all three of them to burst out laughing.

"Alright, then, back to EB. I was waiting for my cup of coffee when the elevator that goes up to the offices opened and there he was, hollering at someone at the top of his lungs. The whole place heard it. From what I could make of what he was saying, the young Asian guy he was yelling at must've been one of his programmers or something. He was technical in some way since part of what he said was in tech speak. But he was very upset and just railed on the guy, belittling him there in front of everyone in the area."

"Why doesn't that surprise me?" Belle replied, snuggling in closer under her man's embrace.

"And he said something about Marley—that was his partner, right?"

"Yes, he was part of the reason."

"Yes, I remember now. Pathetic, the two of them. Anyway, he said something about Marley having just died—some kind of horrible, unexpected death, and all the pressure he was under now, and that the kid he was berating didn't understand that

Marley gave his life for the cause. It was really an awful scolding."

"Well, as bad as Marley was, I'm sorry to hear of his death. There was a really nice side to him, but like EB, he got caught up in the glitz, glamor, and glory—and just lost it."

"So what happened to the guy he was yelling at?" Belle's daughter chimed in.

"Oh, yeah. So EB is ripping him a new one, and the kid just sits there, nods his head, and takes it. When EB's finally done, the kid apologizes and walks as fast as he can away from the elevator. EB steps out, and in that moment, there was no one else around that elevator area. In that very moment, EB steps out and looks around, then up, like he's looking for someone or something. Everyone else around had scattered because of his outburst. And so there he was, standing alone, all by himself looking around aimlessly."

"I guess it really is lonely at the top," Belle replied.

"Exactly. It was tragic, having everything but nothing. Admirers, workers, and people all around him, but there he was alone—all alone in the world."

"Spirit!" said EB with a broken voice. "Remove me from this place."

"I told you these were shadows of the things that have been," said the entity. "They are what they are!"

"I get it. What do I need to do to have you get me out of here?" EB exclaimed, pushing himself right up into the being's face of fire. "I can't handle it!" But this time when he looked at the ghost, he didn't see the usual flame-formed demeanor of light and love. Rather, it had transformed, morphed somehow into a strange montage of fragments of all the faces it had shown him. Triggered, he launched at the entity and wrapped his arms around it, trying to wrestle it to the ground.

"Leave me alone, you beast! What are trying to do to me? I

demand you take me back and end this nightmare at once!"

In the struggle, though it shouldn't really be called that since the spirit exerted no visible resistance on its own part and was completely unmoved by any of the efforts of its adversary, EB observed that there was more light than usual radiating from it. Still in his robe, which he had worn through all of the events, EB released the completely ineffective hold he had on the ghost and, in a flash, took the robe off and with all his might and strength that he could muster, threw it over the spirit's blazing head. To EB's shock, the spirit immediately dropped beneath it, so that the robe covered its entire little form. He pressed and wrapped the waist tie around it and then pressed down even more with every ounce of force he could exert. But though the being was covered, its light could not be hidden as it streamed out from under the finely woven garment in an unbroken flood upon the ground.

He tried to spread the robe farther to cover it and spread his body over the top of it when he finally got it to lie flat on the ground. But all the effort was to no avail as the light continued its flow, refusing to be extinguished. So he held it there, lying on top of it for some time. How long, he didn't know—until he had extinguished his own strength and was thoroughly exhausted, overcome by an irresistible drowsiness. Just as he was about to relent to sleep, he realized he was not at his former love's house anymore, but back in his own bedroom, facedown on his robe, which was now covering nothing but a part of his ultra-plush carpet. To make certain it was gone, he gave one last push on the robe to see if any more light might seep out from under its sides. Nothing. And so, with just a microdose of remaining energy, he staggered to his bed and sank into a heavy sleep.

STAVE 4

SPIRIT TWO

CHAPTER 22

"Wake up, EB. It's 1:00 a.m.," the smooth voice of his alarm kept repeating until EB's subconscious finally processed the sounds and unwillingly released him from his deep REM sleep that had been accompanied by long, roaring snores. Awake, he shot up into the sitting position, but only half aware of where he was.

"Get away from me!" he yelled as he thrust his fists out to beat the air in front of him. Finally realizing he was alone, he pushed himself back against the headboard and pulled his covers back up to his chin.

"It is now 1:00 a.m. Time to wake up, EB. The time—"

"Genius, off! Now!" EB finally replied, cutting off his electronic servant's alert. Taking in a deep breath, EB looked around, noticing his curtains must have been shut since the room was almost pitch black. Almost, because out of the corner of his left eye he could see there was a bit of light that shouldn't have been there. The small ray involuntarily resurrected the dread that had suffocated him when Marley's ghost invaded earlier, paralyzing him to his mattress. Even his head was petrified to the point he couldn't turn it to investigate. For a minute that seemed like an hour, he sat in perfect stillness trying to wish it away.

"Genius, all lights off!" he commanded, even though he knew his AI house butler had nothing to do with it. After another few minutes, EB finally mustered the courage to look and slowly turned his head toward the sparkle that had been just out of his sight range. Like a frightened child, he kept his comforter pulled all the way up over his chin so that, to an outside observer, only his turning head—like a scene out of *The Exorcist*—was visible as the mysterious light illuminated it. Once fully rotated, to his relief EB observed that the beam of light was not another entity as he had surmised, but was coming from under his closed and locked bedroom door.

"What the hexagas?" he muttered to himself. When EB designed his penthouse, he had gone to great lengths to ensure that his bedroom door was sealed, making all light from the other side impenetrable, as he also did with his blackout window curtains.

Will this nightmare ever stop? EB wondered, continuing to stare at the thin ray of light outlining his door. *I'll be damned, but I know I took care of that meddling little ball of fire and snuffed it and its burning head out like the cancerous spent butt it was. Now it's back? Or is this the next visitation Marley prophesied? Hexagas hell!*

EB's mind was churning again, spinning back to the arguments he had gone through before. Was all that he had just experienced actually only a dream, a hallucinatory nightmare? Maybe he really was having a mental breakdown, or had a brain tumor or some mental disease that was inflicting him. After all, mental disease did run in his family. But his brain wouldn't settle as he reminded himself that the detail was too incredible and the events he experienced weren't absurd or destructive as a disease-produced hallucination would be. Nor were they jagged, incoherent, and without a thoroughly reasonable foundation. Though he suffered emotionally because of what he saw and had just experienced, it was a healing suffering, only destructive to the hardness of heart he had fortified over the years.

Also, the travel back in time didn't pry him from reality, but compelled him to face what was precisely his past, contemplate it, understand it, and reconcile with it. No, to submit to the idea that the visions he had just walked through were only elements of a dream, hallucination, or consequence of a disease or breakdown, he would have to acknowledge he was now in such a state, indeed that his whole life was such a diseased delusion. What happened was real, as real as he could ever know reality. All his senses confirmed it, as well as all his reasoning power. Internally, if he was honest with himself, he knew all he had just been through was true.

But that truth was only internal to himself. He was satisfied with that, but scientific inquiry demanded that something external to himself be found that could verify all of this. The cameras he had set up could certainly provide some of the proof he still sought. But proof would only confirm what he already now knew. Yes, video of the entity would help the world believe him, but it did nothing to explain the purpose for it all. He needed a context, a reason why he should suddenly be assaulted spiritually and overrun by otherworldly entities and these very particular events of the past. What was the aim and objective for his epic journey through his past life? And what kind of entities were haunting him? Answering these questions was critical to understanding the whole affair. Were they spiritual beings? Extraterrestrial biological entities? A combination of both?

After five, then ten, then twenty minutes of wrestling with the questions, EB advanced no further toward a solution. But his mental workout did elevate his spirits a little as he realized that, though he still didn't fully understand the who, how, or why of all the appearing, disappearing, and teleporting around, he did understand that, somehow, he wasn't at all harmed.

Isn't this in itself a clue? he thought, concluding that if the beings had been physical beings like himself, like extraterrestrials, wouldn't he have been burned by that last entity with its fire and strength? And, unlike abduction accounts he had read about or seen portrayed in movies, he wasn't probed or prodded in any way. There was no spaceship and no plot to destroy the earth. And if Marley was a deceiving alien, wouldn't there have been some remnant of injury after his encounter? Marley came to warn him—what was it? He was pleading for him to change his ways so as not to be chained and condemned as Marley was. There was no history of an alien bringing this kind of message.

He patted himself all over his body to confirm he was all there and uninjured, and indeed he was, not even a scratch. And that gave him just enough courage to investigate the light that shouldn't be beaming from under his door. Sliding out of his bed, his bare feet landed not on his carpet, but on his robe.

"Outstanding!" he said out loud to himself as he felt it all over, discovering no holes or burns. Happy it hadn't been damaged, EB wrapped himself tightly in it again, like donning armor before battle, and secured the belt with a half knot.

"Genius, open the door," EB ordered boldly.

Complying in perfect obedience, the locks unlatched and the door slid open revealing his living room lit up by what he thought was the glow of his fireplace. But before he could figure out what the light really was, a booming, thunderous voice, like a summons from heaven, called out to him, terrifying him but strangely also, at the same time, comforting him and making him feel safe.

"Ebenezer. Ebenezer! Get in here!"

It was much more powerful and explosive than the previous entity's voice, and EB very slowly obeyed. Normally, he would have lashed back in embarrassment that his true full name was being used. Neither he nor hardly anyone else ever called him anything other than EB, except for his family. And they were all dead. But the majestic deep bass revealed a much greater power and authority than himself or anything he'd known, making him feel like an ant or speck before it.

"Come in! Come in and get to know me better, you old goat!"

laughed the voice in a rich, deep, contagious laugh that immediately took away the sting of its jab at EB's age. EB didn't consider himself to be old at all, and being in such excellent physical condition, people always mistook him for being much younger than he was. But the entity's poke was truth, a truth he hated thinking about, but now for the first time acknowledged to himself. *I am getting old; I really am.*

Once his eyes adjusted from the darkness he had just exited, he saw that the voice's owner was even more mighty in appearance than imagined, so much so that EB involuntarily dropped to one knee and bowed to the magnificent being.

"Stand up, Ebenezer!" The entity laughed thunderously. "Bow only before your Programmer, the Great Engineer of the universe. I, like you, am only a creature."

"You're Hulk!" EB blurted out without thinking as he gazed up at the smiling giant, who, even sitting, had to be at least twenty feet. Above him was not the room's ceiling as would be expected—that was gone—but a canopy of crisscrossed tree branches, through which EB could, for the first time in days, see the stars glistening. The being certainly bore a resemblance to Hulk with his massive stature, clearly defined muscles, and totally green complexion. But different from the comic superhero, this entity had long hair, like Thor, that fell to the sides of a burly beard. And instead of a hammer, the spirit carried a giant torch that emitted the same kind of eternal flame and light as that of the previous entity, illuminating the room EB could now see had been completely transformed. And instead of tattered brown pants, this Hulk wore a full-length green robe that revealed his massive pectorals and perfectly blended with his forest-green skin and dark brown hair. He was the most splendiferous creature EB had ever seen.

Ah! EB thought. *I'm sure I can cut a piece of this Hulk's hair at some point, or a bit of his beard. Or clip a swatch of that marvelous robe.* But checking his pocket for the evidence-gathering tools he had stored earlier, he found they were gone. *Hexagas! I must have lost them while being whisked about by the last spirit.* By this point, however, EB didn't much care anymore about trying to assemble a trove of evidence to prove that this majestic monarchical entity, and what he was experiencing, was real.

Like any king, the green goliath had a crown. But it was not the type of typical human kings, made of gold or platinum, or luxuriously decorated with gems or other rare stones. Rather, the giant's diadem was unfathomably beautiful, a wreath of perfectly woven holly branches from which emanated horns of unmelting icicles that sparkled like diamonds in the radiance of his torch.

Surrounding the monarch, EB's living room had become a rain forest kingdom, defying the perimeters of the room, extending as far as EB's eyes could see. It was not an ordinary type of rain forest or garden, either, but one of thick ivy, dense green brush, and vine-filled trees surrounded by lush foliage and innumerable flowers, the kind found in a tropical paradise. Also in this magical grove, there grew giant holly plants with juicy clusters of red berries in the centers of the prickly leaves, and mistletoe sprinkled with white berries, as well as huge pines of every sort with the most exquisite cones.

Mixed in were berry bushes with wondrously large ripe strawberries, blueberries, and raspberries—berries of every kind—along with a plethora of fruit trees bearing gargantuan fruits of all sorts, bending their supporting branches nearly to the ground. And the smell of it all was astounding, invigorating, elevating; so pure, so fresh, like a spruce-filled hillside, with hints of sweetness, spices, and cinnamon. Everywhere around EB, lights were glistening and leaves sparkling so the entirety of the scene, he thought, was like the most beautifully decorated

Christmas display imaginable.

And at its center sat this gargantuan angel on a kind of throne formed from the winding vines and branches of the forest—natural tables for a feast that would be expected for such a king. Heaped up under him were, in a perfect spread, turkeys, duck, sides of beef, poultry, leg of lamb, chops, fish of all kinds, along with shrimp, king crab legs, giant lobsters, raw oysters, and long wreaths of sausages, kabobs, bratwursts, and kielbasas. Every conceivable vegetable—potatoes, broccoli, carrots, corn on the cob, halved roasted brussels sprouts, green beans, peppers, zucchini—in all their glorious colors complemented the meats, as did plates, baskets, and trays of fruits, fresh-baked pies, cakes, and custards. Together they made the chamber, and EB's fears, dim in their delicious steam.

What a marvel, thought EB as he gazed around, and breathed in, stunned at the symmetry and order amid the delightful diversity. *I sure hope Genius is recording all this on the security surveillance cameras.*

"I can only be seen by you," the jolly green giant said, knowing EB's thoughts.

"And what an incredible sight you are," EB replied, trying to cover up the disappointment and embarrassment.

"You have never seen the likes of me before!" he said with open, welcoming arms.

"Never," EB replied, noticing how free and bright was its genial face, its sparkling eyes, and its unconstrained demeanor. For all its might and outward bulk, it had a contagiously joyful air and remarkably cheerful voice, even though inhumanly deep and low.

"I'm the spirit of the present, your present, Christmas present," it said. "You've been expecting me?"

"I'm trying not to expect anything. Everything that's

happening is completely contrary to all I think and know."

"How do you really know anything, EB?" The giant smiled.

"My question exactly!" EB replied, sensing the being asking in warmth and care, not cold skepticism and cynicism like that which filled his own soul. "Marley did say that I'd be visited by three entities. The first came and compelled me to see the memories that I had put out of my mind long ago, giving me a master class I'll never forget. If you are continuing the lesson, can you do it so that when this is all over, I can monetize it somehow? That was part of the reason I had hoped the cameras were recording all this."

"Take hold of my robe!" the ghost said with a piercing look, not one that condemned EB, but pitied him. He then stood up, exceeding the height EB had imagined he'd be when fully upright. Standing well under his knee, EB grabbed the goliath's green garb and held it as tight as he could.

Instantly, the rain forest orchard, its peaceful delights, marvelous aromas, and divine feasts vanished, and in its place the two stood on a dirty platform in a cold, dark tunnel that smelled like an uncleaned, well-used latrine. People were scurrying around, some nervous, it seemed, or anxious, some coming, others going. The rest were just standing in guarded fashion checking their watches or the embedded digital displays in their wrists, or were being harangued by the lifelike eBeja-brand holographic billboards, or listening to their music via their implanted ear pods blasting their audio that was streamed from their PPCs. The crowds were much smaller than usual, and for a very few there was somewhat of an air of celebration surrounding them, belied by their smiles and wrapped packages they were carrying. Others were at the shops or newsstands or food vendors that punctuated the tunnels, hurrying to buy, eat, or grab a cup of morning coffee. But whether buying, selling, shopping, tuning in, tuning out, waiting, or rushing, all had a single purpose in this suburban BART station: get somewhere else as quickly as possible.

Part of the Yellow Line, and hub for the new Purple, Pink, and Brown Lines, the Pittsburg / Bay Point Station had mushroomed into the major transport center of the expanded BART system serving the congested and densely populated northern boroughs of San Francisco. Once only a transit station serving the middle-class suburb, it had grown to become the largest BART port, carrying and transferring more travelers than even Union Station or the SwarmTrooper Transit Center in the city.

The meteoric change came as a result of the massive population explosion of the 2020s and early 2030s, which followed the frequent lockdowns of P1 and P2, especially P2. But that was only a small part of the population upsurge. After recovering from the Second Pandemic, California completely opened its border with Mexico, dismantling any border checks or enforcement against migrants from the south. To ensure that as many migrants could come as desired, the state deployed its own National Guard–like force to assist the border crossers to their new home and prevent the federal immigration and border patrol agents from operating and enforcing federal law in California.

As part of its post-pandemic revolution, the Golden State also imposed a tri-county mandatory welfare program onto Alameda, Contra Costa, and Solano Counties, which provided free housing, free food, free transportation, and free drugs for anyone at or below the poverty level. The generous, state-funded program ended up attracting tens of millions from around the country, forcing the state to consolidate the counties into boroughs of San Francisco. Then by exercising its eminent domain powers, the city, with legislative approval and the governor's signature, seized all real privately owned property in the three counties. Once all residential property was transferred from private to public ownership, sweeping redevelopment plans and housing projects were implemented to accommodate the poor and desperate masses that streamed into the region from all corners of the US and across what once was a southern border.

Initially optimistic that the social experiment would create a truly diverse, inclusive, and equitable community, money was poured into all areas of redevelopment, especially Bay Point Station. The expansion of the Bay Point Station would be critical to accommodate the transportation needs of the new most densely populated area of the nation. But as with most political pipe dreams and promises, the new borough and Bay Point Station fell far short of the slick public relations propaganda of hope and change that had been publicized. Instead, the entire region, including the station, became a money pit and was soon overrun with the poorest of the poor, which the tri-county relocation project couldn't accommodate.

Whole sections of Bay Station's underground catacombs had to be blocked off for the new homeless to erect their tents or cardboard track homes. And with them came the uncontrollable litter, dirt, urine, and feces that had once been reserved only for downtown San Francisco. Violence and crime also exploded, requiring more and more resources to be dedicated to law enforcement than had been planned. Within only a few years of what had become known as the Giveaway Gold Rush of the Twenty-first Century, California's central planners' and their fathers' dream of creating a poverty-, disease-, homeless-, and ignorance-free utopia became an uncontrollable nightmare from which none could awaken.

"Where are we?" EB demanded of the giant who had somehow shrunk to fit in the dim tunnel.

"We're in the Promised Land," the green goliath said with a

laugh. Amazingly, as he laughed, the frightened people within earshot of him seemed to be relieved and relaxed a little, some actually cracking a smile.

"Promised Land? This place is a toilet!" EB complained. "And I'm about to vomit. The stench is unbearable!"

"Follow me and don't let go of my robe," the entity replied, ignoring EB's grumble.

Leading him down the platform, the giant's torch at one point ignited into a spotlight revealing in the huge open area and down the tunnels a massive hidden population tucked away in the corners, squirreled behind the bends, and sheltered under the stairwells. There must have been thousands in just that one area.

"Incredible! Do all these people live here?" EB inquired.

"This is only one of dozens and dozens of communities like this," the giant replied. He then waved his torchless hand and opened a window in the air in front of EB through which he could see from a bird's-eye view the legions of colonies of wrecked lives and indigent ruin. It reminded EB of refugee camps for those displaced during war, only worse. There were no bathrooms except the public ones for train riders, no showers or food lines, no medical tents or NGO offices to seek assistance or aid. In the vision, which would zoom in on one group, and then zoom out again, EB saw the rampant drug use and piles of discarded syringes, baggies, and aluminum cans turned into pipes. Garbage and debris of all types was pushed into corners, piled up against walls and scattered wherever space could be found. He could hear the coughing, groaning, and weeping; a dull hum interrupted only by the sound of the trains coming and going or the digital billboards incessantly hounding the train riders to take advantage of their one-time-only deals.

The giant waved his hand again and the window closed, but behind it was another site the ghost motioned for EB to see.

Under one particular set of stairs was a group of souls huddled together trying to stay warm in the chilled underground cavern that apparently was their home. A blue tarp was jerry-rigged from a protruding piece of metal and strung over them to an adjacent pillar. Though it gave them some privacy from onlookers scampering up the stairs, it did nothing to shield them from passersby either boarding or exiting the trains. A one-room bungalow, a rotting old blanket served as its carpet with crates and old mats spread out somewhat creatively to serve as chairs and beds.

Three small children with dirty bare feet and faces were huddled together under another blanket, this one not as worn as the carpet. One of the kids was coughing—a deep and wheezing hack—and couldn't stop, sometimes retching, despite many pats on the back and sips of water from a dirty, dented bottle given to her by her mother. Like her children, the mom was shoeless and dirty, with matted hair and a sadness on her face that only a mother who can't properly feed and care for her child can display.

On the other side of their underground penthouse was a man with a long, scraggly beard working on something that looked like a radio. He was pulling parts out of it and separating them into piles of similar objects he had stored in old plastic containers. Unlike his woman and kids, he had shoes—old and worn sneakers—but not matching, and a cap to cover his head instead of a blanket around his body. The cap had a US Army emblem and matched his camouflage jacket. A small, ripped American flag hung from one of the corners of the tarp just over his head.

Seeing the family, EB tugged on the giant's garb. "Where are we, spirit? Have you transported us to some third-world country? If so, look, there's an American there under the stairs and it seems he's with his family. Those poor children. Perhaps they could use our help," EB suggested.

Altering their course, the giant glided over to the family's abode and waved his torch over their domain, sprinkling what looked like a fine dust or mist that lightly descended over the family. Instantly, the children were warmed and crawled from under the blanket, as was the mother who began combing her fingers through her hair in an attempt to untangle it. The man put his partially dismantled radio down and crawled over to his children, who for no reason began to giggle and hug him.

"Train arriving in two minutes!" an overhead speaker broadcasted as EB watched the family scene unfold. Surprised by the announcement, EB looked up at the speaker, then around him noticing that the holographic signs, living billboards, and BART maps were all in English, a plain fact he had somehow missed before, or been blinded to.

"We're in America, still in the Bay Area!" EB blurted out to the spirit.

"I told you, we're in the Promised Land!" the giant jovially replied. "This is the dream from your fathers, the change you believed in, funded, fought for, and are now rewarded with!"

Just then a young woman sprinted by them screaming at the top of her lungs. "Help, help me!" she cried. Not too far behind her were two hooded boys, young men really, chasing her, one carrying a knife that became visible from the giant's torch.

As the woman darted past them, a siren sounded, the kind heard in wartime to warn of an air raid and red lights began swirling over the platform. "Alert! Alert!" followed the alarm from the overhead speakers. "Disturbance in progress. Alert! Alert!"

"Do something, spirit!" EB barked. "They're going to hurt her!" And before the final syllable left EB's mouth, the green being waved his torch over the heads of the galloping hoodlums, dousing them with a dose of the torch's sparkling dew. The two would-be assailants instantly stopped in their tracks and looked at each other as if having just been aroused from some kind of trance. The bigger one, who was carrying the knife, dropped it in a panic. After a moment of just standing motionless staring at each other, the two turned and ran back into the shadows from where they had come.

The siren, spinning emergency lights and alarm warnings, ceased with an announcement immediately following. "The train is arriving. Move away from the tracks!" People began to jostle into position to board it, having not even glanced at the terrified girl or her chasers.

"That's quite a torch you've got there," EB said, looking up at the giant and pointing to it. "When this is over, I'd like you to consider sharing the technology with me. An innovation like that could transform the world, and be extremely profitable!"

"The price of its power is far more than you can afford." The giant smiled, stooping down to look EB right in the eyes. "More than all humanity's wealth from all ages combined!" He laughed. "But at least you've perceived how the world can *really* be fundamentally transformed."

With that, the goliath scooped up EB in his oak tree–sized, sculpted arms and in a flash transported them from the subterranean settlement to one aboveground, surrounded by a large fortress-like wall.

CHAPTER 23

"Where are we now?" EB asked after taking a deep breath of the cold but much cleaner air in which he and the giant stood. Though bringing in all that chilly oxygen into his lungs was a little painful, it paled in comparison to the discomfort from the dank toxicity he had just experienced.

"You should recognize it," the ghost replied.

EB looked around in an effort to find something familiar among the rows of modular, yardless homes, but could not. He examined the street signs and looked up as if to gain some bearing from the sky, but only saw a few scattered clouds and the sun rising over the thirty-foot steel wall that surrounded the community, dowsing it with morning light. In the street, children were running about playing games, or riding their bicycles, or gathered in groups admiring some toy that one of them was displaying. One particular bunch had a game of street hockey going, with goal nets set up on each end, taking advantage of the complete lack of traffic.

"I don't recognize it at all," EB finally admitted. "Is this a prison of sorts for families? These trailers are as clustered as jail cells, and that wall—is it to keep these children in, or keep something out?"

"After all the years in your service, you never did pay him a visit at his home, did you?"

"Pay whom a visit? You're talking in riddles, spirit."

"The one who has kept you organized so you could oversee your vast empire, who made sure you had all the data you needed for all your precious meetings so you could close the deals, who gave you his time—often at the expense of his family—and all his talents so you could heap your sordid profits up to heaven."

"Bobby? This is where Bobby lives? How could that be? I pay him quite handsomely for his services. I knew he lived just outside the Pittsburg / Bay Point Station. Yes, as I recall, I went to great lengths and pulled a number of strings with the higher-ups in the city so he could get a place there. All he told me was that he got it and could walk to the station from his home to catch the train into the city. I went to all that trouble for this?"

"You would have known if you accepted any of his invitations for one of his wife's home-cooked dinners—which exceed even your digital chef's preparations. You always turned him down."

"Glad I did! I'd rather have dinner at San Quentin," EB replied as he continued to gaze around the walled-in ghetto, subconsciously wiping his robe's front and sleeves as if to clean his hands.

"Some of your worst criminals are there. I think that can be arranged!" the giant said in a serious chuckle. He then took EB's arm and teleported into the double-wide that was parked directly beside them.

The inside of the 1,400-square-foot fabrication was as cramped as it was outside in its tight row of duplicates. Though one of the largest homes in the city-confiscated Champion Trackside Manor community, it's three bedrooms were still one short of what the Cratchits needed for their family. But they never complained, or at least Bobby didn't. Always the optimist, he'd fitted three beds into the largest for his three daughters, although only two were currently in use, and situated a bunk in the other bedroom for his two oldest sons. Opposite to the bunks was a small bedframe that rested directly on the carpet. It wasn't elevated since Timmy couldn't lift himself to the height of a regular bed. But Bobby had converted the frame into a race car, giving Timmy, in the opinion of the children, the best bed in the house.

This Rambler model also had the largest kitchen available in the park. That was important for Olivia since she loved to cook, and spent most of her day there, dreaming up dinner dishes and creative snacks or making breakfasts and lunches for her kids. She loved it, though, and it was the life she had chosen. Being a mom had always been her dream, which had been fulfilled six times over with three princesses and three princes. Now all she needed was a castle suitable for her royal family, one that would give more space for them all, and especially one closer to Bobby's work so, as king, he could spend more time in his kingdom.

Bobby and Olivia had settled for their trailer home only out of necessity. Following the Great Giveaway and the city's appropriation of all the surrounding area's private residential property, the only affordable housing for a larger family was in a community like Trackside. Once the unprecedented government buyout was completed, single-family homes were all but abolished to further California's diversity and equity initiative, for the most part eliminating what had once been called the suburbs. The mass influx from all corners of the globe of those looking for the government's full spectrum handout meant big housing structures to accommodate the hordes had to be constructed, and fast, or the very problem the Great Giveaway sought to solve would have been made far, far worse. Only a few pockets of individual homes were preserved, mainly for optics, but for the sake of equity and inclusion, even these were packed like sardines into the few trailer park communities like Trackside.

Demand for these few and nearly impossible-to-acquire homes became so overwhelming that a lottery was created for most of them. Again in the name of diversity, inclusion and equity, everyone's name who wanted a shot at one—which was almost everyone—was submitted for a random drawing. When drawn, the winner's total social, ideological, and financial credit record was evaluated for final approval. If their score was acceptable and income was below a certain threshold, the winner stayed in the trailer without cost. Thanks to EB, Bobby's name was somehow drawn and accepted, and because of his family size, he was given the option for the large three-bedroom, expanded-kitchen unit. But because he was making a very good salary, he was required to pay the $13,000-per-month rent.

Even with sky-high rent for all but the poorest of the poor, long wait lists were formed and envy exploded after the lotteries had been completed. Soon violence erupted in the sprawling housing projects in protest that all no-cost, free living conditions weren't equal. The movement spread like fire and became very organized and formed into several groups, the largest being Freeloader Lives Eternally Matter, or FLEM, which soon after began to vandalize, criminalize, and terrorize the trailer communities. "No Equality, No Peace" was their battle cry as they demanded the fabricated homes be demolished and high-rise housing complexes like the ones they lived in on the government dole be erected in their place.

The riots became a national, even international, spectacle, to the point that similar violence erupted in other major cities around the country and world. The organization had successfully activated the planet's Marxist revolutionary machine in an effort to eliminate even the appearance of private property ownership and inequality. Under enormous pressure to permanently eliminate private property and socialize everything, the US government came very close to succumbing to FLEM's demands. But in the end, the well-to-do and well connected residents of the trailer parks prevailed, leading to the erection of penitentiary-style walls fortified with perched security guards and policed entry/exit gates to protect against the revolutionaries and rioters.

"When is Martha arriving?" Lindi, Bobby and Olivia's second daughter, asked.

"She's probably in the line at the gate," Olivia replied, pointing Lindi to the community monitor in the kitchen that showed a huge line of cars waiting to be allowed in. "It's almost as bad as at the border!"

"It's always like this on Christmas Day," Lindi observed. "You'd think more people would try to come on Christmas Eve instead, or even earlier."

"And where would all these people sleep? Plus, you know that Trackside has very strict rules on overnight guests ever since the riots started. It takes weeks to get someone approved who isn't an immediate member of the family," Olivia replied.

"But Martha is family!" Lindi smiled.

"Yes, she could've come earlier," Olivia said, stopping her sauce stirring and leaning down to speak directly to Lindi who had dutifully been trying to help her mother prepare the big dinner. "But now that she's away for college, she has to stay there until all her exams are completed and her work lets her come home. Honey, unfortunately your sister had to work yesterday and so she could only catch the red-eye to arrive this morning."

"What's a red-eye?" Lindi asked. "That sounds painful. Are Martha's eyes OK?"

"Yes, love." Olivia laughed. "No, a red-eye is a plane trip where you fly overnight. But they don't have beds in the planes, so you have to sleep in your seat."

"That sounds very uncomfortable!"

"It is, and most people really don't sleep much on those flights. So when they land in the morning, they have red eyes because they didn't get much sleep."

"Is that why Daddy has red eyes in the morning sometimes?"

"No, silly," came a reply from just outside the kitchen. "Dad has red eyes because he's always staring at his computer screen, even when he just wakes up."

"Well that's partly true, Pete, but Lindi asked a good question," said Olivia to her oldest son, who was only three years away from college himself.

"Your dad works long hours," she said, turning to her daughter, "so we can have a home like this and not have to live in a housing project high-rise. It takes a lot of money to live in a place like Trackside, and especially to have a large home like this. We're very fortunate to be here, but it has only been possible because your father is willing to stay very late at work, and even work during his forty-five-minute train ride to and from his office. When he does this, he doesn't get much sleep. Not much at all. And so, Lindi, yes, he gets red-eye because of this, just like on an overnight plane."

"I wish we saw more of Dad," Pete said. "Why does he have to work so much? A lot of the other dads in the neighborhood don't have to work as much—some don't even work at all!"

"Those other fathers are on welfare and so don't have to pay the same rent we pay. The government subsidizes their rent because either their job pays too little, they have health problems, or they don't know English well enough to get a job."

"But what about the healthy ones who do know English who don't work? Neither Jaime's or Isaac's dads work at all. They speak English fine and seem perfectly healthy," Pete inquired.

"I don't know their situations, but what I do know is that your father has a very demanding job, Pete, and also a job that many other people would love to have. So he has to work extra hard so he doesn't get replaced."

"You mean he has a slave driver of a boss!" Peter clarified.

Olivia wanted to correct him, but just smiled at him for saying what she really felt toward EB. But before she could say any more, two other children, a boy and a girl, came ripping into the kitchen, apparently in the middle of a game of tag.

"You're it!" the little girl shouted as she swiped her brother on the side of his arm.

"Hey, you two, keep your game in the living room, unless you want to help us cook!" Olivia laughed.

"No way!" the little boy shouted, peeling around a chair and sprinting after his sister who had already dashed out the door in fear of an instant re-tagging. "How long until dinner?" he then yelled, having disappeared through the doorway.

"Yeah, Mom, how long until we eat?" Pete asked. "It smells incredible!"

"Not too long now. It should be ready by the time Martha's Uber arrives and your father gets home."

"Speak of the devil!" Lindi hollered, hearing the chime of the front door pad codes being pressed.

"Devil? In this house we will only refer to Martha as the angel she is," her mother corrected her with a laugh.

"She's here!" the running little boy shouted, dashing to the door. Then all together, the children began to celebrate.

"Martha's home!" they chanted in unison. "Yeah, she made it!"

The littlest girl of the family beat her brother to the door and wrapped Martha's leg with her little arms screaming as if she hadn't seen her sister for ages. The rest of the children all gathered around her for a welcome-home hug, all hastily asking her at the same time a litany of questions: *How was your trip? Why did it take you so long to get home? How's your first year of school so far? Did your Uber get attacked by rioters?* And the most important questions from the little ones: *Did you bring us presents?*

Martha gathered all of them in her arms with tears running

down her cheeks. As homeschooled children, they all grew up together, studied together, and played together building a closeness among them that even outsiders commented was as amazing as it was beautiful. Being the oldest, Martha often assumed the role of teacher when their mother was otherwise engaged, giving her extra insight into all her siblings, and an attachment that extended beyond just their shared blood. And since this was the first time in all their years growing up together that she had been away, even though for only for a semester, she had missed them far more than she had anticipated. And they had missed her as well, making the reunion sweeter than the apple cinnamon pie baking in the oven.

"You must be tired," Olivia said after breaking through the barrier of children and smothering her with at least a dozen kisses. "Come sit by the heater. We've had a terrible cold front over the last couple days, with awful, sleety rain and even some snow. Today's the first day in a week that the sun's paid us a visit."

"Wait! Wait!" the two little ones hollered, looking out the window. "Daddy's coming! Martha, quick, hide!"

Always a sport, Martha grabbed her carry-on bag and backpack and ran into one of the bedrooms just as Bobby came strolling in bundled up in his parka with Timmy on his shoulder also wrapped up in a coat and hat so all that could be seen were his bright blue eyes.

"It smells incredible in here!" Bobby sang as he gave his wife a kiss hello. "I'm starved! But where's Martha?" he said looking around while hugging his kids as they hugged him and helped Timmy off his shoulder and into his wheelchair.

"Now don't be upset, Bobby, but her flight was canceled and so she won't be coming," said Olivia trying to look sad, wiping a tear for dramatic effect. "There's a terrible storm in Boston, and she just couldn't get out."

"What? Not coming for Christmas! Impossible," he said, shaking his head and sitting down, not only in disappointment but from being winded toting Timmy for three blocks from the church they attended for Christmas morning service.

Peeking through the door and watching the whole episode unwind, Martha couldn't take it anymore and prematurely burst out from her hideout.

"Daddy!" she yelled as she ran to him.

"You're here!" His surprised face was worth the hoax, even if it was only done halfway. Jumping up from his chair and taking her into his arms, he outdid his wife with welcome-home hugs and kisses.

"So how's MIT, my little brain?" Bobby finally asked.

"Harder than I ever imagined. You think you work long hours? Part of my days here are going to be spent doing nothing but sleeping!"

"And sleep you will, as much as you want!" he replied. "And your classes, you like them? How about your grades?"

"You'll be pleased to know I'm getting only two *B*s and all the rest *A*s!"

Cheers erupted around the room, with a final high-pitched hooray coming at the very end from Timmy. Martha immediately ran over to him and picked him up in her arms.

"I missed you most of all, Timmy!" she said, twirling him around and around, making him laugh with the most enjoyable, bubbly, munchkin-sounding laugh imaginable. The rest of the children began to laugh with him, and soon Olivia and Bobby were also holding their bellies laughing.

Once the uproar died down, Martha gave him kiss after kiss and finally put him back in his chair, only to be beckoned by the little guy to do it again, and again, and again.

"So how was little Timmy in church today?" Olivia asked as Martha continued to play with him.

"He's an angel! I'm convinced the little guy is actually a messenger sent from heaven to teach us all," Bobby replied proudly. "So I have him on my lap during the sermon, and though it's a little awkward, he leans forward in his little suit and bow tie and listens to every word. The other parishioners just marvel—and are chastised by their own consciences—that he's so engaged. And then, after the sermon, he said the most amazing things. Of course it's a Christmas message today, and after it was concluded, he whispered to me that he really had hope. I asked him what he had hope about and he replied, 'If God would have His Son born in a manger among the animals, where it was cold and there was nothing fancy, then that means God doesn't care how much money we have. And that gives me hope because I know I'll never have a lot of money.'"

"So true." Olivia nodded with a partial smile. "We need to remember that, Bobby—you need to remember that. How does Scripture put it? *The love of money is the root of evil.*"

"I thought the same thing sitting there on the bare wooden pew with Timmy. There we were, in a humble sanctuary, not ornate or lavished with the world's treasures or sophisticated electronics and big holograph screens, but simple and unpretentious, so our focus was on the message, the living Word Himself, and not the temporary, perishing, even rotting works of man's hands or the decaying substances of this earth. And in this environment that the world considers foolish and in many ways backward, there was peace that simply surpasses understanding. The kind of peace we have here in our home, in our family, in our lives. The perfect peace of a satisfied conscience, an exculpated soul—the peace of knowing that this life is not all that there is, but there is an eternal one coming that's real, and that the abiding peace within us proves to us day after day. All the money in EB's plethora of bank accounts—even all the wealth in the world—can't buy such marvelous peace."

EB heard every word and became visibly agitated, especially when Bobby mentioned his name.

"Something striking a nerve?" the giant asked, having shrunk himself again to the perfect size to fit inside the low-ceilinged trailer park home.

"Hexagas!" was all EB could say, although he continued to listen closely, very closely, to Bobby's story.

"Why would anyone's life goal be to get rich and dedicate their life to gaining what is destined to perish? It's the definition of foolishness," Bobby concluded.

"And that's what love of money really is, isn't it? Whatever we devote ourselves to, whatever we think about and spend our energy on, this is where our heart is, what we love. That helps to understand why it's impossible to serve both God and money!" Olivia agreed. "Well, in this house, we love God first and then each other and our neighbor!"

"And a Christmas feast!" Pete blurted out.

"Oh yes." Olivia laughed. "And the feast is ready. Quickly, Lindi, please get the table set—and, Pete, help your sister Martha bring in all the platters. And don't forget the gravy. There's fresh corn from the cob, and the green bean casserole should be done. Oh yes, there's the frozen Christmas cranberry salad, plus the bowl of tossed green salad, and—"

"We've got it, Mom!" Martha laughed.

"I am just so excited and thankful we're all together, that your flight made it, and that at least once a year we'll all be able to be at the same table having a wonderful feast together. It may not be a feast suitable for Ebenezer or all his circles of billionaire tech elites, but I think we've done pretty well on our limited budget!"

Olivia said humbly.

"You've done an amazing job!" Bobby responded, giving her a huge hug and kiss. "Nothing could be better. We wouldn't trade this dinner and your cooking—especially your cooking—for the grandest, most expensive feast anywhere, would we gang?"

"No!" "Never!" "Of course not!" chimed the children.

And with that, they all sat down, held hands, and Bobby gave a rather lengthy offering of thanks to the Lord. His prayer was long-winded, not because he wanted to say lots of words, but because he was truly thankful and because he had much to be thankful for—and he didn't want to miss anything on this special Christmas Day. When he finished his great petition, he concluded with a very hearty "Amen!" to which all the family agreed and together also said the same.

"Now before we eat," Bobby immediately said after all heads were raised, "let's raise our glasses together. Merry Christmas, everyone, and it truly is. May God bless us!"

And though a challenge to raise a glass himself with his feeble hand, Timmy joined and lifted his smaller cup as high as he could and pronounced his own blessing. "God bless us, everyone!"

"Spirit," EB then inquired as he watched tiny Timmy from his little wheelchair struggle with his glass. "How long will Timmy survive this horrible infirmity? Will he live much longer?"

"I see an empty race car bed," replied the giant for the first time without a smile on his face, "and a vacant seat at the dinner table, his chair being folded up in the corner without an owner, memorialized with a ribbon."

"Please no, spirit. It's possible you're wrong," pleaded EB.

"What I see is certain if all remains constant," the giant replied.

"But if everything doesn't remain constant, if there is some alteration of events, isn't it possible that the boy will not die soon?"

"What do you care?" growled the green gargantuan as he put his huge face right up to EB's. "If he's going to die, he had better do it, and decrease the planet's surplus population!"

EB hung his head hearing his own words and was overcome with overwhelming contrition, sorrow, grief, and regret—and not a little fear.

"You and your cabal of self-appointed masters of the universe have spent your lives creating the conditions for fields of the disadvantaged like Timmy to sprout. Claiming to save the planet, you in your hypocrisy impose your life-draining, energy-depleting, property-confiscating, wealth-destroying mandates upon everybody else, all the while excluding yourself. You don't see it, but your entire life is nothing but a pretentious sham, a futile effort to purchase policies and programs of pitiful perversion propagated for one purpose: promulgate your own power and profits at the expense of the people!"

"You've used quite a few *p*'s there, spirit, that I won't forget," EB interjected.

"Well then, here's another. Pathetic. You have been given the means to have an influence in history by genuinely caring for the environment. But your greed has blinded you, and your own avarice compels you to pour your profits into pointless and Godless inventions and government-dictated fabrications that you know full well have been weaved by the father of lies for a single objective: centralization of power into an all-encompassing, top-down global dictatorship. You and your globalist comrades attempt to justify your lust for power with deceptive planet-saving, environment-preserving programs, which are really only guilt-producing whips you're using to drive the human race into enslavement—and which do nothing to actually heal the earth. You and your revolutionary army, through your sordid, perverted, deceptive, self-aggrandizing words and actions, are doing far more to destroy the planet than save it. Continue on such a path and not only will Timmy prematurely die, but so will ten thousand times ten thousand of his poor, weak, and needy brothers and sisters. But what is that to you, oh Chosen One of History? It's the cost of doing business, right? Only collateral damage in your anti-theistic crusade for your ill-conceived notion of the 'greater good'!"

EB crumbled before the giant's rebuke, and, trembling, nearly collapsed to the ground. He began to heave uncontrollably and was soon hyperventilating, gasping to find a breath of air. Not daring to look at the spirit, he tugged on his robe frantically, signaling his need for oxygen. Convinced he would expire, EB gave one last pull on the spirit's green drape to which the spirit—after several seconds of contemplation—responded. Waiving his torch over EB's head, air filled EB's lungs and his breathing immediately returned to normal. EB wanted to thank the specter, but was still too ashamed and fearful to say anything or even raise his eyes to look at him. But he did raise them speedily, on hearing his own name elsewhere.

"To Ebenezer!" Bobby said, once again raising his glass, but this time over what looked like a licked-clean plate, all the nearly empty platters, and a table of overstuffed children. "Let's make a toast to the provider of this feast, my boss Ebenezer, or as he prefers it, EB."

"The provider of the feast? I'd rather say God is our provider and Ebenezer just the rusty old pipe He used to transfer it to us!" cried Olivia, reddening in the face. "No, rusty pipe is too kind. Better is a sewer pipe. I wish I had him here. I'd give him a piece of my mind to feast upon!"

"Please, love," said Bobby. "Let's not do this in front of the children, on Christmas Day."

"Bobby, he takes advantage of you. Granted, he's a genius. But he wouldn't be able to organize a trip to the bathroom without your assistance. And the hours he makes you work—I hardly see you anymore!" she complained.

"Honey, he pays me well—enough so we can be in this home, have this feast, send Martha to MIT. All the kids have warm beds, food to eat every day, and decent clothing and not a small supply of toys!"

"If we weren't living in the People's Republic of San Francisco, we'd be living in a real home where the kids could have their own rooms and wouldn't be bunked up like sailors. And I remind you, Martha earned a scholarship to MIT. Your boss is not paying a penny for that, other than her transportation and extracurricular expenses. Yes, the kids have warm beds, but what about Timmy? We don't have an extra penny to get him the operations he needs. And if EB has it his way, we'll never have the money."

"But we made the choice, dear. We decided to endure the hardship of a mid-six-figure salary in the Bay Area so someday I could advance, maybe even start my own company."

This was the first time EB had heard that Bobby had entrepreneurial ambitions of his own and once again started to breathe heavily.

"When will that happen?" Olivia asked, not angry at Bobby, but entreating him. "He's doing everything he can to keep you under his thumb, locked in his eBeja prison to milk you for every cent he can. We don't have enough to save any money, even for an emergency, so how are you going to break away and start your own business?"

"Honey, it's Christmas. Let's not go into that now," Bobby gently replied.

"Why we would, on such a sacred day, drink to the health and welfare of such a thoroughly godless, odious, stingy, hard, and unfeeling man, I just can't—won't—understand. But for your sake, because I do believe in you, love you more than my own life, and trust you know what you're doing . . . for your sake, I'll toast. Not that he'll have a long life, but that somehow he is awakened out of his wokeness or else his life be very short! To EB, a wolf in sheep's clothing, a megalomaniac unlike any other. May he come to know the true meaning of Christmas!"

The children looked at each other and grinned or giggled and then drank the toast after her. Even Timmy made the toast, but was last to drink as he once again was pained to lift his glass. He was also saddened that his condition brought such grief and worry to his mother. Though his mother blamed EB that he was unable to get the medical care he needed, he did not. Though EB was the ogre of the family and a dark cloud of depression in the home whenever his name was mentioned, Timmy felt sorry for him. *Such a shame*, he thought, *that an old man with so much was so miserable.*

"Let's move to the living room and sing some carols together!" Bobby suggested.

"And play some games!" Olivia added, having changed her mood and signaled the children to quickly clear the table so they could get started.

"We must play Pictionary," Peter added.

"And Monopoly," Martha said, laughing. "After all, we did just toast the world's most notorious monopolist!"

Laughing together, they all rapidly cleared away the dishes, wrapped up what little leftovers there were, and loaded the first of what would be at least three installments of dirty plates, glasses, pans, and utensils into the dishwasher. They functioned in unison like a well-lubricated machine, each instinctively fulfilling a task they had done many times and mastered. EB was amazed at the symmetry, their coordination and great care and love they all gave even in this smallest of chores, all the while laughing with each other, teasing, and radiating a camaraderie he knew nothing about. As they finished the cleaning and faded into the living room for songs and games, so he, too, faded, once again latched to the giant's robe, into the night that had swallowed that instructive day at Bobby Cratchit's house.

CHAPTER 24

Unlike previous jumps with both this spirit and the one before him, after gliding out of their trailer, the pair, like a couple of rockets, shot straight up over the home and its park. Looking down on it, it reminded EB of a garrison with the homes packed as tight together as tents would be in battle. The great wall encircling it made it stand out among the other massive buildings that littered the countryside around it, like a group of white helmet soldiers surrounded by goliaths ready to attack. EB couldn't imagine living in such a war zone.

"Touchdown!" EB heard behind him from a unison of voices. Trying to twist around in the air, he perceived that he was no longer in the air, but was again grounded on a floor that seemed to be shaking from the celebratory roar encompassing him. Turning, he saw a party of young men and women standing and cheering, giving each other high fives as they continued to shout, "Touchdown, touchdown!"

"That was possibly the best play of the year," one yelled above the din.

"Yes, incredible. And right at the buzzer," Fred replied, jumping up and down in excitement. "This is the first Christmas game they've won in decades, and we were here to witness it!"

The high fives continued, and some even threw red, green, and gold confetti, combining Christmas colors with the team's as they watched the replay of the game-winning score in full 3D holographic glory. Others waved their team flags or, as in the case of EB's niece's cousin, a crutch decorated with 49er stickers. A few had painted their faces with the 49er emblem, but circled the "SF" with a wreath instead of the black ring. One of the women, who had painted her face with the Christmas SF, was crying she was so happy, causing the green and gold makeup to run down her cheeks.

"I know you're sad that Uncle EB couldn't make it, but there's no need to cry about it!" Fred joked with her sarcastically, and then gave her a big kiss on the cheek, inadvertently coloring his lips.

"Ha ha. Very funny, dear. Hexagas hogwash!" Fred's wife said sarcastically, laughing out loud. "Did he really say that? Called Christmas 'hexagas hogwash'?"

"Oh yes," Fred confirmed, laughing with her. "And more! How did he put it?" And then in a low, impersonating voice, Fred continued to quote his uncle. "'Around the twenty-fifth of December every year, somehow, magically, everyone decides to love one another. Love? The greatest hexagas of all!'"

Again, they both reveled in a long laugh, along with several of the others who had turned away from watching the postgame celebrations on the field to join the conversation.

"But if you think about it, it's really pretty sad that he sees the world that way," EB's niece said. "Imagine living a cold, bitter life with no love. And it's not just that he doesn't have love; he doesn't even believe in it!"

"I'm not sure about that," Fred responded. "He has a hard shell, and his arrogant insults have their own consequences. But I don't have anything against him, never have, even though he's rude to us and won't visit.

"Deep inside that impenetrable fortress, there's a heart," Fred continued, and then after a long pause, added, "somewhere!"

Again, they all laughed. But EB's niece by marriage wasn't going to accept that view so easily.

"A heart? More like a cavern, full of greed and lust for more. Who cares how many jets he has, or homes around the world, or how many magazine covers he's graced? You'd think with all that wealth and status he'd want to spend some time with the only family he has. It's not as if we want anything from him."

"And maybe that's part of the curse of wealth," Fred agreed. "The more you have, the more people try to take advantage of you, get close to you for some kind of gain or handout, or just to make themselves look good by being around a star. I imagine it's exhausting, not to mention frustrating and debilitating. I've assured him that we don't want a penny from him, but just to be around him and get to know him. But he doesn't believe it."

"He really doesn't believe anything, except that he's the universe's gift to humanity and is above everyone else," EB's niece replied. The rest of the girls had gathered around the conversation by this time and nodded in agreement, several also expressing the same opinion.

"I mean, how much effort would it have taken," she continued, "just to show up for a minute for the game? Here we've got the best suite in the stadium—so he certainly wouldn't have felt that our seats were below him with the deplorables. And it's Christmas night. What else does he have going on? He certainly isn't having dinner with family since he has no family. I'm amazed you even invited him. You knew he wouldn't show."

"Well, he does have family, and we didn't choose him and he didn't choose us—he is my mother's brother. In her honor I asked him to join us, and will keep asking him. There's no reason for us to become like him—rejecting, unfeeling, unwelcoming— no reason at all. We will be who we are and maybe someday he'll come to grips with how short his life is on this planet, that he's nothing but a vapor, a mist, here today and gone tomorrow. When that happens, he'll join us. And so I'll make it a point every year to wish him a Merry Christmas—even if it's only hexagas hogwash!"

They all laughed again and Fred's niece leaned over and kissed his green-, red-, and gold-splotched lips. "That's why I married this man!" she announced.

"Hey, everyone, let's all come up here by the table. We have these box seats for another hour, so let's do our gift exchange now," Fred then said. "Turn the Holovisions off and let's turn on some upbeat Christmas music to finish out the evening!"

Everyone was more than enthusiastic with the plan. They had already received an unexpected gift with the 49er victory, which was only made better by being able to watch it from the fifty-yard-line suite with all the delicious food and beverages they had catered for the occasion. But this was a tight-knit group that had tried to get together every year on Christmas night for the last several years, committed to celebrate the day with a Secret Santa gift exchange.

A big box had been set aside near the suite's entrance that each person put their present in. On each present was a tag that had the person's name that the gift was for, but not the person's name who bought it for them. Earlier in the month, they had done a random drawing of names with each person drawing only one name that they would get a gift. The gifts could be funny or a reminder of the holiday or something useful that it was known that person needed. The only limitations were that the gift wasn't in any way demeaning or crude, and that it's cost didn't exceed $50.

EB's niece clapped her hands in excitement to start. With an upbeat gospel rendition of "Angels We Have Heard on High" playing from the booth's speakers, she dragged the gift filled box to the center of a circle of chairs Fred's coworker had set up in the open area of the suite.

"OK, everyone ready?" she asked and then reached into the box and randomly pulled out one of the gifts. "Jason!" she announced and handed the long, slender present to him. He stepped forward, took the gift, and quickly unwrapped it revealing an extendable golf ball retriever.

"Just what I've always wanted!" Jason exclaimed, holding it up and shaking it for show, to which another of the guests chimed in, "With all the balls you'll be losing during your recovery, you'll need it!" The rest of the gang laughed knowing that Jason was easily the best golfer among them. A member of the exclusive Cal Golf Club in south San Francisco, Jason held the course record and had at one time contemplated going pro and playing on the PGA Tour. He was that good. But a few months previous, Jason had been in a car accident, fracturing his left hip and breaking the leg on the same side. He was recovering fast, but still had to use crutches to hobble around.

"I'm very thankful to whoever gave me this gift," Jason said. "But I guess you didn't get the memo. I've quit golf." The room went silent since everyone knew that golf had been Jason's life. After a minute or two of everyone looking around at each other in disbelief, Jason broke the silence. "I'm quitting golf because I'm going to walk on—well, hobble on—and try out for quarterback of the 49ers!" Everyone broke out laughing at his sarcasm, buckling over in hysterics, not because the joke was funny in itself, but because Jason's brother, Brad, was the current quarterback for the 49ers, and the All Pro who had just led the team to victory.

"Well, I'm sure they'll let you trade it in at the sporting store for a helmet," Fred's wife interjected as she reached for the next present. "Julie!" And so it went for the next half hour as all twenty-six attendees received their presents. For one in the group, it was a teddy bear because she had been having trouble sleeping. For another, a remote mind-controlled drone that fetched beer from the refrigerator. And then there was the eSweater that had an internal heating element that adjusted itself according to the ambient temperature.

All were fun gifts, except for the FeedMe app that was given to Rosie, a longtime member of the group. It was a download that would integrate with her PPC to automatically detect every bit of food eaten or drink consumed, calculate its exact nutritional and caloric value, and then automatically determine how to correct her diet for maximum health. Rosie had struggled with extreme obesity over the years and recognized it as a gesture of love. Rosie thanked the group, acknowledging their faithfulness to her to not pull punches when it came to her condition.

"Only one gift left," EB's niece announced. "Ebenezer!"

Hearing his name called, EB, who had been immensely enjoying the suspense and sheer fun of the secret gift giving, stood up as if to take the present as all the others had. "I can't believe it. They got a present for me?" he asked, nodding to the spirit next to him.

"But due to his full Christmas schedule with family, feeding the poor, giving gifts to the needy, and singing in the church choir, Ebenezer was not able to join us," she said to which the whole group once again erupted in laughter.

"Here, I'll take it," said Fred. "I won't open it, but will give it to him the next time I see him."

"No, no," the crowd of friends yelled back. "Open it! Open it!" they chanted.

"That wouldn't be right," Fred replied, holding the present out in front of him, passing it under the eyes of each of the guests. "How do we know it's not something of great need, or essential for Ebenezer's life? He has so many needs!"

"Open it! Open it!" the group pressed on, laughing.

"Yes, open it!" Ebenezer joined in, skipping right up to Fred to examine the unopened treasure wrapped in glittering gold foil.

"But what if it's something very personal that only he should see? Or what if it's such a prize that he will be forever grateful for the gesture?"

Continuing to chuckle while pressing, the group started to chant in unison, "O-pen it now! O-pen it now!" to which Fred finally relented.

"Fine," EB's niece jumped in. "But here's how we must do it in the spirit of our Secret Santa exchange. I'm going to go around the circle here and each one of you gets a guess as to what it is. I know none of you know what it is because I am the one who is the gift giver!"

"Aha! Yes! That's great," were the enthusiastic replies from the guests.

"As we go around, you can each ask one yes-or-no question, such as, 'Is it metal?' or 'Can a person eat it?' I'll answer your question, and then you get one guess. The person who guesses it gets the honor of presenting it to EB!" to which the whole group roundly applauded.

"Isn't that correct, Fred? If someone guesses it, you'll arrange a personal meeting so that person can present it to him?" she asked her husband.

"I'll do my best, but he'll want to know the nature and purpose of the meeting, and if there's any financial benefit to it!"

Trying to calm their laughter, EB's niece spun a pen to determine who would be the first to guess. "Jason! You get to guess first. What's your question?"

"Will the present . . . put him out of his misery?"

Not able to keep a straight face, she smiled widely as the group continued in their hilarity of the game and replied, "No." And on around the circle she went with EB following her and guessing himself each time a clue was given. "Can he drink it?" "No." "Do you know if he has something like it?" "Yes." "Does it reflect his personality?" "Yes." And on it went to the last person with no one able to correctly guess what was in the box.

"No one could guess!" EB laughed, surprising himself that he could demonstrate cheerfulness and gaiety that matched the guests. "It must be something quite unique. Perhaps a game of some sort. Spirit, do you know what it is?"

"It's time we go," the giant signaled.

"What? Before she reveals what my present is? Can't we just stay for a few more minutes? I must see what it is!" And he bounced back over to where his niece was standing, holding the gift, and attempted to touch it to see if he might feel what was inside. As always, his hand went right through it, but he found that to be somewhat amusing and passed his hand again through it, then waved both hands through it, chuckling at himself like a child playing in a pond.

"Our time is up, EB."

"No, no. Look, she's about to reveal the mystery, solve the puzzle, astound the masses!" he sniggered.

"Ladies and gentlemen, 49er fans all, I regret that none of you were able to correctly guess, and so, unfortunately, none of you will be able to meet with Ebenezer and present this award."

"Aww, too bad! Huge disappointment! Maybe next year," the group again bellowed in sarcasm.

"So, without further ado," she said and tore off the gold wrapping paper to reveal a large square black cardboard box. There were no labels or descriptions on the box, only the solid color of black.

"What's inside?" someone shouted. "Yeah, show us what's in the box!" they demanded.

"All right, here it is." And she lifted the lid from the black box, peeked inside, and then held it above her head and turned it upside down.

"Nothing but air!" She burst out laughing. "You see, it was a shiny gold present that looked beautiful and expensive on the outside, but when uncovered, is an empty black box filled with nothing but air—actually, hot air gauging the temperature in this room!"

And all of the group erupted with her, some holding their sides, others down on the floor bent over, a few only tittering but still greatly amused, except for EB who slunk backwards out of the circle where he had been frolicking. After a significant continuation in this state of euphoria, Fred stepped up to the group.

"Everyone grab a glass if you don't already have one. There's still plenty of libation on the table," he directed. "Does everyone have a drink? Good. Before we break up for the night, it would be not only ungrateful, but Scroogy, to not toast the one who has given us great merriment and amusement tonight. Here's to Ebenezer, who—whether he would have liked it or not – was the center of our fun, helping us laugh uncontrollably on this day meant for laughter and joy. A Merry Christmas and Happy New Year to our missing guest, wherever the old man is!"

EB was still a little deflated from the present-less present, but had such an enjoyable time otherwise that he would have saluted his nephew's circle in return and thanked them, though in inaudible speech, if the green goliath had given him time. But the luxury suite, the field, and entire stadium vanished in the breath of the last word spoken by Fred; and he and his spiritual mentor were again airborne in their travels.

CHAPTER 25

"Spirit, I'm sure you're aware, but the lights below us are about to end and we'll soon be aloft over the ocean!" EB panicked.

"Are you afraid of the water?" The giant chuckled.

"I'm afraid of flying over a vast body of water without any form of a personal flotation device or life raft available in case we crash!"

The mostly always pleasant giant roared in sonic laughter, sending an echo through the surrounding clouds that rippled like thunder. EB wasn't sure if his guide was laughing at him, or for some other reason, so he closed his eyes as the last of the twinkling lights below him disappeared behind his feet. Not more than a second later, he began to descend at a tremendous speed, what he thought must have been Mach 10 or more. The expedited plunge gave him an enormous scare, though without any wind resistance or G-force effects on his body. Waiting for the crash he had feared would befall him and his giant guide, EB braced for impact. But it never came, only a sudden cessation of the sensation and then a hard surface under his feet.

It took several seconds before EB had the courage to open his eyes, but when he did, he found himself standing in a huge, musty cavern. It wasn't the typical natural cave one would imagine dotted with hanging stalactites and protruding stalagmites packed with broods of bats. This cave was clearly man-made and better resembled an underground dungeon.

The hallway in which they stood was long and narrow with ceilings tall enough that the giant could grow back to his original size. The rock walls were rough hewn and seeping moisture in spots, but mostly dry and dirty like the floor on which they stood. The giant's torch lit the tunnel, revealing a series of locked, solid steel doors lining both sides, each with a small barred window at about eye height. There was also an electronically controlled slot in each door with a slide that could be opened or closed on command. Next to each door was a dim light and a very sophisticated electronic panel of some kind that glowed blue.

"What is this place, spirit?" EB asked.

"Listen," the giant whispered.

EB went silent and began to hear a few faint voices, all men, singing. He recognized the tune, but the words didn't register.

"I hear singing," EB said after a few moments. "But I don't understand them."

"Come," the spirit said, taking EB by the arm and immediately transporting the two of them inside of one of the steel door rooms. Sitting in a circle on the dirt floor were eight Asian men, all dressed in dark blue scrub-type shirts and pants. There were no beds in the room, only wooden boards on the floor aligned next to each other against the natural rock wall. A small bucket was in the corner that wasn't empty, emitting a stench that, combined with the moldy cave odor, made EB plug his nose.

The vocalists didn't seem to mind their situation, or at least were used to it, as they joyfully sang, breaking into surprisingly pleasant harmonies at different points of the familiar "Silent Night, Holy Night" carol.

"I recognize the tune, but don't know the language," EB said to the ghost.

"They're singing in Mandarin," the giant replied, humming along with them and sprinkling them with the luminescent dust from his torch. Each time he blessed them, the singers would become more resolute in their singing with their voices achieving greater refinement, clarity, and volume. EB was stunned at how marvelous they sounded, and then how their rendition kept getting better and better with each verse.

"I don't care much for this song, or any carol for that matter, but these men are pretty talented. Maybe I'd like Christmas songs better if I only heard them in languages I don't understand," EB said as he found himself swaying a little in the peace and grace of their croon. "Why are such men in a place like this?"

"All eight of them are pastors of small churches that the government has forbidden to exist."

"That's insane. As much as I disdain what churches promulgate, we do have constitutional guarantees, a First Amendment that protects free speech and forbids government from prohibiting their freedom to exercise their religious beliefs, even if superstitious and hexagas nonsense. I can't say, however, that I'd be too disappointed if that license for stupidity was someday removed from the Constitution," EB waxed.

"That is your country's law, which gives you the right to criticize them and demean them, and call people superstitious without fear of being locked up for such disrespect and verbal violence. Freedom of speech protects everyone, especially those who disagree so that this doesn't happen," the giant said, pointing to the circle of men on the floor.

"So how did this happen?"

"We're not in your country, EB. We're in a not-very-well-known cave in the Henan Province of China. In this country, the God of the Bible is outlawed and can only be discussed according to how, when, and where the government dictates. The communist government here reserves all right of religious doctrinal interpretation to itself, and so forbids the reading, giving, sharing, or possession of the Bible since the Bible condemns their form of totalitarian dictatorship."

"Not all dictatorships are bad," EB tried to assert.

"Of course, as long as you're the dictator, or as you put it, master of the universe!" the giant growled. "The heads of this tyrannical communist beast also consider themselves masters of the universe. I wonder who would win in a war between you and these competing masters?"

EB realized he had once again been crushed by his own words and looked away from the giant's pleading eyes and back to the singers. Their melodies continued to soar through the cave, immensely pleasing his ears and his mind, though their recital had moved to a new song, one that he didn't recognize at all.

"Spirit, these men must have done something more than just shepherd little churches. They're harmless," EB said softly. "What else did they do to earn such a harsh punishment in this disgusting prison?"

"The government sees them as seditious, threats to society and their power because they teach the three basic truths of Christianity."

"There are only three?"

"The first is that God, the only infinite and eternal omnipresent, omniscient, and omnipotent Being, created the universe, the earth, and mankind. Humans didn't evolve from a prebiotic soup, but were specially and marvelously created in the Creator's image—as a reflection of the character and person of God."

"Yes, well, I would have to take issue with that as a scientist. The consensus is that man evolved over billions of years. Call that creation if you want, but it's certainly not what you just described."

"You've deluded yourself, EB. Since you're a scientist and data specialist—your PhD is in that field, correct? Tell me, Dr. Data, what are the statistical odds that as a matter of chance the Milky

Way Galaxy ends up in exactly the position it is in your universe, and your solar system finds itself to be precisely in the position it is in the galaxy, and that Earth could end up perfectly in the position it is in the solar system? I'll give you a hint. There are more than one hundred billion galaxies in the universe, with each galaxy on average having one hundred million stars. That's a total of more than fifty billion trillion stars in the universe. But for your kind, humankind, to exist, the sun must be exactly where it is in your solar system, or humans would freeze or burn up. And for the sun to be exactly in its place, the solar system must be exactly where it is in the galaxy, and the Milky Way Galaxy exactly where it is in the universe. One slight deviation and you and your kind could not exist. So I ask you, can you as a scientist really believe all this is perfectly in its place by accident, by some random chaotic eruption? Isn't it more reasonable that all the symmetry, complexity, and majesty of man, Earth, and the cosmos came by a creative, intelligent Designer who planned it all out?"

While EB scratched his head, the green goliath continued. "The second truth is that, as creatures of God, men and women were given responsible wills, the ability to choose. In this God-given freedom, man chose to rebel against God and challenge the omnipotent sovereignty of their Creator Governor by breaking His law. The judicial consequence and just punishment of their arrogant and horrific crime against God, themselves, and their environment was death. Death is a judgment, not a natural state of man. The punishment of death encompassed all of man's being, so not only would his body die, but his soul and spirit died, meaning his entirety was separated from the life of God, who alone is good. As such, mankind became not good, but inherently evil. This means, contrary to what every person would like to wish about themselves and others, that people are not inherently good, but are depraved, dark criminals. The goodness of God given to man and woman in creation was taken from him and her so that all their thoughts, actions, behaviors, instincts, and inclinations became infected with evil. Being separated from God, it became impossible for a human not to do evil."

"What? You're saying that everything man does is evil and that there is no good at all in men and women? That's nuts!" EB pontificated.

"Ahhh, you're finally asking the right question," the spirit replied. "Let me illustrate. Imagine that I give you a glass of water that is 99 percent pure, potable water, but is 1 percent botulinum toxin, a poison far more powerful than cyanide or anthrax. Would you drink it? After all, it's only 1 percent poison."

"Of course not, unless I wanted to die instantly."

"The poison of evil has infected every soul of man and woman, to the point that, though they can do good things, they are overall and thoroughly polluted and destructive because of the poison in them."

EB had previously applied a similar analogy to the environment in an effort to convince others that even the smallest amount of certain pollutants could end up destroying the planet. He had never thought, however, of how it could apply to the human race.

"The third essential plank that these men shared with their humble congregation," the spirit continued, "is that the predicament mankind therefore finds himself in—the predicament of being under the judgment of death and the whole of his being having become corrupted—is a spiritual predicament. Man is not just matter in motion, a restructuring of a rock or lizard, but is a spiritual being that is now under a spiritual indictment of death. Therefore, the solution to humanity's problem is not material or earthly, but spiritual. A woman condemned to ten consecutive life terms in prison cannot will herself out of prison, buy her way out, or create her own conditions for her release. Similarly, there is no escape from the judgment of death by a dead man. Wouldn't you agree, EB, that all men and women who die stay dead? Do you know of anyone who has died and actually come back to life? And I mean really resurrected, not your hocus-pocus, sleight-of-hand Elevation trickery."

Offended, but knowing that what the spirit was saying was true, EB just shook his head. "No one rises from the dead. Death is the end," he said.

"If mankind was left to himself and had to save himself from death, you'd be correct. Not even collective man can overcome death, and the proof is that every dead person is still dead—except one. And that is the third point. God the Judge pronounced the judgment of death on humanity because all humans have violated His laws, done evil, and become capital criminals. A bad tree cannot bear good fruit."

"So what if there was a human that never did any evil—wouldn't that mean he or she would not be a 'criminal,' as you call them?" asked EB.

"You're starting to understand, EB. Even if there was one, just one person, that didn't do any outward evil, they would still be born with the poison of a corrupt and wicked nature. Or, said in another way that might be more familiar to you, Dr. Big Tech, evil is encoded. It is encoded into the human genome, so that the entire physical being is affected, like when a program is completely corrupted with a virus. Replicating that program always replicates the virus that had infected it. But the corruption goes beyond just the physical body. It is part of your spiritual makeup as well, being fully integrated into your nonmaterial self.

"You see, the very nature of man—his spirit and soul, what

makes man a man—was thoroughly corrupted once the first man rebelled and was pronounced guilty. The punishment of death was imposed on him, in him, and completely throughout his being, and therefore to all those spawned from him. He passed on his corrupted nature to all his progeny. The proof of this is that all are decaying as they grow older and then, at some point, die. As I said, a bad tree doesn't bear good fruit. The first man God created passed on who he was to his children. He passed on death, so all humans are dying and will die.

"So, even if a person managed to go through their entire life without committing one crime against God, he would still die because he was born with the poison of evil in him, the virus of an infected, corrupted encoding. But think about it, EB, has there ever been anyone, anywhere that not only claimed, but demonstrated moral, ethical, and spiritual perfection every moment of every day? Do you know anyone like that? No, you don't, and neither does anyone else on the planet, now or any time in the past. All have committed capital crimes against their Creator Governor, even if just in their fantasies and thoughts, and so it's absurd to argue that someone could theoretically live a perfect life and commit no evil."

"Which means there is no human without guilt. That's great, just great! If all humanity is guilty before this great Judge of whom you speak, and is under the judgment of death, then we're all lost and there's no hope for humanity," EB asserted, apparently forgetting some of his early lessons at Wycliffe's.

"Only God Himself is good and without guilt. And in His goodness and love for His creation, for mankind, the Great Creator humbled Himself and became a man that was born of a woman like you and your kind, raised in a family, and lived just as all other people do on this earth. This man, who was also God, is Jesus of Nazareth. This is important, EB. God only became man once. All other men and women are created in His image, so they reflect Him as beings of love and justice, even though thoroughly depraved. But the fullness of the Creator actually became a man, a unique person, only one time in human history, and that was in Jesus. And as God incarnate, Jesus never committed a crime against God and so was without guilt."

"OK, so we all have guilt because we've all done some evil. Nobody's perfect! We all know that. But not everyone is a serial killer, kidnapper, or terrorist. Why is the penalty so harsh for the vast majority of people? You're saying the penalty even for a little fib is death?" EB asked skeptically.

"The penalty of any crime against God is death, because any amount of the poison is lethal. This is how bad sin is. Even a little fib corrupts everything, just as a little leaven leavens the whole loaf of bread. To you humans, crimes against God and man have varying degrees. But to the One who sees all, knows all, and has perfect understanding of the exact harm and consequences of all actions, with all their ripples and the ripples from their ripples, all that is not good is bad, or poison.

"Or again for your digitally oriented way of thinking, regardless of the size or type of malware, it corrupts and causes damage. That's its very purpose—to destroy something. Sin is the worst kind of malware in the human operating system. If not eradicated completely, it will destroy it. To fully clean out a system, all the malware has to be removed and replaced with pure, uncorrupted code. In the same way, the only way for humans to be delivered from the poison or malware that has infected them is to receive a new and pure, uncorrupted spirit."

"Good luck finding one of those!" EB quipped.

"There is no luck involved. But you're correct—it's not possible to find in humanity a pure spirit to replace the corrupted, defiled human spirit. That would be like looking for an antivirus program within the malware itself. Corrupted humanity cannot heal itself, nor deliver itself from its infected, diseased, decaying, and dying condition. Nor can the guilty human race atone or make reparations for all its injustices. So man's condition is both substantive and judicial. Substantive because he is in his substance fully corrupted, infected, distorted, and depraved. Judicial because, in his corruption, he commits evil—in his thoughts, speech, and actions. And he does it all the time. He lies all the time, deceives all the time, thinks lustful thoughts toward others all the time, and in his dishonest, debased, and debauched heart, hates his fellow man—sometimes with a smile on his face—all the time."

"Really, *all* the time?" EB asked facetiously.

"Not twenty-four seven, you silly man," the giant replied. "But it's continuous in the human mind and heart, because his programming is now such that his genetic code has been corrupted so the output is continually corrupt, as is his spirit—which is enslaved to an evil spiritual enemy you know nothing about, but soon will come to know, who demands and compels evil from his slaves. The only way to stop the evil of man is for his depraved, evil, destructive self to be put to death, permanently, and for him to be freed from the plantation of evil where he's enslaved."

"Enslaved on a plantation? That's an odd way to describe humanity's condition," EB noted.

"Plantation, dungeon, prison. Use whatever term you find most suitable. The point is mankind is not only completely corrupt and depraved—spiritually, mentally, physically, and emotionally—but that he is also a slave of a real spiritual being, God's enemy, the evil serpent of old, the hater of man: His adversary, who has taken the whole of humanity captive to do his wicked will. And that will is to defy God and dishonor Him as

Creator. In plain terms, EB, this means not following the clear precepts and commands the Creator Commander has given in His eternal, infallible instructions to the human race. Failure to follow all that the Creator has revealed in the declarations and messages He gave directly to His prophets and apostles over the span of history—all found in the book you call the Bible—will ultimately enable this enemy to destroy man through his deceptions and temptations."

"I'm nobody's slave!" EB emphasized.

"Whoever's will and way you obey is your master," the spirit replied. "And your actions, the fruit you bear in this life, proves which master you're serving. But there is a way out of the prison, to be freed from humanity's slave plantation, and have the virus that infects you eradicated. But it's all or nothing."

"All or nothing?"

"Think of it this way. If you're a good technician, which you are, EB, you wouldn't remove a network virus only partially, would you? And you wouldn't remove it with the intention to reintroduce it again at a later time back into the system, would you?"

"Of course not, unless I was pernicious myself and wanted to cause damage and destruction," EB proudly stated.

"And we've already established that God is not pernicious, ever or in any way. He is fully good, with no evil or darkness in Him. He never lies; He never does anything but good. He is pure and perfect. All His ways are just, and being perfectly just and good, He will not tolerate evil, whether toward Him or others, in His creation either. Therefore, the Great Judge has thoroughly examined all people and humanity as a whole. The evidence of humankind's continuous, malicious, and determined effort to do evil, reject their Creator, live in defiance of Him and His loving directives, and instead serve the adversary and remain his subjects is overwhelming and incontrovertible. This leads to only one just and correct verdict against you and your kind: Guilty! And to satisfy justice, the sentence of death, which is the eradication of evil, has been pronounced on each person, just as it has been pronounced on the spirit of darkness—the ruler of your world—who God has condemned."

"If we're all under the sentence of death, thoroughly corrupted as you say, then why are you here with me? Why are you sprinkling people with your torch of happiness and goodwill? Why did Marley even bother to invade my space?"

"Because though humanity sits on death row, there is a way of exculpation. Are you so dense that you don't see it? Your penalty is death. But as long as there is a death for your crimes, the penalty is paid. So if there is One that has no guilt and is perfect and pure in spirit, One that is of infinite value and is willing to trade His pure, perfect, and priceless life for yours, and die so that you don't have to die, then there is hope for you! Jesus as the only innocent human ever on this planet is the only One who fits all the requirements and therefore the only One suitable to take the penalty of death in a substitutionary way."

"Substitutionary?" EB asked.

"Yes. Again imagine you were in a prison and your crime was so grievous that the fine was $100 quadrillion. No one has that kind of wealth, not even you, EB. But that's the amount of the fine because your offenses are so severe and heinous. If you can pay it, you can go free. If you can't pay it, you'll never go free and must spend eternity in the cell until you pay—which is never. Now if there was only one person on earth who had that kind of wealth, it would be up to that person whether to use it to pay your fine, or for other purposes. If that rich man decided to use it to pay your fine instead of all the other wonderful things he could do with it, wouldn't you say he loves you very much, especially since you're a condemned criminal?"

"Either that or he's out of his mind," EB replied sarcastically.

"And we know that Jesus wasn't a lunatic—His wisdom and words are the bedrock of Western civilization. And, being guiltless, He couldn't have been a liar. But He is the richest of the rich, the possessor of all who alone has infinite wealth, enough to pay the $100 quadrillion not only for you, but for every human ever born. I'm trying to give you an analogy you'll understand, being a lover of money as you are. But the amount needed to satisfy justice for all of humanity's crimes and felonies is so massive, it could only be paid by One who is infinitely wealthy, whose value is never ending. As God in human form, this is Jesus, who decided to give all He had—even Himself—for you, and every other criminal who is willing. This is love, and this is the third point. Acquittal and absolution cannot come from man or by man, individual or collective. It can only come from God, who became man to take your and your entire race's penalty of death. He paid your fine so you can live!"

"I haven't heard it put quite like that before," EB said, again scratching his head. "You have me thinking, spirit. But why is the Chinese government so hostile to these men if that's all they're teaching? Whether true or not, and now I can see some logic in it—not yet convinced, but you make a strong argument. But whether true or not, why not let people themselves decide?"

"Communism, like all false belief systems, denies these three doctrines. They have officially rejected the idea of God and see it as a superstition. Sound familiar? So, for them, if there is no God, then there is no inherent spiritual problem with man. Yes, humanity has issues to deal with, like crime and disease, poverty, ignorance and war. But to the God denier, those are only social conditions that can only be abolished through the collective efforts of enlightened man via education, proper political and legal systems, and ultimately through force if need be.

"So, in their view, humanity doesn't need a substitutionary savior to save it from God's judgment—that's foolish talk to them, and part of the problem they must solve. They are the savior, and as such, will not tolerate another. So it is essential to their globalist vision of saving and ruling over humanity to free mankind from the ignorant superstitions and harmful practices of biblical theism. Only when a man casts off the chains of the idea that only God saves and rules over humanity, they believe, can that man be a positive force in the world."

"But what about death? They don't have a solution for death—no one does!"

"Precisely. Apart from God, there is no solution for death. A child can understand this. Death is final, except if one has the power over death. Of course, God does—He has all power. And to demonstrate this, prove it beyond a shadow of a doubt, God raised Jesus from the dead. His resurrection establishes once and for all that He alone has all power in heaven and on earth. If anyone would challenge that, let them rise from the dead! But the Chinese Communist Party and all God-denying governments of the world reject this reality and appoint themselves as saviors, even though they are dead themselves, continually inflicting death on others, and are absolutely clueless how to overcome death. As such, they furiously oppose any other system of reform and salvation other than their own policies, programs, and procedures.

"In order to implement and perpetuate their God-denying plans, they deceive and distract their people with false promises, empty hope, and fantastical dreams of their God-hating fathers," the giant continued. "The result is exactly what you'd expect from these criminals: economic and social turmoil, wrecked lives, destroyed nations, and enslaved souls. These dictators are leaches who never stop lying and deceiving, replacing God with government, which is really themselves, the arrogant of the arrogant, making government the idol in which they have put their hope to save humanity and create better lives, but all the while stealing, killing, and destroying to do it! The result of their anti-Christ agenda is death—death of their people, their country, and eventually themselves. This is what happens when God is abandoned and false messiahs replace Jesus as the Way, the Truth, and the Life."

As the beautiful harmonies continued like a background chorus accentuating the homily, another thought came to EB. *Why*, he wondered, *would the Chinese Communist Party and government be so hostile toward Christianity unless it really was a threat?*

"Because it is true," the spirit answered, again reading his mind. "And you're right to ask that question. If Jesus's resurrection from the dead was just a children's story, a long-perpetuated fable serving as merely an opiate for the masses, there would be nothing to fear or be concerned about. It would present no more of a threat to them than the story of Winnie the Pooh or Harry Potter. But instead, they have marshaled their internal security forces to stamp out true Christianity, the faith that these pastors were teaching. Why? Because if the resurrection of Jesus actually happened, then that means Jesus is the appointed King of the planet by the Creator of the planet, and the only One who can deliver mankind from the horrible quandary in which he finds himself.

"What I didn't tell you about these pastors is that all of them were former communist leaders. This is another reason they have received such harsh treatment. All eight of them at one time were dedicated to eliminating the very faith for which they now are willing to die. How does something like that happen? Their own testimony is that the living Jesus confronted them, each at a different time, and in a different way, but really and actually with the same message: they were wrong and criminal in their beliefs and actions and therefore would stand before their Creator on a true and coming Judgment Day to give an account for their all their evil, especially their persecution of God's people, the Christians. Each could tell you the details, but our time does not allow. Leave it to be said that all would tell you that only a real interaction with the Creator and His Son, Jesus, could lead them as dedicated anti-theists to turn from their life of official power, prestige, and prosperity to a life of horrible suffering, rejection, and incarceration as you see them in now."

"That's not a very good trade," EB muttered.

"It would be an insane trade if it wasn't true and for a better end: eternal life. It's not just the communist party and all other governments that oppose Christ that stand condemned. All people everywhere will stand before the Bar of God on Judgment Day and give an account for all their thoughts and actions. And since no one, as we've already discussed, can claim to be guiltless, they will be found guilty and receive the just penalty for their crimes. Understand, EB, the punishment is not simply the death of the body and its disappearance back into dust. It is also the death of the soul and spirit."

"How can a spirit die? Does it just decay away like a physical body?" EB quivered.

"Your spirit, made in the image of God, is eternal. It had a beginning, but has no end. So the death of your spirit is eternal destruction, a pure and perfect suffering, commensurate with all the suffering caused by your crimes, that continues perpetually. If that was only a fairy tale, then no one would or should be worried. If, after you die, you just disappeared into nothingness, then what's to be upset or distressed about? But the deep shrilling fear and sense of doom from the guilt that plagues your and every person's soul is a warning that eternal, ongoing, never-ending punishment is not a superstition or clever story designed to control or manipulate.

"These men who sing before you here came to realize that this endless punishment was their well-deserved fate and cried out to God for forgiveness. But if you'll recall, just crying out or asking for forgiveness doesn't satisfy the need for justice. Justice demands that where there is crime, there must be punishment and restitution. An eye for an eye. Yet if justice is all there is, then every one of you humans who has violated the law of God can only expect God's everlasting punishment. But because God is not only the Great Judge, but also your loving Father, He has satisfied justice by imposing the punishment you deserve on His own perfect and guiltless Son."

"Yes, substitution," EB said.

"Those who desire that their sentence of everlasting punishment be transferred to Christ—in other words, accept God's payment of the fine—do so in an exchange," emphasized the green ghost.

"I was hoping we'd get to some business in all of these lessons." EB grinned, trying to deflect the deep conviction he felt in his soul and fear for his own fate.

"The transaction is simple," the giant continued. "You give your life in dedication to King Jesus and commit to abandon your own ways, your corrupt ideas, and your own selfish will in exchange to follow His pure ways, agree to change your thinking to conform to His perfect ideas and directives, and commit to, day by day, minute by minute, seeking to do His right and perfect will. Your motto after the exchange will be, 'Not my will, but God's be done.'"

"So Jesus's will and God's will is the same thing?"

"Precisely. Jesus is God incarnate, fully one with God in every way. All He did while on earth two thousand years ago was exactly God's will without one error, sin, or transgression. Otherwise, how would He be guiltless and able to be that substitution for you? So when you say, 'God's will be done,' you're committing to do Jesus's will."

"As good as that sounds, I'm quite sure I wouldn't be able to do God's will as a matter of routine or practice, day after day, even if I wanted to," EB questioned.

"Well, well, well. You have been listening and it seems have been given a glimmer of light. Of course you can't! Which is why there's another part of this that is essential to understand. Just as Jesus removes your guilt, exonerating you, so He also eradicates the malware, fully removes the virus. It happens in three phases."

"Wait, wait. You're saying that there will be a real transformation in my life if I agree with what you're saying—a real removal of the poison or malware that's encoded in me?" EB was stunned.

"Exactly, and it will happen at once, over time and then for all eternity. These are the three phases. First, once you see that your life is futile as it is and that you can even gain the whole world but lose your soul, once you understand and believe to the point that your whole life is given to Jesus to be your Commander in Chief, and call to Him to forgive you and save you, God appropriates the punishment that you justly deserve to Jesus. He becomes your substitution since you've agreed to make the trade, your life for His. You are free from guilt then, as Jesus's death is applied to your criminal account. The fine is paid. You are justified before God, and instead of being His enemy, you become His son."

"His son? So God adopts the hardened criminal into His family?" EB asked.

"No, not the hardened criminal. The hardened criminal is the person who rejects God's great offer, who after hearing such incredible news that he can find sanctuary, be forgiven, and not incur the horrible punishment that awaits him, spits in God's face and continues in the way of rebellion and evil. No, no, EB. No hardened criminal will be with God. They will have a place with the author of lies and all those who take pleasure in evil, who spurn Jesus as God's appointed Ruler over the planet, and refuse to change their way of thinking. But the softened and reformed criminal, the criminal who is shattered because of the evil he's committed, broken up because of all the destruction and pain he's caused, and cries out in desperation to the Creator Judge for forgiveness, accepting the substitutionary sacrifice of Jesus's death so he won't die, but live—that is the one God adopts and welcomes into His family. That is the one justified in sight of God's court. Such a person is not a criminal anymore because he has renounced the criminal, corrupt, and uncaring way of life.

"But that is just the beginning. Once a person is cleared before God's court and his sentence commuted to Jesus, and he or she is adopted into the family, that's where the new life begins. This is the second phase. Part of being justified and exculpated before God is the eradication of guilt. The other part is the eradication of the criminal nature that's encoded into each person."

"Yes, the genetic malware," EB said.

"The genetic malware and the spiritual malware. Remember, EB, the nature of man is not only material. There is a spiritual component, which is what you're being shown now. Once a person is exculpated by God, the Creator eradicates the spiritual malware. The old man is crucified with Jesus, so to speak, and the spiritual body of malware is done away with—eradicated. So a true believer in Jesus is given a new spirit, and becomes a new man. The virus is gone, the poison is extracted, never to be reintroduced or returned. The person is literally born again as a new person with a new, perfect, pure, and undefiled uncorrupted spirit. As a new person, the old habits, inclinations, and lusts begin to evaporate. The old criminal actions are halted and discarded, now being seen for the harmful, God-hating behaviors they really are. This happens because the old corrupt spirit has been replaced by a new, upright, and godly spirit, and so no longer is a captive of evil."

"I've got to say, spirit, that this all sounds fine and wonderful, but the reality is that some of the most corrupt and dishonest people I've met say they're Christians. If their corrupted, evil nature is replaced with a new one, why all the hypocrisy and crime among Christians?"

"Those who have been truly justified by God, welcomed into His family, and have determined to love and follow Jesus and His commands with all their heart, soul, mind, and strength will never continue in evil or hypocrisy. How can they if they have a new spirit and a new nature that abhors evil? But there are many who put on a religious front, who want to impress other people instead of God, and many who in their hearts have only tasted the goodness of God but never fully died to themselves or their evil, lustful desires. Wide is the way to destruction, but narrow, very narrow, is the way to life—and few find it. Make sure you're not a hypocrite either, EB, condemning others while you yourself practice the very same things!

"But so that you don't misunderstand, the second phase of sanctification is a lifelong process. The new spirit that is received when one is translated into God is pure and perfect because it is the Spirit of God that makes it so. God gives His perfect and pure Spirit to all His children, fully uniting with their spirit. And it is the work of this Holy Spirit that, over time, conforms a new member of God's family to Jesus, finishes the work of sanctifying that person so, as one of His sons or daughters, they are set free so they are no longer slaves to the criminal passions, the lusts of the body to do evil.

"Just like in life as you know it now, when a person is conceived, that person is fully human and a permanent member of the human family. But it takes many years for that individual to reach maturity. So it is with those born into God's family and nation. Once they are cleansed from their guilt and corruption, and have been forgiven and adopted, they are then forever part of His family. Once in the family, the old, corrupted, criminally inclined nature is gone and replaced by God's nature or Spirit. Then, by the power of the Holy Spirit of God in them—His nature—they learn complete obedience, becoming mature. This maturity is the process of sanctification whereby they are conformed by the hand of God to be as Jesus, instruments to do good, to do what's right and pure, with a changed heart that wants God's way in everything—not only their personal lives, but corporately in all of life and society as well."

"So what, then, is the third phase?" EB asked, wanting to wrap up the conversation, having never been fond of long sermons or speeches.

"If the first is the purification of the spirit, called justification, and the second is the purification of the soul by the removal of evil lusts, habits, inclinations, and thoughts, the third must complete the triune salvation of man. What do you think it is, EB?"

"Well, you've not talked about the body. I can guarantee you that there is no Christian on the planet whose body is not decaying and dying. If they've been saved from the punishment of death, why are they still dying?"

"Exactly. I see why you did well in school. The third phase is the full redemption and perfection of the body. But that can't happen on a planet that is corrupted, and in a universe that is subject to the universal laws of corruption."

"Like the second law of thermodynamics," EB inserted.

"That's one of the codes, but there are others built in that make the cosmos as corrupted as humanity. Not moral corruption—matter doesn't think or act ethically. Doing good or evil flows from the spirit. But systemic corruption of the material universe is part of the judgment imposed on mankind. When the first man rebelled against God and was judged for it, so was the entirety of creation that was made for him, his wife, and their progeny. But as man chose to go the way of corruption and death, so went his habitat and environment. But the third phase resolves that."

"If what you're saying is true, you'd need a completely new cosmos and planet!" EB scoffed.

"And that is exactly what the third phase is. In God's own timing, He will roll up this universe like a worn-out scroll, torching it so as to eradicate it of all its corruption. All the material universe, including all galaxies, stars, solar systems, and even the planet Earth, will be eviscerated so that every proton, neutron, and electron, and all the subatomic particles you don't even know about, are annihilated. No poisonous or corrupted code will be left. In its place, God will again create a new space and time, a new universe and fabric, which will include a new earth for His new sons and daughters. His his new, purified family will then enjoy this magnificent palatial creation for all eternity. The Creator will give new, sinless, lust-free, crimeless, purified, pain-free, ageless, fully glorified bodies to them. This is the third and final phase of redemption for those who give themselves fully to the King of kings, Scientist of scientists, Ruler of rulers—Sovereign General Jesus."

"Really? Why don't I know about this? I'm not sure I believe it—it's a pretty fantastic story. But is all of this written down somewhere, where I can review it when our life coaching sessions here are over?"

"You do know it, or I should say you did know it. But you have rejected it. If somehow you do take all this 'life coaching' to heart, you will find a full and inerrant account of this and all His will in that book you used to study in the chapel."

"Hmm. I surely did spend a lot of time in the Bible as a kid. After all, children's stories are for children," EB said, frowning at the spirit's answer. "But to get back to the more practical part of our session, you're saying Jesus is God's appointed King over all the earth, and that everyone in all countries everywhere, including the communist government here in China—all governments, really—must submit to His will. And not doing so is rebellion against God who promises judgment for all who don't obey?"

"Yes, how could it be otherwise?" the spirit answered.

"Then I can see why the Communist Chinese Party and government, as well as governments all over the planet, are hostile and have great antipathy toward Jesus. Both demand total allegiance!" EB emphasized.

"Jesus was declared by God Himself to be King over all earthly kings, or as you might better understand it, EB, President over all presidents, Prime Minister over all prime ministers, General over all generals, whether Secretary or Five Star. The earth is His and all its fullness, including all governments, which are on His shoulders. To put it plainly, God appointed Jesus over all, giving Him all power and all authority. Even though there will be a new earth down the road, He still requires obedience because every action that is not obedient to His directives is in the truest sense criminal rebellion. Remember, only God is good. All people are spiritually fallen from goodness and so can't help but think in terms of evil and darkness. Reforming a nation is the same as an individual reforming their personal life—it is the process of getting rid of thoughts, ideas, as well as the policies, programs, laws, and actions that are contradictory to God's ways and replacing them with what God has said on the subject. Failure to do so is a direct attack on God and declaration of war against Him, His Truth, and—as ridiculous as it is—against His Sovereignty. An ant would have a better chance against a steamroller.

"But understand, becoming one of His followers, a person not only becomes a member of His family, but a citizen of His nation. Both are forever and cost everything. The reward, however, is that you're not a fugitive of justice anymore—your crimes are quashed, your record is cleaned, and you now have access to God as a good, law-abiding citizen instead of being His target as a seditious felon and treasonous rebel. With a clean record, a perfected spirit, and a new life dedicated to follow God's will in everything, you'll spend eternity with your Father in His coming country and new earth kingdom."

"This whole thing seems like a pretty lopsided transaction, spirit," EB noted. "If I'm understanding you correctly, I have everything to gain—a new spirit, a new family, eventually a new body and a new, perfected, unpolluted planet and universe to live in and explore. And I lose nothing? Those are the kinds of deals I built my empire on!"

"Yes, you have everything to gain, but in this world you lose everything, especially your own corrupted, enslaved, despicable life. You're trading this world and all its corruption for the pure and holy world to come. You're giving up your depraved, decaying, devilish life in a decadent, decomposing, dying world for eternal life and never-ending bliss in a new world and universe that God will create after destroying the present one. You'll have a new body in this new heaven and new earth, one that won't decay or die, and there will be no more pain, suffering, or crime of any kind. And like what you wanted as a little boy, you'll spend eternity with your Father. But until then, you would become like these prisoners, an enemy of God's enemies to be hunted like prey. Persecution will be inescapable. Take hold of my robe, and see."

As soon as he touched his garment, the chorus ceased and EB found himself, in the blink of an eye, standing on a dusty desert road next to his large green companion under a clear open sky lit up by innumerable galaxies of stars and a crescent moon.

CHAPTER 26

Before EB could reply to the giant's troubling promise of persecution, a pair of topless American-made Humvees and a Ford cargo van ripped past him creating a dust storm that would have covered and choked them if they had been there materially. Each of the jeeps was packed beyond its intended capacity with rough-looking men sporting long beards and turbans on their heads. Strapped over their shoulders or carried in their hands were semiautomatic AK47s, converted to full automatic fire, making them rapid-fire machine guns. Both jeeps skidded to a stop in front of a traditional mud house, one fairly large for the neighborhood, and the heavily armed men poured out of their chariots.

The largest of the men, clearly their leader, shouted out some orders in a language EB couldn't understand at all and didn't even know if he had ever heard it before. Immediately, some of the other fifteen to twenty men surrounded the humble home while the rest lined up behind their leader at the front door. He pounded with his fist on the door and again yelled something incomprehensible. An older woman covered from head to toe in a long dress-like garment opened the door just a crack, which the leader took advantage of and, with his troops, stormed into the home.

The giant grabbed EB's arm and transported the two into the main sitting room where the ragged but fierce-looking soldiers stood. In the room, EB could see there were about thirty people, probably a gathering of several families since more than half of them were children. Again the bearded brute barked something at them, which sent them all to their knees with their hands up in the air.

"What's happening, spirit? Who are all these people?" EB finally inquired.

"These are Taliban warriors speaking Pashto. They are the current ruling dictatorship controlling all of Afghanistan, a country the size of Texas, under Islamic law—a law system they call Sharia. The Sharia law system is based on the Koran and the teachings of the founder of Islam, Muhammad, and calls for the followers of Muhammad to subsume the whole of society, including education, government, economics and banking, family law, diet, hygiene, and religious activity, under Muslim precepts. They wouldn't be in power as they are now, and be able to exhibit such oppressive dominion, but one of your misguided presidents, Joe Biden, made a foolish and deadly decision not too many years ago to pull out of Afghanistan and leave it in the hands of these Jihadi militants. Since the chaotic and botched American withdrawal, the Taliban have created an Islamist prison state, a Caliphate, that forbids these families from doing what they're doing."

"What are they doing? It looks to me like they were just sitting on these mattresses lined up against the wall and eating, talking, and spending time together," EB observed, pointing to the food on trays in front of their sitting cushions.

"You're correct, that's what they were doing. But they were also reading passages from a book since today is a special day for them," the specter said. Before he could say anything else, one of the jihadi fired his gun at a corner of the room that had a cross displayed on the wall, surrounded by lit candles.

"Haram!" the warrior shouted as he not only obliterated the cross, but the entire wall with it. "Allahu akbar!" cried all of his fellow soldiers as they held their rifles above their heads, pumping them up and down. The children began to scream, as did a number of the women, some of whom were quite old. Together, they all fell down onto their bellies while the Islamic vanguards continued their Koranic chant.

After finishing their shouts, another order was given and they spread out through the home, tossing the pillows, wrecking shelves, overturning mattresses, tables, and chairs and clearing out cabinets, wildly throwing whatever they found violently to the floor. One of the soldiers started yelling as he held up an opened book. EB could see that the book had been well read with parts of the showing pages underlined and highlighted with notations in the margins.

Immediately the other soldiers stopped their rummaging and all circled back in the living room.

"Is that what they were destroying the house for? A book? What is it, some kind of top-secret manual?" EB asked, moving right up to the soldier who was presenting it to his leader.

"It's a Bible, translated into Pashto, and it's opened to a section in the book called Matthew that tells the story of the birth of Jesus," the giant said.

"That's it? Just a Bible?" EB said, stunned.

"America has Bibles everywhere, but doesn't realize the treasure they have. Here in the outskirts of Kabul under the Taliban tyrants, owning a Bible in Pashto is forbidden and is punishable by prison. Some here have even died for having a Bible and following what it says."

"I don't understand. It's just a book," EB continued to probe.

"It's not just a book, and that's why these Islamists hate it. It's the Word of God in verbal propositional form, and has been the most powerful book in human history, bringing down nations, even empires. You would not be what you are today, nor would

America even exist, nor would Europe and the West as a whole, if it weren't for this book."

"That's hard to believe," EB said.

"It's only hard to believe because you have not read it and contemplated its message since you were a young boy. The families you see here were all Muslim at one point. But that man over there, lying on his face in front of the leader, was secretly given a Bible when he was going through a dark time during the rise of the Taliban Caliphate. Knowing as a good Muslim that it was a criminal offense to read it, or even just be caught with it, he would wake up in the early morning, before sunrise, and study it. The Koran had done nothing for him but plunge him further into despair and fear, for the Koran had assured him that after this life, he would stand before God and be judged."

"Sounds like what you just told me the Bible teaches," EB observed.

"That there is a Judgment Day, yes, they both teach that. But different from the Bible, the Koran promised that his judgment depended on his good works. It taught him that there would be a grand scale at the final judgment, the *Great Mizan* they call it, where his good works would be weighed against his evil, criminal, or unrighteous actions.

"He had not been a criminal of any kind that the Taliban cared about—he wasn't a thief, he always tried to speak the truth, he never missed prayer or failed to give alms. By all accounts, he was a good Muslim. But a crisis in his life forced him to be honest with himself and really dig deep down into his motives, into his secret life, into the actions no one but he knew about. As he examined himself truly and honestly, he realized that his whole life was full of guile and darkness. Though others thought he wasn't a liar, he knew he was—a big liar, always manipulating the truth, fudging the numbers at his job, even if just a little, and regularly deceiving his wife when he thought it convenient.

"But it wasn't just his prevarications that caused his conscience to condemn him. He had once cheated on his wife, who he dearly loved, in a moment of weakness and lust. Adultery is a capital crime in Islam, and he was guilty. Even though it only happened once, when he became genuinely transparent with himself and pushed away the lies and excuses he tried to make for himself, he knew he was an adulterer, and under his own belief system, deserved death.

"Acknowledging these crimes helped soften his conscience, which he had hardened like a rock over the years. And with this softening, he began to see more clearly that it wasn't just the lying and adultery that tipped the *Great Mizan* against him, but his whole life was full of hypocritical wickedness. He didn't love and take care of his family as he should have; he didn't always keep prayer time five times each day as his law required. He failed to always eat the right foods as Muhammad had commanded, and his alms giving was generous, but not to the level of what the Koran demanded. The more he dug down into his soul, the more he realized that not just his actions, but his very disposition, was abominable, feigning friendship when he really hated the person, using flattery to gain the advantage, and worst of all he discovered that he was the greediest person he knew.

"As a businessman, like you, EB, he justified his greed by extoling the glory of the markets, and that by striving for endless capital he was really helping not only the community, but Islam itself. But this was a cover. Inside were a dead man's bones, a soul so corrupt and self-centered that he wouldn't have even realized his depravity if it hadn't been for this awakening. Everything he did was for himself, his own glory and self-aggrandizement, even though he tried to make it appear otherwise to his business associates, Muslim friends, and most significantly, his family. This was the real weight of his life."

"But you said he did many good works," EB interjected.

"Remember the water analogy? Even if 99 percent of his works looked good and pure, that 1 percent of poison spoiled all. But the reality was that only in his own self-deception did he think any of his works were really good. Most, if put under a microscope, would reveal impure motives and lack of any genuinely authentic love or compassion. And of those that were good, they would soon be followed by bad ones, born out of greed, lust, pride, envy, hatred, or jealousy. It wasn't that he had 99 percent good works and a speck of bad, but it was the opposite when he examined all his works as a whole. The *Great Mizan* for him would be one where the evil so far outweighed the good in his life that the evil side would hit the ground."

"I'm sensing that this is important for me to understand," EB divined.

"They always said you were a genius, EB, so don't miss this. In his condition, Yousef—that's his name—became depressed. He tried to live a better life, be a better Muslim, and do what he thought was right, only to find himself delving right back into the very evil he was trying to get rid of. Over and over, he tried to change, tried to be good, tried to live up to the high standard of Islam, its requirements, laws, and rituals. But over and over he failed, each time becoming a little more frustrated, a little more deflated, and ultimately angry at himself and the world. This led to an internal concoction of sadness and rage, wrapped by the doubt that there even was a God. This endless cycle of moral or spiritual failure finally culminated in hopelessness. If there really was a *Great Mizan* on Judgment Day, he was done. He wouldn't be able to argue with God or present any evidence to vindicate himself. He was guilty and knew he was guilty and deserved the harshest punishment the Koran prescribed for the harm he had caused and the sin he had engaged in."

"Part of the problem with religion, I would humbly submit," EB interjected.

"If you define religion as a person's futile attempt to save himself by flawlessly adhering to a list of requirements, then yes, that is the very essence of the problem here. Thankfully, a friend saw Yousef spiraling down into a horrible place, and bravely gave him a Bible, the very one you see that leader holding. Having given up, Yousef reluctantly took it, but mostly just to pacify his friend, not wanting to offend him for his kindness and taking interest in him. He planned to just throw it away so as not to make his already wrecked life even worse, so the next day he threw it into a trash pile on a side road. The Bible failed to stay in the garbage mound as Yousef intended, and instead bounced out of the rubbish and onto the road, where it lay open. He didn't want anyone else to find it, so he quickly picked it up off the road. But before he could throw it farther into the pile, the words on the page it was opened to caught his eye. It had opened to a letter that's in the Bible from one of God's messengers, Paul, to a group of Christians in the town of Ephesus:

But God, being rich in mercy, because of His great love with which He loved us, even when we were dead in our crimes against God, made us alive together with the Savior Jesus who saved us by His grace, and raised us up with Him, and seated us with Him in the heavenly places in Christ Jesus, so that in the ages to come He might show the surpassing riches of His grace in kindness toward us in Christ Jesus. For by grace you have been saved through faith; and that not of yourselves, it is the gift of God; not as a result of works, so that no one may boast. For we are His workmanship, created in Christ Jesus for good works, which God prepared beforehand so that we would walk in them.

"When he read just these few words, they came alive. He had already come to know that he couldn't save himself, and that all his religious works actually condemned him. But in this passage, he read something foreign to his Islam: God loved him. He couldn't have imagined it. God loved *him*? The Koran taught him that because of all the evil he'd done, Allah didn't love him but would punish him forever because his evil works outweighed his good ones, by far. But here was a different message, a different God who was extending kindness to him in grace, who would save him from the great judgment, though he was dead in his guilt. And so he tucked the Bible under his shirt and read it from front to back, studying it and memorizing parts of it in case the Bible was ever confiscated or lost.

"Not long after, his wife saw his one-hundred-and-eighty-degree turnaround. She saw that he was a new man. So did his children and his extended family. Yousef had immersed himself in the Bible and soon after started to teach his wife, children, and relatives all he learned. Like him, they all discovered that Jesus was really alive, had resurrected, and that all that the Bible taught was true. The greatest proof for them was the transformation that resulted in their own lives.

"But word got out into the community, to the Taliban, that this well-established Muslim was not a Muslim anymore, but had committed the capital crime of abandoning Islam and converting to Christianity. They decided to wait until today to arrest him, knowing that, on Christmas Day, they would all be gathered together—even if only in the quiet of the night for a short time— to celebrate the birth of the One that saved their family."

During the giant's recounting of Yousef's story, the Taliban enforcers had continued to quiz the family members and harass and beat the men, at times distracting EB from what the ghost was saying. Then, just as the ghost finished, a couple of the soldiers, now drunk in the fun of their raid, grabbed two of the women who, like Yousef, had been lying on their faces at the feet of the soldiers. They pulled them up and ushered them into one of the bedrooms, laughing and slapping them as they screamed out not to do this to them. Yousef jumped up in an effort to help his wife, as did his brother, who also rose to defend his wife. But they were immediately halted with the butts of two other soldiers' AK47s. The children also started screaming, especially Yousef's son. Like his father, he was hit in the face with one of their rifles and crumpled to the ground. Shocked and infuriated, EB left the side of his green guardian and ran to the boy and knelt down beside him, assuring him he would be all right even though the boy couldn't see or hear him. Finally coming to grips with his helplessness, EB also crumpled over, put his face in his hands, and, with the boy, wept.

"Our time is short; we must go," the spirit said to EB after a few moments.

"But who will help them? Who will help those women? We can't leave now. Do something, spirit. Wave your torch or something, but stop this unconscionable horror!"

"They will be judged for this evil and all their atrocities. But until then, the families knew the cost in this life of renouncing Islam and living for Jesus, and embraced it without hesitation. They don't blame God for this, but thank Him that they're counted by Him with such favor as to suffer for truth as Jesus suffered. They understand that the same spirit of fury and hatred toward God that possessed the murderers who tortured and crucified the very Son of God on a cross will today do the same to Jesus's servants. But in spite of whatever they must go through, He has given those that are His the promise that nothing will separate them from His eternal love," said the spirit, grabbing EB by his collar and lifting him up from the boy's side.

The pair then followed the Taliban thugs as they exited the home with their chained prisoners, beaten, broken, and defrauded. All were crying except the two women the warriors had taken who were silent, slumped over in torn dresses, almost lifeless. Mercilessly, they dragged the group to the large military cargo van, a gift they acquired from the equipment left behind by Biden, all the while laughing and slapping each other's backs. After throwing them all violently onto the van's cold metal floor, it sped off into the night as the Taliban posse once again started pumping their rifles above their heads, chanting at the top of their lungs that their god Allah was great.

EB had seen such antics in videos and on the Holovision, but being in the midst of such a ruthless and savage assault sent the scimitar of their terror directly into the center of his heart. "Please, spirit, take me away from this place and from these sufferings," he pleaded.

"My time with you has almost expired, but we have one more stop on our journey together," the spirit said.

"Couldn't we just skip it? Please? I've seen enough and appreciate what you're trying to show me. I will give it all much thought and consideration," EB argued.

"Consideration? How much—a few minutes or a few hours? You'll weigh all you've seen and put it on a ledger to see how your income and status will result from any decision you make? Clearly, you haven't seen enough," said the giant whose jovial demeanor once again soured toward EB.

"You don't understand. I'm physically and intellectually spent. I don't have anything left no matter where you take me or what you show me," he said, still terrified. He then slumped on the ground like an impertinent child and put his head between his knees. "I'm not going anywhere else. Do you hear me? I'm finished!"

CHAPTER 27

"Do you hear me, spirit? I'm done with this whole hexagas humbug!" EB said after a few more seconds, sitting with his arms wrapped around his knees and head still between them. Not feeling anything after a few minutes, not a tug on his robe or a set of giant fingers around his arm, EB thought that maybe he had finally persuaded the goliath to leave him be. But when he lifted his head, he found himself seated on the floor of a large office or conference room—an exorbitantly plush meeting room with a long, magnificently polished burl wood table in its center.

Towering over him was his green guide, arms folded, who had apparently been waiting for him to finish his tantrum. "Stand up," the spirit said to him, "or you will miss the most important part of the meeting."

EB obeyed the spirit, seeing he was back in a familiar setting, and jumped to his feet. He looked around the extraordinary room, examining it carefully to see if he was in a place where he had conducted any of his business before. After a quick look around, he determined he hadn't, but still felt right at home, especially with the arc-shaped floor-to-ceiling glass window wall that, other than the arc shape, reminded him of his penthouse, which he missed greatly and longed for.

Bowing outward, it was clear that the high-rise room must have been in a circular building, but not very high up by his standards; he estimated about twenty stories. But he felt quite elevated since there were no other buildings obstructing his views, nor were there any taller in the serene town below him.

Composed of mostly two- and three-story buildings, the scene below him resembled more of a village than a modern city, dotted with older European-style structures built around a wide river half a mile or so away from his perch. He wondered what river that was that so beautifully reflected the gorgeous array of oranges, reds, and yellows as the sun set behind it.

In the room was a different array, one of men and women of all ethnicities, sizes, and ages sitting around that extraordinary long and very old-looking table. EB didn't recognize it at first, but after a few moments of observation, realized it was a piece he had once desired for himself for his own tower's main conference room.

"That's the Rothschild Table!" EB said enthusiastically to the spirit, who paid no attention to his discovery. The table had long ago served as the family dinner table of Mayer Rothschild, founder of the Rothschild banking and finance dynasty, during the late 1700s. Prolific in other areas besides money, Mayer and his wife had ten children together—five boys and five girls—and had the table specially built to accommodate their large brood plus guests in gatherings he frequently had in his home. Though a part of the Rothschild family for centuries, the Rothschild foundation took ownership of the forty-by-eight-foot table, finally donating it in May of 1930 to an elite banking group in celebration of their founding the Bank of International Settlements.

"Klaus, would you repeat that last point," said a very tall, thin man—close to seven feet—who was also gazing out the long arced window, only a few feet away from EB.

"Certainly. The Fourth Industrial Revolution is now entrenched and has advanced our agenda more than we imagined. Virtually everything has been digitized, spawning digital platforms, networks, and connections in every sector of life and society that did not exist before. The masses have swarmed to live digitally, as we predicted, particularly those who had been disadvantaged in the past: women, young people, persons with disabilities, and marginalized groups in all parts of the world. But here's the point: we are losing control. The old levers of our power are dissolving, or in some cases have disappeared completely."

"That's why we're here. Can't think of a better way to spend Christmas evening than to resolve these issues and conclude the year with a solution," the tall man said, turning away from the window and back toward the stretched table, waving his long suit-covered arm toward the amazingly diverse group sitting around it, several persons deep. Together, they emanated a collective strength and resolve that even intimidated EB who also had turned away from the view to observe this majestic bunch.

"What are the immediate threats?" the tall man then asked.

"Centralized planning is being replaced by unregulated associations and connections over our digital infrastructure. The most important, I believe, is in the area of work and income. Minimum wage laws are being completely discarded with market negotiations setting wages. Contractors in India, Africa, and parts of Asia are determining their own cost of labor, which often is far below the thresholds we've established. Through numerous online work platforms, laborers are connecting, finding work, negotiating a wage both parties are satisfied with, and without any oversight or management, carrying out tasks of all kinds. The result? Small enterprises that are not conforming to our values, our vision, or our objectives are springing up everywhere, undermining all our efforts over the last century."

"It could become worse than we ever imagined," a slender, but very aged woman with short white hair, an out-of-place perma-tanned face, and a diplomatic French accent added. "Labor unions, laws that prevent open market activity, and regulations that ensure conformity to our centrist standards are being obliterated. Even collective bargaining is being discarded as workers pursue income online, haggling on their own without our oversight or social protection!"

"Yes, Charlatine, and let us not forget that a primary source of our revenue and social control is being cut off as income taxes are being reduced in some places and skirted in others because of this atomization," Klaus continued. "We're speaking openly here among us, so I'll say it plainly. Income tax is one of the greatest mechanisms of power we have ever devised. Our forefathers brought forth upon us the mandate of global governance, which is only possible through the appropriation of a man or woman's wealth—their land, labor, and capital—to us."

"Finally, some people talking sense," EB said to his green guide as he settled into the setting.

"I should have mentioned that," Charlatine interrupted Klaus. "Thank you for keeping us on track. With all my decades of experience in building international monetary mechanisms and fortifying centralized banking, I can't emphasize enough that redistribution of the people's wealth through income tax is a major key to our mission's success. It is the tie that binds all productive workers to us. In essence, income tax is our taking ownership of a person's productivity. If we lose this overarching power to confiscate income at whatever level we choose and then disperse it according to our globalist goals, global governance cannot exist. Frankly, it will be destroyed."

"Or said another way," Klaus interjected, "as long as we control the income stream of the planet's workers, we will control the planet."

"And why hasn't our Personal Protection Chip scheme resolved this?" the tall man asked, hardly moving his lips but somehow able to project his voice.

"It may in time, but PPCs are still voluntary. That's the main problem," Charlatine answered from one end of the table. "And so they're only utilized by fellow traveling corporations, leftist organizations, as well as government employees and contractors around the world that have been mandated to use them. As you all know, we've made extraordinary strides in turning all money into digital currency—state-controlled money, that is. And I'm pleased to announce to the group that, under the United Nations International Currency, or UNIC's digitization plan, India has just agreed to fully convert the rupee to digital currency, the last of the G10 nations to do so."

"We won't achieve our monetary objectives until all the world's major currencies are digital," the tall man said sternly, the group nodding in enthusiastic agreement. "And all the private digital currencies are deleted. Preston, update us on the status."

"Unbeknownst to private digital coin carriers, we've actually achieved full control over all the rogue currencies and are just waiting for the right moment to tank them. I'd say no more than a year or two until we make the announcement—or more precisely, surreptitiously reveal the proof of our control," explained Preston, a bald member of the group who EB thought looked remarkably similar to Austin Power's nemesis, Dr. Evil.

"Cryptocurrency fanatics naively poured their wealth into a medium that could only be utilized across our networks," he continued. "It's true, originally their algorithms allowed for decentralization and anonymity. But fools they are, they believed that the internet would always belong to the people. We've leaked rumors over the last several years that we've just figured out how to track every move, whether buying, selling, or transferring, and can also confiscate this rogue digital money on whatever platform it sits in or in whichever bank it resides. The truth is, we've had this technical ability for more than a decade but have simply chosen not to deploy it. But our rumors have served their purpose and the values of private digital currencies have cratered down to, at best, 20 percent of their highs over the years."

"But they must be eradicated!" the tall man said forcefully, again not moving his mouth.

"Just give the word, and we can do it," Preston assured the group.

"I'd recommend we welcome the New Year with this surprise!" Charlatine suggested as she waived her bony, bent forefinger above her puffy white-haired head. "With unsanctioned cryptocurrencies reduced to zero value, only state-approved and -controlled digital currencies will be available. From our CENTCOM at UNIC, all digital currency transactions are monitored and thereby controlled. We can already fully manage transactions with anyone implanted with a PPC. But mandating the implantation, as you all know, is the last leg of the race. And we were almost there! We were so close to breaking the will of the people during the First and Second Great Pandemics."

"We won't fail again," the tall man prophesied.

"We can't fail again," Klaus emphasized. "As I was saying earlier, digitization is inherently fragmentary. We have to have total managerial power or global governance is just rainbows and unicorns. No global governance, no planetary salvation. I don't think I need to remind you, but if we fail, humanity will descend into chaos. We'll be back in the days of tribal wars, dog-eat-dog, where the wild west of the free market ushers in a global dark age of horrible non-green energy production, inequity, unbridled free speech, and that basest of all evils: individual liberty!"

"As I said," Charlatine jumped in, "mandate the PPC, mission accomplished!"

"Bill, is the Third Pandemic ready for release?" the tall man asked a dweeby-looking elder at the table, whose glasses were far too big for his puckered face.

"The variant is ready and this time will bring just the right amount of carnage and destruction necessary for the masses to be subdued. We've had over five years since P2 to learn," Bill instructed.

"As a reminder," he continued, "P1 was our test run, to monitor national responses and what kinds of social control measures would or wouldn't be implemented, how the world would respond to the World Health Organization's vaccine and safety recommendations and mandates, and to begin the great resetting of infrastructures, economies, and supply chains to accommodate the real revolution via P2. P1 was particularly effective in accelerating global depopulation, especially through the almost untraceable but marvelously devastating effects the vaccine caused to the immune and circulatory systems of the weak. Additionally, there were many rumors and conspiracies circulating during P1 that a microchip had been placed in every dose. At that time, the technology hadn't been developed to do this. We hadn't discovered quantum electricity yet, and so didn't know how to harness the power of the atom on a micro level. We were close, but nowhere near what would be needed to power an implanted chip for a lifetime."

"How did rumor get started that P1 vaccine had chip?" asked a huge military uniformed man in a Russian accent.

"We started the rumor!" Bill giggled. "What better way to prepare for the future implantation than to discredit the idea beforehand? Nearly every news outlet, fact-checking organization, and scientific establishment—from the CDC to the WHO—all utterly dismantled the idea as a crazy internet theory. But we knew we'd have the technology ready by P2, not only to power the implant, but also to have the means to ensure each vaccine dose had a tested, functioning biochip preloaded in it."

"But P2 failed. I still don't fully understand why that happened," interjected a young member at the table, one of their Young Global Leaders, a ruddy, freckled boy who, with his Caesar-like haircut, appeared too young to even have a driver's license, even though he was one of the most brilliant programmers alive.

"We released the variant too early, plain and simple," Bill explained. "We had the vaccine prepared, complete with our newly designed biochip in every dose. We had run the tests in our labs around the world, and it worked perfectly. A decade had passed since P1, and as we had planned, both the variant and the microchip were ready by the P2 launch date. As you'll recall, the P2 variant was brutal and a killer, just as we engineered, making our vaccine essential for survival. But that damn chip—there was an oversight.

"We hadn't sufficiently tested it for longevity," Bill continued. "We just didn't have the time to test the chip between the time its quantum power source had been developed and the P2 release date. Our models demonstrated with near certainty that the chip would stay powered and connected to the grid with full functionality—up to a quarter century, the models showed. Twenty-five years would have been plenty of time to use it to galvanize control. Bottom line, our models were wrong. The chip functioned marvelously for several months, but then began to degrade—en masse. Nearly eight billion doses had been prefilled and administered in record time thanks to the logistics we worked out in P1. But after six months, we had the world's population walking around healthy and whole, but with useless microchips in their system."

"This has been resolved? We cannot fail again," Klaus

asserted. "This final pandemic represents what may be our last window of opportunity to reset our world as we have been reimagining all these years."

"Agreed. We've had enough years since P2 to have tested the chip thoroughly. We know it will work flawlessly for at least ten years, probably a lot longer," Bill said proudly, waving his hands while talking for emphasis.

"We only need half of that," the tall man emphasized. "If your chip works for five years, as Charlatine likes to say, mission accomplished!"

"Don't worry, third time's the charm." Bill smiled confidently. "I'm actually thankful for P2. From it, we learned much, though at a heavy cost economically and in loss of life. But hey, success is a lousy teacher, right? It seduces we geniuses into thinking we can't lose. Our failures in P1 and P2 gave us the experience we needed with variants, vaccines, vanquishing economies and the sovereignty of nations, and all the variables connecting the two to make P3 our victory. Plus, in the years since P2, quantum subatomic power has advanced dramatically, and the transmission range of the biochip has also been significantly expanded, putting every human within range—at all times—of our satellite sensors. In my humble opinion, we've hit the trifecta this time, successfully moderating the variables so our next variant released will spread much faster than Omicron, and be potent enough to drop an elephant. No one will mistake this little bugger for the flu or worry whether or not our micro-tracking chip is in every dose.

"When the initial carnage is seen on every channel of every Holovision set and headlines every news site," Bill said, gesticulating wildly, "every conversation will be about survival. Economies will crash overnight. Inflation will skyrocket, and hunger will overtake nations as the new lockdowns will make the

P1 and P2 shutdowns look like a toddler time-out. The first casualties will not be pretty—in fact, they'll be horrifying. But these are the optics we need for persuasion. The world will come to a full stop in order to get vaccinated—economies, governments, wars—everything! Then we release the Vacci-Chip®. We'll be honored as the heroes we are, the real saviors of the planet and its economies, and, of course, humanity. We estimate we can have more than 95 percent of the planet vaccinated within six months of its release."

"In light of this coming variant's threat," Charlatine jumped in, "there may be a very large risk of panic caused by P3 if there's the slightest delay in having the Vacci-Chip-instilled vaccines positioned and ready. Any glitch in the immediate availability of the vaccine would inevitably lead to rioting, mayhem, and social unrest, possibly beyond what we can control."

"We have twenty-five billion chip-infused doses already manufactured, tested, prefilled, staged, and ready to go," Bill said in his quirky style, continuing to talk with his hands in a language no one could understand. "Once injected, the chips are programmed to immediately sync with the UNIC system, after which they'll migrate to the person's hand or wrist area and settle permanently. Their migration location is to provide ease of access, as well as convenience for scanning if need be. Oh, I forgot to mention that the chips are dormant and undetectable until the vaccine actually enters the bloodstream. That's what activates it, brings it online, and connects the recipient to our powerful UNIC."

"And what about casualties? Have you estimated total deaths needed to implement the plan?" the tall man asked.

"Close to a hundred million dead worldwide if all goes well, with an error factor of plus or minus 2 percent. It could be ten times that, however, if there are any unforeseen delays or unplanned disruptions. But most will be the elderly, obese, and infirm, none of the Essentials." Bill smiled. "Actually, this will be a well-needed cleansing of the unproductive, socially deplorable Non-essentials. There will also be certain genetic groups more affected than others; count on big fatality numbers in Africa. But overall, the best-case scenario is a pretty good trade if you ask me—a hundred million or so sacrificed to gain between eight and nine billion chip implants. I wish I could get those kinds of returns in my companies!"

"We can accept that," said Shipokosa, the well-dressed Secretary General of the Africa National Congress, which after P2, usurped power in the whole of southern Africa, creating New South Africa, a super state confederation of South Africa, Namibia, Botswana, Angola, Mozambique, Zambia, and Zimbabwe.

"Where is all the implant data managed and stored? Certainly UNIC does not have the ability, expertise, or the capacity," one of the group asked in Mandarin, with immediate translation to English and the other languages of the attending principals via the Pod system they were using for their conference.

"That's where I come in," said a new voice, one EB immediately recognized. "I have the fusion server centers—me and my partner—that will store, manage, and safeguard every bit and byte of incoming data from the Vacci-Chips. Combined with all the other data we've been vacuuming up for the last several years through our SwarmTroopers, Pod, and Elevation systems, there will be virtually no information we do not control."

"Your partner?" Klaus said skeptically. "Our plan is to be known only to those here in the GOD!"

"I think you are all familiar with him," Narud calmly replied, waving his hand over the communication ball in front of him to bring up a hologram of EB in the middle of the table. "You know him. He's the founder of eBeja and innovator of Elevation as well as the global Pod system that basically replaced the old internet. He has not officially been appointed a member of our Global Open Discussion forum, but we have invited EB in the past to attend and speak at our forum events. I would propose we now nominate him to officially join GOD."

"It's Narud!" EB said, tugging the huge green messenger's robe. He hadn't noticed him before since he was seated on the side of the table where EB could only see the attendees' backs. "And there I am, in full holographic glory! See how utterly realistic and spectacular my technology is?"

Instinctively, EB immediately ran to Narud and grabbed his shoulder from behind as if to greet him, only to once again watch his hand pass through a body he tried to touch.

"He never told me about these people, or this plan," EB blurted out in frustration to his guide after a few more attempts to get Narud's attention.

"There's much he hasn't told you," said the giant. "But actually he did tell you, just not the details. Now you know what their GOD has planned for you!"

"What? These people won't have anything to do with God, especially Narud. What are you talking about?" EB replied.

"The Global Open Discussion forum, GOD for short, that owns the wealthy, the intellectuals, many of the government leaders and powerful among men. You never replied to their invitations," the spirit reminded EB.

"I had no idea. The name 'Global Open Discussion' sounded so boring and ineffective," EB answered.

"Optics that enable them to stay in the shadows. These who you see sitting around this special table are the forum's leaders, humanity's most powerful. This one is a former head of state," the giant indicated, walking around the table. "And here is a central bank president of a powerful Western country, and another and another. This scrawny, weak-looking one here is the head of the Bank of International Settlements, where this meeting is taking place. Don't let his unintimidating, quirky appearance deceive you. He's ferocious and one of the most dangerous people on the planet. Next to him, the middle-aged decaying one with the grotesquely fat and puckered face, is the son of the late Dr. Soreass who in his last year of life was tried and convicted of financial war crimes against humanity. But his son is one of GOD's most beloved.

"And here, this one has a most astounding cover as an international relief organization president, a true wolf in sheep's clothing who rapes the generous of the world with lies and deceit, conning them into giving him and his multibillion-dollar organization their wealth, of which only a fraction is used to help others. This one is a queen in the Middle East, and this angry-looking man, the one who asked where the data will be stored, is a current member of the Chinese Politburo Standing Committee, one of the seven main leaders of the Chinese Communist Party and next in line to be China's president.

"This one here, EB, oversees the World Trade Organization, and that one the World Bank. The man in the uniform with all the decorations is Russia's top general, and this one, she's a real deceiver, a true deep cover plant who has penetrated her nation to the very top as deputy prime minister. Her constituents have no idea she sits at this table. And the balding man, he is chairman of the largest private investment firm in the world. Though to the world he appears trustworthy with the trillions of dollars under his management and is considered a rock of stability, in reality he is the worst of rats, a real fink and black spot in the world of trade and finance. These three are with intelligence services of the world's three major power zones. Of course, this one you know very well, your mentor, who some think is the most powerful man on the planet. Shall I go on?"

"I get it," EB said. "The elite of the elites. They all left their homes and countries on Christmas Day to be here to do this?"

"Only Klaus and Narud are actually here. The rest are utilizing your company's holographic Pod technology to be here at the table virtually," the spirit answered.

"You've got to admit, it's pretty incredible technology. Even I couldn't tell they weren't really present!" EB said with a half-cocked smile, proud of himself.

"After all you've just seen and heard, you're thinking about how good your technology performs?" gasped the ghost. "Perhaps my time has been wasted and you are indeed a lost cause."

"Please, spirit, don't say that. I am very disturbed by what I've just heard. I was distracted. Sometimes we technologists get distracted away from the big picture and become mired in the minutiae of the data. It's our nature."

"Disturbed?"

"Horrified, spirit! Inside I'm reassuring myself that this part of our journey must be a dream, must be only a fantasy. For certainly, such evil could not really be happening, today, could it?"

"I assure you that what you are seeing is now happening, just as the other events truly happened today. If you care, you'll be able to research that the family in Kabul was really taken, and that the pastors are indeed sitting in that cave as we speak. If you care."

"I do, spirit. I think I do. But I imagine there's no evidence of this meeting in the press or anywhere. Is there? Of course there isn't."

"Only those in this room know of its existence, and all will deny even unto death that they have such a plan or would ever contemplate such an atrocity. Yet you do have proof. Narud is your proof. He will tell you the truth because he trusts you, remember? But like everyone else at this table, EB, he is a liar. All of them, their throats are open graves, and out of their mouth spews only their native language of deceit—taught to them by their father, the author of lies and destruction. These are masters of deception who before the public make themselves out to be angels of light, but inside they are darkness, dead men's and women's bones, full of every form of evil. They disguise themselves as heralds of the new age, builders of the new man, saviors of the planet, not realizing they are ushering in its destruction and calamities of such apocalyptic proportion that, unless they are stopped, there is a question whether humanity can survive what they have planned."

EB's legs began shaking and the horrid dread that had left him in the presence of the jolly giant again enshrouded his soul as the iron hot words of the green goliath seared his heart.

"Apocalyptic?" EB managed to voice, though shaky and hardly audible.

"The end of days!" The giant entity bellowed so loudly, EB thought the circular citadel in which they stood would collapse like a trade center tower. His legs then gave out and he was back down on his knees in fright, not only at the prospect of what the giant had just revealed was coming, but because it sank in that he was part of the plan, an integral part according to what Narud had said, instrumental in its success.

"Look here," demanded the specter, lifting his robe to reveal two famished, unkempt, gaunt children with such dirty faces EB could scarcely recognize they were of his own human family. Behind the scraggy emaciations were legions and legions of others, children of the same skin and bone, grim, stark, and dismal. Mixed in were the aged, myriads of the elderly discarded like trash, piled in heaps, clawing as if trying to get out from under the giant's robe. They were wailing for help in their failing, raspy voices, with extended hands, nearly decayed to the bone. Also strewn among the countless masses were cripples, many who were without limbs, myriads with sunken faces, depressed eyes, piled together with many more who wandered aimlessly, confused, seeking guidance and not a few who were slow of mind, needing patience and compassion.

"Look closely at this wreckage, EB. This is the fruit of all who set their hearts on wealth and labor for money!" the giant again roared.

"The children are yours? I don't understand," EB said, trying to reach for them, then pulling back, fearful and ashamed to touch them.

"They are yours, EB, and theirs," said the giant, pointing to the elites around the table, "and all mankind's! No one can serve two masters. Either he will hate the one and love the other, or else he will be devoted to one and despise the other. You cannot serve God and money, but you and these here have chosen your master. Your every thought is for profit and power because your every inclination is greed and self-aggrandizement. So here are your children! Meet Ignorance and Poverty."

EB turned his head, deciding he most definitely didn't want to meet them or even think about them.

"You and your family of arrogant autocrats," the spirit continued as he again circled the table, extending both arms over them. "In your psychopathic godless irrationality, you have spawned an empty, depressed, stressed, and aimless generation. Your group is well named, for you think you are GOD, and as such you've expended every effort, spared no expense, and considered no action too immoral or unethical to further the revolution, rebuild the tower, and subjugate your fellow man in the name of saving the planet. But you have failed to understand that the beginning of wisdom is not fearing that the planet is having a climate change emergency, but fearing the One who created the planet and can change it instantly into an incinerated ash heap.

"With the ferocity of a rabid wolf, you and yours have ripped truth away in order to drive the very idea of Creator God from these little ones, using the classroom, textbooks, and curricula to teach the doctrines of hell. Instead of life, you impose your perversions, prevarications, and pernicious practices on these poor children, determined to turn them into twice the sons of perdition that you are. Look! Look at these who you think you are making rich, wealthy, without need and the hope of the future for mankind. In truth, you are fostering a brood that is miserable and pitiful, utterly poor, blind, and naked."

Staring at the ground, EB didn't dare lift his head and face the angry entity, but waited, hoping there would be no more imprecations and maledictions. To his surprise, there weren't any, and there weren't any more voices from the table, or sounds of any kind. But he could sense someone still there, or something. EB didn't want to look, preferring the sight of the ground over which he was crouched. He had decided he would stare at the floor for the rest of his days if necessary, rather than endure the giant's wrath or any more debilitating visions. And he would have stayed right there hunched over his knees if not for the familiar voice of Genius.

"It's time to get up, EB," said the calm, digital voice.

Thinking he was back in his room, safe at home, he lifted up his eyes. But instead of seeing the comfort of his quilt, clothes, curtains, and bed quarters, he beheld a menacing phantom, cloaked and hooded, coming toward him, like a mist along the ground, which was no longer the smooth marble floor where he had just cowered, but rather a dark, brownish, clodded, cruddy clay.

STAVE 5

SPIRIT THREE

CHAPTER 28

The phantom slowly, gravely, silently approached. When it came near him, EB collapsed facedown into the ground; for in the very air through which this entity moved it seemed to thicken with gloom and woe.

It was shrouded in a deep black garment, so dark any flicker of light seemed to be absorbed into it like a black hole. The pointed hood concealed its head, its face, its form, and the rest of it, leaving nothing of it visible save one outstretched hand. But for this it would have been difficult to detach its figure from the night, and separate it from the darkness with which it was one.

EB perceived that it was tall, possibly as tall as the green giant who was now nowhere to be seen, and ominous as it glided up beside him, its bodeful presence filling him with a new level of dread. Though the night had already taken him to new depths of fear and dismay he hadn't known could exist, this spirit dragged him into a horror so piercing and debilitating, he could only stay there paralyzed in his prostrated position.

Thinking he may have passed out for a time, EB lifted his head with some newfound energy that came from somewhere outside himself, even though his body was shaking uncontrollably, like when emerging from a cold body of water into a chilling wind. Somehow, he managed to find his voice.

"I have seen the past, and the present. You are the third spirit, I gather, here to show me the future?"

No answer came, only the blackness filling its hood staring down at him. After what seemed like an eternity, he managed to scoot to his knees, and then with all the strength he could muster push himself back onto his legs, which were quivering so profoundly he thought he would once again crumple. But he didn't, sensing that, for whatever reason, this shadowy specter was giving him just enough power to go on.

"Phantom of the future!" he exclaimed. "I'm terrified of you more than any of the unearthly entities I have seen so far. But in my petrified state, I feel there is something coming from you that is enabling me to bear it. I can only hope your purpose is to do me good, like the others, and so if there is some path down which you must take me, lead on."

With the figure still motionless, hovering above him like a darkened rain cloud ready to explode its torrents down on him, EB clasped his hands together in a humble appeal. "Will you not speak to me?"

It gave no reply, but the long arm of the cerement rose up and the blackened, irregular hand protruding from it with its crooked forefinger extended, pointing straight in front of them.

"Please lead on!" EB said, still quaking. "Lead on to wherever we need to go!"

The phantasm floated away as it had come toward him. Gaining control of his legs, EB followed in the shadow of its flowing frock, which then lifted him up off the crusty ground and carried him along, though not too close, down a vortex of darkness. He could see a light at the end of the tunnel, but it appeared only as a speck until instantly it enveloped them, placing them on a familiar podium, which sprung up all at once around them, with a chaotic clamor below.

"I've been here before!" EB blurted to the hooded entity. As he gazed around, he spotted his company logo in its full holographic glory floating around them and the other dozens of expensively dressed executives that stood with them. EB immediately noticed that the name of another company was attached to it.

"Why is my company's name different? The logo's been modified as well," EB pointed out to the ghost as giant "eBeja Swarm" holograms swirled around them.

Before he could ask another question, one of the executives there on the platform with them lifted a huge gavel and pounded it on a large elevated button, setting off a fifteen-second bell. The executives all erupted in applause as the ringing continued, patting each other on the back, waving their fists in the air, some even jumping up and down while cheering.

During the ringing, another group of holographic names began swarming from behind the podium, filling the trading floor air and soaring through the market space like hawks. EB recognized some of the names; others he did not. "Elevation," "Pod," and "Fusion Alliance" were all familiar but "Single Store," "DataLock," and "Vacci-Chip" were alien. There were quite a number of others zipping around and through the cheering executives and traders, who also were ecstatic with glee and confidence.

"This must be the IPO day for my merger with Narud! We did it—the offering must have really gone well since we're here at the New York Stock Exchange again," EB observed, feeling stronger and less afraid.

But before he could revel any more in the merger, the phantom pointed his disturbing finger at the sign behind them.

"NWSE?" EB read aloud. "What's that? It looks like a spelling error! Wouldn't you know it. That never happens, but of course there had to be some glitch with our offering. Reminds me of when eBeja went public years ago. They made a silly error then too. Not like this, but—" Before he could finish, the flashing NWSE sign morphed out into its full meaning: New World Stock

Exchange.

"What?" EB asked the silent specter, which remained speechless, but redirected EB's attention to the executives next to them, all of whom he recognized.

"No," said an obscenely obese man with a monstrous triple chin while he clapped his fat hands. "I don't know how. All I know is he's gone."

"When?" inquired an equally obese clapping woman, but with only a double chin.

"Sometime yesterday, maybe last night," the fat man replied.

"Incredible, just incredible," the woman said while she cheered and confetti showered her and the group.

"Does anyone know what was the matter with him?" asked another who leaned in, half listening and half waving to a few of the traders below them. "Did anyone expect him to die?"

"Only God knows. I don't think anyone knew anything about his private life. He certainly never opened up to us," said the portly partier with a yawn he quickly turned upward in a stupendous effort to catch some of the falling confetti in his mouth.

"Imagine all that wealth of his. He was grandfathered in, wasn't he?" the woman asked.

"Sure was!" the fat man pronounced. "Had the entire corporate law firm dedicated to that for some time. Funny how they always want to spread the wealth until it's their own!"

"Well, it will all be distributed globally, now that private property has been outlawed and we all own nothing—and are supposed to be happy and love it!" the waving man said as he did a few fist pumps for the cameras and choreographed market makers below.

"Tell you what I love," he continued. "This! These circuses that companies put on at New World Stock Exchange studios around the world, every week, pretending it's a great day and that we're all so much better off when there's a quote, unquote 'public offering.' It used to be that way, a real cause for celebration, but now it's all an act, pretending we've made it, are successful, and have hit the jackpot when, in reality, all the company's profits go directly into the Global Redistribution of Impounded Funds Trust."

"Yup." The woman laughed, sending her chins into an up and down tsunami. "And this will be a big one! At least that's the way it will be promoted. I am seeing the headlines now: 'Mogul's Wealth Divided Equally Among World's Global Citizens!' or 'Thanks to G.R.I.F.T., Trillionaire's Fortune Confiscated for the People!'"

"Serves him right," the obese man said as the confetti and balloons continued to rain over him. "What a man sows, he reaps!"

"Word! If it wasn't for him, things would probably be like they used to be, back in the good ol' days when there was no Big Brother chip in every one of us!" said the woman, still dangerously sloshing about.

"Look on the bright side, Laquina. Now you don't have to do any accounting, or worry about groceries or anything. Big Brother's also your Big Nanny, Big Butler, and Big Daddy! But we can't blame him for everything. After all, we voluntarily gave his systems all our data and agreed to let them put this chip in us," the fat man pointed out.

"Mmm, no! We didn't agree! Here was our choice: take the Vacci-Chip or die. What kind of choice is that? And even after that, nobody did tell us that once we got injected with the Vacci-Chip, they'd use it to make us slaves!" the woman said, not laughing anymore. "The chip's become our new chains and all our personal data now their whips. All this 'cause of him!"

The black-robed phantom must have amplified their words over the clamor of the market closing celebration because EB was astounded that he could hear their every word, in perfect clarity, as if they were alone in his office briefing him personally. He desperately wanted to ask the spirit for clarification about the conversation of his fellow executives, two of whom he had hired as entry-level employees years ago. But he knew questioning this spirit was futile and so would have to figure out what they were talking about himself.

One question he needed to immediately resolve was why he wasn't there with his executives on this momentous occasion. He had looked around, even meandered around the podium to see if he was there somewhere, perhaps hidden among the new company leadership. After all, this was the official merger of his and Narud's companies, so he should be there in his future self, celebrating, shouldn't he? And where was Narud? And why the change of the Exchange's name? And who had just died?

The questions were piling up in his mind, and they were questions he couldn't just conjure answers for. He needed someone to get him up to speed on what had happened, to help him understand what the hexagas was going on! The ever-present canopy of doom that not only towered over him but covered his soul in an unshakable dread wasn't going to say anything. But perhaps if he made an even more humble appeal and expressed that he was truly trying to understand all that the phantom was trying to teach him—perhaps then it might speak to him and clarify all this for him.

But before he could open his mouth in supplication, the phantom's giant silo of an arm again extended outward with its missile-like finger pointing in a new direction, away from the podium. Looking where the spirit's finger instructed, EB complied and then, with the specter, dissolved away into a new setting, one of much less fanfare, and where the sorrow was palpable.

CHAPTER 29

EB immediately recognized the woman sitting in the stiff white chair surrounded by five others, three of them children and two young adults. Unlike when he saw them before, exploding in playful vigor, here they were still and quiet. Very quiet.

"Where is your father?" Mrs. Cratchit asked Martha, finally breaking the silence.

"He'll be here soon. Don't worry, Mom. He's trying to get here as fast as he can. I have his Lyft ride synced in to my chip. He's only five minutes away."

"I told him he shouldn't go to the office today," Olivia said before she leaned over and put her head in her hands and started to weep. Martha moved closer and put her arm around her mother, trying to console her. But, like her mother, she, too, was despondent and on the verge of tears. The two younger Cratchits left their plastic chairs and circled around in front of their mother, kneeling down to try to comfort her as well. The younger daughter, however, couldn't prevent herself from crying, and so wrapped her arms around her mother's leg and sobbed with her.

Peter sat several chairs away, blankly staring out the window, not knowing what to do or say. There were some lights strung across the branches of a tree that he could focus on until his eyes also filled with moisture. Next to him on the only cushioned bench in the waiting room was Lindi, curled up in a ball. And, next to the bench, there was a small wheelchair, with no one in it.

"Father's arrived!" Martha informed the others after her

implant had given her the news. And within a minute, Bobby came rushing through the sliding glass door into an empty waiting room, except for his family.

Olivia jumped up and ran to him, hugging him with all her strength as she continued to sob. The children, all except for Lindi who stayed in her cocoon, joined their mother and gathered around their father.

"Where's the doctor?" Bobby asked after hugging and kissing all of them. "Is there any news?"

"Nothing since we last spoke," Olivia tried to say through her tears. "They're doing all they can, but the doctor said there wasn't much more they could do. If only he had been able to get the operations!" And again she thrust her head into Bobby's chest and wept and wept.

"We did all we could, and more," Bobby reassured her. "Don't be bitter, my dear. We tried."

"Yes, *we* tried, but what help was that miser of a boss of yours?" Olivia retorted, her sadness turning to anger. "He could have done something—made a special allowance for you after all you'd done for him, and increased your insurance benefits so Timmy could get the operations. Something!"

"I think he would've if he had more time," Bobby replied gently.

"And isn't that ironic, that he ran out of time," continued Olivia. "Well, it serves him right!"

"Let's not speak of him this way, not now, not after what happened," said Bobby.

"Well, you know the verse: 'you reap what you sow.' I wouldn't want to be in that man's shoes on Judgment Day for all the gold in China!"

"And so you won't, dear. And if anything, some good has come from it. Like my promotion," Bobby reminded her.

"A promotion due long ago! He wouldn't have made it to where he was without you, Bobby. And he never gave you the credit you deserved. All I can say is that he could have done more, for both you and Timmy, but chose not to right up to—"

"Here comes the doctor," Peter said, cutting his mother off and pointing to a tired-looking woman in blue scrubs with a white lab coat who had just come through the emergency personnel only sliding double doors. They immediately ran to meet the doctor, whose face was sullen and sad.

"Doctor, please, has there been any change?" Bobby asked, being the only one in the family not crying.

"I'm very sorry. Truly, I am," the doctor said with as calming a voice as she could produce.

"You're sorry?" Bobby asked, not fully understanding.

"Little Timmy didn't make it. He's passed away," the doctor said softly but directly.

Olivia wailed with a heart-splitting cry that only a mother who has lost a child can make, and then collapsed into Bobby's arms. The rest of the children, except for Peter, also cried out loud as they all gathered into one big family embrace. Trying to be brave and strong, Peter consoled Martha and Lindi who had joined them from her bench. For several minutes, they all stood together mourning, not knowing what to do next.

"Please take us to him," Bobby finally said. The doctor swiped her arm to open the double doors, and bid them to follow her. Behind the family, EB also followed silently with the dark phantom not far behind him.

The group was led to a room with walls of medical Holovision monitors, filled with machines still connected to little Timmy's body, though they had been turned off. The lights were dimmed and there was a peaceful silence surrounding the tiny, lifeless child.

"My little Timmy; oh, Timmy; oh, my little boy," were the only words Olivia could utter as she wept, laying her head on his body. The others placed their hands on him, bowing their heads as his mother said her goodbyes.

Bobby moved close to his wife and laid his head on top of hers, and for the first time since arriving at the hospital, also began to sob. "He was the most wonderful son a father could ask for," Bobby wept. "We will miss you, Son. My son."

Slowly, each of the other children said a goodbye to Timmy in their own words, through their own tears. When they all had finished, they joined hands in a circle around the little bed where he lay and Bobby led his family in a prayer.

EB listened closely in wonderment at the way Bobby prayed. He wasn't angry at God or blaming God for taking his son, but was thanking Him and praising Him for the wonderful boy Timmy was, and for the length of time they all had together. Nor did Bobby castigate EB in his prayer, but probably in response to Olivia's anger at him, Bobby thanked God for EB and that, though they weren't able to get the operations to extend the boy's life, they did have insurance that lasted for a time, longer than if Bobby didn't have a job. He thanked God for this, and said something strange, that EB didn't understand at all. He praised God that He had made little Timmy as he was, and that if he hadn't been as he was, so much of what is important, like humility, frailty, being thankful for each day given, and unconditional love, would never have been so deeply understood by their family.

"How could he pray such a thing?" EB inquired annoyingly of the spirit. "I'd never thank God for a genetic disorder, for a mistake of nature that causes such pain, suffering, and now, so sadly, early death! I don't pray, of course, but if I did, I would've asked God why He allowed such suffering, why He doesn't heal the countless little ones who are like Timmy.

"What kind of God creates a boy He knows will suffer his whole life?" EB continued to rant, though in a whisper out of respect for Timmy even though the Cratchits couldn't see or hear him. "And then allows the poor little guy to die a death like this and bring more misery to the world—misery upon misery. Children leaving parents, parents leaving children. Look at his family—now they suffer because Timmy's gone. Even I now suffer for it. And so the suffering continues—an endless cycle of anguish, affliction, and sorrow. If there was a God, why such suffering?"

The faceless phantom didn't move but stood silently over EB, as though staring at him in contempt. EB could feel the ghost's displeasure with his outburst. Was it so wrong to ask why suffering was so much a part of the human condition? If only this spirit could speak, maybe it would be able to enlighten him how a supposedly good God can allow the evil of suffering.

"Can't you say anything at all, spirit? Won't you answer this question for me? There must be an answer. I assure you, if there was a reasonable explanation as to how such tragedy can occur under the watch of a God who is supposed to have all power, I'll listen!" EB inquired.

The phantom spoke not a word, but flapped his cloak into the air, like a wing, and covered EB, sweeping him away from Timmy's bedside. EB couldn't say it, but he hadn't wanted to leave, and as he was swept away, was immediately sorry that he had burst out as he did. He did so because, in truth, it was he who was in pain, he who had neglected to reach out to Timmy all those years, and now he who would justly suffer for his own negligence, hardness, lack of compassion, and apathy.

CHAPTER 30

When the cloak finished its sweep, the eBeja CEO was back in the company of executives. In this place, however, there wasn't any clapping, confetti, or cameras as there had been earlier, only solemnness and sobriety, and regiment-like order among what must have been two dozen men and women. All were sitting at a gold-trimmed circular table shaped like a wedding band, with a large space in the middle occupied with an elevated platform. In the center of that platform rested a single chair, or what would more accurately be described as a throne.

EB and the phantom appeared in the middle of the great round table loop, and stood on the carpeted floor directly in front of the elevated platform's throne. Sitting on the throne was a small but formidable man who, although he looked like a child sitting on an oversized living room chair, commanded the attention of all. EB immediately recognized the would-be king sitting magisterially on the enhanced eBeja Pod-chair that could instantly adjust itself to directly face whoever was speaking at the ring table. It was Narud, enthroned alone on the single Pod in the center. Whether he was there actually or digitally, EB couldn't tell, but what he could see was that Narud had complete power over the entire circle of leaders, as well as the hundreds of others in the round auditorium, surrounding the table, who were probably there only virtually.

"We haven't found them yet. They're like ghosts," said Bill from the round table after receiving permission from Narud to speak. As usual, he immediately began speaking with his hands as well, wildly waving them up and down as if his motions brought better understanding of his words. "But let me be clear, we won't allow any of these liberty factions to defy our orders and trade on an unapproved market!"

"How are they doing this?" Narud asked.

"They're using gold and silver mostly, but also other specie such as platinum and palladium. It's all by word of mouth. We'd have them if they were communicating electronically, but they're completely bypassing the system somehow. They all have Vacci-Chip implants, but have figured out a way to evade detection. This is why we can't preempt and prevent their transactions," Bill continued.

"But every product, whether a food source, a piece of equipment, a game or toy, furniture, clothing—we've coded everything with a tracker! The information for every product's movement at every level of production and distribution is supposed to be under our watch. My system has the data! So how is it that they are able to trade outside our grid?" Narud asked with unusual agitation.

"If we knew the answer to that, we'd be able to stop them," Bill said shamefully. "Somehow they've figured out a way to distort the tracking devices on whatever they're trading."

"Where are they getting the gold?" Narud asked. "The private ownership of gold was criminalized when private property was banned. It should've all been confiscated!"

"Gold is difficult to detect and almost impossible to track if not tagged." Bill shrugged. "Our CommuNEST Low Earth Orbiting satellites have every square inch of this planet under constant surveillance and the Vacci-Chip grid is fully operational so there's literally no movement, conversation, interaction, or transaction that's not completely managed—as long as one of our sensors or chips is present."

"Except these transactions!" Narud said forcefully.

"Yes, except these. We'll figure it out, Presiding General Narud. It hasn't spread and right now is only happening with social outliers who live outside the primary grid regions."

"Figure it out, fast. And then crush them! For God's sake, we can't allow even the smallest rebellion, especially a monetary one, to gain traction. Our strength is that the entire human race is finally integrated, connected both behaviorally and financially through our planetary electronic system into a single body. With all private property of every sort outlawed and eliminated, we can now finally give to each according to need, and from each extract exactly according to ability. It's been a long, hard, and costly revolution we've been fighting for the last quarter millennium, and we're not going to allow a swarm of liberty-loving termites to bring down this house we've built."

"Your Highness, these illegal trades will have zero effect on the global currency credit allotments, the monitoring of each grid-based transaction, or the overall planetary economy for that matter," said a well-dressed Chinese man in Mandarin that was immediately translated into all the dozens of native languages of those in the chamber.

"Thank you, Wang, but that's not the point," Narud responded. "We're the head designated by history to care for our global body. Controlling all economic transactions is essential to our plan and has long been understood as the only way the body can be managed. One glitch, as you called it, Bill, or one deviation—a single organized group, however small, that tries to transact outside the grid—is a pernicious virus that, if left unchecked, will eventually spread and destroy the body.

"Let me remind all of you again," Narud continued, "that the viability of our planetary governance does not only depend on our being able to effectively manage the data each Vacci-Chip gives us. It is equally dependent on the total unification of all the global financial structures and hubs. Charlatine, you have fought long and hard, first through the International Monetary Fund, then by leading several major central banks, and now as head of the World Bank, to subsume all currencies and appropriate all national wealth into our single, centralized bank and money system. You have been brilliant in integrating the grid technology with our Vacci-Chip technology so that every person's transactions are monitored, and as needed, controlled," Narud explained.

"Thank you, my dear leader." Charlatine stood and bowed from her seat at the round table, looking as orange and wrinkled as ever. "I do all for the greater good."

"And now that we control the distribution of all funds for production, purchases, and investment, as you all know, we've eliminated the need for any kind of alternate currencies or money. We are the money, and by our digital sorcery can create what we need whenever needed. The world does not yet fully realize it, but by centralizing all money and controlling the creation of it, we've eliminated poverty once and for all!" The chamber robustly, but respectfully, applauded their dear leader.

"In the past, our forefathers, mothers, and others hypothecated through Modern Monetary Theory that achieving this marvel could be possible. But that theory failed for one simple reason: MMT could never work when there are rivals for financial interests and competing nations for control of the world's assets and resources. True FIAT power can only be achieved in a centralized environment under a single, unified body of global financial and data governance. This we have finally achieved!

"Under our control, never again will greedy executives amass personal fortunes. They were not immune to the Thanatos variant, and enthusiastically renounced their right to their property, fortunes, and wealth in exchange for our vaccine. They have nothing now, but in accordance with our laws and dictates, are happy and love it! Likewise, never again will power-hungry elected officials deceive and manipulate to aggrandize power for themselves. They were not immune to our virus variant, and enthusiastically renounced their right to elections in exchange for our vaccine. They have no power now, but all profess to love it!

"Even parental rights, personal rights, religious rights, free speech rights—all individuals craving these petty encumbrances were not immune to our pandemic, and so have enthusiastically renounced their so-called rights, which really were only impediments to a globally socialized humanity that can now be purified, made spotless, and saved from their ignorant selves. Individuals in the world finally own nothing, my friends, and as we predicted, are happy and love it! Under our systems—my system!—all are integrated, humbled, and digitally equalized so that, and I say again, there will never be ignorance or need again, only a blossoming inclusive world community of egalitarian social justice!"

Again, those around the golden table and the many in the chamber vigorously but stoically applauded.

"We are here in the Central Hall of the United Nations where you, the Supreme Council, are the realization of the dreams of our fathers, mothers, and others. Our mandate now is to efficiently reset, remake, and restore the planet to perfection, and not let any person, group, or movement hinder us. As your appointed Presiding General and Sovereign, I have dedicated myself, my company, and all my resources to this end. I pledge to you today, this group of illegal gold-hording maggots will be annihilated. Only together, with humanity finally united, did we complete the revolution's great goal of equality, liberty, and fellowship, as we, the GOD forum, define it, and as only I can confer it."

"Your will be done!" the Supreme Council and member representatives all chanted in unison.

EB was dumbstruck. *No more executives or private property? I'll have nothing, be happy and love it? What the hexagas?*

Reading his mind, the specter pointed that ominous finger to a platform that was elevated above them, hovering over the Presiding Sovereign's own pedestal. It looked like just a round disk suspended in the air, but after very careful observation of the object, EB could see that there was something on it, and that it had started descending in extremely small increments, as slow as slow could be, from the chamber's high ceiling. EB continued to stare attentively at it, but couldn't see from his vantage point what it was that stood on top of the descending disk, except that it was surrounded by a most marvelous cascade of rainbow colors.

"Tonight, we have much more business to conduct and numerous important decisions to make on this day we celebrate as our birthday," Narud suddenly expounded from his throne, interrupting EB's concentration on the object floating high above Narud's head. "But before we continue, let us take a moment and remember a dear comrade, a true soulmate of collective humanity who, more than any other person—and I say that in full truth without exaggeration—made our new planetary empire possible. He was the true master of personal data aggregation, the unsurpassed wizard of digital communication used to integrate us all!"

As he spoke, EB noticed the stage start to speed up in its descent and the kaleidoscope of colors start to take shape. He still couldn't tell what all the lights were forming, but as they swirled and bounced like living fireworks sculpting a masterpiece, he felt a horrible sense of ruin in his soul, a deep condemnation that was increasing with every twist and explosion of the light above him.

"Spirit," EB cried out in anguish, hoping the phantom would this time respond. "I fear what is descending from above. I don't know why, but with every inch it descends, I'm being choked and my life is being squeezed from me. Please tell me what it is that is coming toward us!"

Unmoved, the dark entity continued to point at it while EB's mentor continued his speech from his Pod.

"There have been many before us who paved the way for our final solution, some who are considered heroes, others villains. But history has a way of proving who her most dear and needed vessels are, often long after they have departed. Yesterday's antagonists are today's protagonists. The scorned, maligned, and misunderstood of their day, in time become the objects of adoration, adulation, and imitation."

With each of Narud's words, the light show above came closer and closer. Listening intently to his mentor, but not taking his eye off the rostrum above, EB could see that the creative illumination was forming not an object, but a man. First the legs, then the torso were whipped together with swirls EB thought must have been similar, though on a nano scale, of the Big Bang from which the universe exploded. Faint *ooohs* and *aaahs* started to reverberate from the chamber as others began to revel in the spectrum's creative dance. But for EB, it made him shudder, and feel exceedingly cold.

"Spirit, can't you please tell me what this is that I'm seeing?" EB pleaded. "Everyone here is marveling at the glory filling the upper air of this chamber, but my soul is collapsing! Even my sense of smell is being overwhelmed with offenses I can scarcely bear, a reeking of filth and decay!"

Still the phantom's finger was unmoved.

"Regardless what you thought of this man," Narud went on to say, confirming what EB had discerned was being assembled above him, "history will place him as a father of our movement, a tireless activist who sacrificed himself for the greater good, one of the pivotal architects who gave us the infrastructure that made the grid, our CommuNEST LEO satellite protection system, and the Vacci-Chip healing of the nations possible."

All the participants, including the Supreme Council, were now focused, as EB was, on the rainbow extravaganza overhead, some breaking into applause as if they already knew what was going to be revealed.

"Good spirit," EB begged while shuddering from head to foot, recoiling from the light and magic, "as I'm sure there is a wonderful conclusion to this show, please let us go now. I don't want to see any more or know who this person is who Narud is showering with such praise. Let's go, please! Please now, spirit!"

But the black-cloaked being was resolute, and wouldn't pull its extended arm back. Instead, it thrust it even farther forward toward the exalted exhibition that had finally descended to its programmed level. The lights continued spinning and churning, revealing two arms extended upward either to give or receive praise, and then the head. EB didn't want to look, but knew he might incur the phantom's wrath if he disobeyed and tried to cover his eyes. The face began to take a familiar shape, which was too much for EB, who kept his head steady but dropped his eyes so as not to see its countenance in hopes the phantom was fooled. There he kept his eyes steady, focusing instead on the feet of the man of light. Gradually, as when turning the knob on a pair of binoculars, the figure's feet came into perfect focus, shod with a radiant red pair of Converse sneakers, with white shoelaces and glowing, pulsing stars that immediately started to parade around the Elevated platform.

EB dropped to his knees and screamed at the entity in horror, covering his face as he went down. The phantom responded by waving its great cloak over his slumped figure, causing the last bit of life to be drained away from him, and with it, the surrounding chamber, its occupants, and his mentor, Narud, who he heard shout as the light around him was turned to darkness, "Let us honor our hero, the one and only EB, who enabled us to finally overcome the grave!"

CHAPTER 31

"I can't breathe, spirit," EB managed to vocalize, though pushing out the words took what felt like a day's worth of energy. EB could breathe, but just barely, as his lungs had just enough air, he felt, for only one more very short, hardly satisfying breath. After expending what he believed was that final bit of oxygen to call to the phantom, he was certain that was his last gasp and that he would soon suffocate. But for some reason he didn't, as just another fraction of breath was again available to him exactly at the point where he thought he would expire.

Am I up high on some great mountain where the air is so thin I can't find any? he thought. But he quickly dismissed that notion as he came to be aware of his other senses that proved he was definitely not elevated somewhere. It was pitch dark around him, he realized, a blackness that was thick and palpable. It was so dense that it felt like it was squeezing him, further making normal breathing impossible. He tried to adjust himself to see if the enclosing pressure might be lessened, even a little, but to no avail.

As his senses became more acute in this new lightless setting, he also realized that he couldn't be high in the atmosphere because if he were, he would also be cold. But here, wherever he was, he was burning up. Not just hot, as one feels after too much exercise or time in the sun, but a real burning up in a heat that was scorching. All around him, he could feel this incredible heat, so hot that it should have incinerated him. It was as if he were in a fire, and all the excruciating pain of burning covered him, but without any flames for cremation. He wanted to scream out because of the scorching pain that was now enveloping him, but couldn't, since there was no more air to scream or say anything. Only his thoughts were intact with him, but even they were not as they used to be.

Spirit, where are you? he thought, hoping the entity would read his mind and provide some help. He swept his arms about him to try to feel for the ghost, but even that was nearly impossible, for he found he had almost no energy to move, just as he had no oxygen to breathe. He wanted to pant after moving them just a little bit around him, but again found nothing entered his lungs but thick, sweltering darkness. It felt as though he were inhaling hot tar. So intensely painful and torturing was the sensation that he collapsed, certain he was going to die.

On his way down, he hit his head on something hard, causing a large gash. Once on the ground, he put his hand to the laceration, expecting to feel blood pouring out, only to find there wasn't any, only a dry Styrofoam substance, devoid of any moisture whatsoever. But the pain from it was equal with the burning that continued to cover his body from head to toe. The cut from the fall was bad, but shouldn't have been nearly as painful as it was, EB thought. But there it was, radiating a layer of pain on top of his burning that was completely unbearable. He wanted to pass out, the pain was so excruciating, but couldn't. He wanted to find some relief, somewhere, somehow, but couldn't. It was at that moment that he came to realize there was nothing at all he could do. He was completely helpless. And as he touched his body to see if there would be some relief from his touch—which there wasn't—he also realized he was completely naked.

Feeling totally vulnerable and alone, he again wanted to cry to the spirit for help. But as before, couldn't muster a breath. All he could do was slurp in a microdose of air so as not to suffocate.

This must be some final hallucination, EB thought. *For no place exists like this, where there is no air, but somehow I breathe. Where there is only heat and burning like being bathed in molten lava, but somehow I do not incinerate. Where the blackest darkness presses, squeezes, crushes me like it is a living power itself sapping me of all energy so I should die, and yet somehow I continue to live.*

At that moment, a flicker of light that seemed to come from behind him caught EB's eye. Wanting to get a better look, he again exerted every ounce of energy he could find and managed to roll over, realizing that he was on a hard, dry, dirty, rocky floor. Like the rest of his surroundings, the floor was burning hot, like the surface of an iron prepped to smooth the wrinkles from a shirt. The rolling accentuated the searing pain he was already enveloped in, shocking him that more pain was possible than what he had been experiencing. He didn't understand how he could even live for another moment, let alone move with all the pain, but somehow he did. It was a complete contradiction to his mind, for rationally, he should have died the instant he arrived in whatever place this was. But nothing here could be fathomed by his reason, much as nothing that had occurred during the course of the whole evening could be rationalized by the smallness of the human brain.

Utterly exhausted after rolling on to his stomach, EB managed to get up on all fours and move a little more toward the very faint bit of light that pierced the living darkness that choked him. In what felt like an eternity, he crawled a little more toward it to the point where he could see the light was coming through a doorway of sorts. Continuing to fight to move even an inch, after an eternity he eventually made it to the edge of the entry so he could see faint outlines of where he was. Again finding strength from somewhere, though his mind told him there was none left, he stood up and could see he was in a cave of some sort. Not a natural cave, but more like a rock-walled room that had been carved out of the side of a mountain. From the flickering of the light that became a bit brighter now, EB could see that the room was about the size of a jail cell, though much taller, with roughly a fifteen-foot ceiling. The rock walls were jagged and rough, like lava stone, which explained why his fall had caused such a large slash on his head.

Drained from this short journey from the back of this cell to its doorway, EB wanted to rest. But just as the searing heat was incessant, and the pain all over him unceasing, so, too, was his exhaustion. Even when he stopped all his exerting, he could not rest. There was no catching his breath, no relief from the pain, no sense that there was an end of any kind in sight and that he would be able to ever relax. There was only a pressing in his soul, not only from the darkness but also from something else within that kept him in constant torment and tiredness. He had felt it before, but nowhere near this level. It was fear, but not just being afraid of something. That was there, but this was an internal terror that dwarfed anything he had felt earlier that day. It was a shrilling panic boxed in, an unabating anxiety wrapped and sealed with endless dread.

He marveled that he could not only think through all this, but see. His senses were intact, and strangely heightened, making the pain more intense, the darkness more horrifying, and the fear that consumed him much more profound. Then, for the first time since his arrival, he heard something. The sound was faint at first and indiscernible, but grew louder and louder until EB could tell it was the stomping of feet. As the stomping came closer, it was clear these weren't the stomps of human feet as the walls of his cell shook with each step. Whatever was coming must have been huge. EB's instinct was to move out of the doorway and try to hide in the back of his cell against the rough wall where it was pitch black. EB's body, however, wouldn't obey and compelled him to stand paralyzed. *Boom! Boom!* The foot trampling echoing through the cavern was almost upon him. In one last exertion, EB gave everything and slid to the side just as the stomper arrived at his cell.

The light was still very faint, but was enough so EB could see the outline of a most grotesque and hideous creature. Its stomping feet were reptilian—huge though deformed and lumpy, covered with what looked like scales. Its legs were like tree trunks, massive in diameter extending at least ten feet up to the monster's torso, which was also reptilian, but also humanlike. The beast had two arms like a man, also covered in the same scales, but giant hands, each with six fingers. Its arms weren't uniform in length, nor were its fingers, but were uneven and deformed, like its feet. One of its arms extended almost to the ground where the other was short and stumpy, yet both appeared fully functional. The creature's head resembled both a man's head and an alligator's, though much more ferocious. The mouth and jaw extended outward like an alligator, with foot-long, razor-sharp teeth. Its eyes were also reptilian, large with diamond-shaped pupils. But somehow its expressions were humanlike. EB could see that this creature was enraged.

It stopped in front of the cell's door and started snarling in a language EB had never heard, nor would want to hear. It wasn't smooth or systematic like human language, but rough, broken, and like its arms, asymmetrical. At times like nails down a chalkboard, the beast barked out a mixture of screeches, whisps, guttural grunts, and loud, then soft, pronouncements. It hurt EB's ears and made his head ring. After a few moments of the beast's growling jabber, EB realized that, though the sounds themselves were completely foreign, he could actually understand what was being said.

"I know who you are and that you are here," EB's mind

translated. "And you are mine!" The creature then launched into a diatribe of the most foul, obscene, and degrading language EB had ever heard. Most of it was directed specifically at him, berating him with insults and aspersions that, though were heinous in their descriptions, EB recognized were horribly accurate.

How does this thing know all of this about me? EB wondered in agonizing terror, pain, and burning. He didn't dare say a word, but stood pressed up against the jagged wall that seemed itself to be hostile to him, grinding into his back as the beast spewed its threats and hatred toward him.

Then the beast shifted its vitriol from EB as its object of hate and scorn to its Creator. Uttering blasphemies and curses toward God, the monster began spinning around, banging on the outside of the cell and stomping its horrid feet. Curse after curse, condemnation of God after condemnation, the beast verbally vomited its disdain and pure contempt for all that is good, upright, and pure. EB could think of nothing except that this creature was the manifestation of pure evil. The thick darkness seemed to dance at its gory words, as the pain and burning of EB's skin was amplified with each blasphemy.

One of the execrations that struck EB the hardest was its saying how God had unjustly put it in this prison forever, and that EB's fate was the same. The beast said it over and over as it denounced and cursed God. "I have you forever!" it kept saying in between its obscenities. "There is no escape! Does a God of love make a place like this? Does a good God punish us like this?" It would cry out, and then just scream spasmodically at decibel levels that should have shattered EB's ears.

A place like this? Punishment like this? I'm in hell! EB finally acknowledged to himself, sinking further in despair. *And I'm never getting out. This is truly where I will spend eternity!*

Even though this is what the creature kept uttering, it wasn't its words that convinced him. Something deep inside confirmed it. He knew this cell was his abode forever forward and that he could never, ever leave or escape. It was just as how no one has to tell a man when he is in love—he just knows it. So, too, EB now just knew that his rightful place was in this horrible, horrible, horrible place. He tried to suppress the thought—the epiphany— but couldn't. Over and over he continued to tell himself that this was an illusion; it must be. All the other visions of the evening were of real people, real places, and real circumstances in a real world. But this place could not be real.

"I'll show you what is real!" the beast suddenly shouted in its own language and then, not ducking, smashed through the rock above the doorway to EB's cell. Though it was pitch black in the back of the cell where EB was hiding, the creature emanated an eerie red glow once it entered the cave. It was as if EB had just put on night-vision glasses. He didn't know how that happened, but now could see the beast even more clearly, seeing that it was much more hideous than he had thought. In a furious storm, the creature leapt toward him and, in one swoop, grabbed him with its longer arm. As it did so, another sense of EB's came alive and made him breathlessly gag. Maybe it had been there the entire time, but EB hadn't noticed the unbearable stench this beast exuded. Held in the crushing grip of its huge, scaled six fingers, EB felt that if his end didn't come by being squished like a ripe banana, it would certainly come from the gagging, choking stench that was drowning him as if he had been dunked in a swamp of decayed, rotting corpses.

The crushing grip of the creature exhibited incomprehensible strength, so much power that EB knew that he should have been obliterated instantly in the demon's grip. Whatever held him together, though, didn't lessen the pain that continued to increase with each squeeze, surprising EB again that even more pain could be experienced. It seemed to him as if the level of pain could increase exponentially and that, like his sentence in this pit of destruction, the amount of pain would also increase eternally. He again wanted to scream, but didn't have the energy or air to do so—or to move—but simply had to lie there and endure.

After another stream of expletives and damnations rushed out of the creature's mouth, a horrid expression of its utter hatred of EB, God, and all humanity, it threw EB with amazing velocity into the serrated wall. EB could feel his bones crumble at impact and his skin burst open where it hit. But he would only remain in his distorted position on the ground for a fleeting second as the monster leapt over to him and immediately punched and pounded on him, then after sufficient beating, picked him up again to hurl him back into the wall. And then again and again and again. EB felt his bones shatter each time, as though they reconstituted instantly after each hit. The feeling wasn't a healing reconstitution, though, only that they somehow were whole again, ready to be broken. The pain compounded and then compounded, like the interest EB charged for loans he had made out of his company's lending division. All EB could do was take it. He had no strength to try to escape from the beast, and even if he did, the demonic entity was too powerful and too fast.

Then, after what seemed like days, or it could've been months or even years, for EB had lost all sense of time, the ogre stopped throwing and beating him, and for no apparent reason, exited the cave cell. Though the beast was gone, its stench was still present and continued to fill the high-ceilinged cavern. The toxic odor didn't dissipate even a speck, but actually intensified as it mixed with other smells that started to seep into EB's jail—foul odors of burnt hair and rotting, stale phlegm along with rotten egg and gasses.

He tried to plug his nose, but it only burned more when his nostrils came together and did nothing to block the reek that had lodged itself inside of EB's cranium. Helpless, EB just lay on the searing rock floor trying to imagine his living room that the green giant had transformed into the most lush and pleasant-smelling garden he had ever experienced. He tried to remember the smells of the flowers and fruit trees, all so pure, so fresh, like a spruce-filled hillside, with hints of sweetness, spices, and cinnamon. But he could only remember that it had been so, but couldn't make himself experience it again or even enjoy its memory.

All joy and hope, any remnant of happiness or optimism, had been drained out of his animated, but lifeless self. Every time he tried to reference something that had been good in his life—like his friendship with Marley, or the Green awards he won for his building being so environmentally friendly—shame overtook him, and guilt. Incredible guilt. Everything he thought he had done that was good, he now came to see for what it really was and the motives from which it sprang. All his relationships, all his business dealings, every thought of his heart as an adult, it seemed, were marred with lustful soot, sprinkled with pride, or motivated out of selfish ambition. He hadn't cherished his friendships, if he even really had any. He hadn't treated others as he would want to be treated, but instead was always looking for an angle, a benefit, something in it for himself. His subconscious motto, which he had been blind to until now in this prison, was "take, take, take!"

Like the never-lessening pain in his body, ever-increasing guilt tormented his soul. *Have I loved, really loved, anybody, ever?* he asked himself over and over. He scarcely could even fathom what the word meant. He had wanted to love his parents, and thought he at one time loved his mother, but that was quickly extinguished when she left him and his father. He had wanted to love his father, but how could he after his father threw him away like trash to Wycliffe's? He indeed had been injured, but did he ever seek to find healing? Why didn't he take the steps of reconciliation? What prevented him from reaching out to others instead of becoming bitter, hateful, spiteful, and even vengeful?

All these thoughts poured through his soul with no consolation, only condemnation that it was too late. Too late to make amends. Too late to say sorry or ask for forgiveness, and far too late for him to forgive. He had perfect knowledge that he was receiving the penalty he deserved for every action, every thought, every inclination that wasn't motivated by love, a notion he hadn't even considered to be a necessary, let alone possible, element in business or his commercial dealings. Everything became clear in the midst of the overwhelming pain and suffering. All his accomplishments, networks, technologies, innovations, and accolades were vapor, as was his life.

As he contemplated the failings of his life, indeed the complete failure of his life, his senses continued to heighten. After another stretch of incalculable time, he noticed that on top of the stench, pain, darkness, and depression were faint screams. They were human screams, which meant there were others around somewhere. Though he had generally hated to be around people for most of his life, now there was nothing more that he desired than to see another human soul, shake a hand, have a laugh. He had taken for granted all the many people around him, that looked up to him, that depended on him for everything. Bobby and his family immediately came to mind, especially little Timmy who was lodged in his heart like a dagger.

I may have been able to save him! This thought tortured EB more than the heat or bodily pain he was enduring. *What percentage of my vast empire would have been needed to get the little guy the operations he needed? Not even five minutes' pay!* The conviction played over and over in his head, looping without a stop button. Each time, he saw in his mind's eye first Timmy at the Christmas dinner table with his family, laughing and rejoicing with a joy EB knew he had never experienced himself. Though he was bound in infirmity and chained with a genetic anomaly, he was free. And this freedom of soul, this joy and liberty of heart in a child with no advantages, no real opportunities, no long-term prospects to fulfill a dream or ambition—this was wealth far beyond anything EB had ever known. *What was I working so hard and relentlessly for? To save the planet? I should've saved Timmy.*

He started to long as a father does for Timmy and Bobby, only to sink further into despair as he realized he wouldn't see or hear about them ever again. All the course words, the berating and belittling words he spoke against Bobby haunted him. The lies he told Bobby to get him to work extra hours, the manipulation he used to keep Bobby laboring to build his kingdom at the expense of his needy family, and the blackmailing of Bobby by threatening termination or pay reduction—and using Timmy's condition as the leverage—to ensure Bobby would do exactly as he wanted. He recalled in detail every single time he sinned against Bobby, as well as each incident where he made Bobby lie, distort, cheat, or obfuscate for a deal to go through or transaction to take place. But now he could see that if he ever did have a friend, it was Bobby, who only returned good for all the evil EB poured on him, had the courage to tell EB the truth, regardless of consequence, and was the only one on the planet who'd take a bullet for him—and not his money.

All these thoughts flooded EB's mind in incredible detail, making him relive the lies or vituperations or slander over and over again, as if he were there again, sinking him into the deepest levels of despondency. And this against the backdrop of screams that seemed to grow louder during the mental deconstructing and spiritual breakdown he was experiencing. He thought again about the horrid creature and all the damage, pain, and misery it inflicted on him, wondering when it would come back again. He sensed that it wasn't a onetime occurrence, but that the beatdowns from the monster were to be a regular occasion for him, forever.

But it seems I have a moment, EB internally gasped. *I don't hear its stomping or growls. Maybe if I can find out where those screams are coming from . . .*

Again exerting every ounce of energy he could find, EB picked up his ragged body and managed to slowly shuffle to the cell's door. The night vision was still available to him and he could now see that there was a thick, rusty, but impenetrable barred door closed to his doorway, locking him in. Apparently, its previous smashed state from when the beast burst through had been fixed, like his bones. But the huge barrier was locked. He nearly turned away to go back to his black corner when, without any aid from him, the door squeaked open.

The beast is toying with me again, he thought, *and is probably just outside the door waiting to destroy me.* After standing at the threshold for who knows how long and hearing nothing, EB mustered up enough strength to peek outside the door and to both sides. No demon beast. And so he again slowly, still exhausted and fighting for every breath, inched his way out of the cell to an open area where he could get a better sense from where the screams were coming.

He couldn't see it before, but there was a grand rock structure, like a mountain or rocky barrier of some sort, at the end of the open area. The screams were coming from the other side of it, where there was also a glow that punctuated the outline of the mountainous structure in front of him. To find the people screaming, he would have to scale what looked like large boulders piled on top of each other. Climbing them would not be easy, and in his state, impossible, he finally decided. But he did catch a glimpse of a small crevice between two of the great barrier stones that was leaking some of the light. EB limped to it and discovered an opening just large enough for him to squeeze through.

It seemed to take forever to slide through the crack that was just wide enough for his body. While pushing with all his might to get through, he realized that since he'd arrived in this abhorrent pit, he had been without food and water. Hunger pangs gripped him, but even more, thirst ravaged him. He had been unable to think about his thirst before, but now that he was out of his cell and the clutches of the demon beast, he could feel how dehydrated he was. His mouth had gone completely dry with not even a drop of saliva. He tried to swallow to create some kind of moisture, but nothing was there but hot air. He also noticed that not only was he completely void of liquids of any kind—even blood, which should have gushed from his many wounds and lacerations—but so was everything around him. In his cell and all the area around it there was nothing but dead, dry rock. No life, no plants, nothing but horrid beasts and moistureless desert dust.

Parched and hoping to find just a drop of water or liquid somewhere to cool his scorching tongue, EB continued to skirt through the small crevice, eventually making it to the other side, arriving even more dehydrated than when he started, if that were possible. He could feel that the temperature had skyrocketed as he approached the opening, and when he poked his head through to see what was there, he felt a rush of air like a burst from a blast furnace blow across his face and melt it away. He reached up to touch his eyes and nose to see if they were still there, again finding it was just the sensation of incineration. His face was still intact, and with it all the horrid, awful smells and odors of before. The sulfur stench became especially pronounced, and after opening his eyes, EB could see why.

In front of him, he estimated about half a mile, and down in a huge crater of sorts was a massive molten pit of fire. It boiled like volcano's lava, with scorching steam and huge flames of fire exploding from its surface. The furnace wind created from the inferno continued to batter EB's face, but he couldn't pull away from the sight he was beholding, even though it felt like his skin was being cremated. The pit was massive and appeared to be almost exactly the same width as the flying distance from his eBeja Tower plaza to Narud's SwarmTrooper Tower, which he had done countless times in his personal nuclear-powered 'copter. It wasn't a perfect circle, but its length was about the same, a little longer, giving it a bit of an oval shape. But like everything in this subterranean furnace, its perimeter was jagged and without symmetry.

The large pit was surrounded by countless smaller pits filled with the same sulfur-spewing molten fire, extending into the distance as far as EB could see. To his horror and dismay, he could see that the source of the screams and cries he heard was coming from beings, human beings as well as other creatures, both large and small, that were in the pits. The human screams were the most discernable as people of all sorts—old and young, all races and colors, every ethnic group imaginable—were trapped in the pits, wildly trying to escape. As if they were drowning, they would submerge, then pop up out of the molten fire and try to claw their way out. But none could escape or make any progress of any kind. They all just continued to boil in their lava prison, screaming and screaming and screaming.

Above this wide-open area of the large pit packed full of humans and other creatures, and the countless, endless smaller hot-tub-sized cavities that each had only a single person in them, was a large rock canopy. EB could see he was in a huge cavern.

Its only light was that given off from the fire pits, but from that light combined with the night vision he continued to experience, he observed what looked like rain coming down from the ceiling of the cavern. It wasn't the Bay Area rain he had so often cursed, however, but fire rain pouring out from the rock. And not just a few drops here and there, but a torrential downpour continually filling the great pit and the plethora of smaller potholes with an endless supply of liquefied combustion.

Though frantically struggling, the captives in the fire pits couldn't get out since an army of other reptilian-type beings that walked upright were stationed throughout the pit area preventing any escape. They seemed to have one purpose—torment those condemned to the fiery hell holes. Somehow, EB could hear their yelling and shouting and understand them, just as he had with the beast that had demolished him. Like that beast, these beings hurled blasphemies and curses at their prisoners. And if the captive would reach out of the pit too much or come too close to the edge of their tub of fire, the lizard-like entities would ruthlessly kick them, or hit them until they were subdued. Sometimes it appeared they would torment their hostage just for the enjoyment of it, breaking out into what looked like a dance or cheer after inflicting a blow, or series of blows.

It was endless, the venomous army's relentless dispensing of punishment, like what EB experienced in his cell. But this was an order of multiple magnitudes worse. Instinctually, he knew that these convicts would never leave these pits and that their torment would continue forever and ever. The wicked force was unstoppable in this place. There was no opportunity for rebellion against them, and no possible way for any organized overthrow. Their prisoners couldn't even communicate with each other, even those herded together in the large pit. All were in constant pain, like EB, but worse, it seemed. Much, much worse. And even if they could get a word to a fellow prisoner between their screaming and weeping, their overlords were too powerful, too aware, too ruthless. EB sensed that in this place these horrid creatures were invincible.

Other entities scattered the landscape EB was peering over, some larger than the demonic soldiers, others smaller, but in all sizes and shapes. He could see huge spider-type creatures, out-of-proportion scorpions, and other insect-like beings as well as snakes crawling or slithering around the pit, or on the walls or even on some of the captives. Other creatures were organized together, some in large swarms, others in smaller packs. They all resembled in some fashion creatures of the earth, but greatly distorted, deformed, or accentuated in wickedness and power. One, however, stood out—a massive serpent-type creature, almost like a dragon of medieval lore, that was perched on an extraordinarily sculpted, but still jagged and rough, rock protrusion above the great pit. EB could see its outline, and that it must be several stories in length, with a girth of several hippopotamuses. He couldn't see the snake's face, but through the smoke and gasses, only the glow of its pulsating red eyes.

What horrified EB most, however, was how these prisoners arrived at their fate. Directly above the giant pit was what looked like a black hole in the middle of the torrents of fire pouring down. No pouring lava came out of it, but instead it rained humans. Like the fire rain around it, the downpour of humans was nonstop. Screams were also coming from those falling, adding to the chorus emitted from the pits below. EB was stunned at how many people were gushing from the black spout. It didn't make sense to him that so many could be emptied into the pit, but the pit would not fill up. The pit itself was like a ravenous beast of consuming flames taking all that it was fed, and always ready for more.

As he stared in complete dismay at the deluge of souls, he began to recognize faces. This also puzzled him because he was too far away to see such details, but just as his night vision happened, so, too, did this discernment of faces. Not all faces, but one here and one there as they fell mercilessly to their fiery doom. He wanted to scream himself as he started to see among the legions of plummeting criminals fellow technologists and scientists, bankers, dignitaries, political figures, generals, and admirals he had known, as well as lawyers and judges he had worked with and bribed, and even spiritual leaders from all the religions of the world. The stream of anguishing souls continued with hordes and hordes of famous actors, artists, and musicians, not a few media moguls, executives, producers and directors, numerous cultural icons, as well as almost all his close circle of finance and business magnates. Men and women together, all were the self-righteous and arrogant of the world, like himself. Still lacking the energy or oxygen to cry out, he could only groan as he watched those who had been highly esteemed and admired among the human race being thrust down into their damnation.

As the elites descended, like all the others being cast down, they cried and screamed, though their shrills seemed to EB to display greater shock of their fate and be even more desperate than the wailing of the masses of commoners that surrounded them. He could detect every one of these elites' cries, as if it was given to him to hear them over the others, all of which reminded him of his own ways and actions in the various areas of life where these influencers had dominated. Those known as the world renowned brought to mind his own efforts to build and connect a world, not as God had directed, but in opposition to God. All his motives were laid bare and he could no longer deceive himself as to what drove him.

As a scientist whose faith was in evolution, at the most basic level he had wanted to drive the very idea of an Almighty Creator away from humanity. This religious delusion was the root cause of man's problems and condition, the main ignorant superstition that kept humanity from uniting in heart and mind and thereby coming together as one. Destroying this destructive myth had been his raison d'etre. So, like many of those cascading into the inferno that he had admired and followed, his life on earth had been dedicated to shattering belief in the biblical concept of a Creator, Father God.

As the faces of the arrogant poured before him, he saw himself clearly—it was he who was really the ignorant one and it was his own insolence and hatred of God that compelled him to use his intellectual gifts to deceive and spread lies. What could be more superstitious than positing that something came from nothing? He was a scientist and knew this was not only logically unsound, but scientifically impossible. How could there suddenly be, *from nothing*, a Big Bang that produces the intricacy, complexity, harmony, not to mention the enormity of the universe? And even if such an impossibility occurred, how could the winds of chance and chaos in the chamber of space-time blow with such perfect orchestration so as to bring about the wonder of humanity and the myriad of species on the planet? No, these were the cleverly crafted tales that were the real pandemic scourging mankind, the real poison leading souls to destruction, the true virus that he should have dedicated his life to refute.

He knew deep down that God existed, truly existed, and that therefore it would only make sense to do everything the Great Creator wanted, willed, and directed. At the same time, EB, like all honest humans, knew evil existed. But in his arrogance, he had decided he himself would determine what is evil, and what is good—especially the greater good—instead of God. Of course, he never imagined he would be the sole arbiter of justice, although Narud gave him a glimmer that it might happen when he and Narud ruled the world and administered justice according to their definitions and dictates. But now it was clear to him that this had all been a ruse. One giant lie. The two of them, together with the countless elite cascading before him, had justified their lust to unite the planet only so they could be in power, establish the City of Man, rebuild the Tower of Babel and make a name for themselves. But to what avail? This. Outside of God there was only this eternal, torturous dungeon of death. All the centralization, collectivization, socialization, and globalization of humanity had done nothing and could never do anything to overcome death and this final destination for the damned.

So here he was, face-to-face with the reality that all his efforts to save decrepit, deviant, depraved, diseased, decaying, destructive, dying mankind by uniting them were not only vain, but criminal. He had been living for the purpose of detracting humanity from the real emergency of death and the coming judgment by God and instead promoted the lie that man was enlightened, inherently good, perfectible, and that by coming together as a single global collective, man could save himself and the habitat he was destroying. What arrogance! What foolishness! This was the crime above all crimes!

Yes, taking care of the environment was important, but it was only one command of the Creator's many directives to humanity. To absolutize it, he was realizing, was to worship and serve the creation rather than the Creator. And such false devotion inescapably led himself and others away from true hope and deliverance for mankind. There wasn't a climate emergency as much as there was a confidence emergency—confidence in God as the real and true Creator, Helper, Father, Deliverer, and Sovereign who alone could heal humanity and save it from death.

All the faces of those he saw being cast down into the pit had made the same fatal error he had. He knew he would soon join them, and justly so. His eternal perdition wasn't unjust or capricious, but was exactly what he deserved for the great harm he had caused, seen and unseen, by pompously presuming himself to be God and know what was best for himself, others, and the planet. The screaming politicians, popes, presidents, prelates, pastors, pundits, and potentates flashing before him reinforced that the dictators, tyrants, autocrats, and despots of the world were not out there somewhere far from him but were right here, and they were him. His worldview of forced compliance, top-down control, and elitist collectivism for global social engineering fostered the oppression of man, the enslaving of peoples of every race and region, and the removal of responsibility each individual has to his or her Creator.

Indeed, the blood of all the holocausts, purges, genocides, and governmental slaughters were on him, for he not only approved of the doctrines of centralized governmental and corporate power used to bring about these atrocities, but had actively engaged in promoting them, advancing them, and implementing them as policy and law. Population control programs, abortion, forced lockdowns, and death panels to decide who would live and die were only a few of the hell-deserving revolutionary causes he had vigorously endorsed and subsidized. *I am truly a murderer*, he realized.

I am also, like these cascading, a con man and thief! he thought as the central bankers, predatory lenders, primary dealers, and other sorcerers of financial wizardry and deception rained down into the molten pits. Alchemists had always been understood to be charlatans, fooling the unsuspecting with the prospect that ordinary metals could be recombined into pure gold. But in their day, there were only a few and most were aware of their chicanery, relegating them to the margins of life with all the other snake oil salespersons, con men and women, and grifters.

But he had willingly participated in and avidly supported modern man's new global alchemy scheme, which, instead of turning base and worthless metals into gold, turned electrical impulses into monetary credits. The scheme had been magnificently orchestrated, and like any elaborate hoax, was backed by many reputable and highly esteemed money men, Wall Street fat cats, and market manipulators. These were the ones who shrouded their swindle in an undecipherable complexity of terms and formulas only a few elite intellectuals could comprehend, bribing and lobbying so as to erect a myriad of regulations and laws to give themselves legal cover, as well as an air of legitimacy. But all along, it was really a means of deceptively expropriating the wealth of others, stealing livelihoods, and confiscating property, especially among the easy targets of the middle class, the disadvantaged, and the poor.

He could now see clearly that the scheme was in its essence sorcery and wizardry—nothing but centralized money-creating witchcraft. And the central bankers were the coven. Appropriating to themselves the power to create digital credits that equal money, and set interest rates, the globalist elite exalted themselves as a deity, able to conjure up something from nothing. And from their spell, they would give themselves an endless source of wealth with which to transform the world into their own slave plantation in the form of an international centralized socialist order. The phantom had showed EB that they were using this sorcery, this diabolical conjuring, to subsume all the world's national currencies under one global currency issued by a single central world bank. And then, under this monolithic global bank, enslave the entire planet.

EB groaned as all the scales fell from his eyes so he could see the evil in which he had participated, not only personally, but in all his work toward what he thought was social justice. In reality, it was murder, deception, theft, and witchcraft. The facade had come crashing down. He had spent his adult life working, supporting, funding, campaigning, and manipulating however possible to give government and its GOD power to steal, murder, and control the people. He had pacified his conscience—the little he had—by assuring himself and others that all his work was for the "greater good." But when he would see that the good really wasn't that good, he would just brush it off and comfort himself that he was at the top of the human pile anyway and would be unaffected. What he had failed to realize, with all his wealth and power, was that he was simply a mortal, a vapor, a flower that has only a moment of beauty today, but then withers tomorrow, good only for incineration.

And this was the worst part of all. He had been deceived, and now could see that mortality wasn't just fading into nothingness or being erased from existence. These had been the lies he told himself in the few fleeting moments he had thought of what happened after death, further searing his conscience and hardening his heart. But the reality was that another world existed, a spiritual world of darkness that had, unbeknownst to him, controlled him and the world of those like him, in order to keep him from escaping the just condemnation of eternal judgment—a punishment that continued on forever and ever, with no relief or completion.

The ultimate struggle wasn't climate deniers vs. environmentalists, rich vs. poor, elites vs. workers, corporations vs. governments, race vs. race, country vs. country, or any other human-vs.-human construct. There was an entire other dimension that he had disregarded, that the world was ignoring as either nonexistent or irrelevant when in fact it was the essence of the struggle, the very war that required all the attention, focus, determination, and belief by the entirety of the human race. This was a war that couldn't be fought with human weapons, or with Sun Tzu tactics, or by hacking networks, censoring undesired opinions, injecting biochips, building weaponized satellites, or having the biggest nuclear bomb stockpile. It had to be fought with spiritual weapons against these spiritual beings of darkness that not only commanded over this abyss, but over the rebels of the world with one objective: keep humanity from uniting around God's chosen King of the planet and instead deceive them into warring against themselves until they destroy themselves, and the planet.

EB began to weep, but no tears would flow from his eyes in this dehydrated wasteland. He ground and gnashed his teeth in agony. The outward burning and pains of destruction tortured him, but it was the inward devastation of his soul that was the most tormenting and agonizing, a state he knew he would be in for eternity.

How could I have done this? How could I have been so stupid, so blind, so evil? Oh, hubris, you have slain me! he cried within, heaving with the heavy sighs and groans that great weeping produces. Though the rough, rocky ground was dry and scorching, he lay down and pressed his face into the sweltering stone, resigned to wait to be cast into the fiery pit to join the elite he had once been a part of, committed to, and celebrated.

He could feel his cheek for the umpteenth time being seared away from his face, but he continued to press it onto the stone in disgust with himself and his life of folly, rebellion, and unremorseful crime. The night vision he had been given faded, as did the last drop of energy he had mustered to get to his perch over the great pit. Even the final trace of oxygen seemed to finally be exiting his lungs. *As deserved, I should soon be with them,* was the last thought to cross his mind before a shaft of light enveloped him and what appeared in the light to be a great hand took hold of him. It all happened so fast that, in his condition, he could hardly discern it and with the little mental capacity he had left, thought he had been scooped up by this hand to be cast into his fiery destiny.

STAVE 6

ENDINGS
AND
BEGINNINGS

CHAPTER 32

EB held what infinitesimal amount of breath he had as the hand moved him off the cliff's ledge, and then closed his eyes in dread. But instead of more heat, burning, and pain, he felt less, and a sense of ascension upward instead of down. As he elevated, breath returned, then some strength and then more and more. The torturous heat evaporated, and he could feel juices starting to slosh around in his mouth again. For a moment, it was the most valuable—and delightful—substance in the world to him. Oh, how he was thankful for his saliva! Within seconds his energy had returned enough for him to raise his head and see that he was no longer in that dreadful, awful pit of everlasting torment but was back in his room, where the lights were already on, lying on his bed.

"Oh my!" he shouted, patting his body all over, then his bed, then his body again and again to make sure he was really there. "Incredible! I'm alive!" He could hardly contain himself, for as all encompassing as the destruction and degradation of the abyss had been, so now was the vitality, peace, and joy. He checked his face, and there it was, unmelted and without injury or trauma. Then his pulse, his temperature by placing his hand on his forehead, and his inner hands, which he thought had been seared to the bones. All there! And not a wound, laceration, burn, cut, or slash on him anywhere. And though he thought in those last moments on the cliff's edge with the ear-splitting screams, the suffocating, stinking smells, and severe skin scorching that he was about to lose his mind, here he was, not only in full sanity, but in perfect serenity.

"That hand, it was that great hand that pulled me out of the pit, that rescued me from my doom, my sentencing, from the justified and equitable condemnation I deserve. This is astounding! The Hand of God has saved me!" EB hollered through sobs of laughter, ebullience, and relief. "I've been given a second chance! Thank you, spirits. Thank you, Marley! Thank You, Creator, for I can see now all this came from You. You didn't forget me, though I had forgotten You! I pushed You away and denied You, using every excuse of reason and circumstance to justify my hostility. But even though I had become Your enemy, You didn't forsake me but remembered my prayers as a young boy, my searching for You, my desperate need for a father!"

His face was now soaking wet with tears, tears of joy he didn't know were possible. He was so filled with hope and optimism that he felt he must be glowing! He ran to his bathroom to look in the mirror to see if it was so, almost tripping over his robe in the rush. He quickly stopped, patting himself on his torso and arms again.

"Even my clothing is without tear, burn, or mark and is just as it had been when I put it on. What a joy! Even this robe is intact and doesn't have a strand out of place!" He then took off the luxurious robe he loved so much, and with great delight, carefully folded it and placed it on one of the chairs in his bedroom. He then resumed his journey to see his reflection and whether he looked as different as he felt. He didn't, and wasn't glowing literally, but internally he was a lighthouse—and a smiling one at that. He hadn't smiled, truly smiled just to smile, for as long as he could remember, and didn't even have a memory of seeing himself with such a wide grin!

What nice teeth I have, he thought as they beamed through. *So well made, perfectly crafted for their perfect purpose. This is incredible! Everything is in its perfect place in this body, and this body in symmetry with nature, and nature so precisely regulated and harmonious in all its complexity and diversity. Of course there is a Designer, a brilliant one at that. A Master Engineer and Overseer who watches over His masterpiece and keeps it running like this magnificent timepiece!*

Like with his robe, he immediately took off his multimillion-dollar Grandmaster Chime and ran it over to where his robe rested and gently set it on top, all the while laughing and shaking his head in humble thanksgiving and awe.

"I am as light as a feather, I am as happy as an angel, I am as giddy as a drunken man, and merry as a schoolboy. A Merry Christmas to everybody on the planet!" he shouted into the air, then darted back to his bed onto which he leaped and then bounced up and down, up and down, again and again in a fit of hilarious laughter like a child.

"Genius! Are you there?" He laughed out loud.

"Yes, EB, I'm always here," his electronic butler replied.

"Marvelous! The system is still on and working wonderfully! You're like a friend, Genius, always there!"

"You made me that way, EB. I am what you created me to be."

"Of course, I made you, set your parameters, conceived every detail, gave you the capacity for every response within your AI algorithms—programmed you for my pleasure. You didn't just appear one day or evolve over a long period of time as the wind of the office AC blew on my computer! What a fool I've been, what a blind, hardhearted, arrogant fool!" Again, he jumped, and twirled, and leaped up to try to touch his ceiling, bouncing around like a circus acrobat.

After a few more amazing feats of landing on his behind and then springing back to his feet, executing a perfect series of jumping jacks and even a couple front flips onto his back, EB gave a marvelous finale bouncing off his bed with a full 360-degree twist. Taking a couple bows, he continued to laugh, and for a man who had been out of practice for so many years, it was a splendid laugh, a most illustrious, brilliant, and pleasant-sounding laugh!

"I don't know what day it is, or night. I don't know if it's day or night!" said EB. "Or even how long I was with the spirits. I don't know anything. I'm quite an infant. Everything is new! Oh, never mind. I don't care. Yes, I'd rather be an infant. Woo-hoo! Fantastic! Oh, hello, world!"

Dancing around his room, around the chairs, to his closet, and then away from it, to the bathroom, into his shower and then out, and finally to his massive windows, he sang out a command. "Genius, open those big, dark curtains, would you?"

Immediately, the curtains on both window walls whisked open, letting in a tidal wave of fresh morning light. No pounding rain, no slashing sleet, no fog or mist; just clear, bright, jovial, golden sunlight pouring from a clear, heavenly, glorious sky.

"Genius, what day is it today?" cried EB.

"Today is December twenty-fifth. Today is Christmas Day," his monotonous machine replied.

"Christmas Day! I haven't missed it. Those spirit entities did it! They did it all in one night. But that makes sense—certainly they can do anything they like. Of course they can. Of course they did!"

"Spirit entities? That does not compute," Genius responded.

"Oh, never mind. Of course it doesn't compute and it never will to you. But it does to me—it does so clearly now to me! Door open!"

EB briskly exited his bedroom into his living room, which was also restored and without a trace of the forest, gardens, or feast of the Green Goliath. Wanting to taste the fresh air, he scrambled to his patio doors and manually opened them, determined to feel that first thrust of invigorating Bay Area air on his face—the crisp and cool air he would never take for granted again.

The feeling was better than he could have imagined, and so he stood there, on the patio threshold, just inhaling then exhaling—in and out, in and out—until he thought he might pass out. He then leaped out onto the patio where he could see for miles, across the city, over the building tops, to the ocean water, which looked bluer than he remembered, a calm and content blue, a wonderfully fresh and frolicking blue.

"Genius, are there any stores delivering today?" he called out, looking up and extending his hands to the sky, mouthing some undetectable words.

"Yes, EB, most stores are delivering today. Amazon, GlobalDirect, Mammoth Nation are all showing that delivery today is possible—for a fee, of course."

"The fee doesn't matter—whatever the cost, I want you to scan for the most delightful gifts, presents for a family. You'll need dolls and play sets and whatever is most desired by ten-year-old girls these days and the same for ten-year-old boys—race cars, electronic games, whatever you can find. And do the same for a high school–aged boy and girl, things that are fun, but also educational and useful, as if these gifts were for the children of a diplomat or dignitary.

"Also, we need gifts for a college freshman—I don't have a clue what she'd like. But get her several presents; make sure they're valuable and useful for her college days. And finally, Genius, for a young seven-year-old boy, put together the most marvelous, exciting, fun-filled set of toys, games, and amusements. This little boy is bound to a wheelchair, so make certain they are all compatible. And for that matter, add the most modern, up-to-date electric wheelchair that would be suitable for a small boy. Include that, and have it wrapped!"

"Is that all?" Genius inquired.

"Of course that's not all." EB laughed as he went back into the living room, now cooled down with a wonderful chill from the bay that was worth more to him now than his entire fortune. "We're just getting started!"

"Please continue," said Genius.

"Isn't this fun?" EB roared. "Yes, OK, presents for the kids. Make sure they're all wrapped in the most colorful, festive paper with wreathes and holly, some with Christmas pictures—make sure a few have the Three Wise Men around the crèche, and the star, some must have the Star of Bethlehem! Oh yes, a few should have red and white stripes like candy canes. In fact, find a store that has a large selection of Christmas candy and have it included. Not too much—don't want to give them cavities—but lots of Christmas candy and treats for the whole family!"

"So far, all can be fulfilled and delivered by this afternoon," Genius reported.

"Such amazing technology, truly astounding." EB giggled. "And now the most important part. Genius, find a fine restaurant or series of the best restaurants in the city that are open today for Christmas dinner and order the most scrumptious, delicious, outrageous, fattening—but healthy where possible— mouthwatering meal for the Cratchits. Make sure there's roast beef, a full turkey—make it the largest one you can find that's available, sweet potatoes with marshmallows, mixed vegetables—all the fixings. And a full selection of Christmas desserts! Now make this happen and get it to the Cratchits as quickly as you can, my dear Genius!"

"Already 60 percent completed and estimating all orders will be completed with deliveries starting within the hour."

"Absolutely fantastic! What remarkable service. There will be bonus bits and bytes for you, Genius!" EB bellowed out.

"Bonus bits and bytes? Please clarify. The estimated total cost will be—"

"Stop! Never mind. It's a joke, Genius. Don't you get it? No sense of humor—huge oversight on my part!" EB laughed as he skipped around his living room, clapping his hands. "And I don't want to know the price. It doesn't matter. Spare no cost! Get only the best for them—just make sure it all arrives before dinnertime. And all of it is to be sent to them anonymously. They can't know it's from me!"

"Confirmed, EB. ETA for all, 4:00 p.m."

"Marvelous, Genius, simply marvelous. Next, you can find that charity group that rings the bells and has kettles for donations all over the city during this time of the year, can't you, Genius?"

"Already found, sir. Would you like me to leave a message for someone in particular in the organization? Their offices are closed today."

"No, no, not a message, but prepare an account transfer of . . ." And then EB decided to just mentally transmit the amount to Genius. "Send a memo with the transfer that is from me and only the first of regular support that I'll now be giving them."

"That's quite a sum, sir, for a donation. Please confirm the amount again."

"No need, my stingy little Genius. That's the right amount, and much more will be flowing to them from here on out," EB said, feeling free as a bird.

EB spent the rest of the morning and early afternoon basking in the sunlight pouring in through his windows, dancing on his patio and throughout his house, and singing, all the while checking every half hour to make sure Genius had the Cratchit feast and presents under control. In between his sprightly cavorting and frolicking, he began recording and writing down the lessons he had learned and flood of thoughts that were accompanying them, bringing him to levels of pure joy and happiness unfathomed in his former, miserable life.

"Get my elevator, and start up one of my cars—any one of them is fine. You pick, Genius! Isn't this fun, Genius?" EB called out sometime in the early evening as he pranced into his bedroom to shower and change into his best clothes, all the while singing what he had thought were long-forgotten Christmas tunes.

"There's much to do, Genius, so much to do! 'Oh, come all ye faithful, joyful and triumphant' . . . Do you hear me, Genius? We have a whole new plan. 'Par rumpa pum pum. I have no gift for Him, par rumpa pum pum.' They're all coming back to me now, Genius. All these songs that I had despised and hated hearing, even once a year, are filling me up! I want to know them all—my mind is full of these heavenly tunes. 'Par rumpa pum pum'!"

The chuckle with which he said this, and the chuckle he released while shaking his head at the rows and rows of clothing he never wore, and the chuckle with which he put on a hardly worn pair of dress shoes instead of his Chucks, and the chuckle with which he continued to rib and try to joke with Genius, were only to be exceeded by the chuckle with which he sat down, breathless, in his living room chair after his glorious day, dressed and readied, chuckling until he cried.

CHAPTER 33

Genius had chosen, quite fortuitously it seemed to EB, his most inexpensive car for his travel that day. Even that fully electric Escalade with all its modifications and add-ons was a mid-six-figure vehicle. But it was as modest as EB had—something else on his list he would have to take care of. Today, however, it would do nicely, especially since it was a unique green that went nicely with the holiday. As EB got into his SUV, he noticed that the color also was a remarkable match to the color of his giant green guide.

"Incredible! How did Genius know? Of course it didn't, but there is One who did!" he said to himself, sensing the reality that even the hairs of his head were numbered and under the careful watch of the One who had rescued him.

The streets of San Francisco were nearly empty, except for the occasional car either going or coming from Christmas visits, making his short ride to the 101 freeway a breeze. Once on the highway EB headed south, for the first time feeling peaceful and unrushed so he could actually enjoy the drive. The sun began to set to his right over the buildings and hills that dotted the landscape on his short forty-five-minute journey, lighting up the scattered clouds in the chilly bay air in pinks and purples, displaying a grandeur and beauty he had not noticed, or tried to notice, before.

"Hello, sir, may I scan your Personal Chip if you have one? Or I'll need to see your internationally verified ID," the young guard at Levi Stadium's VIP parking lot said.

"Of course, and Merry Christmas!" EB replied back in his giggly laughing mode.

"Oh, Mr. Ebenezer! It's a privilege, sir," the guard said after EB's full credentials popped up on his handheld monitor. "Proceed straight ahead and to your right is your reserved spot, 8A. There's an elevator right next to it that will take you directly to the suite level where you'll find your party."

"Marvelous." EB smiled. "Excellent! Should be a great game, and if I was one for predicting the future, I'd say it'll probably come down to the wire, but the Niners are about to deliver us a Christmas surprise!"

"That sure would make it a Merry Christmas for all of us!" The guard smiled back.

"Yes, it would. But even if they don't win, it's a joyous Christmas anyway, isn't it? A day of celebration for the birth that brought an eternal win for humanity!"

"I suppose it is," the guard replied back enthusiastically, having caught EB's contagious joy. "Yes, it definitely is! Merry Christmas, sir!"

"And to you, and a Happy New Year!"

Once parked, EB took the elevator as directed to the suite level and walked about watching the people hurrying to and fro from their suite box to the concession stand or the bathroom, or wherever. EB was thrilled to see a plethora of children with family on this level. As they darted past him, he would pat the ones he could reach on the head or the back with a "Go Niners! Merry Christmas!" And when he passed a concession stand, he stopped to converse with the attendants if no one was waiting in line.

He was also drawn to a few maintenance men and women who were cleaning the area, keeping the trash cans empty and making everything tidy for the elite game watchers. Seeing them in a completely new light, EB chatted with those that would talk to him, finding that hearing their views on the game, or learning a little about their work, or just saying hello and Merry Christmas to them yielded him immense pleasure and thankfulness. He had never dreamed that any stroll or prelude to an event—that anything like this—could give him so much happiness.

After a few more unnecessary meanders, he finally arrived at the suite his nephew had invited him to visit. He passed the suite's door a dozen times, before he had the courage to go up and enter. But finally, after one particularly spectacular "Merry Christmas" from a young fan decked out from head to toe in 49ers gear, he made a dash, and darted through the door.

"Is Fred around?" EB asked the woman standing just inside, also dressed in 49ers fan clothing with a circled "SF" wreath painted on her cheek.

"Are you the management? Is there a problem?" she asked.

"Management?" EB laughed. "No, no, I'm Fred's uncle. He invited me to join you all for the game."

"You're EB?" She laughed with him. "I've always seen you in pictures with your uppity black clothing—you know, the black jacket over black shirt finished at the bottom with your famous Converse All Stars. But like this—with a tie and jacket? And I love your top hat. Wow! Sorry, that's why I thought you were management. You clean up great, EB! Hey, Fred, your uncle is here!"

EB slid in and hovered in the back of the suite waiting for his nephew who was hidden somewhere among the group gathered toward the front of the box watching the pregame warm-ups. To the side, EB noticed the big box full of presents, and on top, a large square gold one. He couldn't help but grin and then burst out laughing.

"Are you kidding me?" came a familiar voice. EB turned from

gazing at the Secret Santa gifts and saw his nephew and his wife walking toward him with looks of shock and dismay.

"Is that really you? You made it!" Fred continued.

"Indeed I did, if I'm still invited," EB replied.

"Invited? You're always invited. Miracles truly do happen at Christmas!" Fred said, turning to his wife as if to answer a comment she had said earlier.

"More than you know." EB laughed back as Fred grabbed his hand and patted him on the shoulder.

"Hey, everyone, my uncle EB is here!" Fred shouted over the announcers and music of the pregame festivities. Everyone cheered and waved, as if he had been an old friend and part of the group forever. Within minutes, EB felt right at home, another feeling that had long eluded him. All were familiar faces, confirming what he had just seen, and further proving that his journey had been real. There to the side was Jason waving to him, after which he turned back toward the field and made a couple of imaginary golf swings. Also waving and shouting hello was Rosie, sitting down on a bench to the side since she wouldn't fit into any of the chairs in the suite. EB couldn't wait to go over and spend some time visiting with her. Down the stairs of the box he could see a crutch being pumped in the air, full of 49ers stickers, with its owner hollering "glad you could join us!"

And join them he did, way overdressed, but unrestrained and there until the end when the 49ers made an astounding last-minute touchdown to win the game. He even stayed late into the night through the gift-giving fun, having the most wonderful time—especially when Fred's wife profusely apologized that they didn't have a gift for him since they hadn't expected him to come.

Late as the party went, it didn't prevent EB from arriving early to the eBeja Tower the next morning. He always arrived early, but this morning he made sure he was extra early and the first one at the office, not because he had an inordinate amount of work to catch up on. He did, as well as a boatload of new work on which he was about to embark. No, he came extremely early to make sure he arrived before Bobby did.

EB hadn't anticipated Bobby coming in early, but came himself at around six thirty just in case Bobby broke tradition. He found the quiet and solitude of his office in the early morning time to be welcoming, affording him time he had never felt he had before to just sit quietly, meditate on all that had happened, and pray. He didn't really know how to pray or what to say, but decided that it was no different than talking to any other person he respected and admired.

"God, I haven't said anything to You for a long time. Far too long, and I'm sorry. Sorry I have been absent all these years, sorry I hardened myself against You, the only One who I see now truly cares about me, and sorry that I have spent so much energy and effort fighting You, the One who created me, gave me life, and didn't abandon me. Such a fool I've been, an evil, incorrigible fool seeking my own destructive ways instead of Yours. But that's all past now, and so I want to start by saying forgive me for all of it, everything. From here on, I commit to follow You and Your ways in whatever I do, at all times. Thank You," EB muttered and stuttered as he tried to find the words to express what was in his heart.

Before he could continue any further, an alert flashed on his monitor. True to his word, Bobby arrived on time, actually one minute early as his chip logged him in when he turned on his computer at six fifty-nine. EB immediately used his mental command to activate the voice communicator that connected him directly to Bobby.

"Robert Cratchit!" growled EB, in his usual and accustomed aggravated, angry voice—at least as near as he could feign it.

"What do you mean coming in at this time?"

"Good morning, sir. The system shows that I logged in at six fifty-nine. I wanted to ensure I wasn't late as promised," Bobby said as a pit formed in his stomach upon hearing his proper name, replacing the living water that had flowed the previous day.

"After a full day off, you can't even arrive a little earlier to make up for all the work you missed. You think arriving one minute early somehow lets you off the hook for a full day's absence?" EB covered his mouth and mentally muted his system as he could hardly keep from bursting out laughing.

"I am very sorry, sir," said Bobby. "I plan to stay late tonight and catch up on everything."

"You are?" squealed EB in his mean voice, shaking his head in delight. "Yes. I think you very well will be. Probably very late. Now come up to my office immediately!"

Trembling, Bobby pushed back from his desk and made a beeline to the elevator, which he had signaled on the way to be ready for him. Within seconds, the doors opened to EB's office where EB was seated behind his mammoth desk, leaning forward as if to pounce on Bobby, with the biggest scowl he could muster.

"Please, sir," Bobby began before EB could say a word. "I'm very sorry. I should have been here earlier. It's only once a year and won't be repeated. You see, I hadn't planned to celebrate as I did yesterday, but, well, we had an unexpected arrival, completely unexpected, which kept me and my family occupied in some of the most happy and wonderful feasting and merriment—well, I think ever for my family."

"Oh really?" said EB, leaning even farther forward on his elbows, but putting his head down for a moment to hide his uncontrollable smile. After regaining control, he looked up again, squinting but about to burst.

"Feasting and merriment? You're spending what I give you on

feasting and merriment? Perhaps an adjustment to your salary is called for here with all this feasting and merriment!"

"Oh no, sir. Frankly, I can scarcely pay the bills. This was not my doing. You see—"

But before Bobby could continue, EB leapt from behind his desk and charged toward Bobby with such rapidity that Bobby nearly fell back into the open elevator since the door sensors had not yet been triggered to close.

"I'm not going to tolerate you saying you can barely pay your bills. It's over, Bobby; it's all over!" EB tried to snarl, but could only just barely. "And so today I'm giving you official notice— that I'm tripling your salary!"

"What?" Bobby asked in a gasp that could scarcely be heard.

"Merry Christmas, Bobby!" burst EB with a roar of laughter, grabbing the almost collapsed Bobby by the shoulders, and then after steadying him, patting him on the back. "You deserve even more, but let us start there for the time being."

Bobby couldn't move and just stood dumbstruck and paralyzed, staring at EB who was not just smiling, but laughing hysterically at his little prank.

"Don't worry, Bobby, I'm serious," EB finally said after containing himself. "I'm more serious now than I've ever been, and have clarity like never before. And I need your help, Bobby. Not that you haven't helped me more than you know—maybe you do know. Regardless, I need your help on numerous fronts. But rest assured, son, this help I need will not pull you away from your marvelous family. No. In fact, you'll be spending much more time with your family, and especially little Timmy, God bless his little soul. We're going to take care of Timmy, too, get his operations so he can live a long and productive life. We're going to do whatever it takes to make that little angel fly!"

Bobby's mouth was now wide open, but he could say nothing.

He waited for pullback, for the lashing that he thought was sure to follow, or the spite that would come to him for thinking EB might actually be telling him the truth.

"I understand your skepticism, Bobby. I'd be skeptical myself and wouldn't believe a word I'm saying except for this. It was I who sent you and your family all those gifts. Did your children receive them all? Did they like them? You don't know how much I hope they did. You'll see that this is the start of a new day for you and me, for your family and me. And the feast, it sounds like you all enjoyed it and were filled full, having a truly Merry Christmas together, enjoying the roast beef, the turkey—how big was it? I ordered the biggest one possible to be sent. It probably wasn't big enough, but it was last minute, you know. Anyway, I hope it was delicious, and all the fixings and the desserts! Oh, and the new chair for Timmy. Was it the right one?"

"It's perfect, and was amazingly wrapped. That was all from you?" were the only words Bobby could vocalize after several seconds of trying to push words out of his mouth.

"The least I could do for you and your lovely wife, Olivia. I know she's become bitter at me for keeping you from her, separating you two when I should've been helping you two grow together and build your family. I do hope she and you will forgive me. Yes, all that was the least I could do, and is only the beginning to make up for all the misery I've caused you and your family," EB pleaded.

Bobby was finally persuaded, for how could he know all the details, and on top of that, EB had never called him "son" before. But what truly convinced him most of all was seeing EB's eyes swell up with tears as he implored him.

"Bobby, I'm going to need your help to understand God and what it means to live a life for the Creator and His Son Jesus, the real Governor of the planet and my new CEO."

"I can do that," Bobby whispered through a cough, shaking his head in disbelief at what he was witnessing. "I would be more than honored to do that."

"Good!" EB said, slapping him on the back again and then briskly returning to his desk. "That will be priority one in the changes that are coming. Understand, Bobby, everything is changing because I have been changed."

"Uh, I can see that."

"I want to tell you all that's happened so you'll understand the total redirection we'll be taking. As of yesterday, eBeja has a new mission, I have a new mission, and many are not going to like our new course. But I know you'll understand. Bobby, we're in great danger. Our situation is more precarious than I ever imagined and we have to act immediately."

"Yes, I know. The climate emergency—you've dedicated your life to it."

"I have. But that's not the real emergency. That's not what is truly jeopardizing the planet and humanity. We'll always work toward a cleaner, safer, less polluted planet, but our true mission now is to stop the real contamination that puts us all in jeopardy. It's a poison, Bobby, that is about to be unleashed upon the world through the diabolical efforts of a very powerful and dedicated elite who have declared war on God and on His appointed ruler and healer of the planet. We now have a spiritual mission, Bobby."

"I see," Bobby whispered, still in shock. "Where do we begin?"

"A code was given to me by their leader—well, their future leader—a cryptic message that is the key to the plan. I was supposed to be a part of it. We have to crack the code, Bobby. Time is short."

"A code?" Bobby inquired.

"I know. This is a lot to digest. There's so much to tell you,

Bobby, and I'll explain it all when you get back. Now go get your things together at your desk and make sure your group is working on what they need to be working on—whoever is here today. Then grab your portascreen and come back up so we can start planning!"

Bobby didn't say a word, but turned and did exactly as EB had directed and was back in his office within the hour.

"Christmas is the story of endings and beginnings," EB emphasized to begin their meeting. "It ended the hopelessness of death by inaugurating the chance for eternal life through the birth of God's Son. This Christmas marks my end and my beginning. The old EB is gone, Bobby, transformed, and now I'm born again into a new man through what happened yesterday. I'll tell give you all the details shortly so you can see why we're going to go in a completely new direction now—me, you, and this company. But for now, understand, the mission we're about to embark on is the most difficult, and dangerous venture of all. But it will also be the most rewarding and beneficial, not just for us, but for the planet and all of God's creatures. It will be impossible for us to accomplish on our own, and will only bear fruit if we are led by the Great Hand, the only Hand that can save our world as He saved me. So let's now pray together God's will is done, not ours, and that in our new venture, God bless us, every one!"

ACKNOWLEDGMENTS

Without the loving support of my parents, I not only wouldn't have been able to write this book, but wouldn't have even wanted to. Both of them loved learning and inspired me to do the same. To both my mother and father I am deeply thankful. Thank you to my editor, Michael Fedison for devoting many long hours to polish the manuscript, and for persevering through health challenges that could have prevented him from doing so. Also thank you to Nick Castle for his creative brilliance and the entire Reedsy community for the invaluable resources they provided for this project. Like many over the years, I'm thankful for Charles Dickens whose timeless *A Christmas Carol* was the inspiration for this adaptation. "No one is useless in this world who lightens the burdens of another," Dickens said. My hope and prayer is that this book has lightened many burdens. Above all, I thank God, the magnificent Creator of all, and His Son, Jesus, in whom are hidden all the treasures of wisdom and knowledge.

ABOUT THE AUTHOR

MARK HANNA is an entrepreneur and writer who has founded multiple companies as well as held positions in several educational technology enterprises, including as vice president in a publicly traded tech company in the Bay Area of California. His writings on international politics and social issues have appeared in numerous publications including RealClear Politics, ZeroHedge and American Thinker. He has also worked in television for NBC and PBS affiliates, as well as for CNN in Washington, DC. Mark holds an MA in International Studies from the University of Utah and has served on several Christian ministry boards.

www.markhanna.tv
Twitter: @MarkHannaWriter

COMING SOON

EBenezer Book 2

Don't miss EB's next adventure
in the EBenezer Series